THE MERCIER HOTELS

MAKE HIM

KELLY FINLEY

"The Queen Of Spice"
KELLY FINLEY BOOKS

THE MERCIER
HOTELS

For my readers to enjoy their visit with shameless, one-handed pride

THE MERCIER HOTELS

MAKE HIM PLAYLIST

Desire by Meg Myers
Hotel by Montell Fish
Toxic by Kehlani
On My Knees by RÜFÜS DU SOL
run for the hills by Tate McRae
First Fuck by 6LACK, Jhené Aiko
Masterpiece by Sam Short
Why Aren't We Having Sex? by Liza Owen
All I Wanted Was U by Ex Habit, Omido
salvation by Christabelle Marbun
Hello by Adele
Tears of Gold by Faouzia
blame's on me by Alexander Stewart
Love You Again by PLAZA
Yeah, I Said It by Rihanna
Moths by RY X

Listen On Spotify

THE MERCIER
HOTELS

MAKE HIM

Scarlett

CHAPTER ONE

Sometimes a fuck isn't worth it.

The price you pay for the pleasure is too high—the risk of it breaking your heart too much.

But you can't fall in love with someone after just one night.

Right?

It's crazy. How can a complete stranger, okay, and the sexiest man you've ever met, find that broken place inside you that no one ever has, that place so vulnerable? That doesn't happen in one night.

Does it?

Even though that man gave you orgasms you didn't know were possible. Like all the ones you had before, they were tiny, little sneezes. Even though the kisses he gave you were tender until they were torture because he couldn't get enough of your taste.

That fuck with *HIM*?

His sex was mind-altering, and your body can't forget it, either. It makes you conjure the memory of him at least five, okay, ten times a day.

But the consequence for his fuck?

Apparently, I'm about to lose my job over it.

And I need my job. I love my job. I'm a natural at it, plus I

1

have the best boss. I won't let her down. Although, we just stepped into my new client's palatial office, and I'm suddenly staring again at...*HIM.*

Mr. Fuck You To Death.

"Ms. Ravenel and Ms. Jones of HGR Security for you, Sir." A secretary announces us, grabbing *HIS* attention.

Behind strands of onyx hair, glacial eyes that defy nature sharply lift from the files he's reading on his desk. Plush lips that never smile suddenly smirk with satisfaction.

He admires my beautiful boss first. Then those eyes, framed by dark, thick lashes and dominating brows, aim my way...and...

Yep, it's me.

The woman you broke with your fucks. The woman who loved every minute of it.

Nice to see your beauty is even more brutal by daylight.

His glare makes my heart, hidden under my black blazer and sapphire blouse, start to pound, but I keep a stoic face.

Calmly, he commands, "Come in," and like the night we fucked, I obey.

He recognizes me. And, of course, I can't forget him.

Cloaked in a crisp black elegant suit, his starched white shirt is unbuttoned, revealing his taut, deep bronze skin, and I remember his taste—almonds. His flesh felt like hard silk, stretched tight over his towering, muscular frame, and I remember his scent—citrus and cypress.

He has a birthmark on his shredded left thigh. He's packing the thickest member I've ever seen. He loves pulling my hair and choking me while I come.

I know the savagery he hides while I hide my shock, forcing myself to cross his sprawling executive office though the room tilts, I swear.

Walking beside my boss, memories make my pulse race, sweat threatening my flesh. My ribs heave inches higher in the presence again of this clit-shocking man lording behind his imposing desk.

And I swear my cunt is cursed.

Why can't I have a simple day? Like, ease into it, starting with a cozy cup of coffee and a blueberry muffin? Why can't I be one of those women who gets to meditate, do yoga, and walk my dog and...hell, I don't know.

What do those women do all day?

I got no clue because that's not my life, and clearly not my job for the foreseeable future because my pussy's having a panic attack while he doesn't even look shocked or bothered.

No, he reclines in his leather chair and looks amused, entertained as I draw closer.

This isn't going to be a meeting. This is fresh hell.

My boss continues the introductions while we approach his ebony desk. It's a behemoth piece of furniture, commanding in front of an equally impressive view of the Charleston Harbor and the massive bridge looming outside the wall of windows behind him.

"Ms. Jones," my boss says to me, "meet Mr. Mercier, your new client."

Oh...we've met.

We've fucked. Hard. Hot. Loud and dirty and several times one night at a sex club in front of a crowd. We didn't care. We got off on it. We were strangers, fucking like sex was a fight, and we both wanted to lose.

Or at least, I did. With his dominating kiss, I felt myself changing into a woman I didn't know, and I liked her. I've never submitted to a man before, but I did that night because we felt it.

We were fated to fuck. And I never saw him again.

I knew his first name—Luca. Hell, he made me moan it many times. Scream it, too.

He really liked my screams.

After that night, I could've asked my friends about him. I could've stalked him...I mean, accidentally bumped into him on the sidewalks of Charleston. Or I could've scrolled, obsessed...I mean, shopped online for hours as Luca's image kept innocently popping up in my FYPs.

But pride wouldn't let me.

If Luca wanted me again, he knew how to find me, too.

That was almost a year ago, and now I clench my teeth, standing at the edge of his desk.

This is a H.I.F.—How I'm Fucked.

It's how I measure my life; all the ways it's fucked me so far.

Because *HIF #1*: This man is my new client.

A client I'm not allowed to fuck. Even though he's already buried his face in my pussy like it was an oxygen mask, and he was deep-sea diving for my clit, discovering it like a rare pearl...many times.

And talk about being *fucked?*

I will be if my company ever finds out.

"Mr. Mercier..." My boss, Charlie Ravenel, directs us to shake hands without instruction. She's just powerful and gorgeous that way. "Meet Ms. Jones. She's my best protection officer and perfect for your new detail. Highly skilled. A titled fighter but a local who blends in. I pulled her off another detail because no one else will serve you better."

Did he just smirk at that?

Silently, he stands to greet me, his tall shadow raising the hairs on my arms. Extending his massive right hand, I glance down, noting how his fingernails are buffed. How his corded forearm peeks out from under the stark sleeve of his tailored jacket.

Those arms pinned me down while his knees forced my thighs open, and his cock ruined me, making me stretch and bleed with bliss.

And god, how I begged for more.

What Luca Mercier did to my body was infectious, and I feel his captivating fever start to flame my cheeks. Dangerously, his right hand reaches, demanding mine, and *don't let my knees buckle.* Because the last time I knelt for Luca, I was sucking him off while he ordered other men to watch me serve him.

And I loved it.

I don't believe in love at first sight. Or at first fuck. That's bullshit. I don't know what this emotion is again. I don't know what Luca makes me feel.

But I recognize Fate when she bitch slaps you across the face. Twice.

Because our hands touch again, and I suddenly sway, attracted, pulled to him against my will. He grabs my flesh, and his palm is magnetic. It's like we're locked together. You can't rip us apart. I'm in awe, staring at our connection.

Oh my god, we're like all the romance books I read. Lust at the first meeting. Love at the second. Or vice versa. It depends on the book. We're a hot, forbidden work romance, but we'll live happily ever after together, and...

I suddenly clock it. Gleaming and gold on Luca's left hand.

A wedding band!

What the fuck?

I choke my gasp down, my eyes flicking up to his, and he's aiming that evil smirk back at me, revealing no remorse about it while he starts shaking my hand.

He's married?

The cheating asshole!

I'm going to rip his thick dick off and shove it down his throat. Yes, I have the skills to do it, and no, he wasn't wearing a wedding band that night!

Shock explodes through my mind, but I fake it. I shake his hand back and force my smile, greeting him. "Mr. Mercier."

No, Mr. Motherfucker!

Correction: *Mr. Scarlettfucker.*

Because that's what Luca did. He fucked me for hours and never once told me he was married. He seduced me into taboo acts, but I'd never do that one.

I don't cheat. I don't hurt other women. I don't know what I lost to Luca that night, but I will *NOT* lose my job over a man who cheats on his wife.

I squeeze his hand back like a murderous bitch, flexing my bicep against the power of his touch. It's so familiar and foreign, and *he's a fucking liar.*

"It's very nice to meet you, sir." And so am I.

This dick better play along.

We're strangers turned professionals, and we can do this. We can act like he didn't cheat on his wife, fucking me in front of a crowd, both of us so obsessed that the only eyes we saw were ours.

"Indeed. Nice to meet you, Ms. Jones."

Goddamn, he finally speaks to me, and his accent is a silky snake.

It soothes into your ear, coiling down your body, deep and rich and European, wrapping around you so tight, taking your breath away while it leisurely licks your clit.

"It's a true pleasure," he mocks...

And so our performance begins. Because Luca clutches my hand too long, and I deserve an Oscar for this. I'm staring into his eyes again, and they're not light blue, pale green, or muted grey. They're primal and piercing. They're like no other.

Luca Mercier claims anyone in his sight.

And yes, I was HIS pleasure.

He can hide it now, reaching across his shiny ebony wood desk in his fancy office with loaded bookshelves, fine leather chairs, and soaring windows overlooking Charleston, South Carolina. He owns this hotel, the entire Mercier luxury global chain, thousands of staff, and billions of dollars.

Luca owns it all.

But for one night, I owned him.

Pleasure shook his naked, hulking thighs as I took his cock as far as I could into my gagging throat and devoured him. His creamy desire. His velvety width. His long moans. His lush lips parted as he sunk his hands into my auburn waves and fisted my hair so hard it was perfect. He couldn't let go because he was falling for me, too.

I gazed up at him from my knees and savored our milky cum on his cock, the flavor of our first fuck, and I moaned. I tasted him surrender to me, too, growling my name in front of a dozen aroused witnesses.

He can't deny it. I've never made a man come so hard, and so many times, I couldn't believe his stamina. And I've never had sex before an audience, but now, it's my kink. It's my thing.

Luca's my thing, and I ache for more of him. Whatever he made me feel, I need it, but...

HIF #2: He's married.

HIF #3: He's a cheating dick.

"Indeed, sir, it's a pleasure," I answer, wanting to yank his massive hand, pulling him in close so my left fingers can gouge his gorgeous eyes out. How dare he cheat on his wife and make me a guilty culprit without my consent?

"Welcome to The Mercier, *Ms. Jones*," he lures, secretly trailing his middle finger across my palm and...

Oh fuck.

Why did he do that? And why does he sound indecent? Like I'm being initiated into something dark? Though I crave more of his depravity, I'm no man's bitch. I'm no one's *other* woman.

Because now, there are two of us women and one of him.

Charlie, my badass boss, a former Marine turned bodyguard— a woman I'd never lie to.

Luca, my new, sexy-as-fuck, billionaire client who needs me as a protection officer.

And me, Scarlett.

A country girl. A proud hick who came from nothing. The eldest sister of four who learned to fight to protect my little sisters. Those fights won me trouble before they won me titles—MMA titles—and that scored me an opportunity I couldn't pass up. Now, I'm paid thousands to do what almost landed me behind bars. I can't lose this job. I still take care of my sisters. They can still count on me.

And so can Charlie.

I'd never betray another woman.

Though, as Luca finally releases my hand, my body betrays me. That pussy quiver, that flush, that rush of wet heat surging between my thighs because he just touched me again can go fuck itself. I'm not a cheater, and I don't fuck on the job.

"Please," he gestures to the chairs behind us, "have a seat."

He flicks his finger toward his secretary, I assume, still standing in the office doorway.

"Frappe. Perrier," he commands the man to fetch us drinks, though we didn't ask for them.

"Thank you," Charlie answers politely while I lower into the soft leather chair and harden my heart. Though my body turns to mush, watching Luca sit like the King of FuckDom.

"Ms. Jones and I have reviewed what you've shared so far." Charlie continues, sitting beside me, "Your daughter is five and starting kindergarten. That's a big step for both of you."

"Yes, Gia," he says. "She starts school next week, so I called you."

Charlie smiles warmly at Luca. She genuinely cares about his daughter. We have the same calling—protecting women and girls —and that's why I have to lie.

But is it a lie?

Protection officers, some call us bodyguards, are never supposed to get involved with our clients. Emotionally. Socially. Physically.

And you sure as hell aren't supposed to let them eat your pussy and call you their "sweet little whore" until you come so damn hard that your legs turn to Jell-O. Three times.

I didn't know Luca would be my client almost a year later.

I didn't know the billionaire hotelier that Charlie asked me to work for would be *HIM*.

All I heard was that a client needed a woman protection officer for his young daughter. A big, burly man would only scare the little girl and stand out in a crowd, especially at a private elementary school.

But me?

I blend in.

I can look like her nanny when really... I can punch your throat so hard you may never breathe again.

"My daughter is my world," Luca continues with Charlie, tapping his gold Mont Blanc pen over white linen folders neatly stacked on his desk. "Nothing can happen to her."

"I understand," Charlie assures him.

Who has white linen folders? Not manilla, paper ones?

Luca Mercier, that's who.

It's the signature Mercier Hotel look.

From the moment you step through the glass and gold doors of the Charleston Mercier Hotel, warm white wraps you in a luxurious hug. White marble. White furniture. White walls. The grand lobby of the boutique hotel features accents of gold and dark Grecian blue while I counted twelve guests in the lobby as we were led to the golden elevator by hotel security and escorted up to the third-floor executive office suites.

Funny, I noticed details like exits and head counts, but I was too distracted by making Charlie proud that I never asked to read the client's portfolio before our meeting.

Why should I? I trust Charlie. But can she trust me not to fuck this up?

Maybe. My mind is sure, but my pussy is a mafia wife. She will screw me over, getting me screwed. She's too loyal to the Dick.

Speaking of...

"I hire my own detail when I need it." Luca focuses on my boss. "And when we leave the hotel, my daughter is never out of my sight."

We?

Is he talking about the wife he has, too?

My stomach suddenly sours. I'm usually not a fool, but Luca deceived me. He fucked me like he hadn't been fucked in years when he has an innocent wife he deceived too.

"But now,"—he's still looking at Charlie like he knows *I now* know he's a cheating asshole—"Gia starts school next week, and the job starts tomorrow for their open house. I need to make the necessary introductions to the school staff. Mostly, I will drive her to school myself, but I need backup. I can't always be there to protect her, so I need someone who can."

That someone is *me*, and he still won't look my way.

How ironic.

Luca fucked me like I was the air he needed to breathe. Then he left me like a used condom. And now he needs me to protect the one he loves the most.

HIF #4: I'm so screwed; they sell me at Home Depot in a variety of sizes to fuck my life.

"But you have no active threats, right?" Charlie asks, rubbing her pregnant belly under her black sheath dress.

"Not that I'm aware," Luca answers her. "Just the high-value target of my daughter, who I'd pay any ransom for."

And he earns one check in the right column under "Good Man" down the long list of checks on the left under "Fucking Piece of Shit."

"And your wife?" But I can't help it. Rage boils under my skin. "Does your *wife* need my protection, too, Mr. Mercier?"

From his cheating?

I don't say that last part, but...

I'm sorry, God, but if Luca bursts into flames right in front of me now, I wouldn't piss on him to save him.

No, I'd stick my hand in the fire and crush his windpipe, watching him gasp for his last breath.

Even though...

I've already bit his sexy neck. I felt his pulse thrum against my lips while he growled like a wild animal, "Let them watch the filthy things I do to my beautiful whore," fucking me so brutally that he left me bruised and aching for more.

The man is hung and hot and hella talented with skills my sex can't forget. Because who fucks like that? Who makes you come like that? Who talks dirty like that? Who degrades you and makes you love it? You'd do any taboo act for him because he delivers the pleasure, too.

Luca Mercier, that's who.

He dominates. He defiles. He gives you ego-erasing orgasms that leave you desperate for more. I didn't see the inferno of Luca Mercier coming, but he left me in ashes. Because that's all I've ever known of life. Loss.

And that night, Luca felt like home.

The fiery memory wets my silk thong. My pussy wants to

drop to her knees for him again...but I'm not a fucking cheater. And I'm also not a dumbass who'll lose my job over a man.

Dick don't pay the bills.

My question about his wife forces his crystal eyes to confront mine finally, and what's burning behind his glare?

Fury that I dared to ask about his wife?

Fear that I'll tell her?

Desperation that I'm the only one qualified to protect their daughter?

Or is it the attraction raging between us?

I've fucked so many people; I get what I want. I don't want emotions that leave me vulnerable and exposed. I have my sisters and friends; they get all my love, and it's loyal. But the people I fuck? They get pleasure, that's all.

Until Luca.

"MY. WIFE..." he jeers at me, halting, dragging out my punishment.

He's doing it on purpose. He's fighting back. He's taking control because those two words from his mouth make my throat burn.

I don't know what Luca found inside me that night. I didn't know it was there until he touched it. He found it and made me cry...and I *don't* cry. Then he took it so many times from me until it only belonged to him.

Did I fall in love with him?

No. That's impossible.

That's not this pain, this sudden crushing tender ache in my chest under my silk blouse hiding my sweating armpits. I'm staring into his eyes, and I don't know what's strangling my throat.

But fine. Luca may have won my body that night, but he didn't win my heart. Because I'll protect his daughter, but I won't protect our secret. I'll tell his wife. Some day. Somehow. I will fuck his lying ass over. How dare he hurt her?

And me?

"MY. WIFE..."

He says it again, whipping the words like a lash across my

skin. Like he'll take all the time in the world to make me suffer while his murderous eyes glare at me.

What the fuck did I do? I'm not the one who cheated?

My god, men don't intimidate me, but Luca? He makes evil look angelic. And why does that turn me on? I'm not that horny.

Am I?

I hate him.

I can kill him.

I switch my legs, waiting for his answer, draping my thigh over the other, trying to ignore the throbbing in my pussy his evil elicits. My black pants suit, my uniform, covers every inch of my body except for my exposed ankles, and of course, they catch his unfaithful eye.

I wore heels to this meeting. Usually, I hate the damn things. They're meant to make women defenseless. But on me, they make Luca lick his hungry lips.

The big-dicked bastard.

The truth about his innocent wife sits on the tip of his tongue, but he can't stop the memory of our obscene acts. How his tongue trailed up my ankle, licking my leg, his teeth biting the inside of my thighs until he spread them so wide and gazed at my bare sex like a starving animal. Luca held me splayed open, exposed, and wet. He got off on it, and I did, too.

He told our audience, "Watch. Look at how my whore's pussy pulses from my fuck. Look at how she gapes for more of my cock. Look at my cum dripping from her creamy cunt. It's so sweet." Then, he buried his face in my pussy and consumed every drop of our first time. And then...he did it three more times that night in front of others.

And yes, I fucked Luca bare. Secretly, I knew it then—my heart was the only thing needing protection from him that night.

The forbidden memory flashes across Luca's glacial eyes, too, and he suddenly cracks.

His guilty glare drops, not able to speak of his wife. He taps his gold pen like he wants to stab me because he can't admit it.

Shame has finally found him.

"Will we meet your wife, too?" Charlie eases into his long, heavy silence because she means business. "Her and Gia? We're meeting them today, right? Mr. Mercier, Ms. Jones *needs* to meet her detail *today*."

"Yes," Luca snarls. "I'll take you up to meet Gia. They're expecting us."

They? Gia and his wife?

I bet his wife is such a lady. I bet she's beautiful and polished and must be perfect to marry a rich and powerful man like him. Luca may be Satan, but he's inferno-hot in a black suit. And it's going to burn like hell meeting the woman I betrayed. Then, how much will it hurt to watch him love her, share a family with her, knowing how he made me feel special, too?

But that was a lie, and I was the foolish woman who fell for it.

"We live in the penthouse," he says. "The entire half of the top floor is our home. I live here so I can be close to my family."

Still, he won't look up.

Guilt buries him.

This imposing man lords over an empire, but this truth has him on his knees.

Good.

I relish the idea of Luca Mercier on his knees. I love the idea of punishing him. He needs to suffer like his wife will. Like whatever this is that's suffocating my chest and biting at my eyes.

I'll never fuck him again, but I will fuck his ass up. It makes me smile. It makes me lift my chin higher. I gave Luca Mercier some part of me. I let him inside. I let him take something in me that no one else has, and I don't know why.

But I know this...

I'll make him meet the other side of me. The woman who wins the fight. The woman I'm paid to be.

Finally, his crystal eyes lift and aim at my soul. "My wife is dead," he confesses. "She died four years ago. It's just me and our daughter now."

And still...

Luca wears his gold wedding band.

Luca

CHAPTER TWO

FUCK.

It's all I can think of around this woman, in every expression of the word.

I feel my heart reaching again for Scarlett. For love I don't deserve because...

Fuck: it's what I want to do to her. Hard. Often. In wicked ways that make her scream my name. And yes, I want others to watch me do it again. To witness how I own her pussy, her mouth, her ass, every inch of her flesh.

Scarlett is MINE, and she knows it.

Fuck: that's what my life is—*fucked*—because I already have.

I gave myself permission for one night to lose control, to fuck a beautiful stranger, the hottest woman I've ever met in a sex club. I let myself burn for her. Emotions I no longer allow consumed me.

I was there for my friends' birthday party, not to break my rule. But how could I resist?

When my friends introduced me to Scarlett, she scorched my breath away. Her dark, fiery hair. Her mysterious tattoos. Her fearless stare. That intriguing scar through her eyebrow. The temptation was too great. The beast I cage inside me came out that night, and Scarlett didn't back down.

KELLY FINLEY

No, she was a beautiful beast right back, biting me as much as I bit her. She left scratches down my back and across my ass that I treasured the sting of for days.

And fuck. What am I thinking? She's standing behind me, and I remember every beautiful, obscene thing I did to her as I'm about to take her to meet...

My daughter?

But I have no choice.

See?

FUCK.

Because I don't matter; only my daughter does. Gia's all I have. I'll give my last breath for her, but I'm no fool. I can't always be there to protect her. She's got a last name worth billions, and everyone knows it. The damn paparazzi won't leave me alone. They camp outside my hotels.

"The World's Sexiest & Most Eligible Billionaire Is Also a Single Dad."

That news story went viral and ruined my life—our *lives*. And now, I need help.

I have no life, but my daughter deserves one without me, without the Damning Guilt I wear every day, matching my usual D&G suit.

"This is your security code for the elevator and my front door." I command, "Memorize it, then destroy it." I turn and hand my business card with handwritten digits to...

Scarlett.

Her name.

How I've moaned it so many times since that night. Alone in my bed, on my knees, I grab my headboard while I fuck my fist so hard for her. Like I'm behind her again. Like I'm fisting her alluring red hair and owning her addictive pink pussy with my hard cock ripping her open until her sweet, milky cum glistens down her thighs for me.

She drove me wild.

Gazing at her tight, puckered ass, I spit into it, ready to...

Stop it.

I shake my skull and the carnal memory away, willing my cock not to swell in her presence.

"We each have a unique code to access the penthouse." I fixate on business. "There are cameras, too—the usual." I point to the ones in the elevator and focus on Charlie Ravenel, standing beside me.

When I asked around for the best security company, HGR was at the top of the list. They provide security for the most high-value targets. And when I inquired with my unique need—a woman protection officer—I only heard one name.

Charlie Ravenel.

I've seen the news. I know who she is. She's a bodyguard, now married to Daniel Pierce, the British celebrity icon, bringing her a world of love and trouble.

Charlie took my call but turned me down. She explained she was taking over the HGR Atlanta office and was no longer available for the job, but she assured me she had someone even better.

"She's a former MMA fighter," Charlie told me. "She's a featherweight with champion titles, but you'd never know. Your daughter will love her, I promise. I've trusted this woman to protect my family, too."

I never asked for the name of this protection officer sent to me like an answered prayer. You don't look a gift horse in the mouth. But holy fuck, when that gift walked into my office today.

My answered prayer was *HER*...Scarlett.

The woman I sold my soul for.

It took everything I had not to bend Scarlett over my desk and fist her auburn hair again, ripping those sexy suit pants down and loving how she fights me while I remind her tight ass who it belongs to.

But no.

We have to hide the truth, though I sweat at the sight of her. More than needing the hottest fuck of my life again, I need someone to protect my daughter. And I don't need to read a contract or a statement of conduct to know...*you can't fuck a client*. A protection officer cannot get involved with their mark—the one they are hired to protect.

It's common sense.

Even though Scarlett isn't protecting me, she sure as hell can't fuck the father of the girl she's guarding.

My girl.

My life.

"How many people have access to your penthouse?" Charlie keeps us on topic as the elevator dings to the tenth floor.

"Me. Gia's nanny, Celine. A few on my staff," I answer her. "Only the people I trust. They get unique codes so we can track who enters."

The golden elevator doors slide open to a parlor. White marble floors and ivory grasscloth walls greet us with a fresh, floral arrangement of palm fronds and hot pink hibiscus on a gold console table to our left.

This is my home, my sanctuary, and now it's my hell, too.

"We also enter our code here," I tell Charlie, but I won't look at Scarlett.

Even though I can feel her on my heels.

On my back.

On my skin.

My psyche flashes, taunting me with every dark thing I hide, every forbidden thing I desire, everything I did to Scarlett, and even more I crave to do, but I shove it away.

Not. Ever. Again.

I unlock the front door by tapping the code into the security pad, and the *beep* is the signal. I open the white-paneled door, which always sends Gia running into my arms the second she hears it.

"Baba!" she shouts, and for a moment, while I scoop her up, she's the only one in the world.

Her big brown eyes. Her long, bouncing brown curls. The freckles across her button nose. That cute little bow in her lips. She looks exactly like her mother.

And it kills me every time.

"My kóri." Pecking her cheek, I call her "daughter," speaking Greek to her as much as possible while Celine, her nanny, teaches Gia French.

It's how I was raised with a Greek father and a French mother. I honor tradition. Well, family traditions.

Other parts of my life are very non-traditional, and they're not allowed around my daughter. They hide elsewhere in my hotel. They hide deep in my dark, twisted heart, and death will visit anyone who crosses that line.

Except for one person.

The only one I trust with my secrets.

"Meet my friends." I squeeze Gia tighter, turning to confront this finally. To face the fire of Scarlett standing in my foyer.

"This is Ms. Charlie," I share. "She's friends with Uncle Redix. And this is..."

I freeze, staring at Scarlett while searching through the last hour.

Charlie never introduced Scarlett by her first name.

"Scarlett. My name is Scarlett," she answers with blue eyes that've been murdering me for the past hour. But now they sparkle at the sight of my daughter in my arms.

Tenderly, she smiles at Gia, and I see the glimpse I caught of Scarlett that night.

It wasn't just our raw sex; I noticed the tender things about her, too. How she gently brushed the hair off my forehead. How she comfortably lingered her fingertips over my bare chest when we were done. How she fit perfectly in my arms, making my heart beat alive again.

And FUCK.

Here I go again.

I thought Scarlett ripped my breath away that night in the shadows of a sex club, her hair twirling in long auburn flames. But now, in the sunlight of my home, I'm captivated by the light copper strands framing her stunning face, how they tumble over her shoulders.

Her skin was the softest I've ever caressed—or spanked—but now I can see her slight tan highlighting faint freckles across her sculpted nose. And those lips. They pout, so full and soft in a petal pink, but it's her eyes. They remind me of the Aegean Ocean, where I grew up, and I want to dive into them again.

Scarlett has the feminine face of a seductress, a lethal body I can't forget, and now I know how she got that scar through her eyebrow.

She's an MMA fighter.

That's got to be how she got it.

And that's got to be why she fucked me like it was a fight for her life, for *our* lives. She won me over. And over. And over. And I couldn't break her, though she screamed for me to try. It's why I gave in to her, knowing she could take me, she could survive me.

If only for one night.

There were so many layers to her, and I want to rip them open again, watching them pulse, raw and dripping for me.

But I'm holding my daughter in my arms.

And.. fuck.

Stop it!

My worlds can't collide.

I bounce Gia on my arm, explaining, "Scarlett will help me and Celine take you to school. She's going to help us whenever we have to go somewhere."

"Why?"

It's Gia's favorite question.

"Because I get tired or busy sometimes," Celine answers behind Gia in a sweet voice. "I do appreciate the help." She steps around us, greeting Scarlett and Charlie.

I already debriefed Gia's nanny on what was happening, how I was hiring a bodyguard for Gia.

At first, Celine bristled at my plan, worried about the intrusion and how a big man may scare Gia, but when I told her I was hiring a woman—she agreed, relieved.

Celine was *my* nanny, more like my big sister thirty years ago, but I grew up, and she married and had kids. They're grown, and then her husband died, so when Celine heard that my wife had died too, she came back and saved me from inevitable failure.

I had a one year-old daughter and a life I didn't want to live, but for Gia's sake.

I didn't even know how to make waffles in the toaster.

"Will you stay the night with me too? Like Celine?" Gia cants her head at Scarlett, and here come a million questions. "Will you come with Baba and take me to my new school? Will you drive, or will Baba because he says bad words when he drives? He doesn't like the big bridge."

I don't like that big bridge, the Ravenel Bridge, for a tragic reason. One Gia doesn't remember, but I do. It finds me screaming in my sleep.

"Yes," Scarlett won't let her smile drop, gently answering Gia, "I will drive with your Baba and take you to school. And sometimes if his work is too busy, I'll take you, but I love the big bridge. It has the prettiest view of the water."

Gia pokes my cheek with her tiny finger. "Baba, *she's* not afraid of the bridge, so she can drive us."

"I'm not afraid of a bridge," I lie, feeling the grumpy setting I default to kick in. "It's the damn drivers I hate."

"We're not supposed to say bad words," Gia admonishes me. She's got me wrapped around her poking finger.

"*You're* supposed to finish your lunch."

I set her down, but Gia's not budging.

"But you didn't tell me." Her fists land on her waist. She stares up at Scarlett like no adult intimidates her, and I love it and hate it, too. "Will you live here too? Like Celine? We have lots of rooms. I'll give you one."

I've guarded Gia too closely. I've kept her with me in this hotel because I won't let her out of my sight. She's everything to me. And she knows she'll inherit our family business. She already acts like she's running it, handing out hotel rooms like Halloween candy. But Gia needs friends her age. She needs to be free and five, not fifty as I feel, though that's twenty years from now.

Yes, she spends time with her cousin, but it's not enough.

Our hotels may be my only world, but I won't imprison my daughter in the same legacy. I never got to dream for myself. I had no future but the one attached to my last name. Not that it's a bad life. It's a luxurious one, full of exotic locations and fascinating people.

But it was never my choice.

My wife was my choice, the innocent dream I dared to have. We married young at the courthouse without our parents' blessing, and I'm still being punished for it.

Warmly, Scarlett squats before Gia like she enjoys kids. This is the side I saw of her when I let myself hold her for too long in the ashes of our sex.

It was the most I've felt for a woman in years.

It was a grave mistake.

"I bet *all* your rooms are beautiful," Scarlett answers Gia. "Thank you, but I have my place. I live just down the street, with a view of the big bridge and a puppy. Maybe you can come visit us one day."

Gia yanks my hand. "Can I, Baba? Can I play at..." She pauses, excitement raising her voice. "What's your name again?"

"Scarlett," she softly answers.

"Can I play at Scarlett's house? With her puppy?"

I want to play at Scarlett's house. I want to play *with* Scarlett. I want to be a filthy dog with her. All the dark games I crave with her body.

But the fact that I can't have Scarlett again, and I never should've, twists my face. Guilt tastes bitter in my mouth, igniting my fury.

"Gia, it's time for business, not play right now." I nudge her toward Celine. "Go finish your lunch."

Gia mirrors me, twisting her face, too. "Baba, you're being grumpy."

All it takes is the raise of my eyebrow, and she huffs with a stomp, spinning around and taking Celine's hand as she leads her back down the hall into the kitchen.

For the next hour, I sit with Charlie and Scarlett in my penthouse living room with its wrap-around view over the historic city and church spires.

Charleston isn't my home. It was my wife's home.

I met her here one summer as a waiter at this hotel. Despite being a junior at Harvard at the time, my father made me learn the ropes. By twenty-five, I'd held almost every job in the hotel, from cleaning rooms to becoming the Chief Executive after my father suddenly died from a stroke.

Darby, my wife, was a Southern debutante and hated it. She hid in the corner during her Cotillion, and that's where we met, in the shadows of a ballroom where we weren't supposed to fall in love.

And that's where her memory lives now, in the shadows of my heart that will never stop loving my wife, that will never forgive myself.

That's why this feels so wrong.

And so right.

Sunlight dances through Scarlett's fiery strands, and I try not to stare. The edges of a red rose tattoo peek out from under the left cuff of her blue silk blouse, and I try not to remember everything about her, how I lost my mind inside her.

But I do.

Scarlett Jones was my greatest relief and my biggest regret. Because now it's just business, as Charlie clarifies terms.

"During the hours Gia is in school, where will Scarlett be posted, and what will she do?"

I pause before I answer, knowing exactly why I torture myself.

"I'll give Ms. Jones an office beside mine, and she can be my detail, too, if I have to go anywhere high-risk."

That keeps Scarlett close, near the other temptations I hide on the same floor as my office, and that will only make my torment more satisfying.

"What's my cover?" Scarlett asks me in her tempting voice—deep and raspy with a Southern accent.

Damn, the dirty things I made her say. "Yes, Master," she groaned with my dick fucking her ass, "I'm your whore."

I lick my lips at the memory while I answer her, "You're my personal assistant. That's what my staff has been told. I have secretaries, but I've never had an assistant. They think because Gia's starting school, that I'll need help, and it's not entirely untrue."

But *this* is untrue: me, trying to act professional when I remember how Scarlett's pussy tastes like honey. When I want it dripping with my cum into my mouth again.

I swear she can read my filthy mind, chewing her plump lip while Charlie insists, "But let's be clear. Ms. Jones is *not* your personal assistant, and she's *not* a nanny. I respect those professions, but she needs to be free to perform hers. She's a protection officer and can't be distracted by tasks that endanger your daughter. It's a tricky position, and lines can get blurred. I won't have one of *my* officers exploited or her mark compromised. *Ever.*"

That snaps me to attention.

Charlie Ravenel is a badass and doesn't play. I see why HGR Atlanta made her the boss. Why Daniel Pierce is a damn lucky man. Why they say pregnant women glow. And why they say never fuck with a Marine; I know some of her story.

"I respect that," I answer her. "Ms. Jones has free reign. She tells *me* what she needs to do her job."

"I'll need a room here," Scarlett replies, "and Gia can't know about it. She may blow my cover, but I'll need a place to secure my weapons, change, shower, or stay the night if you have an event or an obligation. We need to cover our bases."

I nod, tempted to give her a certain *suite* I keep locked on the executive floor, but no, *Scarlett's off-limits.* I never should've broken my rule in the first place, but I took a forbidden bite, and now I want to devour her.

This will be more than a job.

This is perfect.

Hunger is a constant state for me, and starvation is my drug. Having Scarlett so close but never having her again will be my favorite addiction. It's my punishment. My secret. It only heightens my senses and feels so right because what I desire to do to her is so wrong. It's dark and taboo, and I need it in my life, or I won't survive.

It fills the room with a brief silence before another *beep* sounds at my front door opening. Then Gia's sneakers squeak across the marble floors, running to greet our guest—the one who usually stops by after her lunch.

"Zar!" Gia's squeals before she giggles. "We have new friends!"

Scarlett turns her head toward the wide doorway of my living room with its ornate wooden molding. Charlie does, too.

And the tall, handsome sight that fills the doorway is my other temptation.

He's mine.

Scarlett

CHAPTER THREE

THERE'S A POINT IN SOME FIGHTS WHEN YOU SHOULD TAP out. When you admit you can't win...and that moment is now.

I don't know who this heart-stopping man is in the doorway, holding Gia on his arm like she's his daughter, too, but *holy sex in a linen suit.*

Seeing Luca again today is like lasting five rounds in a title fight. I don't know how much more I can take. My emotions are pummeled. My heart is exhausted. My aroused body can't fight the effect Luca has on me.

And now this?

This man, too?

I don't need to know who he is because it's clear—he's trouble. A tall, sexy pile of trouble in an ecru linen suit with stylish, dark hair and a trimmed beard. His deep brown eyes flicker with mischief at the sight of me and Charlie. He's almost as tan and imposing as Luca, but he's different.

When Luca scowls, this man smirks. He's a scoundrel, I can tell.

"Who are our new friends?" he asks Gia, and that's one positive for the mystery man.

I can sense it. He's not a creep. He genuinely cares for the little girl in his arms.

"That's Scarlett with the mermaid hair." Gia points to me, and I chuckle. It's not the first time I've been compared to Ariel, The Little Mermaid. But long, red hair is where the similarities end.

I'm not giving up my voice for any man. Or my tail.

Okay, I already *gave* my tail to Luca, but never again.

"And she's Uncle Red's friend, Charlie," Gia chirps, pointing to my boss, "the one with the really fat belly."

Charlie starts laughing while Luca quickly chides. "Gia, Charlie is not fat. That's not a nice word. She's pregnant. She has a *baby* in her belly."

Gia scrunches her nose. "How did a baby get in her belly?"

"Oh shit," Luca mutters, realizing his flub before he answers her, "I'll tell you tonight."

Watching Luca with his arms and legs stretched across his ivory sofa, I like this side of him. The side when his daughter has him against the ropes.

This morning, I went from shock to disgust to rage to compassion for Luca in minutes.

He's not a cheat.

He's a widower.

But still...

Luca made me feel everything. He made me feel special. And then he left me feeling used. That's the pain I fight. I recognize it now when I see this new side of him, the Dad side, and of course, Luca makes it look so alpha and so damn sexy, too; I'd let him breed me a dozen times. And that'll never happen, making this pain even worse.

I'm forever stuck in limbo with him.

"But how did a baby get in her belly, and how will it get out?" Gia asks, "Will she poop it out?"

Gia's not stopping with her questions, and I quickly adore her. So does Charlie. Gia's going to be fun. She will keep me on my toes, and hell, yes, I'd lay my life down for this cute girl.

"Yeah, Baba." Hot-as-fuck man #2 piles on with a smirk. "How *did* the baby get in the pretty lady's belly?"

Luca sneers at him, "Don't start."

He taunts, "But I want you to give me *the talk* tonight, too."

"I bet you do," Luca answers, and whoever this guy is, I like him. I don't trust him...but I like him.

"But Baba, tell us *now*." Gia squirms in his arms. "You're being mean to Zar again."

"I'm not mean to Zar," Luca rumbles. "We're best friends," he huffs, "and Gia, what did I tell you about business? It's not time for playing yet."

"Talking isn't playing," she sasses back.

This Zar guy scoffs, "Wanna bet?"

"Gamóto," Luca mutters, throwing his chin up. And though I don't understand what he cursed, it's like Celine can smell his distress.

She appears in the doorway, saying something in French while she takes Gia from Mr. Playful's arms. Then they disappear down the hallway, rescuing Luca from an impromptu birds-and-the-bees discussion, egged on by his naughty friend. The same one who crosses the room, extending his hand to shake Charlie's first.

"Zar Rollins," he says, "nice to meet you, and sorry for the pregnancy joke, but I take every shot at this asshole I can get."

He nods toward Luca, and my eyes flick his way. Luca's not smiling at him, but his eyes are amused.

"Nice to meet you," Charlie greets him.

But when he aims my way, there's too much damn delight in this stranger's brown eyes...as if he knows my secret.

Did Luca tell him about us?

No, he couldn't have. Luca didn't know I'd be his daughter's P.O. So why the hell is this man shaking my hand as a stranger but smirking at me like he knows that I've already fucked my forbidden client...several times?

But I won't be intimidated.

"Czar?" I ask him. "Like a Russian Czar? That's an unusual name."

"No." He plops into the blue velvet chair beside me. "Zar. For Balthazar, and I'll punch anyone who calls me by the name my parents cursed me with."

I huff...*like I'm threatened.*

"Just don't take a swing at Ms. Jones." Luca slides his admiring eyes my way. "Apparently," he says, "you won't win because our bodyguard is a titled fighter."

He reads it in my shocked eyes.

Did he just blow my cover?

So he explains, "Zar is the only one who knows why you're really here. He'd never let anything happen to Gia either. He's my best friend and CFO. We were roommates in college and have no secrets."

Great, that means Luca will be updating Zar later, over thousand-dollar whisky, I'm sure. They'll talk long into the night about the salacious details. Like how I fingered myself, sucking Luca's cock while three other men with their bare, hard cocks surrounded me too, and it made me come so hard, being that dirty for Luca.

"Such a bad girl for me, aren't you?" Luca praised me that night. "Show them. Suck your sweet cum off your dirty fingers. That's it. Now play with your pretty nipples while they watch you choke on me some more."

I never touched those other men, stroking off at the shameless sight of me, but god, how they wanted me to. And damn, how it got me off how Luca loved the fact—*I was his.*

But not anymore.

Minute by minute, I'm stepping farther into Luca's life, and this job, and there's no turning back now.

Casually, Luca updates Zar, "Ms. Jones will need an office next to mine and a private suite on the executive floor."

But I catch it. They exchange a knowing look, and I do the same with Charlie.

Does she feel it, too?

A couple of years ago, when I was her detail, Charlie said HGR was lucky to have me, not just for my fighting skills. Anyone can learn those. She said it was for my instincts. I've got a good one about people, and so does she.

Our eyes silently speak, sensing it now. There's something between Luca and Zar. History and work, obviously, but something more. A bond. A secret.

Whatever it is...

I have to work between these men?

HIF #5: They're so hot, they'll melt me like the cream in an Oreo.

My panties won't stand a chance of dryness.

"So, how does a woman become a MMA fighter?" Zar asks me, crossing his legs like a gentleman, and I half-believe his act.

I always get this question, and I used to be embarrassed by my answer. But with this job, not anymore. I'm proud of who I've become.

"I took an iron skillet to the skull of my stepfather. I caught him..." I pause at the memory, clenching my molars, "abusing my youngest sister while my mom was at work. It was either him or us, and like hell, I'd let him hurt my sisters. I almost killed him, and at sixteen, that landed me in a judge's chambers. She didn't know what to do with my rage. But instead of juvie, she had a friend who ran a gym. He taught me how to fight with control, and the rest is history."

Zar nods, his eyes combing down my body before his chin juts toward my face. "Is that where that scar came from? The one over your eye?"

"Damn," Charlie scoffs, "you got big balls asking a woman about her scars."

Suddenly, we're all humbled, knowing how Charlie got the scar on her cheek and the ones you can't see. Her story exploded in the press years ago, and I'm proud of how she handled it.

"My apologies." Zar surrenders. "I mean no offense. Scars are survival, something to be proud of in my book."

"I got this beauty from someone's elbow in a fight," I answer him. "But it was a concussion from an illegal knee to my skull that ended my fighting career. Especially when this better job came along."

"We recruited Ms. Jones," Charlie interjects. "Women are rare in this profession, and we need more of them."

Zar drawls, "Well, you sure got your work cut out for you now."

He sounds like he's from Texas but doesn't dress like it. I fight not to admire his washboard abs, thinly veiled by his stylish white T-shirt. I like his style. It's all business casual meets spread-your-legs-for-me, darlin'. While Luca's style is all power, all bend-over-my-desk-like-a-whore-for-your-Master fashion.

I try not to remember how Luca said that exact thing to me, minus the desk part. It was a sofa.

I try...but fail.

"Luca has two paparazzi outside that stalk his every move," Zar informs us, "and one crazed woman banned from our hotel. We have a restraining order against her, but it doesn't stop her. We catch her sneaking in all the time."

Charlie's brows shoot up, challenging Luca. "You never told me about this threat."

"She's not a threat," Luca scoffs. "She's just obsessed. It's harmless."

"Obsession isn't harmless," Charlie warns. "I barely survived it. Twice."

"I can take care of myself," Luca replies. "But that's why I need Scarlett, I mean, *Ms. Jones.* I need Ms. Jones to protect my daughter."

"What does this woman look like?" I ask.

"Oh, we have a file on her. I'll show you," Zar replies. "But it doesn't stop her. She comes up with clever disguises and checks in under different names. Our front desk staff is pretty good at spotting her, but a couple of times, she got through. But even when we catch her, a judge just slaps her hand, and she's back, trying to sneak through our doors again."

"What does she do while she's here?" I have to know because

if I thought my instinct was firing about Zar and Luca—which it is —it's an exploding transformer with live wires popping over this.

Something about this feels dangerous, and Charlie's serious face agrees.

"She left photos on my desk," Luca answers me, making Zar chuckle, clarifying, "Very *explicit* photos."

"And she left something in my car in the parking deck once," Luca adds.

"A pair of her...um...*moist* panties." Zar starts laughing while he shares, "And the biggest dildo I've ever seen. Apparently, she enjoyed herself in Luca's Benz and left the dildo, her panties, and the evidence of her joy all over his leather driver's seat."

Now, both men are amused, but I'm not. "Do you know her?"

They exchange another one of those damn secret looks, and now Luca's laughing. I've never seen him laugh, and if I weren't so concerned, I'd swoon. He's beautiful when he's happy.

"Yes," Luca answers me, "Zar dated her."

"For a hot second," he protests, "until I realized she was unhinged."

"Is that how she knows Mr. Mercier?"

I use his business name because that's what this is: my business. Serious business. I'm not judging dildos and photos and public anything. I got no room.

But disguises? Being banned and having a restraining order issued by a lenient judge? And why is she obsessed with Luca and not Zar if Zar's the one who dated her?

"We don't know." Zar shrugs. "It's tough to say because everyone knows who *Luca Mercier* is. He's global catnip. Yeah, he's got billions people want, but it seems women *really* lose their kitties over single dads."

Luca rolls his eyes.

"And apparently," Zar adds, "Luca's not hard to look at either."

That makes Luca narrow his gaze, and Zar winks back.

Yep, I smell a secret.

Scarlett

CHAPTER FOUR

"I CAN'T BELIEVE IT'S *HIM*."

That's the third time my sister has blurted it on our call, and I don't blame her. Ruby's the only one who knows about Luca.

At first, I didn't want to admit it to my sister or my friends that I may have fallen for a man I fucked in a sex club. A stranger who I never saw again. Not like they'd judge me. I just didn't want to admit it to myself.

Hell, I don't want to admit it *now*.

But after I saw Luca again today? After I watched him hold his daughter like she belonged on his arm and nowhere else. He loves her. He'd never leave her.

That's got to be this shitty feeling nagging inside my chest. I can't catch a full breath.

Even a year ago, Ruby knew something was off. I was acting weird and not listening to her latest drama with her boyfriends, so I finally confessed, "I caught the Fuck Flu."

That's what we call it; when you fuck someone, and it makes you sick with feelings.

"Girl, are you serious?" Ruby couldn't believe it. "After only *one* night?"

"Well, what else can it be?" I asked her. "What else explains

35

this sick feeling clawing in my chest like I'm missing something and this heat I feel, though I don't have a fever? I can't stop thinking about him."

Ruby's like me. We share the same scars and won't let anyone hurt us again. We don't fall for anyone.

Or so I thought.

And yes, my sister's name is Ruby. She's a year younger than me. Then there's Rose and Cherry, the youngest. You get the trend—red.

If you ask me, Cherry got off the worst.

Anyway.

"Yes, it's *HIM*," I tell her again. "And god must hate me because I work for him now."

Pressing my phone to my ear, I stare through my sliding glass doors. Moonlight sparkles over the wide Cooper River.

I love my dockside condo on the tenth floor with its sweeping views. I love my new puppy, a cute mutt I rescued. I named him Crimson, of course. And I love my new red Alpha Romeo Stelvio. I love everything I've worked hard for, earning good money at a job I love, too.

Me and my sisters come from nothing. After my dad bailed on us, my mom did her best. She kept our trailer clean and fridge stocked, but she was never there, working long hours to support us. So I watched over my sisters, and we were fine until *he* came along—the stepdad from hell. Now, I realize he targeted my mom, a woman with daughters.

"God doesn't hate you," Ruby chides. "Maybe it's a hot blessing y'all met again."

"No, it's a *HIF*."

"You and your HIFs," she huffs. "Your life is not *fucked*."

"Fine. Then Luca's a hot blessing with a big dick I can never fuck again, or it will be a HIF—How I'll get *Fired*."

"Honey, with the way you say he fucked you...four times in one night! And the way his tongue cleaned your pussy like a Lysol lover after each time. I wouldn't give a *damn* about my job."

Ruby's the only sister who knows my kinks and deeds. She

doesn't care that I fucked Luca in a sex club.

Once, when she was a senior in high school, I came home and caught her messing around with two football players when Mom wasn't there.

There's no shame between us.

It's Cherry who's the survivor, the sister I almost killed for. She keeps a lot of things private, and I understand.

"Cherry's only a sophomore," I remind Ruby. "I've got two more years of her college to pay for, so no, I'm not getting fired over a big dick."

"Can I at least come to his hotel and meet him?" Ruby teases. "I mean, I know who Luca Mercier is. The whole world does. But I want to shake the hand of the man you called 'Master' because that is *not* the Scarlett I know. You usually want men on *their* knees."

"Yeah, well, get this—" I tell her, "he's a widower, too. He still wears his wedding band, and for a second, I thought he cheated on his wife with me until he told me and my boss that his wife died four years ago."

"Oh, my god," Ruby sighs. "Why does that make him even hotter?"

"Hotter?" I refresh the water in Crimson's bowl before I set it on the floor. He laps it up while I add, "No, that makes him damaged in the most heartbreaking way because you should see his daughter, Gia. She's so cute. She reminds me of Cherry when she was little, all precocious and shit."

"Uh-huh." I can see Ruby shaking her head. "Watch:" she says, "y'all will get married one day."

"Married? Even if Luca wasn't my client, I ain't his type."

I give a treat to Crimson, who eagerly chews it, leaving crumbs and slobber on my white tile floors.

"You sure were his type for a night." Ruby jokes. "He left hickeys and bruises between your thighs. And on your neck. Oh, and on your tits, too, you said. Girl, he marked your ass like a Sex Sharpie."

"Exactly. *One night.*"

I turn back to the one outside, stepping onto my balcony and sliding the glass door back quickly before Crimson can escape. A tanker sparkles on the water, slowly gliding across the wide river, seeking its path to the Atlantic, which I also glimpse.

"Luca Mercier is a fancy billionaire who's all class, and I'm a redneck who's all trash," I remind my sister. "Yeah, he fucked me for a night and loved calling me his whore, and that's why I'm not the kind of woman he'd marry."

"Hush your fuss," Ruby interrupts my logic. "You ain't trash. You're hot as fuck, and you said you could tell he felt something, too. That's why he left you all dickmatized and brokenhearted. I've never seen my tough sister so soft for a man. Usually, you never trust them."

I don't argue with her. That's what I told her the next day because I know what Luca and I felt.

I *did* trust him.

I trusted him to have me however he wanted, and he didn't let me down. Luca took our bodies to heights I didn't know were possible to share with a man, and afterward, he gently held me on the sofa in the middle of the club like no one else was there, resting his chin on my head, kissing my hair and softly rubbing my back. It felt so new and natural. I was open, tender, and exposed to him.

When the bartender announced the club was closing, Luca said he didn't want to leave, and I believed him.

But then he shocked me.

Darkly, he murmured some prophetic words before he got up, grabbed his jeans and shirt, and yanked them on. I sat there, speechless, too proud to ask what had changed because I couldn't believe the sight, silently watching Luca Mercier walk out of the club while he left me there, naked, on the sofa we had shared all night.

It was cruel and not the man I thought I had just met.

Our first time, when Luca was on top of me, thrusting into me, he gazed down, letting me see the passion he felt but the tears he fought, too. It was so beautiful, I couldn't speak.

His crystal eyes were so full of pain and pleasure, and he shared it with me. I swear, I felt it, too. It's like he wanted me to take what he suffered, and I did. Everything Luca made me feel made me come.

Then, he roared with his first orgasm, spilling inside me, bruising the wrists he held pinned above my head before he leaned down, kissing my lips. Then, his brutal body wouldn't relent. He became ruthless and addictive all night.

But our first tender moment was real and raw, and it was my ruin.

Not until Luca was gone did I finally let my clenching heart bleed. My past and present collided, and there was no way I could fight the pain flooding my chest. I sat naked on the sofa, alone.

Luca left without a word. He left me crying.

Just like my dad left me.

And it's tortured me ever since. Did Luca use me? Was I really a whore? A filthy one-night distraction from his pristine life?

I mean, how buck wild can the father to a little girl really get?

I didn't get the impression the sex club was a regular place for him. It wasn't for me either. I was there for my friends, to watch Cade and Redix celebrate their Dirty Thirty birthday with their lover, Silas. I wasn't there to get my heart broken, but I did.

"Yeah, well," I answer my sister. "I was a fool to trust Luca that night. Because he's hiding something, I can tell."

"Bitch, Luca Mercier is so fine; he can hide his Mr. Big in any backyard he pleases." Ruby halts, reading my mind. "And you said that night he also called you—"

My phone beeps, interrupting her with another call. I check the screen. "Oh fuck," I mutter. "It's *HIM*. He's calling me."

"He's got your number?"

"Yes, I work for him now, remember? I gotta go. Bye."

My fingertip shakes, ending the call with my sister and accepting the call from my boss, the cruel maledom I can never fuck again.

"Hello?"

"*MS. JONES.*" Luca needs to *STOP* sounding like an orgasm of the tongue. "Am I interrupting a date?"

I snap, "I'm not paid enough to make *my* dates *your* business."

He pauses, processing my sass. "Indeed. Then, is it too late to discuss *work*?"

"No. Shoot." I try to sound in control, but I'm not. My thighs weaken, so I plop in the chair on my balcony. "Whadayawant?"

That question can be answered a million forbidden ways, and he chuckles at it.

"I called to discuss..."

He hesitates, and I hold my breath.

Are we going to be adults and talk about it? About how he called me his "beautiful whore" while he fucked me against the wall, the second of four times. I clawed at his back, making him moan for more before he grabbed my throat, growling, "Yes, my whore. My beautiful whore. Fight me. Make me fuck you. Your pussy is mine. You'll come for me. You'll kneel for me. Won't you?"

That's exactly what he said. My pussy won't let me forget because it made me mewl, "Yes," before he choked me while I came in his grasp.

But now he says, "Your attire for the job."

Well, knock me out of the chair with a tissue.

"My *attire*?" I snarl. "You want to discuss what I'll wear while I protect your daughter? *That's* the important discussion we need to have?"

"I suppose there are several things we should discuss," he threatens, "like your beautiful boss who can never know about our past. Is that clear, Ms. Jones?"

I shake my head, feeling the rage boil again. "Yes, Mr. Mercier, let's *discuss*." I begin. "First, if you tell my boss about us and get me fired, I'll armbar your shoulder so hard, you won't be able to jerk off again. You'll have to hump your pillow. And second, I'll wear what I can fight in. A business suit with pants."

"You'll stand out. None of the women who work for me wear pants. They wear skirts or dresses."

My eyes narrow. "Why? Is that your sexist dress code? Men get to wear sensible pants, but women must submit and wear dumbass tight skirts? And let me guess—stupid high heels, too?"

He growls, "You've got a lot of attitude in your tone, Ms. Jones."

"You've got a lot of shitty asshole in yours, Mr. Mercier."

That makes him suddenly laugh. "You know I'm an ass-man." Then, he pauses. "And you wore heels *today*."

"Yeah, because it was a debriefing meeting. But I can't fight in heels."

"I disagree. I've seen what you can do in heels *and* a skirt. And you do it very well, I might add."

Fucking dickhead. A really big, thick dickhead.

He liked teasing my entrance with it, making it gape while he circled his thumb over my clit until I was begging for each stretching inch he slowly tortured me with and...

Quit it, bitch. You're thinking with your lusty loins and not your brain because...

Is he flirting with me again?

Yes, I wore a black pencil skirt and a matching leather bustier the night we met. And yeah, I wore heels to a sex club. What was I supposed to wear? Flip-flops while I got railed for an audience?

"It's the culture of my business." Luca fills my silence. "I'd never impose such a rule. But we are a five-star, European line of luxury hotels with select American properties. My staff, men *and* women, bring their mostly French fashion with them. But it's your job, Ms. Jones, your decision."

I'm quiet, feeling my cheeks flame while my heart pounds.

Am I angry or aroused?

"Your luxury suite and executive office will be ready when you arrive tomorrow morning," he continues. "Wear whatever you like when you accompany us to Gia's open house tomorrow, though it's an elite, private school. You may want to blend in there, too."

The bossy fucker isn't wrong.

Yes, I need to blend in. I need to look like Luca Mercier's

French, high-class personal assistant, not like I'm running for president.

The fact that I suspect that's a dirty kink for him—the powerful boss and his sexy secretary—is going to burn through me and my wallet. I can't afford the expensive role-play fantasy or these feelings.

As if Luca can read my mind, he says, "I will give you my company credit card tomorrow. Mercier Hotels will pay for your attire. It's part of the job. Go shopping for whatever you need. Pants. Skirts. Guns. *Black lacy panties.*"

"Stop it."

Luca *is* flirting with me, and suddenly, it hurts. I hate it. I stare at the river, remembering how I wore black panties that night, how Luca ripped them off of me, and rapid tears sting my eyes, catching me off-guard.

I let him do so much to me.

"You got what you wanted that night, and then you left me," I mutter. "And it won't *ever* happen again."

He doesn't answer. The only sound is a distant ship's horn across the water, and now I feel as inky and churning as that river. Deep currents of pain wash through me, and I guess I've been holding this in.

How Luca left me feeling used.

How he did something to me, and I don't know what it is.

How men never get inside me, but he did.

Yes, I have a tough exterior. It's my job. It's how I survived. But I know, my sisters know, how we all slept in the same bed. How I'd sleep by the edge while they slept closer to the wall, so I could protect them. So, if my stepdad came for one of us in the night, it would be *me.*

I never trusted him, and I was right. I acted brave when really...I cried silent, broken tears. I was so afraid, so hurt that our father left us. He left us at risk, and it was like I became the dad.

The tough one.

But I'm not.

I'm very human, and Luca left me very hurt. It's a pain that cuts too deep, and I have no one to blame but myself because I let him do it.

"We both got what we wanted that night, Ms. Jones," Luca cooly replies. "You said it first. You said you wanted to be my whore, so I was honest with you. I told you I wouldn't be gentle. I warned you I'd be rough, and it'd only be for a night. I told you that I would use you, and you could use me, and you agreed to those terms."

"You said you weren't a man," I reply, caught in the memory of how he yanked my bustier down, pinching my nipples for others to watch, to hear him make me moan. "You said you were an animal who'd make me come. That's it."

"Exactly," he soothes. "And I fulfilled my promise. I *did* make your pussy come, Ms. Jones." His accent is ruthless. It's strangling the life from me again, all my emotions surging at the sound of it. "Do you remember how many times I made you come?" He coaxes, "Do you remember the *first* time I made you come for me... Scarlett?"

Oh my god, the way Luca says my name.

He's doing it again. He's storming back inside me, seizing control of what he owns when I know he'll only leave again. It wets my cheeks with tears but heats my core with lust, and why do I love his torture?

Only Luca does this to me.

"Do you remember," he baits me, "how I told you to lift your skirt and pull your black, lacy panties aside so you could play with your pretty pussy for me? And you did. You loved submitting to me. Your breasts were exposed, your beautiful pink nipples got so hard. You let strangers watch you fuck your fingers for me and moan my name while you came before I told you to smear your sweet, creamy cum on my lips before I sucked them clean."

"Luca." I sigh his name again, my body drowning in the memory, my stomach flipping, rousing my pussy with sweet pain.

God, I miss him.

There's no one like him.

"Do it again for me, Belle." That's what Luca called me that night—*Belle*—beautiful. "Play with your pussy for me now while I remind you of how I sat on the sofa and you stood over me. How I spread you open so others could watch how I fucked you with my tongue and sucked your clit so hard, you were dripping down my chin.

"You were so strong, Belle, grabbing my hair and suffocating me in that wet pussy. Oh, and your ass is so sweet, too. I couldn't stop licking it. I wanted to eat you alive, and I did. I made you come three times on my face while others watched me do it, and you loved being my whore for them."

"You loved it, too," I answer, feeling my nipples ache under my tank top.

It's all I'm wearing. I was ready to go to bed before Ruby's call, and now, I tug my thong aside, gliding my finger over my clit that's been screaming for him all day.

I can hate him, and he can hurt me, but still, I want him.

"You loved fucking me while others watched," I sigh. "You loved pulling your hard cock out of my pussy and making me lick my cum off of it before you fucked me more, making me confess to everyone how I was your *whore*. Only *your* whore. You moaned whenever I said it—*your whore*. And you're doing it now, aren't you, Luca? You're getting off on this; you're getting off *on me*."

"To your voice, Belle," he says. "To that pussy I know is so wet for me. I'm hard as hell and lying on my bed, stroking my cock and remembering how you told me to fuck you so hard. 'Harder, motherfucker,' you screamed. You bit my neck, growling, 'Make me your fucking whore.' And we hurt each other until we *both* came. So. Many. Times. My belle."

"Is that what you love, Luca? Giving pain while you fuck?"

"I don't love. I don't *FUCK*," he snarls. "I destroy."

Yes, he does.

Luca bombs your walls. He ravages your world. Any shame, pride, or reason you have? Gone. He fucks like an evil conquerer, erasing who you were before while he claims your flesh and you are...

You're owned.

You're his.

You belong to Luca now.

"Now show me my sweet pussy," he demands. "Turn your camera on and fuck your fingers for me again."

I already am, teasing my entrance and grinding my palm over my clit. I stand up on my balcony to be more shameless about it, pushing my thong down to my thighs.

"Let me watch you, too," I demand. "I want to watch how I make you come so hard, don't I? Your cock's dripping for me, isn't it? I get you so hard, so fast. You can't get enough of my naughty pussy submitting to you, can you? I make your legs and lips shake, Luca. You *need* me, too."

"Fuck," he huffs, switching our call to a video first, and I moan at the sight, desire making me sway, dizzy.

It's been forever and like yesterday since I've seen Luca's naked body. His massive, shredded naked body. He's lying on his bed, his bronze skin dark against his white sheets. Thrusting his swollen cock into his choking grasp, he holds his phone overhead like I'm on top of him again. There's no hair on his chest, so every hard curve of his huge pecs and deep carve through his defined abs flexes for my view while he fucks his fist.

"Fuck, Belle, yes, you make me come so hard." He demands, "Fuck your pussy, too. You love being a slut for me, don't you?"

When I switch to video, too, he groans, surprised. "You're outside."

"Yes, I'm on my balcony." I flip on the electric lantern on the end table beside my chair. It glows over my skin as I lift my tank and leave it resting above my breasts before I pinch my nipple, tugging it for him and biting my lip.

"Oh, my belle," he growls. "You get so dirty for me, don't you? Playing with yourself and letting strangers watch."

"Yes," I answer him. "Now pump that big dick harder. I wanna watch you squirt your cum all over your abs for me."

He grins. "How do you ask?"

And I remember wetting even more to what he demands.

"Please, Master," I entice, "stroke your big dick for me."

"You dirty girl, drop your wet panties first."

I grin, shoving them down to my ankles before I step out of them. When I stand back up, I hold my phone so he can watch me step my thighs apart.

"Yes, my belle," he says, the veins in his forearm tensing as his grip strangles, his strokes getting faster. "Now fuck your hand. That's it. Slide two fingers inside. Yes... Nice and slow... Just like that... Now, pump them in and out for me. *Yes*, dirty girl, let me watch. Let me hear how wet you are for me... Um, yes, roll your hips too. Keep going. Play with your clit, and let me watch. Let me hear you spank that wet pussy for me."

This is exactly how I came the first time for him, and I'm right here again—not caring who can see me. Not worried about what's next. I only want this now and with him.

What Luca conjures inside me is all I need to feel. *Adored. Desired.* It's how I'm supposed to feel. *Cared for.* It's too good to be wrong.

"Keep going, my belle," he urges, and I will skate on the edge of death for him because my orgasm is here. It's right here for him. "Are you my whore? Playing with your pussy for me? Does it feel good?"

I'm shaking for him. "Yes."

"Yes, what?"

"Yes, Luca," I sigh. "Yes, Master, I'm all yours. I'm your little whore."

"Then show me. Let me watch you come for me." His cock is dripping. Its veins are swelling in his pumping grasp, his eyes glaring wild while his lips part with mine.

And it's brutal.

It's torture.

It's incredible how I fuck myself so hard with my fingers; I come for him. My shoulders lurch, my pussy clenching around my fingers. It hurts so good, but I won't break my stare. I look right at him on the screen as I cry out, "Luca," my scream echoing across the water.

"Show me your cum," he huffs, and he's so close. When I hold my milky fingers up, licking them for his gaze, he grunts, "Fuck, yes, Scarlett." Throwing his chin back, he grunts again, his back bowing, locking the muscles on his entire frame while ivory ropes of his release spurt over his hard abs, and he gasps, "Fuck, Belle. *Ma flamme.*" More cum spurts, over and over, from his tip while he moans, "Scarlett," and I swear I could come again at the sound, at the sight.

Luca is so beautiful when he comes.

It's like the only moment he's not in power, he's not in pain.

But I don't come again. My sanity returns, remembering how that night ended because this one has to end, too.

"*Ma flamme,*" Luca had sighed our last time while he was still inside me, making me fight tears. I clung to his back, to a feeling that had no name while he held me.

"Don't leave," I pleaded that night, and he said he didn't want to.

For minutes, we lay on the sofa, with me in his arms, him kissing my hair, and I trusted he'd stay until he muttered, "It only dies," before pulling away from me. "I always kill it," he murmured, leaving my body empty, taking my heart with him.

Sitting in my car in the club's parking lot, I looked it up that night. Crying for the stranger who left me burned, I looked up those words, and they mean "my flame" in French.

And tonight, I'm silent again. I can't move. I'm that same woman, on fire for him, and Luca can see it. It's the same look I had in my eyes the night he left me. It rises from someplace deep inside, and I hate him seeing me like this.

Vulnerable.

Hurt.

"It was a mistake, Belle," he speaks of us now, though he's covered in his desire for me. "We were a grave mistake, and it will never happen again."

"Good night." I end the call because I won't beg him this time. My tears won't fall. This is business now, and I'll get used to it.

The hell of wanting a man who leaves.

Luca

CHAPTER FIVE

IT'S THIRTY MINUTES OF HELL DRIVING MY DAUGHTER TO school.

From the French Quarter in Charleston where my hotel is, a narrow, flat city street leads you up a ramp. As the one-lane road climbs higher and higher, the nose of your car soars while concrete barriers that aren't tall enough close in around you, trapping you in a climbing, tight right curve that never ends until you're trapped...

On the Ravenel Bridge.

It's the third longest cable-stayed bridge in the Western hemisphere, and it's my hell. Soaring over seventeen stories high, the bridge is designed to endure three hundred mile-an-hour winds while I can barely endure driving over it.

My palms sweat. My ears ring. And the memory, like a gust of wind across the bridge, makes me sway with terror.

I've been the only one allowed to drive my daughter across this bridge for four years.

Gia's new school is on the other side of it. Her mother went there, and Gia's cousin goes there now. My wife's sister lives near the school. That's where we were that July fourth, driving home from her sister's house.

We were right here...crossing this cursed bridge.

"Is Aunt Abbey going to be there? And Harper, too?" Gia calls out from the back, where I've secured her into her safety seat like a Formula One driver.

"No," I can barely answer, gripping the steering wheel. "The open house today is for kindergarteners only."

If I weren't so terrified, I'd be embarrassed.

I try to hide my fear from my daughter, but now I have a new audience. Scarlett's in the passenger seat of my black Escalade. I bought the biggest, safest luxury car for this daily torture.

"But I won't have any *friends* if Harper's not there."

Anxiety fills my daughter's voice, and it matches mine as we climb. Only the blue sky fills the horizon as the speeding morning traffic in the lanes around me races my pulse. I have to drive in the middle lane, my glare focused ahead.

"Harper's in second grade. She'll be there next week for your first day," Celine soothes Gia. "And you'll see her this Sunday at brunch."

But Gia doesn't reply with her usual glee. She's nervous. I am, too, because the spot is coming up. The one on my left. The one that makes me sweat, it makes me sick, fighting not to remember.

And the silence watching me from the passenger seat makes this even worse.

Scarlett looks ravishing today.

When she met us in the foyer of my penthouse this morning, I had to grit my teeth, offering her a travel mug of strong Greek coffee, like an apology, feeling guilty after what we did last night.

At what she wore today.

It's my punishment; I know it.

She's wearing the same black pencil skirt, or one just like it, from our night at the club. The heels she compromised with are low but spiky. And her pink silk blouse makes her tan skin glow. She left a few buttons open to torture me. I can see the lace of her bra underneath, making me obsess over its color.

But the worst is she left her flaming hair tumbling down.

All I wanted to do on the elevator ride from the penthouse to the parking deck was sink my hands into her strands, crashing her lips against mine while I sucked her tongue.

I can't stop thinking about her.

What I want with Scarlett is so wrong.

But how I need her is so right.

And like she can sense my vision threatening to blur with my terror on this bridge, she quietly asks, "Is this the same car that woman...you know..."

It makes me grin, the sudden change of subject that's too inappropriate for my daughter, but she can't hear it over the *Moana* soundtrack playing.

"No," I whisper back. "I got a new car. Once she knew which one was mine and I knew what she did, I bought two. This and a Lotus I drive by myself for fun."

I risk a glance at Scarlett, and she's grinning my way.

Relief floods me.

I thought she wasn't speaking to me after last night, after I made it very clear we were a mistake. It won't happen again, but I guess at least around Gia, Scarlett remains professional.

I don't know what got into me last night when I called her. It was to discuss her attire, to offer my credit card. I want to take care of her.

That's a fucking lie.

I know what I want. I know what's inside me—lust for Scarlett that feels like damnation and deliverance at the same time.

My wife never made me feel this way. She was always so innocent and sweet and nothing like me, and that only makes the guilt kill me, too.

Yes, opposites attract. So what do you do when you meet your match? The one who's just like you? I felt it the moment we met. The moment Scarlett said those words to me, "Luca, I'll be your whore tonight."

Scarlett's made for me. She's strong enough to survive my darkest desires, tough enough to endure my degradation, and powerful enough to crave submission.

So it's hell she's working for me now, but at least the worst part of the bridge is past me as Scarlett mutters, "Did you give Gia the *talk* last night?"

Unfortunately, my daughter overhears *that*.

"Yes," Gia chirps, "I know how babies get in bellies and how they come out nine years later."

"Nine *months*." Celine laughs.

"Nine *months*," Gia corrects herself. "And Baba told me about boys' penises and my fine china."

I snort, all hell evaporating as Scarlett laughs, turning in her seat to ask Gia. "*What* did your Baba tell you?"

"Baba said that boys have penises and girls have fine china. And that no one can touch my fine china, and if they do, I'm not in trouble, but I have to tell Baba."

"Gia," I ease, "it's *vagina*. No one but you can touch your *vagina*."

"That's what I said," she replies, and once again, I survive hell for my daughter's sake.

But when I hold her hand, walking her into her new classroom, I don't know if I'll survive this—letting her go. But she does. She runs to the brightly colored toys on the bookshelves under the classroom windows, and I watch my world discover a Slinky.

"She's going to love it," Celine assures me. "You loved school too. You were the smartest in the class."

All while, I notice out of the corner of my eye how Scarlett is scanning the room. She looks like my sexy assistant, but her head is on a swivel.

"Luca, is that *you*?" A genteel voice calls over my shoulder, and I turn around.

"Maren, good to see you." I kiss her cheeks before asking, "Where's Thomas?"

Charleston isn't that big of a city, especially the circles I run in. Bumping into my wife's best friend doesn't surprise me, but her reply does.

"We divorced last year." She shrugs. "And as usual, he's too busy with work to be here for Spencer." She points to a little boy playing with Gia, and I haven't seen him since he was a baby.

"Wow," I sigh. "Spencer's so big."

"It *has* been four years." Maren touches my arm, letting her fingertips linger. "How are you?"

"We're fine," I answer, remembering all our time together and her phone calls and messages since that I never answered.

Darby was close to Maren. They shared everything, including being pregnant, months apart.

"It looks like those two have found each other again." I gesture to Gia, playing with Spencer. I'm relieved she'll have a family friend in the classroom. I introduce Maren to Celine as such. And to Scarlett.

"This is Maren Banks," I tell her. "She was best friends with my wi—"

I choke on the word. At what I'm about to say. At how it flies off my tongue.

This is awkward.

It feels wrong introducing Scarlett to my wife's best friend, knowing Scarlett's the woman who makes me come so hard, I see stars.

"It's nice to meet you." Scarlett shakes Maren's hand, saving me from finishing the sentence, and I don't know why I still do it.

Why do I still say "my wife" when she's been dead for four years? People must think I'm in denial, but I'm not. I just don't want to say "my *dead* wife," particularly around our daughter. But there's no word for it.

What do you call your other half, your first love who died before your eyes?

"Scarlett is my new personal assistant," I lie to Maren. "I'm going to need help when Gia starts school."

Maren nods, smiling, but I know women too well, and I've lived in the South for too long. Maren doesn't believe me and doesn't like Scarlett. It's like she's judging her. She disapproves. It's like she's...*jealous*? But why? She's a beautiful woman, too, but I've never been attracted to her.

"Scarlett," Maren coos. "What a pretty Southern name. Where is your family from, dear?"

Scarlett chuckles. "From a pretty trailer park off Highway Seventeen, just north of here."

Maren smiles. I don't remember her lips being that plump as they purse. "And just how did you find yourself working for *our* Luca?"

"Some friends introduced us," Scarlett answers before I can. "I met Mr. Mercier at a birthday party, and we quickly realized I met his demands."

Scarlett's fucking with me, and Maren can smell the half-truth.

Yes, I met Scarlett at a birthday party. Redix and Cade's thirtieth birthday party. But that was at a private sex club, not a country club where Maren is used to seeing me.

"Oh really?" Maren asks, "Luca, which friends? Leanne and Scott? Hallie and Dave?"

She's asking about my dead wife's friends, and to be fair, Maren doesn't know how much I died, too. I don't do much anymore but be a father. It's too hard. Our daughter is the only thing I live for. The only family I see is my wife's sister and *her* daughter, my niece, who live nearby.

The other company I keep...

Maren doesn't know about it.

I don't blab to the world that I've become close friends with Redix Dean. Redix is too famous, and I'm too protective of him. We've both been through hell and seek solace together on the golf course. Or a sex club.

And Maren hates Zar.

Probably because Zar fucked her sister at a fundraiser years ago.

Darby thought it was funny. She adored Zar. They were close, though Darby worried about him. She always said that Zar seemed lost, like he was missing something and hiding his pain.

My wife had no idea what Zar was hiding.

But I did.

I still do.

I answer Maren, "Scarlett and I met through friends from *work*. No one you'd know. But how is your mother...?"

I barely get out of that uncomfortable conversation and back over the damn bridge once the open house is done. Gia falls asleep on the ride home, so does Celine, and Scarlett doesn't say much.

After she spends the afternoon meeting with Zar, after he takes her up to my penthouse to say goodbye to Gia—I watched them with my cameras—she appears in my office doorway.

"Need anything else today?" she asks.

My needs are so grave, they make me grin. "No, thank you," I answer from behind my desk. "You're free to go."

She slants her eyes, half pissed, half amused. "Am I *free* to use the gym before I go? The pool too?"

"Please, do."

"Will you be watching me?"

She sees the array of flatscreens on my right. With the click of a mouse, I can monitor any of my sixty hotels worldwide.

I smirk. "I always watch what's mine."

Her eyebrow arches. "So, you're a voyeur?"

"No," I answer. "I'm *telling* you I'm watching you. For voyeurs, it's a secret. I'm a scopophilic. I derive great pleasure from you *knowing* that I'm watching you. As you're well aware."

I relish revealing a few of my dark secrets to her while I silently guess she's wearing a pink lace bra under her blouse. It thrills me, knowing how her nipples match.

But now I imagine how they'd look pinched in silver clamps with chains, red from my crop marks.

"You don't mind, do you?" I enjoy the control, teasing her, "Being watched?"

"As you're well aware, I derive great pleasure from you watching me." She grins. "But this is business now, Mr. Mercier. We don't make more mistakes, right?"

Checkmate.

I change the subject.

Sort of.

Reaching into my jacket pocket, I pull out my wallet. "Indeed, so here." I pluck my Black Card out. "Take this. Go shopping. There's no limit, no budget, but you need to keep looking as you do today."

Pinched between my extended fingers, I see if Scarlett will obey. If she'll take the bait.

But she smirks, stalking my way. She knows damn well what I'm doing, and she doesn't care. "So I can go to Ross and spend hundreds?" she asks.

"What's Ross?"

She rolls her eyes. "You're kidding, right?"

"Gucci, Kate Spade, Louis Vuitton," I answer. "They're around the corner, and you can spend tens of thousands."

"Great." She takes my card, eyeing it like a foreign object. "I get to be Julia Roberts for the day."

I shake my head, confused.

"*Pretty Woman?*" she huffs. "You've never seen the movie?"

"Should I?"

"Who are you, and where did you grow up?"

"Your client," I answer. "And Mykonos and Paris. And what's the movie?"

"A lonely, mean rich man falls in love with an escort, a poor, pretty red-headed whore he hires for the weekend."

I pause, letting the joke reveal her truth. "Scar...I mean, Ms. Jones, you are *not* my escort. I'm not that kind of man."

She raises that scarred brow, conjuring all the dirty things I've done and said to her. How that one word—*whore*—sets my soul on fire. It could twitch my cock, but my heart is too distracted.

"You know what I mean," I assert. "That was private. *This* is public. This is my world, and you'll be treated with respect. I respect you, and so will others."

She scoffs, "Watch how they'll treat me at Gucci Charleston tomorrow."

"But you have my Black Card."

"But you," her smirk falters, "weren't raised in a trailer park. Trust me. Women in your world can smell it on me."

Though I know Scarlett's tough, she's the most breathtaking

woman I've ever seen—the snobby women in this city have nothing on her—it's her weak spot. She was raised poor, while I was raised rich. We're from different worlds, and she's not comfortable in mine. I suddenly see it, and it finds my vulnerable spot, too.

"I'll go with you," I offer. "They'll respect you if *I'm* there."

"No." She squares her shoulders. "They'll respect me because I'll demand it, poor or posh."

"You need my help."

"You need to watch the damn movie because that's Hollywood, this ain't." She pivots on her heels. "Besides," she calls over her shoulder, "we're strictly professionals. Right, Mr. Mercier?"

I watch her incredible ass sway, bound tight under that skirt, and this isn't strictly business.

Yes, Scarlett will get the job done. She'll protect the only thing that matters to me. The way she smiled at Gia today, gently guiding her with her hand on Gia's tiny shoulder, like Scarlett genuinely cares for my daughter. I watched the sight, and it gave me a warm feeling. A forgotten one.

A terrifying one.

Though I'll never do anything about it, this is far more than business as I watch Scarlett leave for the night...because she looks so goddamn beautiful doing it.

"She's the one, isn't she?"

Zar swirls his whisky. Stars twinkle above while we smoke cigars on my rooftop terrace, and here comes the interrogation.

"Who?" I play coy, watching tendrils of smoke fade into the warm September night.

"Scarlett: she's the one you finally fucked," he says. "I can tell."

Yes, Zar is my best friend. We share...a lot. But I can't be *that* obvious. Just in case I don't answer and Zar laughs. "I fucking knew it."

"You don't know shit."

"The fuck I don't. You're clenching your left fist. That's your tell when you're lying."

I don't even realize I'm doing it. My right hand is busy with my cigar, while the only thing on my left hand...is my wedding band. I've only taken it off once. Still, I fight the truth. "You don't know what you're talking about."

"I know Scarlett Jones is a zipper ripper." Zar grins. "She's so fucking hot; all the blood rushes from your brain to your cock because *Jesus Christ*—and she's an MMA fighter? In fact," he baits me, "we're sparring tomorrow."

"The fuck you are."

"You only own me on Saturday nights." He leans back in his chair, enjoying our power exchange. "Tomorrow's Wednesday, and I'm sparring with a hot redhead with incredible tits and a mean uppercut."

"She's off-limits," I growl, feeling a vicious jealousy foreign to me.

I've shared almost everything with Zar, from tears to temptations, *but not Scarlett.*

"No," he puffs his cigar, "she's a titled MMA fighter, and I'm a big fan of the sport. You know it. You'll deal with it. And you'll love it because she can whip my ass, too."

"Don't tempt me."

"I've tempted you every Saturday night for three years straight. That's how I know it's her." He taps his ashes. "You started acting weird last December after you told me you went to that sex party for Redix Dean."

I roll my eyes. "Fuck, you know too much about me."

"Apparently, I don't because you never told me what happened at that party, but I knew something did. Your...*requests* changed."

He glances my way, and I raise my eyebrow.

We don't talk about this in my home.

I'm very strict about it.

Only on the executive floor. Only on Saturday nights. Only in *that* suite.

Zar smirks at my silent warning. "I figured it out while we met today," he says. "I gave Scarlett a tour of the property, all the access codes, and I made some introductions. But it's when I showed her the file on your stalker that I knew."

"Knew what?"

"She cares about you."

"She's doing her job."

"Bodyguards don't care like *that*."

Zar sips his whisky, and I barely remember a time before him. My childhood feels like a forever ago, but all I've known since I was eighteen was Zar by my side. While we were at Harvard, my family was in Greece, and his family was too wealthy to care about him. They disowned him, so we became close.

Very close.

When Darby died, Zar was the only one who saw my tears. He found me on my knees in the shower, pink rivulets running down the drain as the dried blood washed away and the agony set in.

He never judged. He had a broken arm, but he never left my side. No, he shared my guilt and grief as he sat silently in a chair beside my bed, and then he kicked me out of it a week later, saying that was enough. I had to get my shit together, for Gia's sake.

That's the kind of love we share. Tough and silent.

"She asked questions about Brooke Turner," he says.

I cut him a look. "You mean she asked questions about *my* stalker, who's *your* fault."

"Pussy just goes crazy for you, man. That's *your* fault." He grins. "But it sure is *my* pleasure."

I don't answer him. Again, Zar's bringing up shit we don't discuss in my home, even though Gia is asleep.

It's been one of my saving graces of single fatherhood; my daughter sleeps like a rock. She's a whirling dervish all day, but once her curly head hits the pillow, she's out.

Celine has her room next to Gia's. She watches her when I'm not here. Usually, I am. I never leave Gia except for work or Saturday nights. Celine never asks where I go because I won't answer.

Only Zar knows.

He arranges it.

"What kind of questions did Scarlett ask?" Still, I like saying her name, and I want to know. I want a lot with Scarlett; all that I can't have, all that I can't admit to myself that she made me feel. *Again.*

"A lot of security stuff," Zar answers. "Mainly about Brooke's background. If she's been institutionalized or has a record, or if she met Gia." Zar gets quiet, his voice deepening. "When Scarlett saw the pictures Brooke left on your desk, she might've figured it out."

I wince, closing my eyes to the humid night. It's heavy. It's peaceful, but not my mind, thinking about those photos. They're dark. They're taboo. They're a desperate plea from a woman obsessed with me, with what I did to her.

Zar explains, "When Scarlett saw those pictures, man, it was written all over her face."

My pulse quickens. "What?"

"She was hurt." He turns, glaring at me. "You fucked her, didn't you?"

I'm in charge. I have the power. Zar knows it; he *needs* it. He knows better than to challenge me, especially over this.

"So what if I did?" I growl. The half confession makes my soul-crushing burden lighten just a bit. It's like I can finally breathe.

Can I tell him more? Can I finally admit what I did? What I feel?

I trust Zar even more than I trusted my wife, and though she died, my guilt never will.

Now it's just me and Zar. I know he has other friends. I do, too. It's no coincidence I've found myself with friends like me, people with nontraditional notions of love...and sex, it seems. But no one knows me like Zar. And no one knows *about* Zar. He's one of the dark secrets I keep.

So when I glance at him to finally confess because he's the one who saved me years ago, he glowers at me before he turns his dark eyes away. They reflect the starry night sky.

"I thought we had a rule," he snarls.

"Rules break."

"So do hearts," he replies, and fuck...

I broke his.

Scarlett

CHAPTER SIX

"You sure you don't want to wrap your hands?" Zar asks. "You're gonna rip your knuckles open."

I grin. I like him. But I need pain this morning. "Uppercuts." So I warn him to switch the position of his mitts before I start punching with my bare fists again, loving the biting sting of leather against my bare flesh.

"Our Luca."

That's what that Maren woman said at Gia's school yesterday. She sneered at me as if I'm white trash and don't belong in Luca's world. And the truth is...

I don't.

I'm the help who had to buy a five thousand dollar Gucci dress this morning with Luca's Black Card. It was mortifying; all the clothes I quickly bought with money that's not mine, and the woman at the Gucci store knew it.

Maybe some people like being kept, but I like keeping my pride. It's free. It's all I've had growing up: pride and clothes from Goodwill.

Women like Maren have made fun of me my whole life.

And it's obvious. She's so horny for Luca, I almost feel bad for her. She can't have him either. It's kinda forbidden, right? Fucking

63

your dead best friend's husband. I can tell Maren wants to, and yes, it makes me jealous.

"Dayum, woman," Zar huffs, bracing against my pummeling. "Who snapped your garters?"

"Bitches like Maren." I don't know why I confess it to Zar. Something about him puts me at ease.

"Don't let her get to you. Join my club," he says. "She hates me, too."

I land a left uppercut and glance up.

We're the only ones in the hotel gym. It's a state-of-the-art facility with a saltwater lap pool.

I may not be familiar with such luxury, but I like it. I like the fancy bronze yoga pants and matching sports bra I bought myself today, too, from that Lemon or whatever store.

HIF #6: Yeah, my pride goes out the trailer window when it comes to expensive activewear. I didn't mind spending Luca's money on that.

Technically, sexy workout clothes aren't part of my business attire, but it sure feels like it. I can sense Luca watching in that camera over Zar's right shoulder.

Can Luca hear us, too?

Because I'm appropriately dressed for a gym but Zar is pushing boundaries. He's not wearing a shirt as men should in here. No, he's showing off his shredded body by wearing soft navy jersey workout shorts that can't hide what's hanging long and not-so-soft.

I'm used to it. All the grappling I've done in gyms dominated by men? Big surprise: some men get off on a woman who beats them.

It's obvious my domination arouses Zar, and I find it kinda erotic, endearing how Zar's letting me see his kink. He has no shame about it.

"Hooks," so I thrill him.

Zar's been kind to me since I arrived. We share a love of the sport, but something makes me wonder if we share more. He grins as I wind up for a rear right hook. I land the punch, asking, "Why does Maren hate you?"

My power makes him flex his sculpted pecs, and I confess, it's a sexy-as-fuck sight.

While Luca's torso is smooth like granite, Zar has the perfect dusting of dark chest hair, trailing down in a narrow line to where I won't let my stare go. Zar's a very tempting man, but I'm too distracted by unwanted thoughts of Luca.

"Because I fucked her sister in the bathroom at a charity fundraiser." He grins. "Oh, and because Maren wanted to fuck me, too. She propositioned me several times. I don't blame the horny woman. Her ex-husband had the sex appeal of a sinus infection, but Maren was Darby's best friend, so hell no." I laugh with another right hook. "And now she wants Luca, but that'll never happen. He's a loner."

I drop my fists, barely huffing for breath.

That doesn't make sense.

I don't know if Luca can hear us, and I'd rather die than admit I'm so curious it hurts, but I need to know.

If Luca's such a loner, why is he fucking women like Brooke Turner? If we're strictly professional, why does he keep flirting with me?

"What about you?" I ask. "Are you a loner, too? Is that why you're best friends?"

Zar smirks, wiping his brow with his forearm. "So, you're investigating me now?"

"Is *that* what I'm doing?"

"You're as covert as a bonfire." He smirks. "And I like it." He leans his sweaty back against the mirror. "Luca and I are best friends because we've shared everything," he explains. "Books. Beer. Harvard. Heirs to fortunes. Except Luca obeyed his father's wishes while I told mine to go fuck himself."

"Why?"

"Because I don't want to run an oil company. My father keeps polluting the planet. He won't change, and I want nothing to do with it. My little brothers can have it. So, once I was eighteen, he kicked me out. That's when I met Luca, and we've been close ever since."

"How close?"

Zar grins as if he likes me digging. "We bond over a lot of things. That's what young men do in college." He raises a teasing eyebrow. "We *bond*."

"I wouldn't know." I shrug. "I didn't go to college. I barely graduated from high school."

"But you're smart," he says. "And you're a badass who can whoop my fucking ass, and clearly, I enjoy it." Every time he grins, I grin back. "But you're sweet, too. I can tell. I saw how you were with Gia yesterday. You can't hide your heart. It's open, so be careful."

"Careful about what?"

Zar's glance flicks to the security camera. I can't tell if he's warning me or baiting me. Maybe both. He cares for Luca and loves Gia like she's his daughter, too, so why is he silently warning me about his best friend?

What is he hiding?

It makes the question rush over my whispering lips. "What happened to her?"

I'm asking about Darby, Luca's wife. A Harvard degree isn't required to connect the dots.

"You've already investigated it, haven't you?" he replies, and that's how smart Zar is. He's five steps ahead of most people. "You used your connections at HGR this morning while you were shopping to get more intel on him."

"It was a car crash, but parts of the report were blank."

He nods. "Luca buried Darby and their story. He's *that* powerful."

I lean closer, so close I can smell his leather cologne, and I like it. "But why keep it a secret?" I ask him. "You know why, don't you?"

He barely shakes his head no. Not that he's ignorant. No, Zar's loyal to Luca, but he has an odd way of showing it.

"And why," I ask him, "did you show me those pictures yesterday? The ones from Luca's stalker. They were...*incriminating*."

Now, he cocks a half-grin. "You asked to see them, didn't you? It's your job."

"But you showed me *all* of them when you didn't need to. Like you wanted me to see *everything*."

The photos were black and white and elegant in their depravity.

Brooke is blonde. She's gorgeous in that high-class way. I'd recognize her now. The photo of her naked and kneeling, drooling with a black bit clenched in her teeth, is burned into my brain.

But Zar also silently slid the photos she left on Luca's desk before me. One with her on all fours, the bit strapped across her mouth while she wore a long black ponytail butt plug in her ass. One with her lying down with a black pony horse dildo in her pussy. One of her on her knees, her hands cuffed with "OUR FILLY" written in lipstick across her mammoth breasts.

Apparently, Luca took lewd photos of her. He did depraved things to her, and then he fucked her. And it shocked me. The photos made me wet. And jealous.

And hurt.

Luca fucked Brooke, too. And now, SHE'S a relentless stalker, but I'M the big mistake?

"Yeah, I thought you should see what you're getting into." Zar smirks. "You know...for work and all."

"So what?" I keep whispering. "You're warning me about Luca? Like he's some semen demon?"

Zar chuckles low. "Semen demon?"

"Yeah, that's what my sister and I call them—men to watch out for. Is that what you're warning me? Luca's a perv?"

Zar shrugs.

"You know what, you're right." I glare at him. "It's none of my business what Luca does because it's *just* business between us."

"All right then, Red." He leans forward, towering over me while his mischief turns sweet. "Then join us for lunch today. Me and Luca. We can talk *business*."

Like I'd ever back down from a challenge. And, whatever. Luca can keep his secrets and his best friend who guards them. I don't care what pervy kinks he's into. *Yep, that's a lie.* I'm curious as hell.

Thirty minutes later, I've taken a fast shower in the Ladies' Locker room. Slipping on the new silk Gucci dress I bought today, I feel ridiculous. I've never worn a five-thousand-dollar dress or felt such luxury on my skin. It's some traditional brown and black equestrian print, like I've ever ridden a damn horse, either. But the long sleeves cover my tattoos, and the dress flows loose enough for me to fight if I must.

Did I buy the expensive equestrian dress because of Luca and Brooke's pony play fetish? No, but now I'm wearing it because fuck it. I'm not intimidated; I'm intrigued.

Securing my damp hair into a simple bun, I slip on new black-heeled ankle booties, too, but I don't bother with makeup. I gotta keep my identity, my dignity somehow.

When I meet Zar by the elevator to take the quick trip down to the lobby, why am I not surprised that Luca's looming there, waiting?

He was *watching us.*

His icy eyes glower at me, then at Zar, who smirks back, pressing the elevator button. "Nice to see you found a shirt," Luca hisses low.

"I found more than that," Zar taunts while I roll my eyes, waiting for the elevator to slide open.

It's like they're jealous boys in a pissing contest, and I'm the one getting wet, and in a golden way. That's *not* my kink, and this is annoying as hell.

"Your hair," Luca growls as we enter the open golden doors.

At first, I think he's speaking to Zar, whose dark waves are damp from his shower. Zar's wearing a light blue linen suit. It looks bright against his tan skin, like he's full of light. While Luca towers in his usual dark suit like he's in a constant state of mourning, sucking all the joy from any room he's in. But Zar doesn't answer him, and I feel a fire on my exposed neck, so I look up, confronting Luca's glare.

I huff, "You're talking to *me*?"

"Yes," he commands. "Wear your hair down."

Oh, hail, no.

"Excuse me, *Christian Grey*, but tell me how to wear my hair again, and you'll wear a black eye."

"Who's Christian Grey?"

Of course, Luca's so Dom he doesn't know fictional ones. He's so rich; pop culture is tacky unless it's for Gia.

"He's a billionaire Dom who trains a virgin to be his sub."

Luca sneers with dark glee. "You're *NOT* a virgin."

So I sneer back. "I'm *NOT* your sub either."

Zar snorts as the elevator dings and the door slides open. I shove past Luca while I hear Zar chuckle. "Slick move, Ex-Lax. She fucking hates you now."

And yet, I let Luca feed me the best meal I've ever had. Saganaki, freshly fried goat cheese topped with honey and nuts. Moussaka, eggplant mixed with potatoes and lamb, finished in a rich béchamel sauce. Pork Souvlaki marinated in oil, lemon, and oregano. Fresh pita bread and Tzatziki sauce to die for.

A dollop falls on the white linen tablecloth in front of me, and I don't think. I swipe it up and lick the Tzatziki off my fingertip, loving its creamy zing, while I blurt, "I'd eat this sauce off of the ass-end of a skunk and love it."

I'm so enraptured that I forget where I am, sitting in a five-star restaurant at the VIP table with Luca and Zar and a bunch of Charleston's elite, staring at me like I'm the only one saddled up to the trough. "Sorry." Suddenly, I blush, remembering my manners.

"Quite alright." *Is Luca smiling?* "It's some of the best cuisine in the world. It's meant to be enjoyed with no shame."

Zar jokes. "I had an orgasm the first time I tasted Luca's lamb chop."

Everything Zar says is loaded with innuendo he *wants* me to hear.

"When was that?" I ask.

Luca answers, "I brought Zar home for the summer between our freshman and sophomore years."

Though he can't shake his alpha vibes, at least Luca's dropped his asshole meter down to a 1.5 for lunch.

And yeah, I may have let Luca display me on his lap, my back against his chest while he spread my legs, letting two couples watch while he fucked my ass and grabbed my neck, whispering in my ear, "They can see your pussy dripping with my cum down my cock that's fucking your ass now. You're so tight for me. Moan, my little whore." He pinched my nipple, and I obeyed. "Tell them you're my whore, *ma flamme*, while I make you burn. Show them how you take *me*." He snarled, "*Only* me."

Yeah, I might've come, all sexalted, letting Luca do *that* and a bunch of other kinky shit...

But no man tells me how to wear my hair.

Zar continues their story. "I thought I was going home with Luca for a luxury Mediterranean summer vacation, but no. We were washing sand off of lounge chairs and picking cigarette butts off the beach."

Luca laughs. "I warned you my father didn't play. If you're breathing, you're working."

"Yeah, well," Zar reclines in the blue velvet chair like The Mercier is his home, too, "I sure liked working on a nude beach."

"A nude beach?"

Luca grins, amused by my question. "We aren't sexually uptight where I'm from," he says. "Nudity is natural. It's beautiful. It's meant to be enjoyed under the warm sun, splashing in the cool water."

"Yeah, Red." Zar jumps in. "*We* would love to watch you try the nude beach at our Mykonos property. *We* have a trip there in two weeks."

"No," Luca barks back, "we don't."

"Since when?"

"Since now."

But Zar doesn't flinch at Luca's ire. "I tell ya," Zar turns to me, "all those naked bodies on the beach; I was like a horny fly to honey. I got *stuck* so many times that summer."

I laugh at Zar's joke. "What about you?" I ask Luca. "Did you get *stuck* on the nude beach too?"

"I was the owner's son." He smooths the napkin in his lap. "I had to be more careful than my amorous friend."

"That's not an answer."

I challenge him, so he licks his lips before confessing, "I was careful, yes, but I got *stuck* plenty."

"On the hotel's balconies was his favorite place, so I could watch him." Zar shares that too quickly, and Luca whips a glare at him.

Yeah, yeah, yeah. Luca's fucked in public, and he's a fan of nudity. Big whoop. That's not a newsflash to me, so why is Luca pissed that Zar's sharing it among our little threesome?

It's odd, but I don't want to trudge through a testosterone tiff all day, so I change the subject. "What did y'all do at Harvard to get so close that Zar wanted to go home with you?"

Luca's stare won't release Zar's. They're sharing something silent and furious. But with my question, Zar's face softens. "I took care of him," he answers, looking at Luca. "He got pneumonia that winter. His hot Greek ass couldn't handle the Boston cold, and he got too sick to fly home for Christmas, so I stayed with him."

Luca still stares at him, answering gently for the first time, "It's not like you had anywhere else to go."

He doesn't sound like a dick. He sounds caring.

"Yeah," Zar agrees. "I had nowhere else to go, so Luca got sick for me so we could be together at Christmas. I brought him chicken and noodles from the Soup Shack every day and bourbon all night, and we binge-watched Lord of the Rings in our dorm while he hacked up a lung for two weeks straight. Ain't that right, my precious?"

He teases Luca, and now I really hear Zar's Texas accent. That's where his family is from. I did confirm *that* intel from

HGR this morning. It's another thing the men share. They both come from families so famous for their wealth they can't hide it.

Zar Rollins walked away from the fifth wealthiest family in the country. All on principle.

Luca Mercier inherited the world's wealthiest, privately owned hotel chain at age twenty-five.

And me?

I inherited my mom's old red Ford Fiesta. The windows wouldn't roll down, and the A/C didn't work, but it got me sweating to the gym and back. It secured my future, and here we are.

Though I don't belong here, in this luxury hotel, sitting between wealth most can't fathom, the way Luca and Zar gently look at me? When it's just me and the two of them?

I feel like I belong. It has me glowing all afternoon while I settle into my office next to Luca's. My laptop is from HGR, so I click through our databases, still snooping for something I can't find on Luca.

As I did the day before, when I'm done, I go up to the penthouse and say goodbye to Gia. I need her to trust me, to listen to me. It's protocol. It usually takes time with your mark, but Gia instantly does, giving me a gooey feeling.

"Will you eat dinner with us?" she asks, standing in the foyer with Celine. Gia's been playing with blue and green markers. The guilty evidence colors her button nose.

It's just the three of us while Luca's still in his office, I assume, while I squat to Gia's height. "I gotta go home and take care of my puppy, but thank you for the invitation."

"What's your puppy's name?"

"Crimson." When Gia's confused, her face twists just like her Baba's. "It's a color of red," I explain.

"You're red!" she chirps.

"Yeah, that's what Zar's calling me."

Gia thinks that's funny as I leave for the night. I check in with Luca, too. As usual, he's behind his desk, and I clock on his security screen that its camera is aimed at his foyer, where I just was with Gia.

"I don't need you." Cruelly, he barks, not even glancing up from his laptop, so I leave, feeling that glow I had this afternoon dim on my quick drive home.

Luca's an enigma.

I don't know who he is, and I don't know why I care as I take Crimson on a walk. It's our usual trip by the harbor, down the sidewalk lined with palms, to the aquarium and its park outside and back. It's our evening ritual, and it helps to clear my head.

Dusk smears up the sky into the night. It's almost dark, but upon my return, I notice a delivery woman standing in the shadows by the glass doors of my building's lobby. She's holding a bouquet, I assume, concealed by a gold gift bag.

"You can leave that for a resident at the reception desk," I tell her.

"I have strict instructions to get the recipient to sign for it," she replies, and my instinct fires.

"Is the recipient Scarlett Jones? Ten D? Because that's me."

The woman smiles, relieved she won't have to wait all night while I sign her digital clipboard and wrap my arm around the concealed flowers, struggling to wrangle Crimson on his leash at the same time.

"Good luck with that," the woman offers as she leaves. "Whoever sent it sure spared no expense."

Once settled upstairs in my condo and Crimson's lapping up his water, I carefully cut the gold mylar bag open and softly gasp.

All the romance movies I watch alone at night. All the books I read on my phone, hoping no one catches me. Though I've never felt it for real, I'm secretly a romantic at heart. And it's a heart that's never had a man give me flowers.

I stare at the orchid, flooded with a feeling I want to keep.

The orchid is red with white splattered across the delicate opening lip of the flowers' pedals. "Miltoniopsis Breathless," reads the tiny gold plant label. It's breathtaking, beautiful, and erotic too.

Then I notice the small black velvet gift box neatly placed under the thick green leaves of the orchid. I open it and bite my lip, not believing the tears welling in my eyes.

No man's ever given me a gift, either.

It's a gold hair clip with golden tonal inlaid crystals. In tiny gold letters, it reads PRADA. There's no card with the clip or the orchid. He's not the kind of man who requires one.

> Thank you, Mr. Grey

I can't resist the joke, the kind gesture, or texting him.

Luca quickly replies, like he was waiting for me to text him. Like he knew I would.

SEMEN DEMON

You're free with me, Ms. Jones

...

Three dots quickly appear, and I hold my breath for more of him.

So I insist

In due time

You call me

...

LUCA

Scarlett

CHAPTER SEVEN

PARKING MY CAR NEXT TO LUCA'S ESCALADE FEELS ODDLY right. I've been on this job for a month and settled into a routine.

I'm on time. I'm professional and polite. I look like a demure vixen with an advanced degree, like Luca's assistant, when really... I'm falling for him and his daughter.

Gia's so cute in her school uniform. Her navy pleated dress melts my heart. Kids get me every time. They can be trusted. Adults can't.

Because every day when I accompany Luca and Gia to school, Maren and her gaggle of school moms whisper. They snicker at me like we're in middle school and not in the middle of a parking lot full of *their* kids.

"Whore." I heard one of them spit at my back. And "white trash," Maren wanted me to hear her hiss it.

But Luca doesn't say anything.

Honestly, I don't think he hears it.

Over the din of screaming kids, Luca's too crestfallen every time we drop Gia off, and he's too elated every afternoon we pick her up. And I'm too proud to let those women know they get to me while I guard Gia with my life.

It's a mistake to assume this is an easy job. Assumptions can get someone killed or kidnapped.

But with each day I work for Luca, it's more than a job. We feel it deepening, but we don't say it.

Silently, I wear his hair clip every day, and silently, every morning, he hands me a tumbler full of steaming hot coffee. We drive Gia to school, listening to her favorite Disney tunes, and then, on the ride back, Luca and I take turns controlling the playlist.

He's into Miles Davis, but I introduce him to Cardi B. When "WAP" played, he acted unamused, but I saw the thrill in his eyes.

Once at the hotel, Luca returns to work while Zar spars with me in the gym. We laugh, we shoot the shit, but we don't talk about him.

It's like Zar trusts that eventually, I'll figure out what Luca's hiding.

His fear, yes. Luca's terrified driving over that bridge; I can see it. It makes his square jaw clench, no matter what music is playing. But that's not a sin. A lot of people are afraid of bridges, especially *that* one.

But there's something else.

I feel it every time I sit in my office or walk the hallways of Luca's hotel. The memory of the photos Luca's stalker left him stalks me too. My suspicions are dark and secretly tempting.

I could tell the photos were taken in his hotel. In one of the shots, you can see the carpet. Most guest rooms have the same dark blue and white Grecian key pattern.

Whatever Luca's hiding, it's here.

And when I'm not shadowing Gia, I'm looking for it. So why am I not prepared when I finally find something? When I see Maren with her cute son, and a trio of other mom/child duos standing in the lobby of The Mercier Hotel on a Saturday morning.

I'm surprised, but I don't greet them. I sneak past Maren, hoping she doesn't notice me while I take my usual trip to the penthouse.

Luca told me he needed me to accompany him and Gia to the aquarium today. I get it. It's a high-risk location.

But I don't like *this* risk. The one that makes me vulnerable and jealous. The one that makes me feel not good enough. Like I'm that girl again who couldn't get a date for prom.

Girls at my high school spread mean rumors that I was too poor to afford a fancy dress, and I was. The boys avoided me, too. They heard what I did to my stepdad, and they eyed me like I was crazy.

But I wasn't crazy. I was protecting my sister.

And now I'm protecting Gia. So please don't tell me that she and Luca have a playdate with Maren and her cunty crew. I'll have to watch Luca live the life he should while I stand, feeling like I'm looking through a store window at all I can't have. Like happiness and love and a family aren't meant for me.

Though, I want it.

I didn't know I did until this job. Everything about me changes when I'm around Luca and Gia.

Pressing in my code, the front door opens to the penthouse, and I look forward to how Gia greets me. She hears the door *beep* and runs to hug my legs.

But this morning, "Hello?" I call out.

Where is everyone?

"Fuck." Luca's deep voice bellows down the hallway where I'm standing, which leads to his bedroom. I haven't seen it yet, but when he appears in his bedroom doorway, I've seen *that* before.

Luca with no shirt on.

"Sorry," he mutters, rubbing his mussed hair. "We fell back asleep."

But I'm wide awake. My pussy just woke with alarm; my clit startled at the sight of his grey pajama pants with a faded HARVARD written up the right leg. The waistband of Luca's pants is like my hanging jaw, barely clinging to his chiseled Adonis belt. The pants are old and worn, but he's not.

HIF #7: Big dicks like that should be illegal to pack. Or they should be required to carry. Pick one while you pick me up off the floor.

Because Luca's dick matches his body. It's thick and long with muscle. It hangs free, suddenly seeking while he searches my eyes, shamelessly groping him. But I can't help myself because he rouses at my stare. Like our silence, it's long and heavy and growing with desire.

"Good morning, my belle," he speaks, and his cock agrees. He lets me watch it rise along with his rare smile, flashing his white teeth, and it makes flashes of those kinky photos hit me, too.

The photos of Brooke surprised me. They turned me on. They made me jealous and curious, but mostly, they make a moment like this with Luca way too intense.

He knows I've seen his kinky photos.

I know what he's into.

He remembers what we've done, too.

Because it's a sudden storm in my eyes, and his quickly darken. We drop our stoic masks for the roles we play and reveal what we really want again. What we can't deny. It's right here, standing in the hallway between us. It's intense. It's aching. It's asking...

Will we break the rules?

Will I submit to him again?

I bite my lip in his presence, staring into his eyes as we swim in the silent questions between us.

"Scarlett!" Gia rushes out from behind him, her dinosaur long johns crinkled from sleep along with her face. "We're going to the aquarium today." She runs to me, hugging my legs and gazing up at me. "And Spencer's coming. All my friends are. We have a playdate."

"That's awesome," I tell her before forcing myself to suffer the gorgeous sight of Luca again. "They're waiting downstairs for y'all."

"Shit," he murmurs, the presence of his daughter quickly deflating his dick. "We got up early, had waffles in bed, but fell asleep watching *The Little Mermaid.*"

What inspired that movie choice? I'm kind of flattered.

"Gia, go get dressed, please. Quickly." He turns and disappears into his bedroom, announcing over his broad, naked back. "I'll call Maren and tell her we'll be down in ten minutes."

$$\mathcal{M}$$

Do you know how hard it is to suck at a job you were born to do?

For the first time, I struggle to keep my face frozen, to show no emotion. I shadow Luca and Gia around the aquarium while Maren and her friends stare back at me. I keep a safe distance behind them while Maren's glued to Luca, with Gia on his other side.

Every time Maren's eyes meet mine, they silently hiss "bitch" as if my presence annoys her, and it does. All of her friends do the same, whispering god knows what verbal diarrhea to each other about me.

"Why would Luca's assistant accompany him on a playdate?" Maren's asking herself, gossiping with her friends that I must be something more.

That I'm his whore.

And it makes me grin, breaking my mandatory stoic stare.

Oh, Maren, if you only knew.

If you only heard all the dirty things Luca said to me while I gave him the reverse cowgirl ride of his life, his fingertips spanking my clit for two couples admiring us.

"Let them see." He fisted my hair in his hand like reins. "Let them watch how my sweet whore fucks a big cock. That's it. Show them how you ride it. How you cream on it. How you love it." His other hand palmed my breast, his wicked pinch of my nipples perfection. "Let them watch how I make you come."

And oh, Maren, I grin at her, how they watched me come for Luca—many times.

"Luca," she snaps his name. "Come for dinner tonight. Just you and Gia. I'll make my famous crab cakes that you love."

"Thank you," he answers with his eyes on Gia. So are mine. She's fascinated by a shark swimming behind the glass before her. "That's very kind. But not tonight. I..." His tone drops. "I have plans."

"Plans? On a Saturday night?" Maren's worried. "What kinda plans? Not a *date?*"

Oh, please, woman. Have some pride. If you want to fuck him, just say it.

And if Luca wants to fuck Maren, please don't.

Please, God, don't make me watch her get what I secretly want so much and can't have.

"Yeah, I have a *date.*" He laughs, his wide shoulders shaking underneath his half-unbuttoned white linen shirt hanging untucked over his worn jeans. I love how Luca dresses on the weekends, all casual and one minute away from bending you over the hood of a car. "I have a date with *Zar,*" he tells her.

"That man." Maren rolls her eyes. "He's profane. I don't know why you keep him around. Darby never trusted him."

I glance at Luca. His smile drops while I look back and keep my eyes on Gia, who's now fascinated by the turtles.

"Darby loved Zar," Luca snarls, defending him, "and so do I."

That's the first time I've heard Luca say his wife's name, and it doesn't hurt. I've seen her in photos in gold frames around his home. She was beautiful, and Gia looks exactly like her. It's got to hurt Luca sometimes. Like staring at his greatest pain and loving it so much.

It's how I feel when I see Rose. She looks exactly like our dad. She's the only one who has his straight dark hair, while the rest of us have our mom's auburn waves.

"Still," Maren huffs, "Zar's a bad influence; I can tell. Some people just *don't* belong. While you... You don't come to the club. You don't come to church. You and Darby used to be there with us every Sunday and—"

"*Maren,*" tension rumbles through Luca's deep voice, "a lot of things changed when Darby died, including me, and I can't go back to how life was with her. It's time Gia and I move on."

"Well, you can't forget her memory, either. Gia needs to know about her mother and—"

"Trust me," he growls. "I remember her mother every day. I can never forget..."

Luca trails off, and my glance darts from Gia, who's giggling at the turtles, to Luca, whose jaw clenches at the sight.

The deep agony twisting Luca's handsome face wounds my heart. *He suffers the grief for two people.*

Gia doesn't remember the beautiful mother she's missing. But he does.

It makes me not hate Luca. It makes me see more sides to him. Like turning a crystal in the light, Luca shines in moments, but he has dark edges, too, places the light can't reach.

"Luca, I'm sorry." Maren caresses his sleeve for the umpteenth time today, and my nostrils flare. "I didn't mean to push. I know you loved her. She was so beautiful, so elegant and smart." She tosses it over her shoulder for me to hear. "Darby was your soul-mate. Your first and only love. She was perfect, and *I* loved her too."

Oh my god, Maren, put a stamp on it, stick it in an envelope, and mail me the message: "Luca's mine now, you red-neck bitch."

I half expect her to lift a leg and piss on him, too, marking her territory.

She and her mom-friends continue quietly bullying me all day, and my strength starts to waver. The bullied girl in me fights back all the emotions I hide. But later, Maren's overflowing with so much venom she gossips loud enough for Luca to hear it finally.

"Wonder how many times that redneck let him yank her trashy red hair to earn that Prada clip in it?"

And that hurt.

Because I love my hair clip.

It makes me feel special. Like I belong to Luca. I'm not supposed to feel this way but I cherish his gift. I feel like it's our shared secret when I wear it for him, and he smiles.

Like every morning, he's softly telling me, "Sorry if I'm an asshole today." And I tenderly reply, "I understand. I won't punch you in the dick for it."

But now, Luca growls aloud, "Excuse me?" Slowly, he pivots, confronting the moms while I don't take my eyes off of Gia, picking a plush animal to buy in the gift shop.

But no woman answers him, especially Maren.

"Ms. Jones is a professional," he defends me. "She works hard. She earns her salary. Do you know what that is, Maren? A job? A salary? Do you earn any money outside what your ex-husband owes you?"

"Luca," she hushes, embarrassed. "You don't have to be so unkind."

"Neither do you," he sneers. "You will treat Ms. Jones with the respect she deserves, or I'll let her show you an excruciating way you'll damn sure give it to her."

I bite my lip, fire burning behind my eyes—half to keep from smiling and half to keep from crying.

All the times I defend myself. All the times I defend others. Proudly, I do it, but I feel so alone.

No one ever protects me. No one ever stands up for me. No one ever loves me enough to fight for me, too.

Something foreign suddenly warms my heart while I watch Gia giggle, holding up a plush sea ray for me to give her a silent nod, telling her that I love it, too.

I love the warmth of Luca protecting *me*.

"What do you think?" he asks, watching as I try to use manners.

"It's good," I admit, hiding my stuffed mouth with my hand. "Really good. What are they?"

"Dolmades." He sets three more rolls of grape leaves stuffed with rice and spiced meat on my plate. I sit on a stool at his kitchen island, and Gia sits beside me, scarfing them down, too.

This evening feels too sweet to be real.

"They're our favorite," he shares. "I make them with beef because Gia doesn't like lamb," he smiles her way, "*yet like every Greek girl should.*"

"Lamb is yucky." Gia scrunches her nose. "Baba, if I eat all my dolmades, can I have my baklava?"

"Yes," Luca pops a dolmade in his mouth, answering while he chews, "dinner then dessert like I promised. And when Celine gets home, you can watch *Moana* with popcorn."

Gia smiles, chomping on her dinner while Luca aims those eyes my way, searching for what in my gaze, I don't know.

"Do you cook?" he asks.

"I had to," I answer. "I was the oldest of four girls. Like a junior parent."

When Luca smiles, the cleft in his chin deepens like the pounding in my heart while he asks, "What's your best dish?"

I twist my lips, reluctant to be honest but fuck it. I am who I am. "Country fried steak and collards." *Is it possible for him to smile even bigger?* "What?" I scoff. "Like a five-star European man would ever eat the luxury of country-fried steak."

"Try me," he teases.

And I want to reply, "*I have, and I'll take more, please. Like the Golden Corral of sex where I can just keep fucking the buffet of you and never get full.*"

But that's not in my Employee Manual of HGR Security, so I answer, "Alright. If you buy the groceries and the grease, I'll teach you how to be a redneck too."

He throws his chin up, his booming laughter filling the room and making my cheeks hurt.

Fuck, I'm laughing, too.

Only with Zar have I seen Luca this relaxed. But feeding his daughter and me has him howling with his mouth full.

And he's the sexiest man ever.

The steamiest dad ever.

The hottest boss ever.

But will I ever get used to this?

Feeling comfortable, like I belong with Luca and Gia. It's a one-eighty from this afternoon when Maren fired an Uzi of insults my way.

But once we left the aquarium, Maren wasn't saying much while Luca insisted on feeding me dinner.

Did he feel bad about Maren being a bitch to me? Or did he do it for Gia's sake because she asks me every evening to stay?

"So you made these?" I ask before enjoying another roll, relishing the savory stuffing and tangy grape leaves.

"I've learned a few recipes over the years," he answers, leaning against the white marble countertops in his gourmet kitchen, crossing his arms across his broad chest.

I like how all his cabinets are Grecian blue, and the sleek hardware is gold. Every inch of Luca's hotel reflects his culture.

"But not the baklava," he says. "Our chef downstairs at Margot's makes it. I named the restaurant after my mother, but it's my father's family recipe. Still, it's too complicated for me to make."

"Scarlett, come to brunch tomorrow." Gia swings her legs from her stool. "You're family now."

I nudge her. "I've only been here a month, kiddo."

"But you're like Celine and Zar," she says. "You're family. And Baba likes you. You make him happy."

I huff, smiling at her profile. Gia's got moxie, and I love it. But when I glance at Luca across the island from us...suddenly...he's *not* happy. I don't know what smokes across his eyes as they dart between me and his daughter before he clears his throat.

"Scarlett *works* with us, Gia. So do Celine and Zar, and we must respect their time off. I'm sure she has a life outside of work. Friends and all."

"Do you have a boyfriend?"

The mention of friends and having a life makes Gia wonder aloud. Me too. *What do I have other than my work?*

"I have my puppy," I answer her.

Gia bounces in her seat. "When do I get to meet him?"

"When your Baba says you can."

"Where's your puppy when you're here?"

"He goes to doggy daycare. Kinda like your kindergarten. They're teaching him not to pee on the floor, too."

Gia laughs at my joke, but Luca won't let it slide, his accent thickening. "You didn't answer her. Do you have a *boyfriend?*"

I look his way, my smile dropping as his eyes narrow.

Is he jealous or mad or flirting?

Either way, he shouldn't ask me that as a professional, as a man I work for, as a man who made it clear that we were one night only.

One night we can't forget.

It makes me bite my lip before I answer, "I don't know. Should I?"

There are lots of things I *should* do, that Luca *should* do, but the way he's looking at me now? *Should sucks.* We want to do everything we shouldn't.

"All big girls have boyfriends." Gia pulls the plate of baklava her way.

I turn to her. "Well, I don't have a boyfriend. All girls *need* is to be what they *want* to be."

I don't know what Luca's taught Gia yet. Because I also want to tell her that girls, I mean women, can have girlfriends, too. And they can meet boys, I mean men, who fuck them so passionately they cry, watching them leave, breaking their hearts like her Baba did to me, but that's not entirely true.

Not every man is bad.

Not every man leaves.

And Luca is a good father, and he's a generous but grumpy-as-hell boss.

Every morning, when I arrive, he knows I like my coffee with sugar and no milk, and he serves it to me with a silent scowl.

Every day, when I enter my office, a new floral arrangement awaits me. Three times a week, he has my car in the parking garage washed and detailed alongside his. He has chocolates and fancy spa products sent to my hotel suite, the one I breeze in and out of as a glorified changing room. He even had a plush white

Mercier Hotel robe monogrammed with an S in gold for me. It hangs, freshly washed, every day in my suite, ready to warm me after my evening swim.

Luca is silent perfection.

He's a shitty not-boyfriend.

And a soul-altering fuck.

"So, you'll have brunch with us?" Gia asks.

Crumbs from the baklava pepper her cute face. On instinct, I take my napkin, gently wiping her smiling cheeks clean while I feel Luca's heavy silence.

What does he want me to say? No to him, but yes to his daughter? I can't win, and I won't disappoint Gia.

"I would love to have brunch with *you*." I flick her cute nose, making her giggle.

Later, when I'm leaving, Luca escorts me to his door, which is weird. This was work today, not a date. It makes me pause after I open it to leave, whipping around to face him after he mutters, "You don't have to come tomorrow."

He speaks lowly so Gia, who's in the living room watching a movie with Celine, won't overhear us.

"Thank you for being kind to her," he says with his hands shoved in his front pockets, "but that's not your job. And I'm sorry those women were cruel to you today. Thank you for being dignified about it. And thank you for being kind to Zar, too. He likes sparring with you." He pauses. "You know, I never told him I *was* well enough to fly home that Christmas in college, but I lied and stayed to keep him company, so thank you for keeping him company, too."

Dark silence is Luca's default setting, so his avalanche of gratitude is overwhelming. It's touching. I've never seen this side of him, but I guess he's taking a chance while we have a rare moment alone and off-the-clock.

"I don't mind," I answer, trying not to get trapped in his crystal eyes. "My stomach's been growling, smelling that brunch spread for over a month, so I'd love to try it." I shrug. "Besides, I know the hotel owner. I won't have to pay."

A smile cracks his mask again. "Is that so?"

"Uh-huh. I also know he has a sexy birthmark the size of a nickel on his left thigh. That's why I don't pay when I use his hotel's gym or swim in his lap pool."

"I think he likes that." He grabs the door frame above me, leaning way too close. "He's got cameras everywhere and likes watching how you please yourself."

Oh god, he flicked my clit.

And he knows it.

"Does he watch me, too? In my suite here when I'm taking a shower?"

I've never seen a camera in my suite or the hotel spa. Luca seems too ethical to violate privacy, but maybe that's his secret. He *is* a voyeur, too. He watches what he shouldn't.

His black hair hangs, long strands kissing the top of his lips as they near, inches from mine. "He *wants* to watch you shower," he taunts. "He *wants* to see you nude every day with your hair down. He *wants* to do a lot to you, but rules keep him from his desires."

His aroma, sex mixed with spice, makes my flesh tingle. It makes me confess, "Sometimes I want to break the rules again. Do you?"

"You know I do."

He glances down, directing my gaze to follow. Under his jeans, he's getting hard, and the surge is sudden, desire flipping my stomach. "So we aren't strictly professionals?"

He glares. "We're whatever I *say* we are."

"Oh?" I cock a grin. "You think I'll submit to you again?"

"I say WE crave it."

We? Me and him and the anaconda in his pants?

Who else is there?

Celine has Gia in the living room. The volume on the flatscreen is high enough, so it's safe for me to indulge, just for a minute.

"If I submit, what will you make me do?"

I turn the tables, needing Luca to need me, too. So, he leans closer, his lips brushing my ear, the steam of his voice, of that accent, drenching my sex.

"I'll make you sit on my desk and lift that skirt and pull your panties aside. You'll sit there while I watch your pussy get so wet for me. Then I'll tell you how to touch yourself, rubbing that beautiful hard pink clit of yours. I'll watch you get so desperate for me; you'll tell me how you're my little whore to fuck anyway I want until you beg me to let you come. But I won't. Not until that tight wet hole of yours is pulsing for my tongue to fuck it, and when I devour you, I'll make you scream my name. I love your screams, Scarlett; my name shredding your voice is where it belongs. Your cum is my water, and I'm the only one allowed to drink it."

I shiver, my pussy clenching as he swears, "Even if you have a boyfriend or a girlfriend—I know you go both ways—it doesn't matter because you belong to me. Even if I *let* someone taste your sweet pussy, it's mine. You can't get me out of your blood. When you come, I own your mind now, don't I, Scarlett?"

My lips graze his stubbled cheek, my nose inhaling his citrusy scent, my fists twisting to grab him.

It floods me with our truth.

"Just like you're *mine*, Luca. You want me. You spoil me. You think about me. You can't find a pussy like mine. One that can take your pounding and your pain away. One that owns your cock, too, no matter where you put it; it's mine now, isn't it? You come with my name burning on your lips."

"I will tonight." He nibbles my ear, and it takes all my strength not to take him down. "I'll come on my pillow thinking about you." I can flip him onto the floor, on his back, and make him mine again. "And you'll send me a video tonight of your fingers buried inside your pussy, needing it to be my hard cock ripping you open again. I want you coming while I watch you scream my name."

He presses his forehead to mine, the brush of his lips hovering over me is so close...

"You ache for me, Scarlett, just like I ache for you. It's torture being around you every day. I feel the same way. I need you again. I'm empty and in pain, wanting me inside you forever."

"Luca."

His name escapes in a stutter, and I can't control it. This hurts so much, and I love it. I need it. He hears it. He sees it, too.

"But I can't," he growls like a war wages inside him and suddenly pulls away.

So I turn and leave him this time.

I don't look back at him in the doorway, though I can feel him there. I step into the empty elevator and stare in the mirrors, seeing him watch me in the reflection as the golden doors slowly close.

Without a word or a single thought but him, I mindlessly follow my new routine. I go to my suite on the executive floor.

And I change.

I become a woman who'll fight for him. Who'll break the rules for him. Who'll lose her job for him. A woman who needs these feelings, his sweet family and his brutal fucks, his tender gifts and dark secrets, his wicked mind games and warm heart.

I don't know why, but I need it all with him.

I slide on my red, one-piece Speedo before slipping into my plush, white Mercier Hotel robe. The hotel gym is at the other end of this floor. The heated, saltwater lap pool there has been my relief from old injuries and new ones, too. The fresh scars of Luca sting as I dive into its depths...

And there...

I scream his name.

Luca

CHAPTER EIGHT

SATURDAY NIGHTS ARE MY ONLY RELIEF, AND I'VE NEVER needed it this bad.

Guilt has me ripped into two men.

I'm one man, the father of a daughter he lives for. So many times, I wanted to jump off that bridge, but I didn't. Gia is my joy. She's my life. I will never abandon her.

We were fine until I met her—*Scarlett.*

And to watch her guard my daughter with her life? To see her endure ridicule from cruel women while she does it? To adore Scarlett as she tenderly wiped crumbs off my daughter's face? It made my throat burn with what emotion, I can't fucking name it.

I don't want to name it because the other half of me is an animal.

I need blood on my hands again. I need pain. I need Scarlett so fucking bad I feel the edges of my mind slipping. All I want is dirty, brutal sex with her. Sex that hurts her, that heals me. Sex that's so taboo anyone can see that she belongs to me.

It's a drug. It makes me feel better. I love it. I crave it. I want it so much I share it.

It's an addiction I discovered in college, and Zar never lets me down. He desires my satisfaction. He needs it as much as I do.

91

We *need* our Saturday nights.

Even when I travel to another property, Zar takes care of me. He travels with me to exotic locations or the glimmering cities of The Mercier Hotels, where they provide a ready supply, always waiting and willing.

But living here in Charleston for so long? We have to be very careful. Rumors flow like the wide river beside this city.

It's midnight as I take the elevator down to the executive level. No one's here at this hour. I insist my staff take Saturday nights off. We have staff at my Paris property ready for emergencies because it will be a crisis if I don't get what I want.

My steps know the path, down hallways of white marble floors with Grecian rugs of blue and white. Silence and barely audible classical music piped through the speaker system fill the air. But it doesn't muffle the giggles.

The laughter I hear comes from my secret suite.

Pressing the access code, I silenced the *beep* long ago as I carefully open the door. I want to watch what they're doing so I don't let the door close behind me. I leave it barely cracked open so the *click* won't disturb what I hope to find.

"Come on," Zar's laughing too, "you gotta pick one. You can't possibly take two."

I grin, leaning against the wall in the dark foyer. The light above me is off, so they don't notice me here. Not yet. Zar enraptures the two naked women wearing black leather collars around their necks, and I love watching his game.

The man is a master.

He collars women every week.

But he's wearing a collar, too—a wide black leather one with a 24-karat gold O-ring. Seeing it adorn his tan flesh warms my heart. His impressive masculine nudity gives me a constant thrill. His long cock, swelling half hard, gives me deep satisfaction. His play soothes my jagged edges because I had that collar made for him.

I'm Zar's Master.

"But they're both so big." The redhead giggles, and I exhale, relieved he finally found me another. It's been months since our

92

last one. "How can I decide?" she teases. "Let me fuck them both for you, Daddy."

"Bad girl." Zar playfully slaps her thigh with an extra long, purple, double-ended dildo. Then he slaps her other thigh with a pink one. "I'm not your Daddy, and you're being greedy. You need to share the cocks, ladies."

The brunette practically purrs at him, lacing her hands into his dark waves. "But we want to share *your* cock, Sir."

He's got them right where he wants them, where I am, too.

No one can resist Zar.

He makes sure his body is a magnet. I do, too. Our grueling dawn workouts keep us in top shape for this. He craves our punishing routine as much as I do, though he doesn't have to follow the rules like me.

I don't know what Zar does on his free nights, but he has my permission to play. Every Friday, he leaves his suite on the fifth floor. I've watched him with my cameras, sliding into his Porsche in the parking deck and disappearing into the Charleston night.

Yes, we're creatures. We have lots of good habits and very *bad* ones, too.

"Ladies," Zar caresses the brunette's ass, "if we're going to share tonight, then let's invite my Owner to watch. He's patiently waiting for us."

He saw me here all along. I swear the man can sense me even when I'm not around.

The women turn, surprised at first to see my shadow looming in the hallway, and that swells my cock.

I love getting caught watching.

Because here's the test.

What do you do when you have this chance? The opportunity to truly be free and submit? To fuck how you're told to and for anyone to watch? Don't underestimate it. It's liberation beyond your wildest dreams.

"Oh my god," the redhead sighs at seeing me. "You're Luca Mercier."

"Holy shit," the brunette mutters. "Are you our Dom tonight? Are we fucking you, too?"

I'm not worried. They've signed NDAs. They know the cost of this secret. Their phones are secure in the safe beside the bar cart. Zar makes sure of it all before I even enter the room.

"You'll do as I say." I enter the hotel suite, aiming for the gold and glass bar cart. "My stud has told you the rules. We honor limits and consent. But I think you're going to want my demands tonight."

In this suite, most of the traditional Mercier furniture is gone. We removed it but left the plush king-sized bed in the bedroom. It's for aftercare, of course. This large living room is empty except for a black leather armchair and a few black leather benches with gold side tables around the room's perimeter.

It's all seating for an audience.

A few glass curio cabinets featuring supplies and toys stand in the corners, while a very large, low platform gleams like a stage in the center of the room.

The dark blue walls are empty of art, too. Instead, gold-framed mirrors are strategically placed to reflect the platform and the black, padded St. Andrew's cross on the wall opposite the windows.

I designed the room, while Zar designed the platform. It's covered in top-grain black leather, like a massive bed, but it's also functional. It has a multitude of gold chains secured underneath with cuffs to restrain ankles, wrists, or necks. It's the right height for us, just below our knees. Zar's six-three, I'm six-five, and it fits us and any arrangement of bodies we desire.

Zar even selected the lighting. It's ambient and minimal but glows bright enough to see all the details. The music in here is different. Zar picks that, too. He's got a playlist of fuck-songs, that I only allow myself to listen to on Saturday nights.

Blue velvet drapes sweep the dark blue and white carpeted floor. They're closed, though I wish I could open them. I wish more could watch us, but the risk is too high.

No one can know about our habits. Our need. It stays in this suite. We haven't even used the benches for an audience yet.

"Yes, sir," the redhead giggles at my warning. "I consent to *all* of Luca Mercier's demands tonight."

I grin, pouring myself an Ouzo with a splash of water.

I'm sure Zar's already fed them and spoiled them with dinner downstairs and one drink; that's it. Again, this is consensual. We don't fuck drunk, and he directly asks them if they want a threesome. He asks about limits and interests and any questions they may have about BDSM. He explains impact play, spanking in particular. He makes it very specific and clear. He makes it so shameless with no surprises.

Well, except for the surprise of me joining them. But the women can always say no to me, too.

But what I love is...

They never do.

Taking my usual seat in the black leather armchair two feet from the platform's edge where all three kneel, I set my milky anise drink on the brass table beside me. Leaning back, I unbutton my linen shirt, sweeping it aside, exposing my abs and chest for this and all three watch, anticipating my first demand.

"Ladies," I command with Scarlett still scalding like fire through my veins. I'm not playing around. I have no patience tonight. "Get on all fours and share the purple dildo. Fuck it like whores while we spank you and watch."

And the show begins.

It's a long one, I insist. It gets me so hard. I love making people please themselves because I can't. But I can tell them what to do, to stop or go slower or faster. Tonight, I demand to watch a thick glistening dildo slowly disappear between eager slick pussies.

Zar kneels on the platform, centered between their bodies and facing me. His hands remain clasped behind his back while he watches them, too.

I lick my lips at his hefty, hungry erection, jutting out at the sound of their moans, at the sway of their ample breasts. They're getting off on giving us a show, and it's having the usual effect.

"Stud!" I bark at Zar.

"Yes, my Owner." He knows he can't look at me yet.

"Spank them for being bad for us."

Zar tries hiding his grin, but we've done this too many times, and I see it as he lifts the red leather paddle from the platform beside him. He's a pro. He's been trained. He doesn't spank them hard. That's not what I want.

I want them thrilled to be bad for me. To be free for me. To fuck for me. To let me watch.

Whack!

Zar swats the redhead's ample bottom, her flesh blooming red along with her cheeks. "Yes," she moans.

"You like it, don't you?" He teases her, spanking her again. "You like being bad for us?"

"Yes," she quickly stutters again, looking over her shoulder at him. "Yes, spank me more."

Zar gives her three more smacks before it's the brunette's turn.

Thwack!

He reddens her bottom, too, making her cry out, but she doesn't use the safe word "Red." No, she writhes her hips, seeking more of the dildo that's fucking her, too.

"Bad girl," Zar taunts. "You're being so bad for us, aren't you? Letting us watch you share a dildo and fuck another slut."

"Yes!" She groans, shaking.

She's close to coming, and I have all night long. I need this to last. I need this always. I'm leaking in my jeans for it.

Their pleasure. Their display. Their submission. I control it when I tell them, "You'll both get spanked for being our bad little sluts tonight until you come, and you're going to love it. Keep telling my stud how much you love us watching your dirty pussies fuck."

Neither woman lasts long. Not with my demands. Not with Zar's measured pain heightening their pleasure creaming from their lips. One comes, then the other does, and I need more.

"Stud," I command Zar, and he loves being used by me.

"Yes, My Owner," he replies.

"Have her suck that big cock, the cock that belongs to me, and make her do it nice and slow until I hear her choking on it."

I gesture to the sexy redhead on all fours. She's still fucking one end of the long dildo while the brunette fucks the other, moaning and watching me.

"Luca," the brunette moans. "I mean, Master, Our Owner, let me suck your cock, too."

She's beautiful. I like that her nipples are pierced, that she has ink down her arm like Scarlett, but I'm not even tempted.

"Silence." I toast my drink to her. "Enjoy me watching that dildo fuck your wet pussy, and I promise we'll make you come more tonight. Because you like obeying me, don't you?" I grin. "You like me watching you. You like being a dirty girl for me."

She moans with my gaze on her, like she's obsessed with my stare, but this is safe. This is controlled as she starts rolling her hips harder, fucking her friend, and amping up her show.

"Do you want this cock in your mouth?" Zar asks the redhead, dragging his swollen tip across her bottom lip as she nods yes, and I'm riveted.

"Say it, my doll," Zar demands. "I need to hear you say I get to fuck all of your holes for my Owner to watch. Say you want to be a slut for us."

"Yes, I want to be your slut." The redhead practically shouts it. "I want to suck your cock. I want you to fuck me."

It makes me unbutton, then unzip my jeans, exposing my hard dick.

Zar takes turns, brutally fucking one woman's throat, then the other's, all while they moan with spit drooling from their chins, while their bodies twist and writhe even more, sharing the glistening dildo. When they finally come again, it's how I feel, too.

Lust owns me, but I won't break. I won't ever break my rule again; I only watch.

"Fuck her hard, Stud," I tell him, and he knows which one.

The redhead.

Zar now knows why I've changed my requests for almost a year. Why I told him I crave redheads to fuck.

For him to fuck for me.

I'm obsessed with it.

But this is the first time since Zar's known about Scarlett that he's found her substitute. A mere shadow of the woman I really crave.

I start stroking my hard cock to the truth, watching what I won't do with Scarlett ever again, but I'm desperate to.

The denial. The punishment. The loneliness and pain of no true satisfaction is what I deserve.

Zar directs the women's bodies, turning the redhead around and grabbing her hips as he guides her to the edge of the platform. Lifting two chains underneath, he binds her ankles in black straps to the edge so she can't escape. She's on all fours, her pussy waiting and open for his cock while he stands behind her, and I lick my lips again, remembering a similar sight one night at a club.

After Zar rolls a condom down that tempting dick of his, he starts fucking her as I tell her what to do to her friend. "Now eat her pussy. You know you want to. Be a bad little girl for us and lick up her cum while my stud fills your pussy with his."

The women grin at me like they've done this before, and I swear Zar has a spidey sense for bisexual women. Or for ones curious enough to try.

I have so many sights I crave to watch. Usually, I want to dominate, I want to torture with pleasure for hours, and Zar's done it all for me. It's like he enters a trance, being told what to do, being controlled by me, on fucking for me while I whip his ass, but tonight's only for him. This is his favorite scene, and though he didn't say it, I owe him.

I broke my rule.

I broke his heart.

It's not a rule he made or asked me to keep, but Zar knows what my rule means to me. How it brought me back to life, how it brought me back to him.

For years, I've only been his, and now he knows who I broke

my rule with, and he gets to make me watch the punishment I crave.

Zar and I have been together for so long, since college, so he knew it the second his eyes met Scarlett—*I fucked her*—so now he wants to fuck her, too.

And this time, I'll kill him if he does.

Zar always wants what's mine. That's the punishment he craves.

I've been watching him and Scarlett around my hotel. When they spar in the gym, they're happy, relaxed, and like best friends.

But his arousal around Scarlett is obvious, too. It's starting to bother me in ways I'm not used to. I can't stop staring at how his cock gets hard around her, knowing I've fucked her.

When it's business, their security meetings are chatty. They sit in the lobby with their laptops open, discussing how to mitigate risks at my various properties, but they laugh too much.

His eyes linger on Scarlett's stunning smile too long. His hands twitch to caress her hair. He licks his lips when he watches her walk away, his stare equally captivated by her ass in a tight skirt as mine is.

I sit in my office and watch them all the time through my security cameras, and every so often, he glances up and smiles at the lens, feeling me do it.

Zar lives for me to watch him, and I live through him.

So he starts fucking the redhead with a feral passion I've never seen in him before. With lust, she cries out at his brutality, at his hips slapping against her ass, and his discipline falters, glaring my way.

My jeans are open. I never wear boxers on Saturday nights. I need full access to do this. It's my only relief.

But tonight, as Zar's lips part like they always do when I permit him to stare at my hard cock, to watch me jerk off, something's changed in his eyes.

I know he feels something about me fucking Scarlett, but we won't talk about it.

We're men. We do. We fuck. We fight. But we don't talk.

The brunette is in heaven. She's been screaming so loud for minutes with her eyes closed, her legs spread wide while her friend leans over and devours her pussy. The redhead's tongue swipes across the brunette's clit in tempo to Zar's unrelenting thrusts, and I can't stop licking my lips, remembering the taste of Scarlett's honey.

I'm parched for her. Starving for her. I've never known hunger like this, and the deprivation is what I need.

"Eat that pussy," I command her. "That's it. Bury your nose in it. Smell her lust for you while you suck her clit and make her scream. Make her come so hard on your tongue that she fills your mouth with her cream."

It's what I did to Scarlett, and the redhead moans, obeying my demands. She's jutting her hips high, seeking even more of Zar's cock that curves up, long and thick. It hits a spot in women every time.

But his eyes are on my cock, swollen and leaking in my grasp.

"How does her pussy feel?" I stroke my tip, always demanding he taunt me.

"So fucking tight and wet for us," he growls, his thrusts slapping against her ass. "She's a good little slut for us, eating pussy and loving it while we fuck her pussy, too." The women moan. The brunette grabs her friend's head and holds her there as she thrusts her hips up for more of her tongue.

"Look at her," Zar taunts me. "Look at her red hair, her tongue eating pussy for you, and her tight little cunt taking this big cock that belongs to you. She loves it, my Owner."

I love it.

Now that Zar knows, he's going to torture me, and it's what I crave. Yes, I want Scarlett, and no, I can't have her, so this is what I deserve.

I love this pain.

"What a sweet whore she is for you, Luca." Zar keeps going, his jaw clenching. He's close. I'm close. The women are having their orgasms, and now it's our turn.

I stand up with my jeans open, my hard cock fisted in my

grasp. Stalking toward Zar's taunts, I drip because the sight of my arousal enraptures him.

It always has.

Zar loves my cum shooting over his hard dick. I know he wants it in his mouth, too. Probably in his ass, as well, but this is all he ever gets from me, and it tortures us with the denial we love.

"She'll let you watch her." He keeps serving me. "She'll let us fuck her. That's what you want? Right? To watch your sweet whore fuck for you?"

Yes, it is. I lock my eyes on him because Zar knows my soul; he knows my desires and demons. He licks his lips to them, his eyes on my swollen cock about to come, and whenever I do, it makes him come, too.

"You want her, don't you?" He takes me there. I'm swelling in my grasp, jerking my fist faster, and falling into my favorite hell. "You want to fuck her and make her your whore for all to watch. For *me* to watch. For everyone to watch."

Yes, yes, fuck yes, I do, but I can't speak.

The answer is my pumping fist, my thrusting hips, my mouth open, about to release a painful roar from my soul.

"Luca," Zar coaxes, "you want to fuck Scarlett, but you can't because you're a fucking devil."

Fuck, yes, I am.

I come so hard to her name, to him taunting me with pain, with denial, with truth. Ropes of my cum spurt over Zar's abs, drizzling down to the base of his pumping dick. He didn't know my weakness—*Scarlett*—and now that he does, it only makes me come harder, grunting again as more of my torture escapes, splattering his flesh, and it takes Zar's guilt away, too.

He grabs the redhead's hips. "Fuck yes, take us. Take us," he grunts. His body, dripping with my cum, shakes while his eyes won't leave mine as he releases his deepest secret into someone else.

Zar's never confessed what he feels for me, but we know it, and we'll never say it.

"Wanna join us?" The brunette giggles, and it jerks me out of my haze.

I rip my focus off of Zar, his head also whipping around to see who's hidden in the shadows of the foyer.

But she can't hide the flames in her hair.

They match the fire in her eyes.

Scarlett

CHAPTER NINE

I'M SITTING IN A CIRCLE OF HELL WITH ONE LITTLE SPOT OF heaven beside me—Gia.

She's devouring a chocolate croissant while Luca smolders on the other side of her. He sits at his round table for eight, like a king. But we haven't spoken this morning, not since I caught him last night.

Now...his eyes avoid mine.

Is he embarrassed? Angry? Aroused? Who knows? He's just silent and fuming again.

But when I met everyone for Sunday brunch in the restaurant at noon, Zar sure let me know how he feels. He slid into the chair beside me, uninvited, leaning over with a "Morning, Red," his grin shameless, "you look hot as usual."

"Fuck you," I muttered.

But he whispered in my ear, "Now you finally know it would be my pleasure to fuck you because that's *exactly* what he wants to watch."

Of course, Zar looks hot in his linen suit and satisfied, too. He should be after last night. And I should hate him for being part of Luca's cruel, kinky game, but I don't.

I didn't answer Zar's tease after we sat down because I don't have one. I don't know what I feel about what I saw, but my tingling pussy sure has an opinion.

HIF #8: *My V needs Luca's vitamin D so bad...she's considering a double dose while I call Luca "Master" and let his sub use me however he wants.*

Zar keeps grinning at Luca about it. Like he's already mailed the gold-embossed printed invitation to me:

PLEASE JOIN US FOR A SATURDAY NIGHT OF DEGRADATION IN OUR SEX SUITE WHERE YOU WILL BE THE MAIN COURSE

But Luca squirms because I know his secret, while his sister-in-law, Abbey, sits to his left, along with his niece, Harper, beside her.

It's like Luca's worlds are colliding, and mine are too. After what I saw last night...

Stop thinking about it!

I was tempted to cancel my plans to join their family brunch, but I'd never hurt Gia. Only for her will I go through this awkward hell.

Sitting on the other side of Zar, Celine keeps the conversation going. She and Abbey exchange gossip about the girls' school while I sip coffee, wanting to bite the delicate porcelain cup.

I'm in a storm of emotions and can't find the way home to my truth.

Last night, I stayed later than usual, taking extra laps in the pool before returning to my room to change into dry clothes to drive home.

Then I heard screams, not tortured ones. They were muffled shouts of pleasure as I followed the sound down the empty hallway, turning left and left again until I saw the white door barely cracked open.

For minutes, I stood in the dark foyer of that suite watching—

just as Luca was—Zar fuck a woman who was going down on another one.

Marveling at how they all wore collars for Luca, how they fucked for him, seeing the desire in his crystal eyes controlling them, lust struck me like lightning.

Luca was stroking his mouthwatering cock and staring at Zar. And when Luca stalked Zar's way, lording over him with his hard dick inches from Zar's mouth, Zar said *my* name. Taunting Luca made him come all over Zar, and I couldn't even gasp.

Shock silenced me.

When they saw me standing there, all I felt was...*rage*.

It hit me so hard I had to turn and leave without a word because...

Why am I angry?

Though I want him, I've fallen so hard for him; Luca doesn't belong to me.

We work together and do these sweet, silent things for each other, but he doesn't have to be faithful to me. He can get off however he likes.

But apparently, Luca likes using me, once again, for his pleasure. He enjoys using Zar, too, watching him fuck women who *look* like me.

And I saw the toys, the BDSM gear in the cabinets and the whipping cross on the wall, and the red paddle and used dildos on the platform, too.

I know Zar played with them while Luca watched. Did Luca whip the women? Did he whip Zar, too? Did he punish him before I arrived, before Luca let him fuck his "whores" too?

And what? Does Luca fuck them first? Did I miss that part? Or does he fuck them last?

I barely graduated high school, but I don't need a psychology degree to figure it out. Luca's a Dom, and Zar's his sub, and Luca uses Zar to find women they fuck.

Add what I witnessed last night to the photos I saw, the tempting ones left on Luca's desk by his stalker, and my hand shakes, lowering my cup into the saucer.

"Scarlett, you look like a princess today." Gia gazes up at me, grinning with flakey crumbs on her face again. "You look like Ariel."

I smile at her. On instinct, I take the napkin in my lap and gently wipe her cheeks clean. "Thank you, kiddo. And you look like the princess of chocolate croissants because it's all over your cute face."

Gia giggles, and she's my only comfort. She's the only reason I'm here because I'm dressed for war. The fact that Luca paid for this dress is extra ammunition.

It's emerald green and strapless, hugging my curves in simple lines and skimming my thighs. My sleeve is on full display. It's my armor, and like me, it doesn't belong here in this posh Charleston Sunday brunch crowd.

Women like Maren sit around me in conservative dresses and elegant hats worn at church while I look like a temptress from hell because, apparently, *I AM.*

I know who Luca is now.

Zar too.

I thought Zar was my friend, but was he grooming me? I thought Luca secretly cared about me. But is he just using me again?

Fine.

If they want to use my name and my image as some kinky game between them...*then how do you like me now?*

If they can break the rules, so can I. If they can get dirty and fuck around, so can I. The problem is, I can't fuck who *I* want.

Luca keeps rejecting me. He called me a mistake. He used me and swore it would never happen again like I'm *something* he's ashamed of.

But then he defends me. He does sweet things for me. He whispers in my ear how much he wants me. He almost kisses me, confessing how he aches for me. But then he won't touch me? But he watches Zar fuck women who look like me? And he fucks them too?

Why?

I don't know.

But I sure can fuck *with* Luca.

I feel the public glares. I smell the judgment in the room. The lecherous stares of most men in the restaurant aim my way. They want me. They desire me.

They'll fuck me.

I don't know how it makes Luca feel, but the women in the restaurant obviously disapprove. I'm trash to them. The only women who seem comfortable in my presence are Celine and Abbey.

Celine's been nice to me since the first day. I know a good woman when I meet her.

It's Abbey who surprises me. She's the opposite of Maren. You'd think Luca's sister-in-law would hate me, too. That she'd see me as Maren does, as a cheap seductress. Abbey's the sister of Luca's dead wife, and I get it; hers is the only judgment I respect. She has a right to be protective of him, of Gia, too.

But no, Abbey's kind to me, asking, "Scarlett, I understand you have a new puppy."

"What little angel told you that secret?" I grin Gia's way, and she smiles, guilty.

"Both girls," Abbey glances from her daughter, Harper, to Gia, "they're begging for puppies. It's all they talk about."

"Baba says I have to be *ten* before I can have one."

Gia pouts it, so Luca explains, "You have to be old enough to walk the dog outside by yourself."

"But Scarlett can help me. She walks with me outside every-where I go, and *she* has a puppy."

It's automatic. Luca finally looks at me, and he can see past my smile right through to my fiery eyes, demanding his answer.

What game are you playing?

We can't fuck; it's against your rules. But you can watch your best friend fuck women who look like me after you fuck them, too? You said I was a mistake, but you come so hard to my name and all over your best friend saying it?

"Yeah, Baba," Zar chimes in, "let *Scarlett* help you."

And this guilty fucker.

When I turn my chin, Zar's grinning at me. He's so cocky and warm, it's cute, and I can't stop myself. Dammit, I grin back.

I like Zar. Underneath his swagger and bad-boy smile, he's a good man. We've gotten close, sparring every day, and I trust him. I don't want to, especially now, but I do.

I can sense it. Zar wasn't grooming me to use me for sex; he wants to share Luca with me. Getting off on kink doesn't make you a bad person, I should know.

But I also know when someone's trying so hard to be happy, they're not. When someone acts like nothing bothers them, something haunts them.

There's more to Zar than his sexy smile and quick wit.

Zar fucks a lot of women. He's clearly *very* good at it. Because with those dark eyes, those thick lashes, and that body that rivals Luca's and that cock? That curve in it? I got an eyeful of Zar last night, and he loves it. He's leaning back in his dining chair, giving me a gander at more.

"What do you say, Scarlett?" He taunts us, "Will you help Luca with his little problem?"

It's an inside joke Luca's daughter doesn't get.

"Will, you, Baba? Will you?" Gia bounces in her chair. "Can we get a puppy? If Scarlett helps us, she can—"

"No!" Luca pounds his fist on the table, barking so fast it's cruel.

It makes Gia's bottom lip suddenly tremble, and Abbey looks at Luca with shock. He doesn't usually lose his temper with Gia. It's obvious, and it makes her cry. Silent tears start spilling over her cheeks, and they burn my eyes, too.

Gia reminds me of my little sisters. I can't help it. I lean over and kiss the top of her head. "It's okay," I soothe. "You'll get a puppy one day. And you can play with Crimson until then, I promise."

When I glance up at Luca, wanting to punch him for hurting her feelings, his feelings punch me back.

There's a storm in his eyes, watching me comfort his daughter —guilt churning with grief and something else. I don't know what it is as he reaches for Gia.

Quickly, he lifts her into his lap. "I'm sorry, my kóri." He wipes her tears with his thumb then kisses her cheeks. "Baba's sorry he made you cry. I love you so much, okay? I promise I'll get you a puppy one day, and you can name it whatever you wish."

He cradles her head to his chest and closes his eyes, kissing her curls, and hot rocks choke my throat.

Why can't Luca just be an asshole? Why does he have to make me feel used but be so willing to share his love?

All the love he has for his daughter.

Why didn't I have a dad like that?

I'm not jealous.

It just hurts like hell.

"Can we name him Baklava?" Gia asks against his chest, and he laughs. We all do. "Yes, my kóri," he mutters into her hair, "you can name your puppy Baklava."

It's cute. It breaks the tension enough so I can finally eat the delicious Greek omelet before me.

As I chew and chat with Abbey and Celine, I feel the intense looks exchanged between Luca and Zar, like they're silently fighting over me. It's not that I suspect Zar wants me to himself. No, Zar clearly serves Luca. He wants to give him what he desires. He wants to fuck me while Luca watches, and why?

Why does Zar need to serve Luca, and why does Luca deny himself? And would I let them do it? Would I let them use me that way?

I'm so confused, but I won't look at them. I stay focused on the conversation until something over Abbey's shoulder catches my eye.

That woman?

Sitting at another table, she's wearing one of those fancy Sunday hats, the wide brim disguising part of her face, but I catch her stealing glances. A man in a grey suit sits with her. He's wearing a wedding band when he lifts a mimosa to his lips, but that doesn't stop the woman from looking.

She's devouring Luca's profile.

Setting my fork down, I talk to Abbey while secretly watching the woman behind her. Finally, my instinct is too strong. I lean over, my lips seeking Zar's ear like he's my date, while I tell him, "In a minute, barely look to your two o'clock. The woman in the yellow hat. Isn't that Brooke Turner?"

Zar gently kisses my cheek, surprising me because I like it. It warms me, but he's also wicked smart. He's quickly playing along.

I don't look at Luca when I pull away from Zar's lips. It will break the ruse, and why should I care? I don't—not right now. After Zar glances to his right, he glances back at me, nodding yes.

Like she knows she's been spotted, Luca's stalker quietly rises from her chair. Grabbing her clutch from the table, her steps are quick. She's headed to the Ladies' Room or a back exit, but I'm hot on her heels.

Darting down the hallway, she looks over her shoulder.

I toss my hair like this is an innocent trip to fix my face, too, and she's stuck. Two waiters stand by the emergency exit, so she darts left, disappearing behind the swinging door of the Ladies' Room where I'm right behind her.

Shoving the door open, a punching blur crosses my face, but I'm too trained for this. With an arm block, I evade her punch with my left while my right hand grabs her neck.

"Hey, Brooke." Slamming her hard into the wall behind her, I knock her hat off. The shock in her eyes delights me while I squeeze her throat—just a bit. I'm not in kill mode. *Yet.* "You've been banned from this property, so it seems I'm gonna have to choke you till the cops come."

"Let go of me, you bitch."

She's blonde and beautiful and a snake caught by its tail.

"Nah, nah." I laugh. "Don't be stupid. I'm the bitch with my hand choking your neck. You really want to dance with this devil? Because I promise you, I'm your hell."

MAKE HIM

"Are you fucking him?" She doesn't care. "Are you with Luca because he's *mine*? Luca's *mine*. He belongs to *me*. He loves *me*."

Her blue eyes shake. I vaguely recognize a mania in them because I feel it, too, for Luca, and it makes me ask, "What happened with him?"

Because something did, I can tell, but I don't get her answer.

The bathroom door slams open behind me, and Luca and a team of hotel security take over. Like he knows better, Luca doesn't speak to Brooke. "Take her away," he instructs his Chief of Security. "Discreetly," he growls low while they put zip ties on her wrists.

"Luca." Brooke's desperate for his attention. "Luca, I'm sorry. I'm sorry. I know you love me, and I'm sorry. Please, look at me. Talk to me. Tell me how to serve you. Tell me you love me, too."

The desperation in her eyes is sad and scary as security drags her into the hallway, and the door swings closed behind them.

Now, Luca and I are alone in the Ladies' Room, and I glare at him. "What the fuck did you do to her?"

"Nothing." He glares right back.

"We're in a room for shit, but you're the only one full of it." I step into his shadow. "You fucked with her, didn't you? Like you did those women last night? Zar gets your victims, and you break their hearts. Right? But let me guess; you couldn't cast your happy pussy spell over Brooke, could you? No. You fucked her, and that fucked with her head because now she's delusional."

His molars clench. "She wanted it. We *didn't* hurt her. She came back for more, a couple of times, but then..."

He can't say it, but I can.

I feel it. I understand Brooke.

"But then, when you told her it's over, you hurt her. You told her she was a mistake and left her like that, and she didn't know *what* to feel. What to think. You play your fucking games with women, and some can take it. They love it. Some can let you go, Luca." I hate this pain. I hate how he makes me pound his chest. "And some can't. You leave them, and they get hurt. They feel abandoned. They feel used."

He grabs my punching wrist, his other hand sinking into my strands, tugging my hair until our eyes are locked.

"I didn't mean to hurt you, Scarlett."

"But you did. You used me, and now you use women who look like me. You play games with them and me, and I don't understand. Why?"

The truth overwhelms me.

I have no filters, only rare feelings flooding my heart, welling in my eyes. I don't care if he sees my pain; he's the reason I feel it.

"You act like you care about me, Luca. You say we're professionals, but then you do romantic things. You leave me gifts. You defend me from others. You make me feel special like I matter to you, but then you're so cruel. You call me a grave mistake, but then you fuck women who look like me because...I'm what? I'm just trash you threw away? I'm not good enough for your rich world? I'm not worth keeping? Worth loving?"

My past and present pain drown my chest. I can't breathe as my tears finally escape.

Luca presses his forehead to mine, his grip on my wrist and hair squeezing so tight it hurts.

"Scarlett, you're the only one."

"The only one...*what*?"

Passion burns in his eyes. The heat of his towering body pressed against mine confuses me even more. The intensity of it melts his mask, falling to the floor in flames as he confesses, "You're the only woman I've been with since my wife died. No one else but you."

If time could stop, it would.

If my breath could cease, it does.

If he could cry, he'd do it. It's in his eyes. They're full of grief and guilt and pain and searching mine for forgiveness. For an answer and...

"Why?" I ask. "Why me?"

"I knew it the moment we met."

"Knew what?"

"That you were strong enough to take my pain."

"But I hurt, too. I have a heart, too."

"I know you do. I see it all the time." Tenderness softens his face. "You don't know what that night meant to me, why you're the only woman I've been with, and what you're becoming to Gia now. I need you for this job. I can't lose you. Your company can't find out, or you're gone, and that's what makes this so fucking hard."

"Makes what hard?" I shake my head, confused. After what I saw last night, I know this isn't just about work or remaining professional.

It's about something more.

"Luca, I'd never violate someone's marriage or commitment. And she was beautiful. I've seen the pictures of Darby around your home. I see why you loved your wife so much, but..." *Why am I pushing him? Why do I care so much?* "But it's been four years. It's okay to move on. Even if it's not with me."

HIF #9: It's that bad.

I've fallen for Luca so much. I guess it's love because I only want him to be happy, even at my expense.

"Never." His thumb lingers across my wet cheek. "You're my passion, Scarlett, and that's my punishment. Even if you didn't work for me, even if I met you in a café and I fell for you, which I would, I made a promise by her grave, and I'm keeping it. I broke it with you once and—"

"Why?" I grab his shirt. He's sweating; I am, too. "Why did you break your promise? Why did you do it with *me*? Why did you do this to *us* because it fucking hurts?"

"I know. It's killing me."

"Then why? Why did you use me like that? Why did you fuck me like that? Like I belonged to you. Like you couldn't get enough of me." The logic starts falling into place—that night and what he just told me. "Was it just me? I'm the only one who felt something? But you, you were just what? Just getting laid after so long? Is that why you fucked me like that?"

He tugs my hair. "I fucked you like that because I couldn't believe it. I'd never felt that before."

"Felt what?"

"I never even felt it with *my wife*. Ever. With any woman."

I don't care how big he is, how much money or power, or goddamn sex appeal he has; I can drop him to his knees.

"Felt *what*, Luca? Be a man and name it. What did you feel with me?"

Because I know the name for what I feel, but I won't say it. Not first.

"This—"

He slams me against the wall, his hand still fisting my hair. He crushes my body against the cold marble tiles, but we're not. We're ablaze, flames licking with desire as he starts rutting like he wants inside me again, pressing his lips to my ear, his other hand clutching my hip.

"When I call you 'my whore' it means everything to me because I'm finally free with you. I've always wanted a woman who's like me. You're the *only* one for me. I'm man enough to know what I feel for you is so fucking strong; it *has* no name." Even with guilt in his eyes, he growls, grinding his swelling cock against my center, spilling heat through my veins. "Because you feel this too, don't you, Scarlett? We match. We belong together. It's insane between us."

"Yes." I grab the back of his neck and a fist full of his long black strands and yank hard so he can feel my strength, too. "I feel you, Luca, but I'm not afraid. I can take whatever's killing you inside and make you live again."

With a clench of his jaw, he grabs my thigh, slinging my leg to wrap around him before he shoves my dress up to my waist. Exposing my black thong, he thrusts hard into my wet lace, lifting my heels off the floor.

His hard cock is so close. I can feel his hungry tip under his pants, urging against my covered pussy, and all he has to do is drop his zipper, rip my wet thong aside, and thrust inside me where he belongs.

I'm throbbing for him.

He dusts his lips over mine, and my knees almost buckle. Grinding against my aching cunt, his thick cock is rubbing my clit, torturing us.

"Fuck," he grunts. "Fuck, I want you so fucking bad, Scarlett; you're the punishment I deserve."

"Then let me punish you." I yank his hair again, rubbing my slick thong over his linen pants, feeling his painful need. "Let me fuck you again so hard, I promise it'll hurt us both."

His eyes slowly blink, lust flooding them as his hand seeks where I'm spread open for him.

"You torture me, don't you?" His fingertips play with the hem of my thong. "You tease everyone looking like this today." His touch is fire, licking the edge of my wet lace, sliding it over, and exposing my aching pussy. "You're so beautiful. They all want to fuck you, my belle." Barely, his fingertip brushes my clit, and it kills me. It makes me shake, moaning for him. "But this pussy is mine. I claimed it. It belongs to me now, doesn't it?"

"Yes." I can't take this need. I'll do anything. "Yes, Luca. What do you want? To watch me? To play with me? To be my master again? Do you want me for yourself, or do you want to watch me with Zar? Or do you want to share me with him?"

He groans, panting over my lips, tickling my clit while I'm breaking the rules and losing my mind. My pussy is soaked and aching for Luca, any part of him, please.

He's a prisoner, too. He clenches his jaw so tight. "I need everything with you." His fingertip lightly circles my clit, making my leg wrapped around him shake. "But I can't. I won't." His thick middle finger teases into my entrance, not even an inch. "I meant it that night." He does it again, barely piercing me with his finger, and I groan in sweet agony. "You are *ma flamme*, my flame, because you fucking burn inside me, Scarlett, and I don't know how to get you out."

"Because you can't, Luca," I sigh, rolling my hips, needing more of his touch. "You've burned me as much as I've burned you, and now what? What do you want, Luca?"

"Good question."

A voice bounces off the marble. We turn our startled stares to see Zar standing in the doorway.

"You two better decide what you want because Gia's asking for you." He warns. He's not smiling. "She's asking for *both* of you."

Luca

CHAPTER TEN

"What do you want?"

That's not a question I can answer.

My life isn't about what I want. From the day I was born, I was told what that is—I want to run a global hotel empire. Then, when my daughter was born, my life became about what she wants and needs.

Besides, from the moment Gia's mother died, I didn't want anything but bone-breaking grief.

But time changes everything because the grief is gone. Like cancer in remission or cured, I don't have it anymore, though it constantly threatens to return.

But the guilt?

It's here.

That's what I want—*guilt*.

Because if I keep that emotion wrapped around me, desire won't win. I can keep my grave promise if I can keep my guilt. Because if I let it go...

All I want is Scarlett.

What did that night at the club mean to me? Why did it mean so much to me to have Scarlett innocently offer to be my "whore"?

I'll never tell her.

Because when I was inside her, I realized I could feel again, live again, love again, and it terrified me. I felt my pain threaten to heal, so I had to let her go, though it was the last thing I wanted to do.

"Hello?" The sound of her sweet, raspy voice calls out almost every morning from our foyer now, and I need it like the sunrise.

"In here," I shout out from the bedroom floor, trapped with my eyes closed and dreading this.

"Baba, be still," Gia bosses me, and I love it. I'm raising her to be a CEO. "I'm not done."

"Gia, you're going to be late for school."

"But you said if I took a shower like a big girl and not a bath, I could do your makeup."

She stabs my eyelid with a Q-tip, and I wince, answering, "I'm wiping this off the minute you're done. And that's it. You've got one more minute."

"Well, my, my..." The voice I crave sings like a song, but...*I'm not looking.* "Don't you look as pretty as a pumpkin but twice as smart."

"I'm doing Baba's makeup for work," Gia answers Scarlett, and I'm not opening my eyes to witness Scarlett's glee.

"Baba looks so *purdy*." Scarlett chuckles. "All glittery and colorful, like a grumpy unicorn."

I will triple her salary if she'd stop.

Gia pokes my eye again, almost blinding me with a Q-tip. "That's it." I open them, insisting, "Enough, my kóri. We're going to be late."

"But, Baba, you need lipstick too."

Gia lords over me and the shit I do for my daughter. Humiliation is at the top of the list, but usually, only Celine sees this. Zar did once, and I never heard the fucking end of it.

And now Scarlett looms above me, too.

My gaze caresses from her black heels up her bare, shiny calves. Her skin glows under a black sweater dress that falls below her knees. The damn thing covers every inch of her but leaves nothing to the imagination. Today's poison is a one-shoulder dress. One long, knitted sleeve covers her right arm, while her left is exposed, the one adorned in a sleeve of colorful tattoos, and I find myself curious about what they mean.

"Yeah, Baba." Scarlett tilts her head, her flaming strands pulled into her usual high ponytail wearing *our* hair clip, and my cock twitches. "You need some lipstick."

She sounds too much like Zar. What did they do? Exchange notes last night?

Since Zar busted us in the bathroom, I don't know if it was a blessing or a curse. We didn't talk about it. I focused on Gia the rest of the day, Scarlett went home, and Zar let me stew in it like he always does.

None of us said a word about how close I got to breaking my rule again with Scarlett.

Every time she's near, I feel my resolve falter.

Maybe I can have Scarlett and my guilt.

She knows my secret now, what we do on Saturday nights. Maybe I can punish myself doing it with Scarlett instead.

"Baba, wear this pink one." Gia shoves a tube with butterflies on it in my face.

"Men don't wear lipstick." I lurch to stand, and my torturers step back.

"Yes, they do," Gia answers me. "Rocco, the concierge, wears makeup, and he's a boy."

I brush white carpet lint off my black pants. I have a meeting this morning; I can't believe I got suckered into this.

"You're right," I answer. "Our staff can express themselves however they desire."

I'm fine with my employees being themselves. I sure as fuck don't get what I desire. I'm happy at least they do.

But when my eyes confront Scarlett with her sexy pink pillow lips cocked in a half-grin? "You look beautiful, Mr. Mercier," she teases, and even Gia giggles at my torment.

I storm into my ensuite bathroom, growling over my shoulder, "Gia, get your backpack. And Scarlett, I need you to drive her to school. I have a meeting I can't miss. Our Bali property had a fire."

Scarlett's on my heels, her face serious, while I glimpse mine in the mirror.

Fuck me.

Purple, pink, and blue makeup?

I look like a clown who went down on a pussy that glitter-bombed all over my face. Because yes, that's what I think about when Scarlett's this close—eating pussy.

"Is everyone okay?" But she keeps it professional.

"Yes." I wet a washcloth to remove the ego damage. "Just a few rooms were damaged. The guests got out safely, but with the time difference, I can't miss this call. It's getting late over there."

"Okay," she eases. "I'll drive Gia to school."

Dragging the warm cloth down my face, I confess to her in the reflection, "No one's ever driven her but me. This is my hell. I need you to protect her. To be careful. I need you to—"

"I understand." Scarlett softly grins. "*I'm* the titled fighter who's completed three defensive driving schools. I'm overqualified for the job. What skills you got?"

I could slam her against a wall again and show her my hard skills. All I could punish her with and fuck her with, all I crave to do with Scarlett, to torture her with pleasure and—

Fuck.

Stop it.

I can't take much more. Scarlett's blurring the lines that keep me safe. "Please." I close my eyes, dragging in a painful breath, because the guilt returns. "I can't lose her, too."

A gentle touch lands on my shoulder, and I let this moment be. I let Scarlett comfort me because I can't open my eyes to what I know I'll see—a woman I need more every day, and I've never trusted one like this.

Not since...

"Luca," her voice weaves into my soul, "I won't let anything happen to her. I promise. Gia's more than a job to me. I love her, too."

Hot boulders suddenly choke my throat, the memory of Darby's gravestone exploding into my mind, and I have to open my eyes so I can breathe. I have to turn around, dropping my washcloth on the marble floor while I cup Scarlett's cheeks, lifting her blue eyes to mine before I stare at her lips.

God, to hear her say that. What I want at this moment. What I feel at this time that's stopped.

Her lips part, her eyes searching mine, and I know exactly what I should say, and how I should change, and how I should kiss her and—

"Baba, where's my backpack?"

I drop my hands, letting Scarlett stagger back seconds before Gia waltzes into my bathroom.

"You left it under the piano," I answer her as I pick up my washcloth. "Gia,"—*this is hell*—"Scarlett is taking you to school today, and you must behave. Don't distract her while she drives."

"I won't." Gia chirps, "We'll sing *The Little Mermaid*."

I roll my eyes, dread pumping through my veins as Scarlett adds, "I'll text you once I drop her off."

"And meet me in my office when you return," I order. "I want a full report."

Scarlett salutes with a grin.

Ten minutes later, I start my video meeting with my Bali office while I'm focused on my security cameras, on the one sight that imprisons my breath.

It's a beautiful auburn-haired angel in the parking deck, whisking my daughter, my soul, away in a black car headed toward that bridge...and *my* guilty heart crumbles into dust.

"Revenues are down in Mykonos."

Zar tosses the quarterly report on my desk, almost knocking my plate of orange slices onto the floor. "We're not canceling our trip. We need to find out why. It's our crown property and makes no sense."

I open the folder, thumbing through the pages. "We don't need to go. It makes sense. My father put his unqualified best friend as the manager there years ago, and this is what we get, mixing family with business."

Zar plops down in the chair across from my desk, stacking his feet on top of it.

"Well, I'm family." He smirks. "I'm your best friend, and when we mix, our numbers are *always* up, and you're very welcome."

I grin, scanning the numbers, but I don't answer. I don't need to address the truth.

"Speaking of," he pushes. "Are we still doing that field trip to Delta's this Saturday? Maybe Scarlett can watch the private demonstration with us."

He taunts me, and still, I won't answer. My mind is flooded with worry.

Scarlett texted me twenty minutes ago that she had safely dropped Gia off. Glancing at my screens, *she's back*; I spot my Escalade parked in the garage.

She's on her way to my office, and Zar's stressing me out with some plans I've made, too.

Last week, I took a stroll down the street to visit a friend of my friends who's opened a new store in the French Quarter. Lucky for me, it's an exclusive sex store disguised as a boutique—Delta's.

The owner is Stacey Evans, the former wife of that evil monster, Senator Gentry Evans. That man's trial is all over the news, but it doesn't bother Stacey.

She and I had a great meeting. She showed me around her new store, giving me a pre-opening tour. You'd think we'd be uncomfortable drinking mint juleps in a room full of high-end sex toys, but we weren't.

I've met Stacey before.

She was at Redix and Cade's thirtieth birthday party with Silas. But Stacey was busy that night with the three men she loves while I was busy having my world flipped.

Yes, that's the night I fucked Scarlett at a sex club.

And I swear, it's like destiny loves tempting me because now, Stacey Evans's new adult store, Delta's, is like a beacon down the street.

I was planning to take Zar there. I asked Stacey for one of her private demonstrations of the sex furniture she has on the third floor in a parlor-turned-showroom. I saw the sex bench, the sex chaise, and the sex swing, and I thought Zar should see them, too.

The fact that we can *watch* Stacey and her men demonstrate how to use them thrilled me even more. I figured Zar and I could shop at Delta's for more furniture and toys for our room.

And fuck.

What am I thinking?

I'm not controlling my temptations; I'm making them stronger.

I say I won't do something, then I half do it, and Zar's right there, taunting me to go all the way.

It's too much. Like an addiction, it's getting out of hand. Like a drug, I won't be able to resist.

"No," I answer Zar. "No more. No trips to a sex store. I'm canceling our *demonstration* there. I'm canceling all Saturday nights. We're losing control."

I glance up, and Zar's furious. He seethes, "When are you going to stop this shit?"

"What shit?" I glance over his shoulder, noting that my office door is ajar, so I lower my voice. "Quit busting my fucking balls. They're *my* balls to bust."

"Exactly." He rips his feet off my desk and leans forward, lowering his voice, too. "They're your balls, and it's time. You can break your rule with Scarlett because you already have, so quit fucking punishing yourself. It's been long enough."

"It'll be until the day I die because I deserve it."

"It wasn't your fault."

I glare back at him. "Yes, it was."

"I loved her too."

I snarl, "I'm reminded every day."

But he doesn't back down. "I lost her, too. But she'd want us to move on."

Zar did love Darby, and she loved him—just not as much as she loved me. I was the first man she was with, and Zar watched from the sidelines of our brief life together. My love with Darby was pure and innocent. She was never part of what Zar and I had shared in our dorm room. She never knew about it. I hid it from her.

It was dark and tempting, my drug, *our drug.* Zar and I didn't plan it. We stumbled across our addiction.

First, we brought two women back to our shared dorm bedroom. Zar was fucking one on his bed, and I was fucking the other on mine. The women tried to hide under our bedspreads. They were shy. But once I saw the lust in Zar's eyes watching me fuck, I was hooked.

He was hooked.

Then it became about him watching me fuck. My dates thought Zar was asleep, but he was stroking off, secretly watching us. Zar would also try to date the same women, and most did. They couldn't resist him either, and I craved acting like I was asleep, but really, I was relishing him enjoying my seconds, and he loved having them.

The power exchange started to build between us. We've always had a bond. Then, an admiration. Then, an attraction.

Finally, one night, Zar's date realized I was awake, and she didn't freak out. She was on her knees, sucking Zar's cock, and begging me to join them. She wanted to fuck us, and we did. But it was when I fucked her first and how I growled in Zar's ear, telling him exactly how to fuck her next, that we were born.

"Feel my cum inside her?" I pressed my chest to his back while he knelt, fucking her while I taunted him. "Pump your hard dick into where my cock stretched her pussy for you. Keep going. Don't stop. Feel how I made her wet for you."

Controlling him like that made me so hard again. I wedged my swollen cock between his ass cheeks, and Zar got off on me doing it. "Yes," he groaned. "Make me. Own me."

"Pull your dick out. Let me see my cum on it. That's it. Look." We both did. "Damn, my cum looks good on your cock. Now, fuck her harder. Fuck her with my cum. Fuck her while I watch. While I make you do it."

The power between us was clear; I needed control, and he needed to submit.

Both Zar and I were ruled by names, by legacies we didn't want, so we shared the sex we were forbidden to have. But he doesn't always obey me when we're not in scene. I like it because it pisses me off, too.

"I don't get what I want, and neither can you," I growl low. "If I can't fuck Scarlett, you can't either. I told you, she's off limits."

Zar leans back, his eyes narrowing. "She wants to. I heard her in the bathroom with you. I heard what she said. It sure sounds like she wants us to play with her limits."

"We're not fucking playing with her. We're not using her. Not that way."

"You're full of shit, and you know it. She's perfect for us. She's tough as fuck." Zar grins. "She's a badass and beautiful, and she can take us. She's not another Brooke."

"No, she's not. She's more than that, and that's why it stops. We can't lose her. We need her." My worlds threaten to crash again, and here comes the soul-crushing guilt. "Gia needs Scarlett. She's fallen for her."

His grin grows. "*You've* fallen for her." I stare him down. He's mocking me. Tempting me. Zar's too damn good at it. "Admit it." Zar doesn't whisper. "You've fallen in love with Scarlett."

A gentle tap interrupts us. Speak of the beautiful devil. There she stands in my office doorway.

"Listen…"

Scarlett demands, sitting in the chair Zar just left. He has a meeting, and my world won't stop unraveling.

"I've proven you can trust me," she says, "and I'm sick of the secrets. I can't do my job protecting Gia if you don't tell me everything, every risk. So fess up before they release Brooke from jail today." Her scarred eyebrow points. "Tell me right now what happened with her."

My exhale is long. She's right. My stalker is a risk, so I confess, "Zar met her first. Like he always does."

"Where did he meet her?"

"Playing golf with her husband."

"She's *married*?"

"Yes."

"Does her husband know about—"

"Yes," I interrupt, trying to get this over with. "Brooke would go home and tell him about it. He got off on it. The first time, it was the usual—her playing with another woman while Zar fucked her, and I watched."

Fuck, my dick has a mind of its own.

I'm getting hard telling Scarlett this.

"But Brooke wanted more." I try ignoring it. "She asked to come back and wanted us to take pictures. *She* wanted the whole pony play thing. She said her husband wanted to jerk off to it. He's some rich equestrian. So I got a photographer, and she came over and took the shots."

"So a photographer knows about what you and Zar—"

"Yes," I keep interrupting her, shifting in my chair, trying to will my cock to stand down. "Vivian. She's an incredible photographer. She did our advertising shots here, and she can be trusted. Don't worry. They all sign NDAs."

She crosses her arms. "How long ago was this?"

"Nine months or so."

"So what happened with Brooke?" Scarlett crosses her legs. *Is she getting turned on, too?* "Why did you end your arrangement with her? And why is she fixated on *you* and not Zar?"

"Because the third time she came back after she showed her husband the photos, she said she used our names to cuckold him. And she wasn't supposed to reveal our identities, so I ended it. We can't afford for it to get out."

"But in the bathroom, when we caught her, Brooke acted like she's in love with you," Scarlett persists, "not like she's mad at you. Why?"

I really shouldn't tell her this...

But I'm too tempted.

"Because Brooke had Zar, but she never had me. Zar fucked her hard from behind while she looked into *my* eyes. I told her to scream *my* name and to say, 'Fuck me harder, motherfucker,' and she did, and I guess, somehow, that—"

"That's what *I* said to *you*."

It suddenly dawns on Scarlett. She understands my obsession now, what's making my cock so hard again. My fists clench, and my tongue licks my lips because she licks hers, too, at the memory.

She asks, "How many women have you made say *my words* to you?"

My edges are cracking. "All of them since you."

"How many women have there been?"

"Countless. Ask Zar. It doesn't matter to me. I never fuck them."

"But..." Something troubles her blue eyes, her tone wavering like she doesn't want to know. "You had Gia. You had sex with your wife. Did you and Zar ever—"

"Never," I bark. "I never cheated on my wife. I never shared her. She was too pure and innocent. She wasn't a whore."

Scarlett flinches like I slapped her, like I insulted her, and I immediately regret it. "I mean..." I try to explain. "Zar and I discovered our fetish before her. But Darby wasn't a very...*sexual* person. I loved so many other things about her, so I hid that part of me from her. That part of me that needed that in a woman."

"She never knew you were a Dom? That you're Zar's Dom?"

"No, she never saw that side of me, and it wasn't until a year after she died that I couldn't take it anymore. I made my promise to her grave, but I needed something."

"Why did you make a promise to her grave?"

I gnash my teeth. "Next question."

I'll never tell Scarlett. She'll hate me. No one knows but Zar. Our secret died with my wife.

But Scarlett nods as if she needs more intel, so she asks, "So what happened after a year? What did you need?"

"I kept my promise but needed to watch, and Zar needed me back. We both needed something, so he suggested the suite we made and the Saturday nights we share. I collared him, and now he picks the women, and I control what he does to them. Watching him is my relief and his reward."

My chest pounds. My dick throbs hard. I'm aroused telling Scarlett but afraid for her to know all this.

Is she disgusted?

Will she hate me like I hate myself?

"Do you love him?" Gently, she asks, surprising me, and it makes this worse in the best way.

I want her so bad.

"Do I love Zar?" I twirl the gold band on my finger. "Yes, but we don't say it."

"Do you fuck *him*?"

The way she asks, she's not judging us. Scarlett's perfect for me, made for me. She's mine, and it ignites my veins. It turns my resolve to ash. She's so damn beautiful, I can't fight it.

"No," I answer. "I'm looking at the only one I want to fuck. Every day. In beautiful and brutal ways like my whore. *Harder.* Like a motherfucker."

Her pink lips part with a soft gasp, so I let go. "Remember? That's what you said to me," I coax, "while I fucked you the third time like a rabid dog." *Just a little taste.* "While our cum dripped down your thighs, you screamed at me to fuck you even harder. To hurt you." *I can control it.* "So I fingered your ass, getting ready to fuck it, too, while people watched me make you scream. I love your screams, Belle." *I won't break my rule.* "And I want to hear them right now." Her eyes flood with lust. "I want to watch you be a whore for me, Scarlett. Is that what you want?"

She nods like she's been waiting for me to crack, so I do.

But not all the way.

"Get up, Ms. Jones," I command. "Close my office door and lock it."

When she rises, it's with triumph. When she walks, it's for my gaze. When she turns around, after securing our privacy, it's for me.

All of her is mine.

"Sit on the edge of my desk." I push my chair back. "And do a good job for me."

Scarlett sits in front of me like a lady, crossing her legs at the knee. "I'd rather do a very *bad* job for you, Mr. Mercier."

"I can get sued for this." I spread my legs. "And you can get fired."

"Well then." She frees her hair from our clip, shaking her fiery mane for me. The sunlight streaming through my office windows makes her glow like the fire she is inside me. "If I'm going to get fired, Mr. Mercier, then make me come so hard; it's worth it."

I demand, "Pull your dress down and show me your nipples. You're not wearing a bra today. You've been teasing me like a dirty little girl, and now you're going to play with them for me."

Pulling her sweater dress down, she frees her arm from its one sleeve, leaving her dress around her waist.

"Fuck, Belle, your tits," I groan, rubbing my cock, hidden by my pants. "Your pointy, pink nipples. Play with them. Pinch them for me."

"Like this?" She doesn't take her eyes off me. Arching her back, she rolls her body while her palms cup her breasts, her fingertips thrilling her hard nipples, and we're both enraptured.

But when she glances over and sees my orange slices on the plate beside her, she picks one up. Squeezing sticky citrusy drops over her nipples, she makes them drip, and I'm in hell.

I love it here.

"I get so juicy for you, Mr. Mercier. Is that what you want? To drink my sweet juice again?"

"Rub it on your nipples. That's it." I watch the fruit graze her pink peaks, covering them with nectar I need to lick off if I want to live. "Now eat the orange for me," I command. "Lick it like a pussy. Have you licked pussy before, Ms. Jones?"

"Yes," she sighs into the juicy flesh before showing me her experience with her tongue, and I'm dying. I moan, unzipping my pants. "Is that what you want to watch, Mr. Mercier?" Juice drips down her chin, her tongue licking between her taunts. "You want to watch me eat a woman's pussy for you? Like a good little slut?"

She's going to torture me, and it's exactly what I need.

"It makes you wet, doesn't it? The thought of being my whore again." Using the slit on my boxer briefs, I free my cock, and her eyes get wide at its size. "Does this make you wet, too, Ms. Jones? Seeing my hard cock again?"

"I *make* you that hard, Luca." She grins with her glistening chin. "You *need* me to be your whore, and I will. I want to."

Setting the orange down, she reaches, shifting and lifting her dress. My dick drips at the sight on my desk; that pussy I can't erase from my mind. Glimpses of it tease from under her black lace thong.

"Pull your panties down your thighs, but leave them on," I demand. "In case we get caught. In case someone sees you being my dirty little whore." I love the idea. "Now lean back, prop up on your hands, bend your knees. Put your feet on the edge of my desk." She obeys. "Good girl. Now, spread your legs for me."

"But with my panties like this, I can't do it all the way for you."

"Exactly." I smirk, stroking slowly, wishing it was her hand but loving the naughty sight of her pussy. "We don't get all we want, Ms. Jones. We get just enough."

"Is *this* what you want, Mr. Mercier?"

With one hand, she reaches between her thighs, spreading her lips open, her middle fingertip with a French manicure circling her firm, pink clit, and makes me stroke harder. It makes me regret so much. It makes the world outside disappear because this is my world—Scarlett's pussy in my face.

"Fuck yourself," I sigh. "Fuck yourself like I fucked you."

Our hands start matching tempo, our eyes fixed on our desire —her fingers pumping into her wet cunt, and mine pumping my hard cock.

I've gotten off so often like this, just watching Scarlett, but it's more. I'm not watching her; I'm *with* her. She pulls me into her gaze, into her tight, wet heat, and I don't exist. The guilt is gone. I'm hers. For minutes. For hours. Forever, I'm with her, and it's almost good enough. I can almost get by like this.

"Say it. Say who you are. Say who I am, Scarlett."

"Yes, Master, I'm your whore. Your only whore." Her two glistening fingers start pumping harder, just like my fist over my cock. "Play with me. Use me. I'll submit to you."

"If I play with you," I warn, "I *will* use you. I'm a Pleasure Dom. I will torture you with intense pleasure. I'll make you come so many times until you can't take it. It will torture us both. Is that what you want?"

I can't believe I'm offering this. I can't believe I will do this, but I have to. I can't go back to a life without Scarlett. There's no oxygen there.

"Yes," she gasps. Her nipples point hard, her pussy is so pink and wet, her milky cum coating her fingers, and it swells my cock.

"You'll be so dirty for me," I insist. "I'm going to do lewd things to you and let people watch, and you'll obey my commands, but I won't fuck you. Is that what you want?"

"Yes, Sir." Her thighs shake.

Fuck, I love this hell. "Say it, my whore. Say what you want me to do to you."

"Fuck me, Luca." Her voice. Her eyes. "Fuck me harder, motherfucker."

Scarlett can take every inch of my cock and pain. But when she sighs, "Luca," with her two glistening fingers disappearing into the place that brought me back to life, I need more. "Luca, please." Her eyes droop, and she needs more, too.

"Come, Belle." My fist keeps pumping, the fire in my veins white hot. "Come on your fingers, then put them in my mouth. Let me taste your sweet cum on my tongue again."

"Oh fuck," Scarlett groans, "I'm coming." Her thighs, bound by her panties, shake feet from my face, and I can hear it. I can smell her sweet lust. "Fuck, Luca." She buries her fingers inside and keeps them there, jerking harder inside her pussy as I watch with hunger.

I want to be inside her again. I want to feel that pussy take my breath away again. I want to give her everything inside me. Her orgasm is my home, but I can't join her there, and suddenly, the punishment isn't sweet.

"Luca, please," she sighs again, her shoulders lurching. Her orgasm won't stop, and it's torture for her too.

"Ma flamme, give it to me," I grunt. "Give me that pussy. Let me taste your fingers."

I stand up so fast, pumping my swollen cock as she slides her two tangy fingers over my lips. Tasting her again, I'm barely hanging on. The flavor of her cum returns to my tongue, to my memory, and I break for her.

"You can fight me, Luca," she sighs, pumping her fingers in my mouth while I suck them, and I'm right here, staring into her eyes, seeing her wet pussy exposed to me. "But I'll win. You can watch me. You can torture me. You can degrade me and use me. You can come all over me, but you're mine, too. I will *make* you mine."

Fuck, yes, I groan, sucking her fingers so hard I splatter her pussy with my creamy cum. I grunt, spurting more, watching Scarlett, my erotic dream. Her fingers hover over my lips while I confess, "Yes, Belle. Make me."

I want Scarlett to make me. To fight me. To fight *for* me. To break my rules. Scarlett's the only woman who can, and I can't get enough of her.

I'm not as guilty if Scarlett *makes* me love her.

"This Saturday," I murmur, wanting to kiss her, but I don't. I lean forward and kiss her hair, knowing what I need, what we *can* do. "Join me."

"You and Zar?" She reaches for me, her palm caressing my pounding chest, and I hold her hand there.

"No," I answer. I don't think I can handle watching Scarlett with Zar. I can't even think about it, not with how her touch over my heart soothes my pain.

"Join me at an adult store," I command, "where only *I* will play with you first."

Scarlett

CHAPTER ELEVEN

Ruby sighs in the pedicure chair beside me. "Girl, you have died and gone to slut heaven."

I feel inspired, getting the same red polish as she does, but I keep my voice down in the salon.

"It ain't heaven," I huff. "It's hell; Luca, not fucking me yet."

"With how you say he wants to take you to a sex store for some games instead? Shit, I'd let him play in my kinky park all day." She opens her eyes, aiming her stare at me. "Besides, I thought you weren't fucking your client."

"Think again," I scoff.

"Interesting." She grins. "You always say, 'Dick don't pay bills.' Where's all that sisterly wisdom now?"

"Sounding dumb to my pussy."

The technicians giggle, and why should I care? I want to try this arrangement with Luca so bad I'll advertise it on an interstate billboard.

**SCARLETT JONES IS NOW
LUCA MERCIER'S SUB**
Disclaimer: His *second* sub.

Or am I? Is it official? I don't know much about his world yet.

"See," Ruby laughs, "you're dickmatized. One day, y'all will fuck again, and then you'll get married and be his happily-ever-after slut from that day forward."

"Not happening. Luca's got too much guilt over his wife dying."

"Guilt? Why? He didn't murder her."

"I don't know. But he feels guilty, so I get it. We go slow."

"Slow?" Ruby leans my way across her chair. "Since when is finger banging yourself for him to watch, going *slow*? And tonight, he's taking you to a sex shop for a circus show? If that's *slow*, Girl, fast is gonna scorch your kitty to a crisp."

"Shhh." I keep no secrets from my sister, but the whole damn salon doesn't need to know my kinky plans for the night. "It's slow for *him*."

Ruby lowers her voice. "Slow cuz' he's got a *watching* kink. And what about his friend, Zar? The Oscar-Winner of Orgasms? Where does he fit in?"

"I don't know. I don't know how this whole Dom/sub thing works."

"Want me to Google it?" Ruby reaches for the phone in her back pocket. "Like AskAnastasiaGrey.com?"

"Hell no. I assume Luca will answer my questions, but I can't figure Zar out."

"Ain't no math to figure there." Ruby chuckles. "Luca's best friend is a typical man wanting a flesh sandwich with two women and for others to watch what a big dick he has while he eats it." Her eyes dance. "You gonna do it? Are you gonna be in a three-layered cake with Luca's friend and a woman while Luca watches?"

"Isn't that like...*cheating* on Luca if he's not in it?"

"Not if it makes him paint the ceiling! Not if they have some kinda agreement. It's hot as hell."

"Okay, fine. It's kinda hot. And it's not like I'm a prude, but it's more. The way Luca and Zar look at each other sometimes. They share more than women."

"What? They're dickmatized too?" Her eyes roll. "Fuck, that's so hot if they bowl from both ends."

I can't answer her.

Luca, I sort of understand now. He has guilt over his wife dying. He feels like he's cheating to fuck again, so he watches Zar do it instead. And that's why he loves Zar. They're more than best friends. They share an erotic bond.

But Zar puzzles me.

What's in it for him? Doesn't he want love, too?

I heard what Zar said to Luca before I knocked on the office door. "You've fallen in love with Scarlett." Zar sounded happy about it, and Luca didn't deny it.

Why?

Is Luca in love with me? Is that why *I'm* doing this? I'm breaking every rule, and getting thirsty for whatever he wants, and putting my heart on the line for Luca...again? Because I'm in love with him, too?

"Well then, at least answer this." Ruby nudges my arm. "Who's bigger?"

Damn, this could be fun, too. I can't help but smile. "Zar is hung. He's got this curved-up cock that I bet comes like a fountain, but I swear, Luca is two stacked soup cans."

"Bawk, bawk, Bitch. Chicken soup *is* good for the soul," Ruby jokes, and we double over, laughing so hard we have a disapproving audience.

But as our smiles fade, Ruby knows the look in my eyes. My sister knows the fear I hide because we share it.

Our dad walked out on her, too.

I was eleven, Ruby was ten, and Rose and Cherry were so young. Mom was at work, while Dad made his unemployment feel like a vacation for us. I thought we made him happy, but darkness would fall over him, and I didn't recognize him. He'd sit, like a ghost, on the sofa for hours and not speak to us.

Then, one afternoon, after all of us girls and Dad played in the sprinkler, he made grilled cheeses for dinner and spoiled us with Tater Tots and ketchup. Then he kissed the top of my head and said, "I'm going to the store for some beer. Watch your sisters."

But I ran to the window, watching him drive away in his white truck because he didn't say, "I'll be right back, kiddo," like he always did.

Because he didn't come back.

And my heart is still eleven. It's still broken. It's still waiting at that window for him to return.

"You're really gonna do it?" Ruby reaches for my hand, and I let her hold it. "You're finally gonna trust a man?"

"I'm gonna try."

I LIKE the sidewalks through the French Quarter of Charleston. The historic buildings. The brightly colored, narrow single homes. The Spanish moss in the trees. And I like the palms in the porch planters and the ferns and pink geraniums spilling over the iron window boxes.

But I like this more, and it's my *HIF #10: I'm becoming a helpless romantic. You'd think I was walking beside Ryan Gosling, holding a notebook.*

But no, I'm walking beside Luca like he's sort of my date.

We stroll side-by-side in the warm evening October air, my shoulder brushing his arm, and I want him to reach for my hand. It's like he's itching to do it.

But we don't.

We aren't there yet. Maybe we'll never be.

But I know where we're going—Delta's. It's just a few blocks from The Mercier Hotel.

I met Luca there, outside his place. It's technically my day off, but I didn't want Gia to see me. This part of me is for adults only. I keep it separate.

So does Luca. Escaping for the night had lust swirling in his eyes when he met me outside the glass and gold doors of his hotel, kissing my cheeks for the first time. He greets everyone that way, but with me, his lips on my skin aren't polite. They make me blush with salacious memories.

It has me chewing my lip. My pink lace panties are already wet.

Yes, I want to trust Luca. I want to try with him. Secretly, I want everything with him, but for now, I want to make him let go of his guilt. And if we have to play kinky games along the way?

It'll be my pleasure.

"I have a wager," I say, seeing Delta's coral single home come into view.

"Which is?" Luca sounds intrigued.

And he looks 120 in the shade. His white starched shirt is unbuttoned. His bronze chest gleams. His black hair hangs seductively over his sizzling eyes, and he always wears dress pants that make his ass look like a peach I want to bite.

I went with my usual temptation for him: the naughty secretary in a black pencil skirt, heels, and a pink silk blouse.

"Whoever comes first tonight loses."

He laughs at my bet, and it turns my head to gaze at the sight I'm afraid to want, but I do. I'm falling so fast for Luca, gravity can't keep up.

He grins back at me. "What do they lose?"

"Whoever loses has to let the other do *whatever* they want to them."

"We're *not* fucking," he warns, and...

We'll see.

"Mr. Mercier," I tease as he opens the iron gate of Delta's for me, "I thought you were a sexpert. Don't you know how to play all the games that aren't fucking?"

"I do, and I have the advantage here." He gently holds my elbow, guiding me up the porch steps beside him. The long, narrow side porch, the piazza, overlooks a blooming courtyard. You'd never know this place is a luxury sex shop inside.

"I've already been here twice," he confesses. "I know the owner, Stacey. She's friends with Redix and Cade. And I've already spoken to one of her men, Ford. I told him what I want you to watch tonight."

"I remember Stacey," I tell him, "from the first night we fucked."

His eyes darken. "The *only* night we fucked."

He keeps insisting, and that tells me he's fighting...and I'm winning.

"What do you want me to see tonight?" I ask, standing with him before the tall, black wooden double doors. The brass house plaque on the right reads,

DELTA'S
WHERE SATISFACTION IS GUARANTEED

"I want you to see how gratifying it is to watch," he says. "Why I like it, and maybe you will too. Or maybe you'll be like Stacey. She likes others watching *her* with her three men. They all love it. We all have something we crave."

"What do *you* crave?"

He stares at my lips, at the question between us. "I don't get to have what I crave, *Scarlett*."

I love my name in his accent. His Ss are lush, like silk on his tongue, like he wants to keep me in his mouth.

And his eyes sparkle like light dancing on the water because tonight we're about to enter his domain. A place to watch. A place to explore. A place where pleasure is a bottomless ocean.

"Then we have a deal?" I ask, and Luca nods yes.

But I don't win tonight.

Not after I meet the gorgeous Stacey. Not after I meet her three sexy men: Ford, Mateo, and Luke. Not after we're in the third-floor private sex parlor where Ford takes Stacey's robe off, and she's wearing a black BDSM bikini with thin, gold nipple chains attached to the black and gold collar on her neck.

This is what Luca wants me to watch?

Is this what he wants to do with me, too? With Zar? Is that what he's trying to tell me but feels too guilty to ask?

Because I want what Stacey's doing.

She's on her knees, moaning on the plush, white fur rug and riding a dildo attached to a saddle while her men watch. While I watch.

And while Luca watches me.

Ford, one of Stacey's hot-as-fuck men, hands me the remote control for the saddle. "Have fun with her," he says.

So I do.

I've been with a woman before. Two actually. I've been with way more men. But it's all been the same. It was sex. It was pleasure. No one got my heart. No one could leave me and walk away with it.

But now, it's in the hand of the man standing behind me as I click the remote, and Stacey cries out, "Yes" with lust.

Because, yes, Luca has my heart.

Every day that I see him, it beats in his palm. Every day, he wants me to try some delicious Greek food he's made for me, or he plays the piano with Gia as she sings for me, or he kicks his feet up on his desk in a meeting, grinning when he sees me walk past his office door.

I see his life, and I want to share it.

"You like this, too, don't you, Belle?" Luca's heat presses against my back, his lips whispering as we watch Stacey get off, and I crave this side of him, too.

The dark side. The dirty, Dom side whose kink is so taboo, I love it. I sit on a bar stool, watching Stacey ride a dildo for us, and it's getting me so aroused.

"I'm going to buy one of those for you." Luca steams over my ear so only I can hear him. "I will put it in my office, by my desk. I will call you in, and you'll do as I say. You'll unbutton your blouse and play with your nipples for me. You'll lift your skirt, and pull your panties aside and show me how you've been wet for me all day and..."

Stacey's about to come. I can see it in her eyes, especially when Ford tugs her nipple chains and tells her to come for us, and I'm about to as well.

I'm going to lose our bet because I'm crossing my legs, rubbing them together, letting my clit love the friction. I don't need much, not with how horny this makes me.

"You're going to kneel for me." Luca overwhelms my mind, flooding my sex. "You're going to be a dirty little girl like Stacey, and let me watch as you ride a dildo for me every day, aren't you?"

"Come for Daddy," Ford tells Stacey. "Show our lady friend how that naughty pussy comes."

"Yes," I gasp, answering Luca. I come at the taboo, at the intensity in Stacey's eyes as she comes, too.

Then Mateo, Stacey's other man, straps her body belly-down to a sex bench.

Luca returns to his stool, sitting beside me while I recover from my loss, and I can't wait for my punishment.

Because it's obvious Luca wants this, too, watching Mateo play with a glass dildo, toying with Stacey's ass for all to watch. It makes Luca stroke his hard cock under his pants. He's got to be remembering when he fucked my ass, too.

And it makes me braver. It makes me desperate. I want to break Luca until he's mine.

So I use what he just told me and unbutton my silk blouse, slipping my hand under my pink silk bra, knowing it tortures him. I pinch my nipple for Luca while I watch Mateo smack Stacey's ass and tell her to squirt for us.

I can't stop watching Stacey because I want all the kink, pleasure, and exhibition, too. And when he gets up from his stool again, standing behind me with our eyes locked on Stacey staring back at me—she's about to come—Luca keeps delivering his poison.

He nibbles my ear, and I tremble, feeling his lips on my skin again. "I'll make you squirt again, too, Belle. Do you remember? Your pussy dripped with my cum after I'd fucked you three times. I pumped my fingers into your tight ass that I'd just fucked, too, and I made you squirt in front of a dozen people before I fucked you the fourth time. Our cum was dripping down our thighs. Do you remember being my cum whore?"

"Yes, Luca," I sigh. Pinching my nipple hard, I rub my thighs together, but it's Luca's lips brushing my ear; it's his voice taking me again as Stacey screams, coming for us all to see while Luca dives into my mind. "What does my whore see?"

"Oh my god," I gasp. "My god, that's so hot. They make her squirt."

"Yes. You do, too, Belle. Do it. Come for your Master."

I moan and obey, coming and taking the edge off. It's almost satisfying. It's almost enough as I sag in my stool, letting my hand flop by my side.

But it's not enough.

Luca's not satisfied.

When he sits down beside me, torment is in his eyes. It's the same look he had the night he left me—the same one after our phone sex, or in the bathroom, or on his desk.

Then, Luca makes his pain worse.

He tells Ford he wants them to demonstrate the sex chaise for us. As her men prepare Stacey for more, Luca asks, "Where may we excuse ourselves in a moment if we need privacy?"

I chew my lip.

Is he asking for him or us?

Stacey has the same question in her eyes as Ford tells him about the rooms down the hall. How Delta's special guests, like us, can use them if we need privacy.

But as I watch Stacey's third man, Luke, sitting on the sex chaise, start to fuck her ass with her back to his chest and her legs spread for us to watch, I need privacy. I need *that* again. I need Luca so bad it makes me lift my skirt and pull my panties aside so I can at least have this. I can share my pleasure with another woman, watching her get fucked.

The sight of my pussy exposed to others makes Luca rise, prowling behind me again.

"You love it, don't you, Belle? You're just like me. You crave watching. Being watched." Luca presses his lips to my ear. "Leave your pussy exposed. She's looking at it while she plays with her clit and gets her ass fucked. I bet she wants to lick your pussy, too."

Oh my god, I'm going to lose control, and I love it.

Sitting at an angle, I can watch Ford, one of her men, mount Stacey. Two men fuck her, one in her pussy and one in her ass, and I confess, whispering, "Luca, I want that. I want you and Zar that way."

I start fingering my pussy, showing Luca how far I'll go; these people can watch me get off too. I don't care. I'm so close to my edge again. Once Mateo, the third man, starts fucking Ford's ass while Ford's cock is fucking Stacey's pussy; I lose it.

"Oh my god," I rasp, coming at the sight of two men together. Two men fucking *and* fucking a woman who's also getting fucked by a third man. All four bodies together. Holy fuck, they're so hot and beautiful. They move like they belong together, like they love each other.

I want to cry at all I don't have and want so much because it makes Luca mutter some curse in French in my ear: I don't know the meaning, but I know the emotion—desire denied.

It's killing him, too.

"Fuck her," Stacey calls out, pulling me out of my haze. In the middle of her pleasure, she sees my pain. "Luca," she cries out, "take her down the hall and fuck her now. Do something. You belong together."

Yes, we do.

I don't care how long I have to wait or what I have to do with Luca to get there. I want to. I need to. I will. We belong together. No man has ever been strong enough to take me until him.

And he does.

Luca snaps.

He picks me up, my body still trembling from three orgasms. Draped in his arms, I wrap mine around his neck as he silently carries me out of the room.

It's so romantic. I've never been carried before, and I don't know what we'll do, but the anguish on his sexy face is beautiful. He needs this, too. Carrying me down the long hallway, he kicks open a wooden bedroom door, and without a word, he lays me on the bed.

It's all white in here, just like his hotels. White walls, white bed sheets, and white silk draping from the ceiling; it's like a dream. But as Luca searches the side of the mattress, it gets dark.

It's like he planned this.

"Give me your wrist," he demands, and I do. I watch him wrap a black cuff around it, then he walks to the other side and cuffs my right wrist, then my ankles until I'm strapped to the bed, helpless to whatever he wants.

I don't say a word; I want him to keep going. He mounts me, straddling my body, ripping my blouse open. Then, my bra; he yanks the silk cups down, leaving them there, exposing my breasts, making my nipples pearl for his hungry stare. He eyes my skirt, bunched high around my thighs.

"Do it," I tell him. "Fuck me while I'm tied down," but he doesn't.

He gets up, gazing down at me from the edge of the bed. "The winner gets whatever he wants; do you consent, Scarlett?"

"Yes," I answer with my eyes on the erection bobbing long in his pants.

Then he smirks with such evil and silently...

Luca walks out.

He leaves me alone in the room.

The lamps around me softly glow, but I try not to let it creep in. The shadowy fear that he won't come back. That Luca's left me. The room is warm, but my fear is bitter and cold. It shivers my lonely flesh.

Please, don't hurt me like this.

Don't leave me again.

I hear his footfalls trod down the grand wooden stairs. We're on the third floor, and I clocked what's on the second floor: a showroom full of sex toys and lingerie. I pray that's where he's going.

Please, come back.

Minutes feel like forever, and I don't even care that I'm strapped to a bed. I let it happen. I can't fight the rush of emotions that leave me so vulnerable that I crave it, too. I need to feel this,

145

finally. I'm so used to being the one with no emotions, the one who has to fight, but now, I can't.

I have to trust Luca.

Emotions break me when I finally hear his heavy steps, climbing stairs. Tears threaten as he opens the bedroom door. Carrying a black cotton woven basket, I don't care what's inside it; all that matters is *he came back*.

He sets the mysterious basket on the nightstand and removes a shiny pair of steel scissors.

"Ma flamme," he stands at the edge of the mattress, gliding the dull end of the cold, metal blades down my cleavage, "do you trust me?"

"Yes, Luca," I answer from depths I've never been to.

"I'll let you prove it," he says.

Slowly, he cuts my bra open, then tugs the cups away, freeing my breasts before he calmly drags the sharp edge of the cold blade under my warm, erect nipples, but not enough to cut my flesh. Obsession claims his eyes, watching the power in his act as I exhale, relaxed yet aroused.

"Who do you belong to?" he asks.

"You." He cocks a dark eyebrow. "You, Master. I belong to you."

"Good girl." He glides the steely blades gradually down my belly, making it quiver with trust before he aims the sharp tips at the fabric of my skirt. "What can I do to you?" he baits me.

"Anything," and I mean it.

Lazily, he cuts my skirt open. It falls from my body along with my resistance.

Then he slides the cold blades over my warm silk, drifting the weapon over my covered clit before he presses down. But he's not watching his torment; he's watching my eyes, how my ribs heave, and my thighs jump, but I won't break his stare.

I'm not afraid. I answer before he asks, "I'm all yours, Master."

My submission hoods his eyes as he glides the sharp blades under the string of my delicate pink thong. He holds them there, poised and ready to reveal what he desires, like if he cuts the string, he'll cut his resolve, too.

Finally, he licks his lips, snapping the blades together, snapping the string free, and I shudder, watching him. He's enraptured, cutting the other string as air rushes my exposed pussy. My clothes lay in ruin under me.

All that remains is my trust.

Silently, he sets the scissors down before slowly unbuttoning the rest of his shirt and tossing it on a side chair. As he gazes at me lying here, open and helpless. His hands work, removing his dress pants next, and a breath catches in my lungs at the sight. At how his black boxer briefs can't contain his hard cock. His thick desire strains the fabric. It's practically see-through.

He turns to set his pants on the chair while I can't stand the silence. "Luca, you can fuck me like this. I want you to. Please."

"Oh, my belle, *I* can't fuck you." He turns back, grinning from the edge of the bed. He reaches into the basket. "But this will."

He pulls out a thick, ten-inch flesh-like dildo, making me gasp. "Luca, it's huge."

"Precisely." Suddenly, he's smiling. "It's like me." And almost not lying.

Then he pulls out another toy. It's black and fits in his palm. I know what it is. I've been tempted to splurge on one before. It's one of those toys that gently sucks your clit. The soft silicone tip surrounds it, and it's like you're getting eaten out...at up to fifteen different mind-erasing speeds.

But first, he surprises me, putting it over my nipple, clicking the sucking toy, and making me cry out, "Yes," at the exquisite pressure.

"It's like my mouth, isn't it, Belle?" He plays with my nipples, making me writhe while he taunts, "We need these little nipples excited too. Every part of you is mine to play with."

"Luca, please," I call out, and he stops.

"Use these words, Belle. 'Red' to stop. 'Yellow' to slow down. But you say *my* name when you want more."

"Luca," I answer him. I give consent, and his deep smile is almost evil.

He thrills my nipples with the toy until I'm tugging at my restraints. My pussy is in pain to be filled, to come, and I almost do, but then he stops. "You come when I tell you to. Do you understand?"

"Yes, Master," I gasp, curious as he lifts the sucking toy away and lays it on the bed. Reaching into the black basket again, he pulls out little black cups, a little larger than sewing thimbles.

"They say these feel like sucking snakes biting at your nipples," he tells me, smirking. "Do you want me biting your nipples, my whore?"

My pussy drips. "Luca," I answer.

Whoever "they" are aren't kidding.

He cups my first nipple, squeezing the soft, black rubber, and when he releases his pinch, it creates a vacuum, sucking my nipple so hard I groan, slamming my eyes shut. I groan again when he tortures my other nipple, taunting me. "It's my mouth, biting and sucking your pink little nipples that belong to me, isn't it?"

"Yes, Luca." I crack my eyelids open to watch him walk to the foot of the bed. Kneeling between my naked legs, he stares at my sex splayed open for him.

I've been so wet all evening; arousal soaks my thighs.

He picks up the huge dildo from the bed, gliding its cool, velvety latex through my lips, smearing my arousal around, and I pant. When he teases its fat tip into my entrance, I moan. Slowly, he penetrates me, and it burns so sweet, stretching me open, just like he did, and all I can do is growl his name over and over so that he doesn't stop.

"You want to be my whore, don't you, Scarlett?" He kneels with his hulking legs between mine, and he's so close to where I'm desperate for him.

"Yes, Luca," I answer, stretched wide with inches of a dildo inside me.

"Your pussy gets so wet for me, I can see it. You want me. Your cum is all over my cock."

He starts sliding it in and out. It's so erotic, so lewd and intimate, the sound of my arousal smacking against a thrusting dildo. Then he picks up the sucking toy on the mattress and hovers it over my screaming clit.

"If you let me, I'll torture you with pleasure, Scarlett. That's who I am," he promises. "Pleasing you punishes me, and that's what I need. Giving you pleasure but not being allowed to fuck you or taste you or kiss you destroys me, and that's what I want, do you understand?"

"Yes, Luca."

"Even if I let someone else play with you or taste you, this is *my* pussy, and watching them touch it when I can't is *my* pain. The pain I want. Do you understand?"

"Yes, Luca."

But it will be him fucking me one day, loving me one day; I know it.

I will *MAKE HIM*.

Luca won't be able to stand watching me with someone else. I remember how he devoured my kiss, how he growled my name when he was inside me. Luca won't be able to fight me forever, and I never lose.

"Look at how hard my whore's clit is. It's so swollen for me." He gazes down at the dildo he's sliding in and out of me. "You're going to look me in the eye while you come on my cock. If I let anything fuck you, you always look at me. You always come for me when I tell you to. You always scream *my* name. Look at me. Answer me."

"Yes, Luca." I'm shaking. "Yes, Master."

Clicking the sucking toy, he presses it firmly over my throbbing clit as the muscles in his corded forearms strain. He starts brutally fucking me with the big dildo, thrusting faster and faster, making my body receive all his power, and I thrash, loving it, begging him, "Please!"

"Come, Belle!" He commands, and I scream his name. I come so hard my wrists yank at my restraints, my nipples stinging so sweet, my thighs shaking, my back bowing, and I can't help it. My eyes slam shut.

"No, no, my whore." He spanks my breast. "You always watch me." I open my heavy eyes. He's staring at me, the ice in his eyes hardening as he growls, "You need to be taught until you learn. Do it again."

He starts training me, fucking me with different dildos.

Next, it's a curved jade glass one that he leisurely drags in and out of my pulsing walls. Then it's a thick steel one that he coldly leaves inside me, always torturing my clit with that sucking toy, then it's back to the stretching, ten-inch realistic one, making me come three more times for him until I learn to keep my eyes open.

I have to force my stare on him while he watches me crumble into a soaking, throbbing mess before his satisfied glare over and over.

But when he goes for a fourth time, pulling the real-looking dildo out of my clenching pussy and sucking my cum off of it like he's giving it head, I groan at the sight.

Does Luca like dick, too?

But as he starts to slide it back into my tender opening, "Red," I tell him, and he stops. "Luca, no more. Not unless you come with me too."

"Scarlett," he sneers my name like a curse, but it's in his eyes; he's aching to indulge in the sin.

He's so close that when he pushes his boxers down, his cock that's been hard for hours, I swear, hangs heavy and throbbing with need. It makes my mouth water. It makes me feel empty without him. My chest aches because he won't give us what we need, but he gives us this.

Leaning over me, he surprises me, unstrapping my left wrist. "Fuck your pussy like it's my cock inside you," he says, guiding my free hand to grab the dildo he's made warm with his mouth and my lust.

Then he kneels between my legs, tenting his gorgeous body over mine. He braces his mass over me with his left hand, his shredded muscles glistening but able to take his weight, but I don't know if I can. It's like Luca's on top of me, about to fuck me, but he's barely letting his body touch mine.

"Do it, Belle." He gazes into my eyes. He won't look away. "I'm the one fucking you. The only one."

He starts jerking his hard cock with his right hand while my left hand does the same, sliding the life-like toy in and out like it's his real cock that's only an inch away.

"Luca." I can't help it. I want to cry at his beauty above me, at the lust and torment in his eyes. He won't stop staring at me, and it has to match mine.

Because I feel it, too. This is what he needs: someone else to share his pain—someone to join him in his lonely hell. I don't want to break him; I want to wrap around him. I want to take him inside and never let him go.

We can't say a word while our bodies build fast and hard because he's been holding it back for so long, but *I* won't hold back.

"Yes, Luca. It's you inside me." I start panting because it's true, even if this is as close as we get. "Yes, it's you. It's you inside me. I'm yours now," I confess because he's groaning like we're connected, like he can feel himself inside me, too. "I always will be yours. Oh, god..."

I anchor my eyes to his and stare at an emotion churning so deep inside him that it ends me. I come again, trained now to lock to his crystal gaze as I do, gasping his name and making his lips shake.

"Scarlett," he grunts, his muscles seizing, his body locked above me before his warm cum coats my pussy, splattering my belly. There's so much pain he's been holding back; it covers me. His grunts sound like excruciating ecstasy, and I can't help it. My tear escapes.

"Ma flamme." Barely, he kisses my wet cheek like he can take away our ache for the other. Like this is the answer, but it's not.

It only leaves me with questions.

Why does he punish himself?

Why won't he let himself live again?

Love again?

Once he catches his breath, he leans back, kneeling between my legs. Like he's lost in thought and can't decide what to do, he trails his fingertip through his cum puddled on my trimmed mound.

Silently, I watch him suck his taste off his fingertip, his eyes burning at mine before he growls low. "Is this what you want with me, Scarlett? Do you accept our arrangement? Because let me warn you now, tonight was easy. As your Dom, I will only be worse from here. I will use you. I will degrade you. I may share you, and I will *always* watch you. You're mine. I own you, but I will never fuck you, or taste you, or kiss your lips. I will torture you with pleasure until you beg me to stop, and sometimes I won't. Not unless you say, 'Red.'"

Red.

The poetic irony isn't lost on me.

It's a sign because I answer him, "Luca."

Luca

CHAPTER TWELVE

"She's *Penthouse* in person. Or even better, she's porn served on a plate. And I bet..." Abbey keeps going while we watch Scarlett across the room, "you won't take a bite of her, will you?"

I shake my head, always shocked by my sister-in-law.

Standing on the edge of a massive blue padded floor in a karate dojo, we're supposed to be adoring our daughters in their little white gees learn how to kick, and we do.

But we're also admiring Scarlett.

She's standing on the other side of the mat, between my daughter and the doors to the building. She's acting like she's distracted by her phone, but she's not.

I know her methods. Her focus is on Gia.

But I don't answer Abbey.

It's like we *are* siblings. I never had any, and when I married Darby, I met her polar opposite, her older sister. Darby was innocent; Abbey was bold. Darby was elegant; Abbey is edgy. She just hides it under her yellow cardigan.

And now she's like Zar, pushing me to break.

"I bet she's a hellcat in bed." Abbey nudges me. *She's so fucking right.* "You still like them, don't you? Pussycats?"

"I'm a widower," I huff, "not a corpse. Yes, I still like pussy... *cats.*"

"It's okay if you like dogs, too." I cock my eyebrow her way, and she smiles. "I mean, you and Zar are inseparable. I know he's a bad boy, but I think he wants to be your best man, too."

I scoff, "We're best friends. He's not attracted to me that way."

But we've shared women and get off on watching each other's dicks, and he likes my cum...but hey...sharing is caring.

Abbey shakes her head, making her long, curly brown ponytail swish. She looks like Darby, but she doesn't talk like she did. Darby was sweet; Abbey is salty. When I'm around her, I can't stop the comparisons to her sister.

And now I can't stop the questions Abbey's shoved into my mind.

Is that what Zar wants? To be my...*man?* Isn't that what he already is? He's my best friend by day and my sub on Saturday nights. Does he want something more? Something romantic?

"Luca," Abbey huffs, frustrated by my denial, "*everyone* is attracted to you except me. You're not my type. I like them burly and Sea Captains and gone most of the time, like John."

I like my brother-in-law, too. But true, we rarely see him. John's gone months at a stretch, and that finds me and Gia spending a lot of family time with Abbey and Harper, my niece.

At first, Abbey and I grieved together. We raised our daughters together, too. But then Abbey bounced back faster than me after Darby died.

She started laughing again and joking around. After two years, she told me I needed to live again, too. But this is the first time she's told me to fuck again.

And she's telling me it's okay to fuck Scarlett?

Or Zar?

And Zar?

What the fuck is happening to my life?

One night at a sex shop, after watching three men fuck a woman and the men fuck each other too. After accepting Scarlett as my second sub, with Zar as my first, I feel the energy cracking over my skin.

I'm changing.

I *am* living again, but I don't know as who.

And though some things may change, I will never allow myself the joy of loving again.

I've watched my close friend, Redix, fuck the man he loves, Silas. And I've watched them fuck Cade, Redix's wife, too. They did it several times at their party, where I met Scarlett.

They're so in love with each other. I think it's hot and beautiful, too. I'm a sucker for love. And clearly, those three—Redix, Cade, and Silas—are in love. Clearly, so are Stacey and her men after the show they gave me and Scarlett last weekend.

I'd rather watch anyone in love because I know pain. I wouldn't wish the kind I have on my worst enemy.

But sometimes, I don't know what I feel for Zar. I love him like a best friend. I can't imagine my life without him. I need him. I trust him. But is that all?

Yeah, I think he's an attractive man. He jokes that I am, too. It's normal for us to get off watching each other fuck or come, right? We live every man's fantasy; well, he does. I just watch now. We're secure in our arrangement, not seduced by it.

But Scarlett?

She seduces me.

She tempts me.

I almost fucked her again last weekend at Delta's. I was so close. When my body was over hers, feeling her heat, I wanted to let go and fall into her fire. If she's hell, then let me burn there forever.

"You know," Abbey fills my silence, "Zar was attracted to Darby, too. He was in love with her. It was obvious."

Where did that come from?

And why is Abbey bringing it up while we're watching Scarlett?

"I know he loved her."

I answer while watching Gia run to Scarlett, asking her to

retie her white belt. Scarlett kneels, patiently showing her how to do it again. When Gia found out Scarlett was a professional fighter, she begged me to enroll her in "fighting" classes, so Scarlett suggested kids karate. And now the sight is too cute to bear.

"Darby knew how Zar felt about her," I tell Abbey. "We all knew, but it was just me and her."

Except for one time.

"Because that's Darby." Abbey tightens her ponytail. "She was the sweet one."

"So I was the *bitter* one?"

Gia runs back to the line of kids, proudly taking her place beside her cousin.

"You are now." Abbey's half-joking. "You're all grumpy and bitter, worse than you were when Darby was alive because now, you aren't getting laid."

"*You're* not getting laid."

"Yes, I am," she laughs. "When married to a Sea Captain, you have many toys to keep you company and a helluva sexting game."

"Same," I tell her. "I got my fist. I'm fine."

"What's fine is your new assistant, Scarlett." Abbey leans against my arm. "And when your fist finally gets old, I want to see your sparks fly with her."

I chuckle. "I thought you were Team Zar."

She laughs. "Oh, so you finally admit it? Y'all are a thing, too."

"We're not a *thing*. I told you, we're best friends." She cuts her eyes my way. "Okay, fine," I confess. "Zar helps me dabble a bit. But we don't fuck. *I* don't fuck. I don't cheat on my wife."

"Luca," Abbey whips her glare my way, lowering her voice, "I love you. You're my brother, I swear. But I want to slap your sexy face into next week when you say that. You're *not* cheating on my dead sister."

She makes me swallow hard, chastising me, "She's gone, and you're not. You're right here, looking fine as wine, with all those mothers across the mat wanting to fuck you senseless, so live again. And, god forbid, love again. I don't care who: Scarlett, Zar, one of those moms, or some rando you meet at a bar. If not for yourself," she nods towards Gia, who's running to Scarlett again, "then do it for her. She deserves a happy father."

I let Abbey's bitch-slap of my heart sting for a while. She replies to a few texts on her phone while I watch Gia and how she's drawn to Scarlett.

So am I.

I wake up thinking about her, excited to see her almost daily. I think of the little things I like to do for her, like sending her a monthly dog food subscription. Like finding a photo of her last title fight and having it framed for her. But Scarlett's proud, so I have to restrain all I want to do.

Fuck, I don't know what I want. Guilt or gratification. What's the difference anymore, because guilt has been so gratifying to me?

Snickers flutter the air, making me move my stare from Scarlett to the group of six women across the mat. Maren stands with them, their eyes darting my way.

They catch Abbey's attention, too. "Feel that?" she asks. "That's a bunch of cats licking their lips for you."

"Maren's a friend."

"Oh, you've got *lots* of friends who want to fuck you."

I grind my teeth, determined to never fuck again.

"And," Abbey adds, "Maren and her clowder sure want to sink their claws into Scarlett. They're so jealous of her. It's no coincidence that once you signed Gia up for karate, her entire class also showed up to take the same class. Those women stalk you; they want to fuck you. They're sweet to *you*, but damn, they're catty, talking shit about Scarlett right in front of her face."

My eyes dart back to Scarlett, who's ignoring the women, but you can feel their claws swiping in her direction.

I shouldn't make Scarlett suffer this again, but I can't help that Gia told her friends about starting karate lessons. The class is brimming with kids, and the dojo is packed with parents on the perimeter. You can't even see the glass front doors.

The truth is, I'm proud Gia wants to be like Scarlett. She even colored her arm with markers the other day, saying her flowers matched Scarlett's tattoos. Yes, she got in trouble for it. I grounded her from screen time, but secretly, I thought it was cute.

I don't know how I will do this, but I have to try. I'm changing, and I can't go back. I'll always be a father, and I can still be Scarlett's client, too.

But on Saturday nights? Tomorrow night?

I'm not a dad.

I'm a Dom.

"Want a cigar?"

All evening, I've tried making up for the abuse Scarlett endured today. I fed her Moussaka. We played Charades for Kids with Gia, and I let Scarlett watch me make a complete ass of myself.

How fucking hard was it for me to act out "Wings" and get Gia to guess it?

Impossible when Scarlett rolled on the floor, laughing so hard at me, she said she was "gonna pee my panties." Gia was way too amused by that. It took forever to get her to sleep tonight.

"Can Scarlett spend the night?" Gia kept asking me since Fridays are Celine's night off.

"I have to pick up Crimson," Scarlett told Gia, I know to save us from an awkward situation.

No, a *tempting* situation.

"But he's playing with his friends at doggy daycare." Don't argue with a five year-old on a mission. "So you can stay with me and Baba tonight. Like family."

Gia looked too cute in her dinosaur pajamas, her long curls everywhere. I can't resist her crazy requests, and apparently, neither could Scarlett.

"Okay," she said. "I'll stay and sleep on the sofa."

"You're *not* sleeping on the sofa," I grumbled. "I will, and you can sleep in my bed."

I fought to make that sound innocent, and to Gia's ears, it was. But now that she's sound asleep, I'm too tempted with Scarlett in my home at this hour, so I follow my trusted routine.

"Let me guess." She sniffs the cigar I offer her. "Cuban."

The night is mild. The humidity is gone with autumn here. The full moon shines through thin clouds as I try not to stare at the sight across from me on my terrace.

"It's an international blend, like me." I take her cigar back and light it for her, puffing while I tell her, "Dominican. Mexican. Nicaraguan. But not Cuban."

I hand her back the glowing cigar before I light my own.

"Do you ever miss Greece?" she asks. "Or Paris? They're a far cry from South Carolina, I imagine."

"Indeed." It makes me chuckle. "The first time I saw pickled pigs' feet being sold in a jar by a gas station cash register, I knew I was far from home."

She laughs. "Then why do you stay? I'd love to live in some fancy European hotel or a Bali resort."

I'd love to take her there, to every one of my properties.

I'd be proud to have Scarlett on my arm. She looks sexy wearing a silk emerald wrap dress and nude high heels while smoking a cigar.

"I stay for Gia," I reply. "So she can be close to her aunt and cousin. I never had siblings, and since my father died, my mother won't leave France. We visit her often, but we live here, so Gia has a cousin to play with. Family is important to me."

"I like Abbey. She's not a snob like those vanilla women at the dojo." Smoke curls over her blush lips. "Bless those bitches; they think the sun rises just to hear them crow."

I chew my cigar, amused by her sayings. It makes me curious. "Why do you stay in the South? You can go anywhere with your job."

"I got family here too. Three sisters."

She toes her heels off, tucking her bare feet under her on the patio sofa. I like her feeling comfortable in my home.

"What about your parents?" I ask.

"My mom is on marriage number three. She lives in Memphis with her husband. He makes her happy, and she deserves it."

"Because of your stepdad, the one you almost killed with a skillet?" Scarlett falls quiet, tapping her ashes. "I don't judge. I would do the same. I'll kill for who I love." She shrugs, her eyes glancing toward the moon. Something makes her frown. "So where's *your* father?"

She takes three more puffs before answering, "He left eighteen years ago to get beer, and I'm still eleven, waiting at our trailer window for him to come back."

The lump in my throat is sudden. Pieces fall into place. Scarlett won't look at me. Her gaze is far away while I sit close to her, letting the hard truth in.

Scarlett's dad abandoned her.

That's her real scar.

I imagine her as a beautiful girl, crying by a window for her dad, just like my Gia did for Darby. For months, she cried for her "Mama." It was excruciating.

So when Scarlett cried and said I used her, it was about more than the woman I left that night at a club. I hurt the little girl inside her, too. I can be so cruel, I know, but I would never hurt her like that.

"I'm sorry," I mutter, wishing I could say for what because it's so much. "I—"

"Mind if I intrude?"

A deep voice turns my gaze on Scarlett to see Zar standing at the threshold, where he usually does at this hour. Cigars on the terrace—it's another one of our habits.

He doesn't wait for me to answer. He's already grabbed a Traveller from the humidor and filled a snifter with whisky. "Hey, Red." He saunters over and plops down beside her on the sofa. "Told you," he winks at her cigar, "you're smokin' hot."

"Shut up." She elbows him. "And call me 'Red' again, and I'll put you in a triangle choke."

Zar cocks his devilish lips. "Oh, I'd love to die choked between your legs with my face in your pussy."

"And I," Scarlett crows, "just won a sexual harassment lawsuit. Thank you very much, Mr. CFO."

"I'm off the clock," Zar quips, "and free to honor pussy after hours, not harass it."

He makes her light up, her eyes sparkling while she laughs. "Last I saw, you're not the one who had his face buried in it. *She* did."

It's fast. Their ease. Their banter. The memory of her catching us with two women. And it swells my cock instantly, imagining Scarlett with us instead.

"Oh, rest assured, Ms. Jones. I'll clam dive all night long." Zar loves this: a cigar in one hand, a whisky in the other, and his flirt aimed at Scarlett. "I don't even need a mask. Just let me dive into your pink ocean while you wear my beard for hours."

She laughs again. "You're horrible."

"And you're bicurious." Zar is smitten. "Wanna go for sushi with me?"

Me? I'm getting horny as fuck. Suddenly, I *can* see how the three of us could work.

SO. DAMN. WELL.

"I prefer a cunt *lap* over a cunt *snack*," she gibes.

And Zar winks, teasing her back, "I bet you do."

Scarlett puffs her cigar while they smile, staring each other down, and what the fuck am I watching? My attractive best friend, my loyal sub, is trying to seduce the woman who...

The woman who...*what?*

What is Scarlett to me?

The woman my daughter is attached to. Celine is more like a grandmother to Gia. Abbey is always her aunt. But Scarlett is young. She's the age Darby would be now, and Gia won't stop hugging her legs like she's found the mother she doesn't remember.

Zar's taken with her. Though he flirts off the clock, he respects Scarlett. I've never seen Zar get close to any woman but Darby. They used to see rom-coms together because I can't stand those damn movies, but Zar loves them. He recites them.

Celine likes Scarlett. They laugh over coffee all the time. And Abbey likes her too. Hell, she wants to see my "sparks fly with her," whatever the fuck that means.

And Scarlett and I remaining professionals?

That line's been crossed ten miles back. If we're discreet, we can hide the secret of our new arrangement. Her company doesn't have to find out, and she won't get fired. I can keep her on this job for years.

As what though?

"The question is," Zar keeps taunting her, "do you like eating club sandwiches?"

"Ahem," I remind him who's boss, "we will have this conversation *tomorrow* night."

"Oh?" Zar's surprised.

I haven't had a chance to tell him about last Saturday night at Delta's, what I did with Scarlett and our new arrangement.

That's a lie.

I've been reluctant to tell him. I wasn't sure how he'd take it, sharing me with Scarlett. The truth is, I can't bear to lose him either.

"You're joining us in the suite?" Zar asks Scarlett, again forgetting who's in charge.

"Yes," I bark, answering for her. "She is. But we're not discussing it here. Remember the rules?"

"What *are* the rules?" Scarlett asks.

I turn my glare her way. "Never in my home. Never around Gia. Never around anyone, not even my friends. No one knows. It stays on Saturday nights, and it stays in the suite."

Scarlett nods like she agrees with most of it. "But why not our friends? Cade and Redix and Silas? Stacey and the guys, too? They'd never judge."

"Because I'm his big dirty secret." Zar chuckles. "He's ashamed of me."

"I am not."

Why would he say that?

Even though, deep down, I suspect it's true.

I'm not ashamed of my kinks. I'm a natural Dom. It's the air I need to breathe. But what I'm ashamed of is why I deny myself, why I live through Zar.

If my friends knew, particularly Redix, he'd worry. He cares about me and would wonder why I'm punishing myself.

Redix and I have shared so much. Whacking at golf balls and walking miles across the manicured greens of my golf resorts, I've shared my grief with him while he's shared his recovery with me. Though Redix finally told me the harrowing story of how he got those horrific scars on his backside, I still haven't told him why I have this scar on my soul. How Darby's death was my fault.

I killed my daughter's mother. Not directly, but I still remember her blood on my hands.

Try living with that guilt.

You wouldn't want to, but you do. *I do.* First, I lived for Gia, then for my nights with Zar, and now I live to see what my days with Scarlett could be like.

Yes, I will bind her tomorrow night; I have a special new device for her if she permits. But even more...

I want to see Scarlett roam free through my life. She's a natural with Gia. I adore seeing her around my hotel, in my home. She's so much like me. What a relief it is to the soul when you find your reflection in someone else.

That's how I feel with Scarlett. I feel seen. I feel understood. I finally feel like myself.

"If you're not ashamed of me," Zar challenges, "then why won't you take me in my collar and have a scene with me in that sex club? The one where you and Scarlett met?"

Scarlett darts her glare my way.

"He figured it out," I tell her. "He figured *us* out. I didn't tell him."

"You didn't have to," Zar interjects. "When you and Red are around each other, it's like mating season on the Serengeti. She nuzzles your dark mane until you mount her, biting her neck while you breed."

"We're that obvious?" Scarlett sounds worried.

"To me, you are." Zar warns her, "So be careful the next time your hot boss is around you two because she's going to smell your pheromones in the breeze."

"We'll be discreet," I growl, feeling like the mating lion Zar equates me to.

The fact that I know male lions can mate with females up to fifty times a day, and they sometimes mount other males to show their dominance only hardens my cock more.

"What else do you know about us?" Scarlett challenges Zar.

"He's a vault." Zar nods my way. "He doesn't say anything about that night at the club, so I'll ask *you*." When Zar lays his gravelly Texas accent on thick, it tempts me every time, and now, he's tempting Scarlett. "Did you get on your knees for him that night?"

"Yes," she answers.

"Did you *taste* him?"

"Yes."

"Did he taste *you*?"

"Many times."

"How many times did he *fuck* you?" Zar drawls slowly, and he doesn't sound mad. He sounds aroused by Scarlett's confession.

I am, too. I like him knowing I've already taken her. She's mine. And if I let him play with her, too—that's Zar's favorite game.

The man was born into more money than god. His family's wealth is colossal, and he wants none of it. He gets off on giving up his power like it's a burden to him, and I'm thrilled to take it, too.

"Four." Scarlett sounds aroused as well. "Luca fucked me four times and not again until last Saturday at Delta's. We..."

She stops herself, not sure what that was between us, but I know.

In my mind, I fuck her all night long.

"I didn't break my rule." I add, informing Zar, "We reached our agreement. Scarlett will be joining you on Saturdays. If she earns her collar tomorrow night, you're both mine."

Zar licks his lips. His stare aimed my way burns with lust. He's never had another sub join him, not one I've collared. He's always collared the others. They were his. They weren't his equal.

Scarlett joining us will fulfill Zar's fantasy, and now I can see what Abbey meant today because he's staring back at me like he's finally getting what he wants. And yes, his satisfaction pleases me. It's *very* attractive.

Zar has always wanted a woman to share our darkest bond, a woman strong enough to take us, to connect us. But we've never had a woman like Scarlett before, not one who knew about us, not one we cared about...not one who survived us.

I just hope we don't lose her, too.

"YOUR SHEETS SMELL LIKE YOU."

Scarlett nestles into my pillow, gazing up at me while I stand at the edge of my bed. Zar left for his suite an hour ago, so she showered, and now she's climbed on top of my sheets like she's home, and it sure feels like it.

"You belong in my bed," I tell her.

I'm wearing my usual pajamas, no shirt, just a pair of my old joggers from college. I let her borrow an old HARVARD t-shirt of mine to sleep in, and I'll make sure she wears it every night in her bed, too.

"You've really been alone all this time?" she asks. "Like, even on your Saturday nights, you've never slept with anyone? Not even Zar?"

Worry bends her stunning face. Her damp hair flames over my pillow. Her panties are white and lacy; I can sneak a peek at them.

"Why would I sleep with Zar?"

"Why wouldn't you? He loves you. You love him. Even if you've sworn off women, is being with him breaking your rule?"

"I told you before," I loom over her, "I don't fuck Zar."

"I'm not talking about *fucking* him." She squeezes my pillow like a teddy bear. "I'm talking about holding him. About letting some warmth into your life, into your bed."

"You're the warmth in my bed now," I confess. "You're the warmth I'm letting into my life. I'm happy watching you here. I don't need anything else."

I'm sharing more with Scarlett than I have with anyone in years, and this has to be good enough.

Her face softens. "No," she answers, "you think you don't deserve it, but you do *need* it. I'll follow your rules, Luca, but I control my mind. I know what I see. I see a father devoted to his daughter. I see a boss who takes care of everyone. I see a man who protects his friends."

Her legs, carved with slight muscles, rub content over my sheets. This is a new side to Scarlett, soft and vulnerable and honest, and it's breathtaking on her.

"I see a man," she says, "who needs love again. He's in pain without it."

I stand by the bed that only Gia is allowed in on the mornings we watch movies and share waffles or when she has nightmares, which is rare. Otherwise, I sleep alone, if I sleep at all.

But the sight of Scarlett lying in my bed is so natural, it's dangerous because she's right. I do need love, and I won't let myself have it, which makes her the perfect punishment.

"So, do you sleep alone, too?" I ask, knowing I'll kill anyone who dares to hold what's mine. I already see blood on my hands.

"No, I don't," she answers. Then she laughs, all husky and deep, reading the murderous rage rip across my face. "Calm down. I sleep with my dog sometimes."

"So when you're alone in bed, what do you do?"

"I think of you. I use my vibrator, and I come, moaning your name. I do it at least twice, sometimes three times a night before I fall asleep, hugging my pillow like this, wishing it was you."

Her tender candor has my cock getting rock-hard. I'm tenting my joggers a foot from her sweet lips. "You're toying with me," I groan.

"Yes." She starts lifting my T-shirt she's wearing, revealing her panties. "I'm your toy, Luca. So how will you play with me tomorrow night?"

"It's a surprise."

"Is Zar fucking me?"

"No," I scold, annoyed and aroused that she's trying to control our scene before it's even begun. "I'm blindfolding you tomorrow night. I'm tying you up, and then I'll play with you however I want."

"I want you to." She doesn't back down, lifting her shirt higher, exposing her aroused nipples. "I want you to play with me, Luca, every Saturday night like you promised. Then, every Monday, I want you to get that dildo with a saddle and make me ride it at your feet. I want you to lean me over your desk every Tuesday, and lift my skirt and pull my panties down and fuck my ass with a glass dildo. Every Wednesday, I want you to—"

"*Fuucckkk*, Scarlett."

She's killing me.

I'll have to use a ball gag tomorrow night on her because she fights back; she fights my self-control, just like I told her to.

"Yes," she stares up at me, tugging her nipples, "you can fuck me, too, Luca, however you want. Whenever you want. You can take me to any balcony, any window, any shop or club and fuck my pussy and come in my ass for all to watch. Let them watch how I belong to you."

She's racing through my mind, clocking all my dark kinks and winning. She's using everything she knows about me so far to make me crack.

I could take her now. She wants me. She belongs to me, but I won't. I have to know. "Why do you want this with me? Why did you agree to my terms, knowing I'll never fuck you again? Or even kiss you?"

"Because," she replies softly, "I like how you make me feel." She drops her toying hands. She drops her seduction and answers me thoughtfully. "I had to be strong my whole life. It was lonely because I had to fight for me and my sisters and I was scared. I've never had anyone take care of me or defend me until you did. And I don't get to show emotions on my job. I have to act like I feel nothing, but I do. Whenever I'm with you, you make me feel everything, good and bad, and I like it. I feel alive with you. I can be the woman I really am."

"I made you feel bad because your father left you like I did that night. Right?"

Silently, she nods before confessing, "That's what my tattoos mean. Flowers for my sisters and mom. Flames for how I feel. Skulls for my dad leaving us and crosses, praying he'll return."

The pain Scarlett hides is suddenly revealed. It's written down her colorful arm and across her beautiful face. Like a wave receding, she's showing me all her broken shells left in its wake.

It overwhelms me how much I want to take care of her, how she belongs with me, in my home and family. She was sent to me like a divine punishment. Like hell cements my feet, and heaven fills my eyes.

"I'm sorry about your father," I tell her. "And I'm sorry if I hurt you like he did. I didn't know, and I won't do it again." Tears well in her eyes, so I caress her cheek. "If you are mine, Scarlett. If you obey my rules, I'll never leave you."

The swallow in her tender throat is visible. The tear sliding down her cheek finds me leaning over to kiss it. I can't stop myself.

"What happens if I break your rules?" she asks while my lips lift away.

"Don't," I warn. "Don't make me end us because I don't want to."

"We haven't even started."

"But once we do, in time, you'll hate me."

"Why would I hate you?"

"Because I'm a man of my word." I lick my lips, tasting her salt on them. "I will pleasure you in many ways, but you will never fully have me because I will not break my promise to my wife." She flinches. *I've done it again.* "My dead wife," I clarify.

"Luca," she gazes up at me, "why did you make a promise to her grave? Why is it a secret? Why won't you talk about how she died? It was on that bridge, wasn't it?"

"Stop."

"Why?"

"Because some words are too awful to say."

"The only *awful* thing is the truth you hide."

I don't answer her. I control the silence while allowing my fingertip to trace over her eyebrow and the scar in it.

"Will you ever tell Gia the truth?" she asks, letting me barely touch her. I map the light freckles across her tan nose, over the silky skin of her high cheeks, and the blush on her petal lips. *I could get lost in her.* "Luca?"

"Her mother will remain a perfect angel, and I'll be her hero, her father. That's the lie Gia will always believe."

She snaps up, her breath gasping, "You're not Gia's father?"

I step back, shocked out of my trance. "Yes, I'm her father."

"Then what do you mean? *What's* a lie?"

"Her mother wasn't perfect, and I'm not a hero. I may be a good father, but I was a bad husband. You say I'm devoted, a generous boss, and a good friend, and maybe I am, but I'm more Scarlett. Believe someone when they tell you who they are—I'm *not* a good man."

"Yes, you are."

"Fuck, you're stubborn."

"Fuck, I'm right." She shrugs. "So you're flawed, Luca. And so was she. Who isn't?"

"Some flaws are fatal."

"Life is fatal, Luca, so quit fighting it. You have the privilege of being alive; she doesn't, so live in her honor."

"Don't speak as if you knew her." I'm not mad. I'm suddenly flooded with an ominous feeling. Like even when I fight with Scarlett, it feels right. It feels natural.

"No, I didn't know her." And she softens again like she feels it, too. "But I know Gia. I know Abbey. I know Zar. I know everyone she loved, and she loved you, too, and I see why."

"I loved her as well. Very much." I twirl the gold band on my finger. "That's why I'm keeping my promise to her."

"Okay." Scarlett surrenders. "Okay, keep your promise to her, but make one with me, too."

"Which is?"

Her stare weaves over me like my naked chest is her fabric, and slowly, she'll cut me open. I know Scarlett can, and I won't let her, and this will be the war I need.

Proving my point, she gently wedges her fingertip under the waistband of my joggers, tugging them down, and I don't stop her. I'm naked underneath. My dick springs free, and I start getting hard again, letting her stare at me.

I can't deny the passion between us, whether we fuck or fight. I feel alive with Scarlett, and it's so tempting, the urge I feel to put my swelling cock in her mouth that's inches away, but she surprises me. Leaning forward, she doesn't aim for what I will undoubtedly refuse if she tries.

Gently, she kisses the birthmark on my thigh, the one she remembered from the night we met, and I hold her there. Sinking my fingers through her silky waves, I let her kiss my flesh, pieces of my heart healing against my will.

Yes, I need her warmth. I need her. I need Scarlett's love, but this is all I'm allowed.

"Promise me," she whispers against my skin, "that if you ever break your promise, you break it with me."

"Lie down," I tell her, with visions of her breaking everything inside me. "Let me tuck you in."

"Is that a promise?" she asks, obeying me.

Tugging my joggers back up, I answer, "Yes," but I'm not smiling because this is excruciating. It feels wrong while I do the right thing. I tuck her into my bed, then linger the back of my fingers across her cheek.

"Good night, my belle."

"Good night, Friar Fuckless."

Laughter bursts up my throat, surprising us because it's funny. *She's* funny. I do feel like a monk, and leaving Scarlett in my bed does feel like church. Like I'll worship her forever.

"I'm going to the sofa now."

"And I," she announces, unfazed by our fading tension, "will fuck your pillow once you leave."

"Please do," I grin, "and save some for me. In case you hate me so much that you armbar my shoulder, and I can't jerk off anymore. Right? That's what you said. That I'd have to fuck my pillow."

"Well, at least it wouldn't be fucking your fist anymore."

"Kiss it." I hold my palm up to her lips, and she smiles, kissing my flesh before giving it a little tongue. It tickles. It shoots straight to my cock and keeps me smiling. "In five minutes, I'll close my eyes, and I *will* be fucking you, Belle. In my dreams."

But after I crawl under a blanket on my sofa, I don't fuck my fist. I just let Scarlett's kiss tingle on my palm as I fall into dreams with no nightmares.

Scarlett

CHAPTER THIRTEEN

"CAN I POKE HER AND WAKE HER UP?"

"Shhh, my kóri. Let her sleep."

I can hear them. Though my eyelids weigh a ton, my grin rises, feeling a light weight crawling across the mattress.

"But how do you know she's sleeping?" Gia's voice draws closer.

"Because she's snoring."

I'm not. Luca's teasing me, and I like it. He knows I'm waking up. But I wait until I can sense Gia inches from my face. It takes everything I have not to laugh when she tries to lift one of my eyelids.

"Wake up," she insists, but I start fake snoring. It makes her giggle before I blindly snatch her into my arms and snort against her neck, making her squeal with delight.

"Who dares to wake up the monster?" I growl, tickling her waist, too.

"Baba, Baba!" She laughs. "Save me!"

The mattress sinks even more, and I open my eyes to the best dream—Luca, lying beside me with Gia between us.

"Good morning, Belle."

His smile is brighter than the sunlight streaming into his

bedroom. He's still wearing the same poison: no shirt and those sexy joggers. Gia's in her long johns, and I'm in his T-shirt, and warmth like I've never known fills me.

"He called you beautiful," Gia informs me, playing with a lock of my hair.

"Is *that* what that means?" I tease her. "Cuz' I sure got a lot of eye boogers this morning to be beautiful."

She laughs. "No, you don't."

"Are you sure?" I widen my eyes for her full inspection, so she crawls over me, sticking her nose in my face.

"No boogers," she says.

"What about my morning breath?"

She sniffs, taking her job seriously. "Smells like fruit."

Now I laugh while Luca asks, "Who wants waffles?"

"Me!" Gia exclaims. "And *Moana*."

I roll my eyes. "Not *Moana* again?"

"Then *The Little Mermaid*," she insists.

"Really?" She can tell by my tone that I'm playing. "I know a movie we can watch, and I promise you'll love it."

"What is it?"

"It's called *Bugs Life*, and it was me and my sisters' favorite."

But my new favorite becomes sitting in bed with Gia tucked under my arm and Luca on the other side of her.

A wooden tray loaded with waffles sits by our feet. Luca made them from scratch and served them with real maple syrup, orange slices, and my favorite Greek coffee. Gia doesn't touch the savory Spanakopita bites filled with spinach and feta that Luca serves, but I devour them, too.

"You have crumbs." Smiling, he reaches over and gently brushes the phyllo bits off my lips before I can use my napkin.

"You do, too." Gingerly, I reach over, and he gazes down, watching me brush them off his pecs, swishing them onto his sheets, but he doesn't care. We're too focused on my hand touching him.

"Shhh!" Gia fusses at us, daring to speak during her movie.

So Luca and I exchange silent smiles, and I know his foot brushing mine under the sheets isn't an accident.

Luca speaks of promises and never, but I know it's not true. This feels too perfect to be a lie. This feels like family and forever. It feels like something I won't stop fighting for.

"Where's my girl?" A familiar voice booms down the hallway. With the volume up so high, we didn't hear the front door beep.

Zar appears in Luca's bedroom doorway, wearing jeans and a white T-shirt, and stops at the sight of me, Luca, and Gia in bed, innocently watching a movie. I can tell he's shocked...but then...he smiles.

"Shhh!" Gia fusses at him, too. So Zar grins and eases his way to the foot of the bed, where he makes himself at home.

Resting on his back, he snacks on waffles and silently watches the last thirty minutes of the movie with us.

Once the credits and the hilarious blooper reel rolls, one that has Gia laughing and jumping on the bed, Zar finally snatches Gia into his arms.

"There's my girl!" He grabs her, gently tickling her neck while she tickles him back, and I wonder.

Is it possible? Is Gia Zar's girl? Is that the horrible truth Luca doesn't want to share? I can't tell. Gia looks just like her mother, and Zar and Luca look alike. They both have dark hair and tan skin. The only difference is their eyes, their features.

Either could be her father.

Luca says his wife was innocent but flawed. But how flawed? Did she cheat on him with Zar, of all people? Or did they agree to it? Were the three of them together? But Luca said he never shared her, but what if it was another type of arrangement?

Either way, is that why Zar is so dedicated to Luca? Does he feel guilty about whatever happened, too?

I glance at Luca for clues. He's watching Zar with Gia with nothing but love in his eyes, and I'm so confused.

What did Luca do that is so bad that he swore himself to celibacy in his dead wife's name? Well, sort of celibacy because he's into some very kinky pleasure torture instead.

"Hey, Red." Zar snaps me out of my haze. "I had to place a call this morning to HGR. Your boss is on her way. We need to meet about an *incident* last night once Celine gets home to watch Gia."

Luca and I exchange glances but don't say a word, hearing Zar's disguised tone around Gia, but this sounds serious.

Zar starts playing Legos with her while I get dressed in Luca's bathroom. I slip on my emerald dress from yesterday and pray Charlie won't notice that I should be doing the walk of shame this morning.

I didn't fuck our client. I didn't even sleep with him. I slept in his bed and *wanted* to fuck him, and he's going to do kinky things to me tonight, so I fear Charlie will sense the deception.

Luca gets dressed, too, and then we quietly sip coffee, waiting in the kitchen for Celine to get home. Apparently, she spends her Friday nights off at Luca's Hilton Head Island resort, enjoying a full menu of spa services.

Her relaxed smile greets our silent tension when she gets home. Quickly, Celine senses something is awry, so she distracts Gia while me, Zar, and Luca slip out.

Zar debriefs us on the elevator ride to the third floor, to the boardroom, where we're meeting Charlie. "Brooke was here last night," he says. "She was in the gym."

Luca starts to seethe. "How the fuck does she keep getting in?"

"That's what we're meeting about." Zar points to the camera in the corner of the elevator. "Because she's been here enough to know about your cameras everywhere. She's getting off on performing for them."

"What did she do?" I ask.

"She uhh..." Zar twists his face, trying not to laugh. "She kneeled on a workout bench, right in front of one his cameras, and fucked herself with heeldo."

"A *what*?"

I think I heard Zar wrong while Luca whips the phone out of his back pocket and opens the app that controls his cameras.

"It's a dildo," Zar explains, "attached to a strap that you wrap around your foot. If you kneel with your feet behind you, the dildo, I mean, the *heeldo*, fucks you from behind."

"Fuck," Luca mutters. "Like this."

He holds his phone screen so I can see the footage Zar found this morning. It's Brooke, naked in the gym. It was late last night when no guests were in there. She's alone and on a workout bench, grabbing the weight bar in front of her and kneeling, leaning forward so the camera has a prime view of her fucking a purple dildo strapped to her heel.

But that doesn't upset me. It's the name LUCA tattooed like a massive stamp above her ass that fills me with concern. I bet her husband loves to hate it. To hate Luca.

The elevator *dings*. The doors slide open while we don't move, and I ask Luca, "How long has she had your name tattooed on her?"

"It looks like fresh ink," Zar defends him. "Zoom in and you can tell."

I don't need to hide my feelings for Luca when we meet with Charlie because I'm too worried, and it's warranted. It's my job.

Charlie enters the boardroom a minute behind us, and I'm surprised, asking her, "How did you get here so fast?"

Her home is two hours away, but she looks relaxed, *and* like she's about to have that baby in ten minutes.

"HGR helicopter," she says. "Perks of being the boss." She takes the chair Luca pulls out for her and jumps straight to business. "I have another officer joining us, too. He should be here any minute."

"Another officer?" Zar asks, taking the seat across the table beside Luca while I sit beside my boss.

"Yes," Charlie answers, tapping the tablet she pulls out of her bucket bag. "This is serious. This is an obsession, and she won't stop. You need to secure all access points to this hotel, all floors, too."

"I agree." Luca's solemn. "But by law, stairwells must stay unlocked, and doors must be accessible due to fire code. But you can't access our upper floors from the stairwells. Those doors are exit only for the guests on each floor. They all lead to the lobby and fire exits. So she's getting in through the elevator."

"Exactly," Charlie says. "So, on my way here, I sketched up two options. That's all you have." She slides her tablet across the polished mahogany table. "You can install a keycard system in the elevator so guests can only access their floor. I've tallied the cost and the timeline to implement it."

"No," Zar dismisses her first suggestion. "We're a five-star luxury property, not a hotel by the interstate. That's the wrong look for The Mercier."

"He's right." Luca taps his gold pen. "It sends the wrong message to our guests. That we can't keep them secure."

"Well, then swipe." Charlie gestures to her tablet. "I found another solution. It's an old-fashioned one that you can sell. You hire an elevator operator."

"A lift man?" Zar's not convinced.

"Or a lift *woman*," I remind him while I watch Luca study Charlie's tablet before he shows it to Zar.

"They still use them in New York," Luca says. "At some museums or corporate buildings, too. We can pull it off. Make it look like a nod to nostalgia. Our Stockholm and Paris properties used to have them. Tokyo, too."

"I like it," I add. A trained operator is likelier to spot Brooke than trusting a card access system to stop her. Besides, she can get ahold of a card too easily. But there's only one elevator, one access point we can monitor twenty-four-seven."

"And that's where your backup comes in," Charlie turns to me. I catch her wincing like her baby just kicked her, but she moves on. "You continue to cover your mark, but we get officers covering the elevator. We'll catch her that way."

"What does it matter, though?" Zar snarls, exasperated. "She keeps getting arrested, and she keeps getting bail with no punishment."

"Her husband gets her out," I inform them.

"But we don't know how," Luca adds. "He's not a judge or a

lawyer. He's an equestrian. He owns a ranch west of Charleston. We already looked into him."

"Yes," I challenge him, "but did you look into where he goes to church?"

"Did *you*?" Zar's shocked.

"Yes," I admit. "I followed them a few Sundays ago."

Luca exclaims, "*You* followed Brooke and her husband?"

Is he impressed or disturbed by my sort of stalking?

"Hell, yes, I did." I don't care. I'm not embarrassed. "They're a threat to you. A threat to Gia. I don't fuck around, so I followed them. I had a hunch. Because if you don't do deals on a golf course around here, you do it in church, and they don't call Charleston the 'Holy City' for nothing. Brooke's husband is a deacon at a church, along with three judges. The same judges that keep springing Brooke free."

"Damn, Red." Zar smirks. "I'm so impressed, I got a stiffy."

I widen my eyes while Luca coughs, and Zar catches his slip. "Pardon me, ma'am." He lays his accent on thick for Charlie. "I'm just impressed with your talented staff, Ms. Ravenel."

"So am I." Charlie's a former Marine. She doesn't give a shit. "But Ms. Jones is right. Even if we catch Brooke, we can't keep her behind bars if she's connected."

"Not if her connections are persuaded otherwise." I lean back in my chair, sharing my plan. "If Brooke and her husband are into some kinky stuff, I'm willing to bet their god-fearing deacon judges are, too."

"Done," Luca says. "I'll hire PIs and have them dig up some dirt."

The irony doesn't escape me. Bribing judges to do the *right* thing, making them feel ashamed for any kinky stuff they may be into, when I know damn well, Luca has some kink planned for me tonight.

Luca's phone pings with a notification. He glances at it. "Your backup is here. The concierge is sending him up."

I don't think anything of it. I assume it'll be Rob, Wade, or one of the HGR P.O.s I've worked with. But when Jameson Grant steps into the boardroom, I'm on *HIF #11*.

How am I fucked?

Well...

I've fucked Jameson.

He's one of the few men that made it past one night with me. On paper, he was perfect. He's a former cop. A helluva detective. He used to work with Cade, my close friend. He was in love with her, but nothing happened. She belongs with Redix, and they're with Silas, so Jameson tried hard to make it work with me.

But we didn't. We split as friends, and he took a job with HGR, too, but still, I'm fucked.

Because Jameson is a pussy pleaser. Yes, he's that hot and makes it obvious—we've bumped uglies.

Charlie introduces Luca and then Zar, but Jameson isn't formal when she gestures to me.

"Hey babe," he says softly, shaking my hand but quickly leaning down to kiss my cheek. "Long time, no see."

"Hey," I mutter.

"You two know each other?" Zar asks on Luca's behalf because I glance at Luca. He's too good at watching everything, particularly me, and he can sense the connection.

He's got murder icing his eyes.

"Yes," Jameson answers, taking the chair on the other side of Charlie, "Ms. Jones and I are familiar."

"Good." Charlie pushes right past the tension. She's either well aware of it or, again, she doesn't give a shit. Probably both because there are more important issues. "You'll make a good team. Mr. Grant will—"

"Please call me Jameson," he says.

"Fine," Charlie continues. "Jameson will cover the night shift."

"He'll cover the day," Luca cooly seethes.

"No, he shouldn't." But I understand Charlie's logic, explaining, "Brooke's forming a habit. She likes to do her deed at night, on the weekends. It's like an addiction."

Luca knows exactly what I'm covertly referencing because *he* introduced her to this habit. He shares Brooke's drug. He uses his cameras, too. He needs his Saturday nights. He craves kinky games with dildos.

I don't know what Luca will do to me and Zar in his suite, but I know he doesn't want Jameson anywhere near it.

"We'll have different officers during the day," Charlie adds. "They can rotate so as not to make it too obvious, but at night, especially the weekends, we need Jameson. He has experience with this."

"What kind of experience?" Now Zar sounds pissed and possessive, too. He's not serving it as lethally as Luca, but I'm getting to know both of them too well.

What Luca feels, Zar expresses.

"I had a mark with stalkers," Jameson explains. "She had one in particular who blended in too well. But once the stalker got into my mark's corporate building, she made herself known. The stalker had some...*ahem*...proclivities for making pretty obscene public displays until I stopped her. I guess I've developed an ability to sense it coming."

"Well, Brooke's not obscene," I interject, "she's obsessed. I don't care who or what she fucks, she's getting too close, too often, and she knows about Gia. It's a matter of time before she goes after what matters to Mr. Mercier."

That lowers Luca's brow.

Like a wolf, he's protective of Gia. I am, too. So is Zar. I may not know all their secrets, but I know this is true. We'll die before we let something happen to her.

We meet for an hour.

It's almost amusing watching Jameson keep a straight face while Zar shares the photos and video of Brooke with him. Charlie's unfazed, while Luca says nothing. He just glares my way.

I know he's jealous, furious about Jameson, but he has no right to be.

Zar calls in the Head of Security and Human Resources and shares the new protocol with them—an elevator operator will be stationed in the lobby now. Jameson and others have been ordered the signature blue Mercier Hotel jackets and gold name badges so they'll blend in as staff.

And if Luca would stop seething over Jameson, I'd feel bad for him.

Gia is his weakness.

She's his world.

And now he's paying the price for his "proclivities," as Jameson calls them, and I wonder if this is Luca's greatest guilt.

Is this why he insists that he's not a good man? Because somehow, his dark secret cost him someone he loved? And he fears it will happen again?

Brooke may seem harmless, like this is only her fetish that Luca's inspired, but we can sense it. It's more. Luca will never give Brooke the satisfaction she craves, so she will eventually crave to hurt him back, and there's only one way to do it.

Go after the only one he loves.

Once we establish that Jameson will begin his first shift tonight and have a room to use here to sleep during the day, he leaves with Charlie to prepare.

The other staff leave the boardroom, too, and it's just me, Luca, Zar, and one big angry jealous elephant in the room.

Hang on.

Make that two elephants.

"Y'all get your boxers out of twist." I kick off my heels, propping my bare feet on the table. "Don't be dicks to Jameson. He didn't do anything wrong."

"How long?" Luca snarls. "How long were you fucking him?"

"A million years and one hot minute," I answer. "It don't matter. It was before you. Before...whatever we are, so get over it. You and Zar went on beaver patrol every Saturday for years, and I ain't a little dick about it, so I'm not apologizing for the grown cocks I've craved in the past."

"Don't speak so crass." Luca pounds his fist against the table. "*I'm* the only cock you'll crave, and your *beaver* is mine."

He makes my snark sound even worse in his rich accent.

"Listen here, Mr. Citified. I'll speak Redneck whenever I please." So I pound the table back. "I may be your sub or your whatever, but I am *not* your slave. You don't own my mind or my past, and if you keep acting like a caveman, you won't have my future either."

His lip curls. "You have a lot to learn."

"Yeah, well, maybe I'll *let* you teach me. But as long as you two keep your secrets," I point to him, then to Zar, who's smirking with glee, "I have mine. So don't dig up more snakes than you can kill."

"Dayum!" Zar woofs. "You two are gonna be hotter than a honeymoon hotel when you finally fuck again."

"We're *not* fucking!" Luca barks at him before glaring at me. "And you're *not* going near your colleague."

"Which one?" I ask. "You? Zar? Jameson? I'm surrounded by men everywhere I work. Get used to it. And I want to be with *you*, Luca,"—I pause, letting the truth pound his thick skull—"and with Zar, or whatever you have planned. I'm trusting you, so you have to trust me, too, or we won't work."

"We need to have the talk," Zar urges, resolved. "Let's have it now, before tonight, so everyone is very clear."

"What talk?" I ask.

"VICSS." Zar explains, "Voluntary. Informed. Consensual. Safe and Sane. We talk now about our boundaries and rules and words before we begin because you two are a powder keg, and that shit is dangerous when he's holding a whip."

I nod, relieved. Glancing over my shoulder, I make sure the doors to the boardroom are still closed. They are, and yes, it's time.

"He gave me my words," I share with Zar. "Red. Yellow. And 'Luca' for green."

"Nice touch." Zar glances at Luca. "So *your* name is green for her?"

"Yes." Luca sounds like he's calming down.

"Can I just order your wedding cake now," Zar quips, "or are we gonna play this waiting game for years?" Luca cuts him a glare. "Fine. What else?"

"You don't kiss her. You don't fuck her," Luca demands. "No one does. You only touch her when and how I say."

"Are *you* touching her?" Zar probes, and despite my irritated edges, my core melts. I want to know, too.

"Some," Luca asserts with his gaze on me. "I'll play with her as I wish unless she says 'Red.'"

"Well fuck," Zar huffs, rolling his eyes. "There goes my cute nickname for her."

"Thank god." I grin. "Quit calling me 'Red.'"

"Don't worry." Zar grins back. "I'll come up with something derivative. Like Pinkie. You know, for your pink hole, your pink flaps, your pink Cadillac or—"

I toss my chin up, laughing. "You're so bad."

"Alright, you two." Luca's lightening up. "Enough. Is there anything else?"

"Yeah," I answer. "I want both of you to do my whole aftercare thing, not just Zar."

Luca smirks, tenting his fingers. "You've been doing your research."

"Yes, I have."

Slowly, he rises, pushing back from his table. Quietly, he walks around to my side, racing my pulse while Zar sits still in his chair. We both sense it, watching shadows fall over Luca's face. A wicked resolve ices his eyes, and it shoots straight to my cunt. It's in control because...

Hello, Daddy Dom; look who just entered the room.

Once Luca's looming over me, he commands, "Kneel."

The pussy rush is instant. It finds me lowering to my knees, my eyes trained on his. But when he gently grabs my chin, I'm not prepared for his touch. I gasp. When he slowly pushes his thumb over my lips, *oh sweet Jesus*, I moan without instruction, sucking it while he pumps it in and out of my mouth until his cock gets hard, inches from my face.

"Tell me," he finally demands. "Tell me what my whore wants tonight."

Spit webs from my lips to his thick thumb while I answer with no shame, "I want to wear your collar, Luca. I want to earn it tonight. I'm not afraid of you. I want you to put me in a thigh harness with wrist cuffs. I want you to use rope and one of those steel anal hooks I saw at Delta's and—"

"Oh, my belle," he praises, "you're going to be so perfect for me, aren't you? Where did you learn all this?"

"After Delta's," I rasp, confessing to his towering erection at my eye level, "I went home and started watching BDSM porn. I've been reading websites and blogs, too."

Zar shifts in his chair like he's aroused while Luca gazes down, admiring me. "Do you want me to spank you, Scarlett?"

"Yes, sir."

"Do you want me to torture your pussy with pleasure?"

"Yes, sir."

"Do you want Zar to play with your ass?"

"Yes, sir."

"Do you want strangers to watch me train my whore?"

Oh my god...

"Please, Master."

He caresses my hair. I never put it up this morning, and he looks captivated.

"Listen to me." He vows, "I will be as possessive as I wish, and you will love it. I will kill anyone who touches what is mine, and *you* are. You may have your past, Scarlett, but I am your every next breath. I will never leave you. You belong to me, and I will please you until you scream. Do you understand?"

"Yes, Master," I answer, not understanding the desire drenching my panties, and I don't need to.

I'm soaked with the emotions only Luca can make me feel, and I need this too much. I finally feel trust, I feel wanted, I feel loved.

"Now, go to your suite," he orders. "I will send a masseuse, my spa staff, your lunch, your clothes for this evening, everything you will need to prepare. You will wear what I send you and meet me and Zar for cocktails at eight downstairs."

"Yes, Master."

"And then," his hand sinks deeper into my waves, yanking them just enough to make me mewl. "I will escort you to *my* elevator, right in front of your colleague, before I take you into *my* suite, tie you up, and make you *my* whore, tonight and forever like his cock *never* could. Do you consent?"

"Luca."

Luca

CHAPTER FOURTEEN

When you add a splash of water to Ouzo—the clear, Greek licorice liqueur I love—it blooms into a cloudy liquid like magic. The sight always soothes me as Louis, our evening bartender, sets a crystal tumbler of my favorite drink garnished with a lemon twist in front of me.

Silently, Zar sips his coveted Rip Van Winkle twenty-five year old bourbon beside me because we're celebrating tonight.

Sitting on dark blue velvet bar stools circling the bar in my hotel's exclusive lobby lounge, we say nothing, while tonight means everything to us.

I try to let nothing ruin it. Though, out of the corner of my eye, I glare at the tall figure stationed in the lobby, standing guard by my elevator.

Rage and relief fill me.

I hate imagining Jameson Grant fucking Scarlett, but I know how much he loved it. *Did she scream his name? Did she scratch him, too?*

I sip my Ouzo and swallow, clenching my teeth because I'm also relieved. Jameson's skilled. He won't let Brooke slip through, and safety is what matters.

Will Brooke go after Gia one day?

It's not a risk I'll allow—over many dead bodies will that never happen.

"You're hot when you're jealous," Zar taunts. "Maybe I should be jealous that you never get jealous over *me*."

I glance at him, noting how he's trimmed his beard and styled his dark waves to look very appealing tonight.

"I don't get jealous," I answer, "because you've always been mine."

Half a smirk lifts his lips. "You sure you can handle two of us?"

"Can you?"

He swirls his bourbon, studying me. "It's all I ever wanted. You know that."

I know it in the most painful way, and he reads me too well.

"She'll be different," he soothes. "She won't get upset, and she won't get obsessed. I like her, and you're in love with her. It's perfect."

"I'm not in love."

He sucks bourbon across his teeth before he drawls, "Damn if you won't be after tonight. I've followed your instructions. Everything and everyone's ready."

Glancing at the crystal clock over the bar, I see it's eight o'clock, but I can't focus on tonight. He suddenly makes me worry about the past.

"Will *you* love her after tonight?" I ask. "Or will you finally be able to keep it straight? Who belongs to whom? Or will you break again?"

His stare flicks down to his glass. "It was a mistake. It only happened once, and I'll keep apologizing to you forever."

"I forgave you long ago."

I mean it. I've told him a dozen times. We may play our games, but Zar means too much to me. He found the real man inside me, and I'm forever his, too.

"Maybe," he doubts. "But you never forgave yourself, and it wasn't your fault. Darby loved you. She loved you the most; she just got lonely."

"So did you," I agree. "You were lonely, too."

Some people are a part of you; the edges of you are woven into them. You can't hate them, no matter what they do. You will always forgive them because that's how real love works.

That is Zar. That was Darby. And that will be Scarlett, too. It already feels like she owns my heart even though I can't give it to her.

"Sometimes," Zar says, "I don't regret it because we didn't have to fight. We could've talked about it. We could've figured out how to make us work, but other times...*I* made the mistake. *She* made the mistake. Not you."

"I became a CEO at twenty-five," I object, "and I changed. Work consumed me, and stress made me mean. I ignored the ones I loved. It *was* my fault. Loving someone isn't good enough if you don't prove it."

Zar shakes his head like he doesn't have the energy to keep fighting about this. He knows he'll never change my mind, my heart.

I claim responsibility for what happened.

You may love someone, but you have to show them. You can't ignore them for months and take them for granted. It's not good enough to peck someone on the cheek and quickly say it.

Love is proven.

Love doesn't say cruel words that kill someone.

"Just promise me," I tell him before tossing back my last sip, "you won't lose control this time. You know my rules. We follow them, and no one gets hurt."

"Oh," he grins, "I'm not fucking this up. I've waited too long for it." He aims those deep brown eyes my way; they always do something to me. "Just promise me something, too."

When he turns, aiming his body at mine. When he looks that good in a navy Gucci suit. When I know all Zar will be wearing later is my collar, "Okay," I answer him.

"Promise me," he lowers his voice, "that if you finally touch her, you'll touch me, too. I need you. I miss you."

The memory rouses me.

I used to touch Zar. I used to kneel behind him while he knelt and obeyed my demands. I used to caress his back, his thighs, his ass while I felt him flex, fucking a woman on my command.

It was intoxicating. To control not only my body but also his. To let him feel my pleasure with his submission, my hard cock wedged against his thrusting ass while I watched him. While I reached around and squeezed the base of his cock, making him groan while I felt his shaft swell in my grasp, and I controlled when he could come, too.

I miss him, too.

I miss so much.

I can't answer him. I nod, unsure if I'll keep the promise before I feel that itch, that sense in me whenever she's around. I turn, and our dream stands at the bar's threshold.

Wearing the black satin and lace corset D&G minidress I sent up to her room, it's dangerously short, and Scarlett's bare legs race my pulse along with the strappy black heels she's wearing for me, too.

Watching her stalk my way, this is how I crave Scarlett, how I met her—dripping with lethal sex appeal. Her sexy tattoos. Her dark, fiery hair tumbling in waves. That scar and those eyes.

She's a bullet, and I'm her bull's eye.

"Good evening, Ms. Jones." I stand to greet her, pulling a stool out. "You look ravishing."

"Thank you, Mr. Mercier." She lets me kiss her cheeks before she nods toward Zar. "Mr. Rollins."

"Join us, please." I love this performance as she gracefully takes a seat, crossing her bare legs, but I correct her. "Uncross them. You're not a lady tonight."

She hesitates, surprised I've already begun as I lean down, whispering in her ear, "You're mine now, so lift your dress all the way up and lean forward, putting your elbows on the bar."

The mahogany bar is cantilevered over her. Zar gets up and sits on my empty stool beside her while I lord behind her.

Guests chatter and sip their drinks. Candles flicker in the dimmed lights. Jazz music softly plays from the quartet in the corner. Eyes are on us because I can never escape the attention, while Scarlett only adds to my display. But really, no one can fully see what I'm making her do but Zar and me.

How her training begins...

Now.

Discreetly, Scarlett wedges the short hem of her dress up. I watch over her inked shoulder, thrilled by her naked thighs and the peek of her glistening pussy, brushing against the plush velvet stool.

"My beautiful whore, you're already wet," I whisper. "Did you get aroused getting ready for me tonight?"

"Yes, sir," she sighs.

"Good girl. Now start rubbing your pussy for us." My lips brush the shell of her ear. "Rub your naughty little hard clit against the stool while I order a drink for you. Do it, my belle. Prove your cunt is mine."

Slowly, she starts circling her hips while I flick my finger for Louis. "Another Ouzo, please." He nods at my request while Scarlett glances at Zar, who's watching her, too.

I taunt her ear, "Let my stud watch what he gets to play with tonight. Keep rubbing that pussy for us." Her breath stutters. "Is that what you want? For us to play with you tonight?"

Her hips don't stop moving. "Yes."

"You look beautiful, Pinkie." Zar swivels her way on his stool.

"Don't," she huffs, but her hips don't stop. "Call me that, and you'll get a Flying Knee in the ribs tomorrow."

He toasts his glass. "I tell you what—I'll call you 'darlin' because I'm a Southern gentleman that way." He leans forward, ogling her breasts bound in a corset. "But when it's just us three, I won't be minding my manners, ma'am."

"Please don't." Her tone is amused, her hips grind, and their ease warms me.

Once Louis sets a crystal tumbler in front of her, I'm in her ear again. "Sip your drink and enjoy the taste I love on your tongue. Feel your nipples, too. I can see them. They're getting hard while my stud toys with you, and I control you."

Silently, she obeys, rubbing her pussy in public for minutes. I love this about Scarlett—how she doesn't back down.

"Spread your thighs wider," I whisper. "Grind harder." She sips her drink, obeying. "That's it. Such a sweet slut, you like this, don't you? Rubbing your hard clit for me in public?" Her soft moan is the only music I hear. "My spa staff waxed your pussy for me today, didn't they?"

"Yes, sir," she stammers.

"Did you show them what belongs to me?"

"Yes, Master."

"Good girl. You're nice and bare for me, so I can watch everything I'll do to you." Her flesh is raised at my voice. "You're wearing my plug in your ass, too?"

"Yes, Master." She arches her back, the mention of her ass making her hips circle harder, faster. It's getting obvious.

"You like me in your ass, don't you, Scarlett?"

"Luca," she affirms.

"I had the plug made just for you. What does it say?"

Ordering the custom slave plugs for Scarlett thrilled me. I ordered several, in increasing diameters, and sent the smallest one to her suite tonight as part of her attire. I ordered the words, stamped in white on the red plugs, for her, too, because I'll be toying with her forever.

"It says 'My Whore. My Belle,'" she answers.

"Because you are, aren't you, Scarlett?"

"Luca," she rasps, so I press my lips to her ear, taking her right to the edge.

"I have so many plans for you tonight. There are guests in this bar watching us. We've invited some to help me make you my whore. My stud has arranged it." I glance at Zar. He licks his lips because he hears me. "Now, grab your breast and pinch your hard nipple. Show them. That's your signal to them that you consent to my torture, my belle. Pinch it right here, over your lace if you do."

She obeys, bracing one hand against the thick, wooden edge of the bar. Trying to be discreet, she pinches her nipple, covered by couture fashion, while surrounded by dozens of people, a few of whom will be joining us later.

"That's my whore. Don't stop," I praise while she moans. "Is your pussy excited? Are you being a naughty girl and smearing your cum all over my stool for everyone to watch?"

"Yes, Master," she moans, and I glance down. Her thighs are shaking.

The sight of her pleasure is branded on my soul, so I grab her arm and pull her off the stool, gently reminding her, "You come when I tell you to."

"Yes, Master," she gasps, trembling in my grasp, but her stare meets mine, and she looks thrilled.

"Bad girl, look at the mess you've made." I make her turn and glance back at her stool. Her dress has fallen, covering her, but she can't hide the milky smears she's left on the dark blue velvet.

Zar swipes his finger through it before he grins, sucking it off his fingertip.

"Come with me." I press my hand over the small of her back, guiding her flushed body in front of all watching us, controlling our steps through the bar and into my white marble lobby.

I want to hold Scarlett's hand. I want to pull her to me and kiss her, proving to all that she belongs to me. I meant it; I've never had a woman like her. A woman I've craved for so long, but I'm on a mission. I have plans.

We reach the elevator, and I won't take my hand off of her, pressing against the satin over the top swell of her ass.

"Good evening," I greet Jameson, who studies us with an intensity I relish.

"Good evening, Ms. Jones, Mr. Mercier," he answers gruffly, his eyes scanning my smirk to Scarlett chewing her bottom lip.

"*My* third floor," I demand, letting him pass through the golden elevator doors, sliding open. "Ms. Jones and I have a long, arduous, private meeting tonight."

Per the protocol, Jameson enters the lift, pressing the guest's floor before he exits again, staying at his station in the lobby. He steps out after Scarlett and I step in. I turn her around. I do, too, knowing we have three seconds before the doors start to close. Jameson could look away, but he doesn't.

I knew he would watch as I lean down, glaring at him while I bite Scarlett's neck, making her gasp. "Mine," I growl over her flesh as the doors close, and his eyes narrow, glaring.

But once the doors close, I back off. Jealousy makes me lose control, and that's what I require tonight. *Control.*

"Careful," Scarlett huffs, aroused by my possession but worried. "He's a good man. He won't rat me out unless he's worried about me."

"No need to worry." I linger my fingertips over the colorful crosses, flames, flowers, and skulls down her arm. "I'm a *bad* man, and I carefully torture what I own."

The doors *ding* open, and I grab what's mine. I reach for Scarlett's hand. It's instinct at first, and then it's everything.

There's only one other woman whose hand I've held. In tender moments, yes. This feels like that, too. But I've never held my woman's hand, taking her to a destination like this. I've never been myself like this, with my partner, with my match beside me. And Scarlett's silent, letting me lead her while she glances down at my grasp wrapped around hers, like she knows it, too.

I press the code to enter the suite, then tap a switch on the wall. A dim glow lights up the room. Erotic music starts to lull. The temperature is programmed. The suite is warm and ready as the door closes behind us.

"Where's Zar?" she asks while I lead her across the room.

"He'll be up later with our guests. He knows his orders."

"What are we doing now?"

She sounds so curious, so I turn and press my finger to her lips. "You don't speak in here. You only use our words. Understood?"

Confidently, she grins. "Luca."

I can't help it. I grin back while I guide her to my first major purchase from Delta's. It stands beside Zar's St. Andrew's cross— the giant X padded in black leather with wrist and ankle restraints on the wall. It's where Zar likes to be whipped.

And now...he's not alone.

Standing beside it is a Forced Orgasm Tower. It's a black metallic structure. It's a tall, thick, vertical bar where a sub stands, restrained against it, with padded neck and wrist straps. At its wide rectangular base are ankle straps, holding legs open, straddled over a thin metal bar at the center. The center bar holds any vibrating massager, wand, or dildo, stimulating the sub's clit, cock, pussy, or ass, forcing them to have orgasms for as long as you command.

Scarlett realizes what I'm about to do with one look at it.

"I won't blindfold you yet." I guide her to stand in place. She silently watches while I bind her wrists to the pole behind her first. It thrusts her breasts in the corset out, and I lick my lips. "You're going to do as you're trained. You're going to look at the only one who makes you come when I tell you to. Say it."

"Luca." There's a thrill in her voice, not fear, while I squat and spread her legs, caressing her ankles arched in high heels while I restrain them next.

She can't move while I'm tempted to graze my touch up her bare thighs, but I don't. I rise, reaching for the neck restraint last. It widens her eyes, but she doesn't protest while I carefully secure the leather collar around her throat. She's trapped. She's helpless, and she has to trust me now.

And hers is a trust I covet.

I know what this means to Scarlett. To trust a man to take care of her. To never leave her.

And I won't make the same mistakes again. I've told her how cruel I can be. I've tried to make it up to her, too. I will never take her for granted. And with her, I don't have to hide who I am, even though I can't give her everything she wants.

The sight before me is one I'll worship forever. Gently, I touch her bound neck, feeling her hammering pulse, before I hook my fingertip over the center boning of her corset and yank it down, just like I did to her bustier the first night we met.

"I'll always watch you, Scarlett." I gaze at her nipples pebbling before my eyes. "I'm going to watch you come until it drips down your thighs."

Carefully, I lift the hem of her dress, harnessing all my restraint not to touch her sweet pussy again. I didn't give her panties to wear, so I leave her dress like that, bunched around her waist while her ribs heave, her flesh prickling for my gaze.

"Oh, my belle." I adore the lewd sight, stepping back to admire every inch of her. "You look so beautiful. You look like such a whore for my torture, don't you?"

She pauses, her stare dropping to the heavy erection I proudly display under my black trousers. I'm not wearing boxers, and I'm already dripping for her. She licks her lips. "Luca."

I let her watch me take my black jacket off before I drape it over my chair, my steps aiming for a glass curio cabinet. Rolling up my starched white sleeves, I leave them cuffed around my forearms while I open the cabinet and reach for another new purchase.

It's been my ultimate fantasy to use one of these on a woman, but I've never done it. The white Hitachi massaging wand is iconic for a reason. It relentlessly satisfies anyone using it, the torturer included.

Covering its soft, large head with a condom, Stacey at Delta's told me this only adds to the wand's sensations, I grab a bottle of the lube she recommended, too. This entire cabinet will be filled with new toys. Toys only allowed for Scarlett.

Scarlett doesn't flinch at what I'm holding when I turn around and stalk back her way. She knows exactly what I'm about to do to her, and her lush lips smile.

"Dirty little girl," I tease, "you're going to like this torment, won't you?"

She doesn't answer while I strap the massager to the center bar designed to secure it to the tower. The bar is adjustable, and she gasps when I press the soft head of the wand right against her little pink clit, peeking from between her shorn pussy lips.

Damn, I have to hold back. I have to find a new level of control around her.

She watches as I grin, shamelessly pouring a ribbon of lube over the device where it's poised over her pussy. Then, I set the bottle down before I hover my fingertip over the blue buttons on the charged device. It has four intensity levels, and she's about to endure them all.

But something powerful grabs my heart.

A warm, new, deep feeling makes me meet her gaze. I don't know what it is as I search her eyes for an answer.

This isn't breaking one of my rules, the promise I made to a grave, but it feels like it. It feels like Scarlett is about to become everything to me, and Zar warned me this would happen.

She senses it, too. "Luca," she speaks, disobeying me, "it's okay. You're still keeping your promise, and I want this with you. I want everything with you, however you want."

I reach, gently grazing my fingertip over her bottom lip. "Don't hate me, Belle. Don't hate me for what I'm about to do to you."

She gets that look in her eyes. She's bound by her neck, wrists, and ankles. She's completely vulnerable, but she's a fighter.

"You think I can't handle a little torture and a lot of pleasure?" she asks with her scarred eyebrow cocked. "I'm about to *love* your pain." Her smirk grows. "*Luca.*"

So I press the blue button and...

She screams.

The wand hums against her clit at the perfect spot. She's been too aroused all night, all day, for over a month, maybe for a year, like me. Her right leg violently shakes. She tries to obey, waiting for my command, but can't. Her shoulders lurch, but her neck's restrained while that stone look seizes her eyes. Staring at me, her lips part, and she groans, disobeying me in less than a minute while her first orgasm shatters through her.

The sight?

An erotic masterpiece.

"Oh, my belle." I press the button, turning the wand off. "Bad little girl. You'll have to be punished now."

I leave her shaking and bound while I aim for her cabinet again, reaching for the gold chain with two tweezer nipple clamps on each end. But when I return and get so close to her, my fingers about to pinch her pert pink nipple between the coated soft tips, I sweat. I can hear her panting breath and smell her arousal. Memories of filling my mouth with her nipple, sucking and biting while she rode my hard cock arrest my mind.

I want to kiss her mouth. I want to lave my tongue over her nipples. I want to taste her again, but I taunt, "You liked watching Stacey and her men use these, so I ordered one just for you. It's fourteen-carat gold. It's my kinky treasure, just like you are."

It makes my mouth water, pinching her nipples with the clamps and hearing her hiss, watching the soft carve of the muscles down her abs flinch at the luscious torture.

"Use your words," I insist.

"Luca." She tries throwing her head back to survive the sensation but can't. She's stuck while I press the button on the wand again, and her shriek is a symphony.

"Yes, my belle." Gently, I tug the gold chain connected to her aching nipples, and I won't let go of her stare. "Fight it," I demand. "Fight the pleasure. Fight the urge. Wait for me."

I press the button again, going one intensity higher on the vibrator, ruthlessly thrilling her clit, and she can't help it.

"Oh god," she groans.

"Yes," I snarl, "I *AM* your god."

I yank her chain harder, rattling it, delighting at my tug, at the skin of her breasts pulled taut by my indirect grasp. I want to lick the sweat blooming across her dewy, heaving chest.

"Luca," she cries. "Luca, please."

It means she only wants more of me, so I give it to her. I unzip my pants with my free hand and lift it out, revealing my cock, heavy for her stare.

Her eyes drop, then her lids. "Fuck," she huffs at the sight of my proud arousal for her, so I swipe the next drop for her dripping from my swollen crown.

Holding my fingertip to her trembling lips, she's dangerously close. I want those lips on mine, but I order, "Taste who you belong to while you feel me in your tight ass, too."

She does more than taste. She sucks my finger so hard, rolling her eyes. Shuddering with a moan, she comes in front of me, breaking another rule.

"Belle," I growl, "look at me when you come!"

"I..." She pants. "I..." She lifts her heavy lids and sighs with a satisfied smile. "Punish me, Master."

Yes.

I am falling in love.

I stride across my room with my exposed erection pointing the way. Grabbing the leather riding crop from her cabinet—we'll build up to the paddle and the flogger—I can make this sting, too.

When I return to her, I turn off the massager and pull it away from her pussy, relishing how her cum is glistening across her lips. It's starting to drizzle down her thighs.

"You want to be punished, my belle?" I tickle the crop across her flushed cheek, then through her flaming hair. "You want me to spank you for being my dirty little whore who can't stop coming for me?"

"Luca," she growls with demand in her eyes, so I deliver.

I lick the flat red leather tip of the riding crop for her gaze, covering it with my spit before I wedge it between her swollen lips, rubbing back and forth while I train her. "Whose tongue licks your pussy, *ma flamme?*"

"Yours, Master." I raise my eyebrow. "You. Luca."

"Does my tongue feel good? All firm and wet and rubbing on your naughty little clit? Is it making your pussy ache for my hard cock to fuck you?"

She writhes, trying to squat and open her pussy for more, but she can't. She begs, her voice labored with lust, "Luca."

My god, I want my name tattooed on *her* and no one else. I can't hear enough of the sound of my name screaming from her throat.

Lifting the glossy tip of the crop back to my mouth inches from her face, her eyes are riveted, locked to mine while she watches me lick her cream off, and my dick does it again. It drips in agony at the taste of Scarlett's forbidden honey on my tongue.

"Your cum is mine," I tell her. "Every creamy drop or every watery gush from your cunt belongs to me." Swiftly, I smack the hard tip of the crop against her clit. "Who do you drip for?"

She cries out, "Luca," and it's torture for me too. In perfect strokes, I rub her clit with the crop while I tug at her nipple chains, too, and I won't stop until she's dying to come. It's in her eyes, and I'm right here with her, but I have too much discipline.

I start brutally smacking her clit with luscious, quick stinging whacks, and I don't let up, demanding, "Who's pussy is this?"

"Luca's." Her gaze anchors to mine like I'm the only truth she knows, and *yes, I am.*

I rattle the crop over her clit and demand, "Be my little whore and come all over my tongue."

It's only fantasy, but she obeys. Scarlett moans, jerking at her wrist restraints while she stares at me, her abs constricting with her next orgasm, and mine threatens, too.

I'm in that trance with her. That euphoria you get from pain and pleasure, but I so rarely feel it. I reach this state only when I'm with Zar and only when I truly let go.

But with Scarlett, it's my new world, and I don't want to leave.

I drop the crop and push the massager back to her slick pussy. I ask with my finger poised over the button, "Can you take more of me?"

The next clicks will be orgasmic agony for her. Her lips tremble with "Luca," like she'll never give up, and Scarlett's too beautiful like this. Mine and broken and lavished with so much pleasure, she feels my suffering too—the hell of not having all you need to breathe.

She understands me now.

But still, I need more of her.

I press the button four quick times, and she's stunned and silent. Her bound neck strains, her teeth clenching, her gaze shattering, so I caress her warm cheek. It's flushed and dewy with sweat, like our first time together.

"Feel my pain, my belle." I step into her breath, straddling the massager between her legs and mine. I pump my painful cock in my grasp and groan at the coming relief that won't satisfy us. "Stay with me until our end."

I know this is a sick game. I know this is so brutal and beautiful, too. But it's all we can share, and I'll give it to her.

We don't speak. I don't even taunt her. I nuzzle my forehead to hers while we gaze down at everything we can't have until it's the only thing we desire.

But I can't do this without her touch.

Not anymore.

Quickly, I reach, ripping her right wrist strap open before guiding her hand to my cock, aching for her. Without a word, she obeys, choking my swollen shaft with her touch again, and I groan from depths I forgot.

Her touch on my cock makes white heat blaze through my veins for her, the exquisite binding pain of all that's pent up inside me, demanding relief.

This is *not* enough with her. I need so much more with her, and for the first time, I hate it.

I hate that I'm this way. I hate that guilt has twisted my soul. I hate the secrets I hide and the truths I won't admit. I hate everything I didn't do and every sin I've committed. I hate the blood on my hands and my hand cupping her tender cheek. I hate it all while I let it go because it's killing me, and I'd rather die with her.

I love again.

I love Scarlett.

"Ma flamme," I groan, my thighs and lips shaking, and Scarlett knows because she's inside me, so she lets go, too.

I cover her mound with all I wish I was filling her with, and she comes with me, crying real tears. I lift my eyes to see them, so I press my lips to her wet cheek while I groan because the brush of my lips over her flesh causes my body to release even more for her. I can't hold it back. My cock pulses with cum, with pleasure in her grasp, and I can't bear her pain, too. Not like this. I turn the wand off and urge, "Scarlett, we can stop."

"Never." Her rasp is instant. "No, Luca. I want more of you." She nudges her cheek against mine until I lift away and look at her. "I mean it," she says. "Give me all the pain you have. Show me who you are and what you desire. Never hide from me, and I *won't* hate you."

I brush her lingering tear away with my thumb. I'm almost stunned, silent, staring into her sapphire eyes because my dream is coming true. "You want more? You want to see the real me?"

"Luca," she softly answers.

So I blindfold her.

Scarlett

CHAPTER FIFTEEN

I'M FLOATING.

This must be the trance state I read about. I feel suspended in Luca's touch. Black silk covers my eyes while I crave his every subtle touch as he releases my nipples from their clamps, and I whimper at the painful rush of blood to them.

"No more pain, my belle," he eases. "The rest is for your pleasure. You'll come when you want to."

Carefully, he frees me from the tower. My wrists and neck are tender from the restraints. When he releases my ankles last, he silently guides me to step off of the metal base, and my knees buckle beneath me, so he gently grabs my waist, and it feels right every rare time Luca holds me.

Leading me a few steps, he makes me halt before his hands start tugging at my dress. I sway while he silently unzips it, wedging it down over my hips until it falls to my feet. The fine fabric smears the cum Luca painted across my mound. It's sticky down my thighs, too, and I relish how he doesn't wipe me clean. He leaves me dirty, covered in his desire.

Fingers caress my ankles, and gently, he helps me step out of my dress and heels.

I stand naked, except for his plug thrilling my ass, while I sense air cooling my sweating flesh and the rug, soft and plush, beneath my bare feet.

"I'm going to prepare your body for our guests before I let them in."

Those taboo words entice in Luca's accent, and my tortured pussy, which went numb after my last orgasm, starts to rouse again.

I didn't know that being forced to have multiple orgasms can be an assault of pain and pleasure, and I want more. But his promise of only pleasure seduces me, too.

Carefully, he leads me. All I can focus on is his hand caressing my waist, my steps blindly following until my knees brush against the soft, padded leather platform.

"Lie down," he commands, guiding me. "On your back," he insists. "I'm going to use a thigh sling on you. It wraps around your thighs and loops behind your neck. It has wrist restraints, too. It comfortably holds your body helpless with your pussy open for all to see."

Oh my god, what saint did I fuck to deserve this blessing?

I know.

Saint Luca the Pussy Patron.

My sister was right. I have died and gone to slut heaven.

I hear his steps across the room while I lie on supple leather. I saw the cabinet he filled with toys, and I hope they're all for me, for Zar, too. I don't mind sharing Luca with him.

It's like Zar and I want Luca in ways Luca's unwilling to allow. So Zar and I bond in our starvation. We don't compete. We'll submit and get what we can from Luca.

I don't know how the three of us will be, but we'll work. Our bond feels so natural.

"Come here, Belle." Thick hands lift my right leg, and for a man so tough, his skin is soft, brushing against mine while he wraps a strap around my upper thigh. It feels padded and soft while I hear a metal buckle securing it.

"Sit up," he urges, and I obey, feeling something even softer wrap behind my neck, like a padded pillow. Then he binds my wrists in padded cuffs to the sides of the strap, tucking my elbows in before he takes my left thigh and hoists it, binding it in the padded strap, too.

It leaves me suspended with my thighs spread open, my knees bent, and my pussy fully exposed to the thrilling rush of air. But I can't balance on my ass for long without my hands. I'm like a Weeble Wobble fuck toy, and I don't hate it.

I fall over on the platform, giggling.

"What's so funny?" He sounds amused, too.

"I can't sit up." More laughter hits me, and I need this, too. It's so dark and passionate with Luca and kinky, too, but we've also shared funny moments. "I'm gonna keep falling over. My pussy will be like a moving target."

He laughs, and I wish I could see him. He's beautiful when he rarely laughs.

"I'm going to sit behind you while the others are here," he says. "I'll hold you open."

He'll what? He'll hold me? While others do what to me? I don't care. I'm still stuck on the first part.

I lie on my side, hearing the sound of rustling clothes like Luca's stripping.

HIF #12: If your naked body is going to be devoured on the platter of the hottest man you know, you should be able to see it.

I'm leaving a one-star review of his sex suite.

But it's sweet. It's tender as the cushion sinks behind me, and I feel Luca gently pull me between his strapping thighs and into his naked lap, aiming our bodies toward the foyer where guests will enter.

His warm body envelops me. My head rests comfortably between his beefy pecs. His cock presses into my lower back. So much of my flesh, more than he's allowed in almost a year, touches his and...

"Red," I rush. "Red, Luca."

"What's wrong?" He makes it worse, gently sweeping my hair off my shoulder.

"You're making this all sweet and hot and humiliating and

hilarious at the same time. My emotions can't take it. I can smell your cologne and feel your heartbeat near mine. Your body is so fucking hot and hard, but I can't see it. *And* your huge dick that never sleeps is waking up against my back. Pick a lane for your torture and stay in it."

"So," he sounds too entertained, "me holding you is torture?"

"Yes...I mean...no. I mean, I'm fucking naked and blindfolded in a thigh sling, and this is supposed to be kinky, but you're making it sweet, too. You're a sexy asshole because I like you holding me so much that I don't care if a priest, a rabbi, and the entire U.S. Army enter the room. And..."

And I'm fucked.

HIF #13: Something this slutty feels sweet with him. Only Luca can make extreme raunch feel romantic.

His chuckle is deep before he confesses, "I like it, too, Belle." His voice gets soft, not sadistic. It lulls over my shoulder. "Your skin is soft against mine. Your hair and your perfume intoxicate me. You're the most beautiful woman I've *ever* seen, especially in a thigh sling, and you're perfect for me; you fit with me. That's what I feel, holding you like this." He pauses. "That's what my heart feels, too. Know that."

A light caress brushes the inside of my thigh, and I jump, then relax at his touch as he soothes me with his fingertips, brushing them up to my pussy, spread wide open.

"Does this help?" His voice gets that tone, his cock jumping against my back. "*You* are my lane, Scarlett. You belong to me." His fingertips barely tickle my thrilled lips. "It's sweet that you trust me like this. It's hot how your pretty pussy is spread open. It's humiliating that strangers are about to enter and see you like this, my beautiful, proud whore in my lap, blindfolded with my plug in her ass and her pussy still covered in my cum, but it's *not* hilarious. It's degrading and kinky and under my control, holding you the whole time while they pleasure you however I tell them to because you're mine. *I'm* all you feel. Say it."

A tsunami of emotions surges through me, conjured by the rip current of his feathery touch teasing my splayed sex with his taunts, his warmth, his control flooding my mind.

So I let go and drown. "Luca."

"Enter!" he shouts, startling me, but then I settle.

I submit. I recline against him, my masculine throne, while I hear the door *click* open, and the muffled moans and soft gasps at my salacious display thrill me, though I have no idea who my audience is.

All but one.

Knowing that Zar is seeing me like this suddenly thrills me, and my body responds. Two hot men want to use me? To play with me in their Dom/sub game? For whatever reason, my pussy loves it. She's leaving a five-star review.

"Join us," Luca says. "Please come in and taste my whore."

Wait? What?

We're not easing into this?

No, he's using control. He's using shock. He's saying that I'll submit as cushions sink around us, multiple bodies approaching. I can sense them.

But it's when a warm tongue greets my pussy that I gasp. In one long lick, it glides from my aching entrance up to my clit, slowly circling it before giving it a gentle suck. Then I feel tickling whiskers, too. It's Zar, eating my pussy on Luca's command, and "Oh my god," I sigh, so Luca yanks my hair.

He holds it tight in one hand while Zar's tongue won't relent. He's flicking my clit to delight.

"That's it, my belle," Luca cajoles. "Just be my sweet-tasting whore and let him devour all the cum you made for me. He has my permission. He loves tasting what's mine. He wants to clean my cum off your pussy, too."

Zar moans, licking over my bare, sticky mound, tasting what's left of Luca before Zar returns to my folds, and Luca lets go of my hair. Lifting me higher, he hooks his arms under my bound thighs and hoists me off the platform. Every part of me is open while he challenges Zar. "Whose pussy is this?"

"Yours, My Owner." Zar's drawl is laced with desire.

"Whose ass is this?"

"Yours, My Owner."

"Can you play with my whore without my permission?"

"Never, My Owner."

"Take my plug out," Luca warns, "*carefully*...and have a taste of every hole I've fucked."

Bodies surround us. I can hear their panting breath while Luca offers me like I'm Zar's punishment and reward at the same time. It's the same for Luca.

And suddenly...

I understand them.

I feel the pain Luca feels of never truly being satisfied. And I feel Zar's submission, too, needing to pleasure Luca, to please him. I don't know what happened between them, but I feel everything they're trying to satisfy through me, to heal through me.

And it feels right.

It feels like I belong with them.

Laving over my clit, Zar gently tugs at Luca's plug, and I groan at the sensations. At the luscious weight in my ass before the slight stinging burn of the stretch while he pulls it out, never abandoning my clit for pleasure.

"Who does she gape for?" Luca taunts Zar.

"You, My Owner." Zar's voice strains with lust. *God, he's so aroused.* "I can see her pussy dripping for you. I can see her pink little holes open for you."

"Lick her ass," Luca demands. "Trust me; it tastes so sweet."

Dragging his tongue down my cunt that aches for anything inside me, Zar's tongue pierces my entrance, taking as much of my taste as he can before he lavishes my tender ass next, and deep moans erupt from my throat. They make Luca's hard dick jump against my back while Zar's mouth obeys him.

"That's it, my stud," Luca's voice darkens, "show us how you love licking every little hole my big cock has fucked."

Shamelessly, Zar groans, darting his tongue over my puckered hole, just like Luca did forever ago, and it makes me remember. It makes me groan for him. "Luca."

I need more. I'm in pain for so much more.

"Taste her, too."

I don't know who Luca commands, but a warm, soft mouth claims my dangling foot and my other foot, too. Two strangers gently suck my toes, and the only one who's ever done this to me before is Luca, and again, it's like it's all from him.

He's every pleasure I feel.

It's like he told them how to lavish me.

No, to *ravish* me because another mouth, another tongue, slowly circles my tender nipple before; yes, I gasp as another stranger gently sucks my other nipple, too.

The sweet sucking pressure on my toes. The gentle licking of my nipples. The sensitive circling tickle around my ass. "Oh my god, yes," I sigh, wanting to cry at the pleasure. At the taboo.

Five people are worshipping my body with their mouths while I rest on the throne of Luca like his sacrificial offer, and it's my honor. Long hair tickles my ribs and stomach. I don't know if it's a woman or a man. I can't feel any sensations but warm mouths, wet tongues, and rousing touches.

"That's it," Luca urges in that coaxing accent. "Pleasure her."

Bodies surround me. I smell perfume, cologne, rich wine, and sweet whisky. Their erotic attention suffocates me. They steal my air, and I don't need it. I don't need anyone but Luca in my ear, owning my mind, holding my heart while offering my body to others.

"Make her come, each of you," Luca demands. "Make her come at least five times."

Zar goes first. I know it's him because he wants me to know. Growling, he buries his beard in my pussy again, snacking on my clit like he said he would while his two long fingers slowly enter me, and I gasp...and gasp again. I'm going to come so fast. My clit is a firecracker. I needed something inside me, and now it's Zar's stroking touch.

"Harder," Luca commands him. "Fuck her harder, motherfucker."

Luca honors us with our past, with my words. He's sweating

against my back while Zar's fingers start pounding into my sex, his tongue whipping across my clit while dripping mouths suck hard on my toes and tug at my nipples, and I explode.

"Luca!" I scream so loud; his name forever marks my voice. My bound thighs, dangling over Luca's arms, violently shake. My orgasm is excruciating and heaven. I let it wash through me while one of the mouths lavishing my toes leaves and...

"Yes, fuck her with that," Luca says before kissing my hair. I can imagine what he's watching, and it's so erotic. I trust him so much when he directs a stranger, "*Gently.*"

I don't know what it is, but it's not a real cock. It's too ribbed and thick and getting wider and wider as someone slowly urges it into my pulsing walls, and I groan.

"Her clit," Luca orders. "Lick her clit too."

It's Zar again. His whiskers tickle. I feel his shoulder brushing my thigh. Secretly, he kisses my clit, too, letting me know it's him before he gets brutal, sucking it so hard while mouths flick my nipples and someone impales my sex with an amazing sensation, and I convulse in Luca's arms, coming with another deep groan.

"Now go slow," Luca soothes. "Give her a break. Take her slowly next time."

It's beautiful. It makes me want to cry into my blindfold. Luca knows what I desire and need next because it's him. He's controlling my pleasure. Though his hard cock drips against my back, filling me with painful urges, it doesn't need to be his body when at last, I'm giving him my trust, I'm under his control.

Mouths leave my nipples and toes, too, and bodies shift while Luca tilts me. He turns me on my side in his lap, his erection pressing against my arm while his arms hold me splayed open so two mouths can gently start their devotion.

One is Zar again. It's like he'll always be here with Luca. It's his soft whiskers nestling into my ass crack before his tongue starts teasing me as another tongue gingerly plays with my sensitive clit.

It has to be a woman, someone who knows our sex can only take so much sensation before it's a burning numbness, so you have to be soft next. You have to gently awaken the clit again.

I whimper, flooding with lust and gratitude and not believing this.

"Luca," I sigh, thanking him.

He's more than my word; he's my world.

"This is for you, my belle." His voice weaves into my mind, caught in the most sensual blind dream. "This is the pleasure I will always give you."

This time, Zar and the woman slowly take me there. They work together, tongues and mouths devouring my every exposed inch. I wonder if Zar is touching the woman, too. I wonder if she's stroking his long, curving cock. I wonder if Luca is ever going to come to this because his cock has been urging hard and thick against me for so long.

"Enjoy it," Luca gently urges me. "Come, my sweet whore, because you deserve it."

So softly, after minutes, I shamelessly fall into my next orgasm, washing over the mouths beneath me. It's so sensuous and relaxing until Luca says, "Now, everyone, get her ready."

I groan as he maneuvers my helpless body to where I'm centered again in his lap and hoisted high. This night is lasting forever, and I don't want it to end. It's almost good enough since I'm not fucking Luca until he demands, "Get her ready to take two of my cocks, to take at least two orgasms, back to back. Give her all she can take. I'm going to break her."

"Oh my god," I murmur.

"Is that what you want, my belle?" Luca's voice urges above me. "Like when you watched Stacey take all that cock, and you came too? You said you wanted me and Zar like that. You wanted to be my dirty little whore with a dick in your ass and cunt. Say it."

Hell, I'll sing it. "Luca."

But if I thought I was in a trance state before. If I thought I had died and entered erotic heaven, that was just the waiting room.

Warm tongues and fingers and mouths blanket me, resting on Luca's hard lap. They find my nipples and toes and sex again until

I'm a moaning mess of sensations. I can't find logic; I don't know where I am, but cradled against Luca's body until the sucking sensations leave my toes.

Bodies shift before one slick dildo slowly slides into my pussy, and I groan at it, stretching my aching walls. Then another dildo presses gently against my ass. I don't know if I can take it until a body brushes against my thigh and Luca's. It's Zar. I know his touch now, feeling his generous mouth take care of my clit.

"Put my cock in her ass, too," Luca commands someone, and the dildo burns entering me. The pressure is immense as someone urges it slowly inside while Zar's tongue lavishing my clit makes it orgasmic. The pain, the pleasure, it makes me heave, and yes, I die.

My body convulses. I can't control it, bucking and jerking while sensations rip through me, dildos thrusting in and out of me. Zar's warm hand presses down hard over my mound to hold my clit still for his attention while I'm helpless and being fucked senseless.

"Yes, my whore, take all of me." Luca's voice invades me, too. I keep coming so hard I lose count through the explosions. My blindness goes from black to white. White light is all I see. Euphoria is all I feel. I can't hear. I can't find a thought. "Luca," is all I can say; it's all I'll ever know.

Like a god from above, his voice presses to my ear. "I'm always inside you, Scarlett."

"Please, Luca," I whimper, tears threatening, too, because I wish it were true. I need him so much as the last tremors of my orgasms wreck through my body.

"Leave us," he calmly commands the others.

I'm vaguely aware of every touch, every person and toy withdrawing from my body. Then I hear lusty, murmured voices exiting the room before buckles clank and velcro rips. Luca frees my thighs and wrists, but I can't move. I can't stop shaking.

Shifting our bodies around, I'm draped over Luca's arms while he carefully stands. I sense gravity, our bodies rising while my cheek rests against his pounding chest.

"Scarlett?" He sounds worried. "Belle, are you okay?"

"Yes," I sigh, feeling him carry me to the bed, I hope.

"Thank you." I barely hear Zar say it across the suite before the door *clicks* closed.

Did he leave?

"Luca," I rouse, "I want to see you now. You and Zar. You promised."

"You will," he replies, gently setting me down on the plush bed, my legs dangling over the edge. "Let's do this slowly," he insists, gently tugging at my blindfold. "The lights are low, but take your time."

Once he removes the silk, I rub my eyes until I'm brave enough to open them.

There is a warm glow in the room. It doesn't hurt my eyes, but the sight slowly filling my focus is an assault on my heart in the best way.

I start blinking, staring up at a towering, naked Luca and an equally naked Zar. They stand, almost shoulder-to-shoulder, gazing down at me with a sheen of sweat glistening over their chiseled muscles, the gold gleaming on Zar's thick collar, too. But what really attracts my attention is their hard cocks, almost crossing like thick swords in front of me.

It's like God and the Devil stand before me, and I don't know which is which.

They look worried about me, but I'm fine. I'm high on orgasmic opium, and I'm not coming down. Not until they do, too.

"Well, hello, my big boys," I rasp. "Ready for the final round?" Zar chuckles, making his hard dick bob, and that makes this even better. "Now that you've permanently rearranged my DNA into happy whore mode," I demand, "let me help with your two huge problems."

"Are you okay?" Luca asks.

"I'm thirsty," I answer. "And not for water."

"No. You'll have some." He turns toward the nightstand and turns back with two glasses of water, like he planned our care, offering one to me and one to Zar.

We drink while he watches. Silently, we hand him back the empty glasses, and he sets them on the table.

"Now, can I have what I'm *really* thirsty for?" I know I'm supposed to be a sub and not speak, but that bitch is tired, and this bitch needs dick, real dick.

"No," Luca growls. "It's time for your collar." He sounds serious, but tell that to his dick. It wants to play.

"Okay." I grin, wedging my ass off the bed, slowly lowering to my knees. They step back while I stare up at Luca and demand, "Collar me, Master."

Luca can't help it. I make him grin, turning again for the nightstand. Of course, he's planned all this while Zar keeps staring down at me, so I hook my finger and say, "We're equal, right?"

"Quiet," Luca huffs over his shoulder. "I have some proper words prepared." He unfolds a piece of paper.

So, Zar winks at me, quickly joining me on his knees. Once he's this close, I can see my milky arousal, slick on his beard, and I feel like I should thank him for giving me so much pleasure, too, but I don't.

We're silent. We're too focused on Luca turning around with a white velvet necklace box and a piece of paper in his hand.

But when he finds us *both* on our knees, he clears his throat, sounding surprised. "What are you doing?"

I taunt, "We're serving you, Master."

Don't think I didn't notice when I sat at the bar that Luca wasn't wearing his wedding band. That added to my thrill, to my hope that everything changes tonight. It makes me brave as I lean forward, kissing his thigh, his birthmark, and he doesn't pull away.

"*Scarlett*," he warns in a low growl.

"If you want to collar me, too," I move my kiss higher, thrilled because his cock jumps, "then let me completely serve you, Master." Then I remember our roles, feeling Zar's knee brush against mine. "Let *us* serve you."

I give Zar a look. I hope that, given all the laughs and talks we've shared, he can read my mind by now.

This is our chance.

We do this together.

We can make him change.

Zar leans forward, slowly pressing his kiss to Luca's other thigh and Luca grunts. I lift my gaze to his, and he stares down at us with his hands frozen, holding his gift for me. He doesn't step back or protest.

It's like we have him trapped in his hard truth.

"If it's the three of us, now," I soothe, "then let us serve you. We'll promise to honor some of your rules, but some need to change."

I move my mouth, hovering before his swollen crown, and Luca doesn't stop me. He lets me see the crystal in his eyes crack. He needs me. He's dripping for me, so I dart my tongue, taking his first drop, and he hisses with pleasure, so I keep going.

I remember what he craves. I linger my tongue under his crown, over his sensitive seam, and down the thick vein in his shaft, and he swells even more. I do it over and over, and he doesn't say a word, but his heavy breath speaks volumes.

So I grab his base. He's so thick that my hand can't wrap around him, but I squeeze what I can as I stare up at him, letting him watch while I slowly stretch my lips, swallowing his fat crown. I take my chance; I take every inch of him I can until I gag on him, and he groans.

He finally speaks, "Fuck, yes, Belle." Tossing the paper and velvet box on the bed, he frees his hands to yank my hair, pulling my mouth off his swollen cock. He growls, "Do you want to serve me?"

"Yes, Master," I rasp.

"Then fucking suck it all." Brutally, he grabs my skull, forcing his cock over my lips, as far into my throat as he can, and I gag again, loving it. Loving his surrender. Loving the shadows across his face.

He's unleashed. He's unbound. He's furious that he desires this and can't fight me either.

"Suck it," he snarls. "Gag on my fucking cock." He controls my movement, his big hands trapping my head, my mouth stretched open, my lips cracking, my jaw aching while he pumps his hips, fucking my mouth like a feral animal until spit drools over my chin. "Oh, my fucking dirty whore," he jeers, watching me. "You're serving me now, aren't you?"

Yes, I am, and I'm so wet. I'm choking and aroused. I don't regret anything because Luca, like this, is the perfect sight lording over me. Tears stream from my eyes, loving his pleasure and my degradation, and then I hear, "It's my turn to serve you."

Suddenly, Luca releases me.

I grab a drooling breath, my lungs huffing for air while I watch Zar stare up at Luca.

The men, the best friends, exchange this long look, the tension between them unveiled. It's dark. It's dominating. It makes the love between them fall away while Luca's eyes fill with a storm of lust and rage. Like something he's been holding back for years, but Zar's not submitting. He's demanding.

"Fuck my skull," he taunts Luca. "Choke me on your cock and fucking punish my throat. You know you need to. You know you want to punish me finally."

Heat blazes in Luca's eyes. He seizes Zar's head. "You want my punishment?" With both hands, he captures him. "Are you my cock whore, too?"

"For you, *we* are," Zar answers, staring at him while plunging his hand between my thighs, surprising me, defying Luca's orders by fingering me right under Luca's nose without his permission.

I moan, I can't help. Zar's too good; the two of them look too hot, and this feels so right.

"Get your hand off her," Luca snarls.

"Make me," Zar jeers back. "Punish me for touching her."

"You fucking, Skull Pussy." Luca fists Zar's hair, and Zar opens his defiant mouth for him, making a show of removing his hand from my pussy. And suddenly, Luca looks possessed. He starts fucking Zar's throat like he fucked mine. Brutally. Cruelly. Painfully. Every muscle on his hulking frame is tensed as Zar endures; he delivers. "That's it. Take my fucking cock," Luca growls. "Take it like you *took* her from me."

Luca gives Zar the punishment they need, making Zar moan. Sucking Luca's cock has Zar's surging hard and swollen. I see him dripping with satisfaction.

How long has Zar wanted Luca like this?

How long has Luca needed this from Zar?

You can feel how this has been tormenting them. You can hear how much it satisfies them, too. They grunt. They groan. I can see they belong together, so I help because I need this, too.

Leaning down, I start licking under Luca's base at the rigid vein above his swollen balls, and he groans so deeply with need.

"Oh fuck." He starts to break. "Oh fuck, yes." He slows down his claim of Zar's mouth. "Yes, my belle."

Zar takes the cue, jerking his head back and grabbing a breath. With spit trailing from his lips to Luca's tip, he offers Luca to me next.

Slowly, I start sucking Luca again, gazing up at him, letting him hear me moan with his cock filling my mouth while he watches. Then Zar starts lavishing Luca's balls at the same time, and Luca's destroyed. The tension and rage drop from his muscles as if all he feels is pleasure now.

"Oh fuck, you two," he groans, sinking his hand in my hair, his other in Zar's. "Oh fuck, yes, you're mine now."

Forever, he lets us serve him, taking our turns. Discipline is all Luca's known for so long, and he uses it tonight. My jaw hurts, and Zar's throat gags, but my pussy is loving this.

It's beautiful. The three of us are connected. Luca's pain is gone. Only pleasure is shared. Still, it's not enough. We need relief, so I reach, wanting to pleasure Zar, too. I fist Luca's shaft in one hand and reach for Zar's beside me, but Luca growls low, "Never. You only touch your Master's cock."

But Zar needs release. I do, too. I don't care how many millions of orgasms Luca tortured me with tonight. This is different. This is the three of us. This needs to be perfect.

And Luca can see it. "Pleasure yourselves," he demands. "You'll come with my dick in your mouth."

He gives it to Zar first, letting him pace himself and enjoy it. They both do.

Zar slows down, moaning while he fists Luca's cock, sucking his swollen tip, his tongue, flicking his sensitive underside. Zar lavishes Luca, and it's so hot to watch. So beautiful, too. The pleasure they're feeling. Their love returning. It's in their groans, and I start fingering myself, tugging at my nipple, too, and Luca watches us in awe. He lets himself enjoy it. He likes Zar sucking his cock.

"Yes, my stud." He guides him, cupping his head. "Take me. Suck my cock like you've always wanted, haven't you?" Zar moans louder, jerking his cock faster. "That's it. Let me fuck your throat. My cock belongs in your mouth, too. Show us. Show us what a cock slut you secretly are for me, aren't you? Come on, show her how you're mine, too."

The groan from Zar's throat is deep. Plunging his mouth as far down Luca's shaft as he can, he holds it there, staring up at Luca while feverishly jerking his dick. Zar looks blitzed out. He's going to come, so I turn my body, and he tries to aim his, too.

I want Luca to watch this. I want Zar to have this. I coax him, "Come on me. Show me how you're his, how you have me too. You get us both now."

The shudder of Zar's ripped shoulders is violent, his grunts so satisfied. With Luca's cock in his mouth, he splatters my stomach with his cum, and I'm so fucking aroused, I need him.

"Master," I beg. "Luca." He knows.

Dragging his length out of Zar's panting mouth, Luca keeps his hand in Zar's hair while he offers himself to me last.

"I'm going to come in your mouth, my whore. Then you're going to show me," he says. "You're going to open your mouth and make yourself come while I take pictures of you sharing my cum with my stud."

Oh my god, he's so depraved, and I love it.

I love this side of Luca. It's him, lewd and controlling, gentle and pleasing, and it's really beautiful.

And it's not long.

Not once Luca sinks his hands into my hair as he gazes down

at me with that look he gave me the night we met. "Yes, my belle." He's not furious. He's mine. I take as much of him as I can, over and over, until my chin drools, my eyes cry, and his thighs shake. His lips, too. "Yes, *ma flamme*," he grunts. "Scarlett, *fuuuuck!*" He cries out, grunting and filling my mouth with more than I can hold.

It spills over my lips while Zar caresses my hip, praising, "*Dayum* woman, you're so beautiful."

Luca's still shaking but he pulls out, reaching for his phone on the nightstand. Aiming its lenses at me, he says, "You're our only woman now, the only one we want pictures of. I may allow others to please you, but you are ours, and we are yours."

His promise makes me moan before I proudly open my full mouth. Jerking my hand in my swollen pussy, I rub my raw clit, making it deliver one more time tonight, one more time for Luca to watch.

And he takes all the pictures he wants. Of me on my knees. Of his cum on my tongue. Of me, poised, spitting over Zar's eager lips, sharing Luca's desire with him.

Then Luca kneels with us, cupping my head and Zar's as he vows, "We won't do this every time. We can't. But I promise, we're together now."

Then he looks at me. He knows the one thing I need to hear.

"I'm never leaving you, Scarlett."

Scarlett

CHAPTER SIXTEEN

POURING LAVENDER-SCENTED BATH SALTS INTO THE TUB BIG enough for four people, Zar fills the bubbling water before he climbs in with me.

"You're a godsend," I sigh.

My muscles ache from last night, and my sore pussy is checking into early retirement, too.

But who are we kidding? She'll be healed and back on the job by next Saturday.

I don't remember much about falling asleep last night. Exhaustion claimed me. I wanted both men to crawl into bed and hold me while we slept, but that didn't happen.

I rested my head on Luca's chest while he had Zar rub arnica gel over the places where my body had been bound. It soothed the soreness and helped with bruising.

I drank a Gatorade for Luca and snacked on banana slices and pistachios for him, too. He made Zar do the same. Luca made sure we were nourished before he said, "I need to be there when Gia awakes."

I understood. I would never argue with him about that.

But before Luca left, he opened the velvet box and presented me with a thick gold link necklace. At its center hung a square-cut ruby surrounded by tiny diamonds. When Luca wrapped it around my neck, it fit like a collar, and I touched it, not knowing what to say.

"I had words prepared," Luca said, "but you leave me speechless, Belle." He leaned down and kissed my hair. He lingered there before he said, "And you broke my rules." He lifted, eyeing us. "Both of you. So I'll give you this—if you honor me and wear my collars, you're promising you won't try to break me again."

He looked from me to Zar, and for a moment, Luca was humbled, asking us not to tempt him again. Like my heart, the moment felt too fragile to speak, so I just nodded yes.

Luca kissed my forehead, "Goodnight, *ma flamme*," before he climbed out of bed.

I looked at Zar, wondering if he'd stay. His smile was gentle, but he climbed out of bed, too. If Luca couldn't sleep with me, Zar wouldn't either. The two friends healed something last night, and Zar wasn't risking our future.

Luca tucked me in while Zar promised, "I'll be back in the morning with coffee."

"We're doing brunch tomorrow," Luca pronounced, "as a family."

They left together, turning off most of the lights, and I hugged my pillow, content, knowing they'd come back.

Sloshing in the tub, Zar reclines opposite me, sipping a mimosa while I sigh at the warm coffee he brought, too. It soothes my throat. I don't know how many times I screamed last night, but broken glass fills my neck.

And is it weird being naked around Zar?

No, nothing feels weird with him. We're not best friends. We're not lovers. Yes, we're subs together, but we're also just...*us*.

It's pure silent relaxation until Zar informs me, "He sent me with the suitcase from your suite and your clothes for brunch, too, darlin'."

I roll my eyes. "That name's not sticking either."

He flicks water at me. "Why not?"

"Because," I flick him back, "you sound like Matthew

McConaughey saying it, and it's weird now because you've licked my pussy, too."

He chuckles. "So you don't want my boy, Matthew, licking your kitty?"

"You *know* him?"

"Yeah, he's a good fella," he drawls. "When your family owns the state of Texas, you meet all its prestigious residents."

I study Zar, like *really* study him. He's beyond sexy. Yes, his dark hair and eyes are seductive. His body is drool-worthy. His cock is incredible.

But it's him.

Zar can go from sounding like a Harvard-educated CFO to a Texas cowboy in a flip of a phrase. He's a southpaw who throws a vicious left hook. He can be stern, but he's so sweet with Gia and polite to everyone, but he doesn't put up with Luca's grumpy bullshit unless it's Saturday nights.

"Do you ever talk to your family?" I ask.

"I talk to my little brothers." He swirls his mimosa. "I let them bitch about their billions. My mom sends me birthday cards, but to my dad, I'm a ghost, and it's fine by me. We never got along."

"Do they know about Luca?"

He cocks a grin. "Well, now, how do you mean? Do they know that my college roommate and best friend is my boss, the CEO of The Mercier Hotels? Yes. Do they know that I get off on him yanking my collar and whipping me until I come? No. Do they know that I really like the taste of his hard cock in my mouth? I sorta didn't know it myself until last night."

"So, that never happened before? Between you two?"

"A lot never happened before last night."

I brush his leg with mine. "Are you alright with it? Like, it's what you wanted, right? You're not mad at me, are you?"

"Nah," he says. "You're what's making us finally work."

"So you weren't working before? You weren't happy?"

He sets his flute down on the wide edge of the spa tub before raking his fingers through his coal waves. The late morning sun fills the high window in the luxurious bathroom. We have two more hours until brunch, and we need this talk.

I need to know more about Zar.

I don't want to hurt him. I don't want him to feel second to me, but why does that already feel like the case, though I don't want it to be?

He takes too long to answer me, so I ask, "Zar, what do you get out of this? Why do you want this with him? With us?"

"It's simple." He reclines, draping his arms over the edge of the tub. "I was raised to be a Grade-A entitled asshole, to use my privilege to use others—the good ol' American way. The problem is, when an even more entitled asshole raises you, you start hating everything he stands for. You want to be nothing like him. So, I get off on giving it away. Power. Privilege. Pussy, too. I like submitting because honestly, I have enough trust fund money that my father can't touch that I could dominate all, but I don't."

"So that's why you like submitting to Luca?"

"Yeah." He grabs the bottle of shampoo on the edge of the tub. It's nestled beside an array of Mercier Hotel spa products. Filling his palm with pearly liquid, he says, "No one else has enough power to do it. I'd laugh in their face. But Luca has that way, doesn't he? He's so damn Dom he doesn't need dollars to own you. That's why I get off calling him 'Owner' and you call him 'Master.' We're free under his control."

"But you love him, too. I saw it last night." I reach out, silently asking for the shampoo. He hands it over, his other hand sudsing up his waves.

"Yeah, we love each other. Like best friends and all."

I dunk under the water, saturating my hair before I emerge with a little splash and he declares, "Dayum, you look like a mega-babe mermaid."

"Shut up." I grin, pouring a dollop of shampoo into my palm. "And keep lying to yourself that y'all are just best friends because I know what I saw last night."

"I know what I saw, too." He gets playful, forming his hair into a shampoo faux hawk. "You two are falling in love. You know it, right?"

I shrug. "Just like you two are."

"No." He laughs. "We're different."

"How?"

I amuse myself, too, dividing my hair into two sections, trying to form horns on my head but my hair's too long, and they flop like donkey ears, making Zar chuckle.

"Because," he says, "I don't want a wife, kids, or a picket fence. I don't want a husband either. Look up 'traditional' in the thesaurus, and I'm the antonym."

I twirl my bubbly horns. "Then what do you want?"

"I wanna live my life like I damn well please. No rules. No expectations."

I look him in the eye. "No love? No family?"

"Is that what you want? Love? Family? A husband? Because careful," he gently warns, "he may break your heart. You may never get it with him."

I pause, searching my heart, imagining how I'll be sitting beside Gia with Luca on the other side of her and Zar on the other side of me in a couple of hours.

We will feel like family, like Luca's version of the family *he* wants, but will it be enough for me?

"Yeah, I want it," I answer, not knowing how I'll truly get it. "You want it, too; you're just afraid to admit it."

Sheepishly, he grins, and it's cute. Zar ducks under, all the way, yanking my ankle so hard that he pulls me under, too.

We emerge laughing, bubbles streaming down our faces. The shampoo threatens to burn my eyes, so I don't open them. But I sure hear the deep "ahem" of an amused man watching our splashing spectacle.

"Do you need rubber duckies, too?" Luca asks while I wipe my eyes so I can open them.

"No," I answer, blinking up at him. "But I sure did like those rubber *fuckies* you used on me."

"Rubber fuckies?" He laughs. "That's what we're calling dildos now?"

"Hell, no," Zar chimes in. "Y'all already ruined 'red' and 'pinkie' for me. I ain't sayin' 'rubber fuckie' in a scene. I gotta draw the line somewhere."

Luca walks to the vanity. Dressed in his usual dark suit, white shirt, and no tie, everything he wears is Dom By Design, I swear. Grabbing two rolled towels, he offers one to Zar, then holds one open for me.

I obey, rising from the water, bubbles streaming in rivulets down my naked flesh. Both ogle me, but Luca holds me in his admiring gaze. Silently, he makes me stand there, nude and dripping, while his stare marks every inch that's his, making me feel beautiful before I let him wrap the towel around me.

"I need to shower, too," I insist, and they watch.

Zar stays in the tub, his towel resting on the edge as Luca sits beside him. I rinse off in the steamy glass enclosure, adding conditioner to my hair. Their silent admiration is turning me on, but I'm not breaking Luca's rules. It's Sunday, and apparently, only Saturday is Sex Day. Well, *Sorta* Sex Day.

"How do we do this?" I ask, shutting the water off. "At brunch? From now on?" I pull open the glass door, taking the towel Luca has stood to offer me again.

"We do it like we have been," Luca answers while Zar climbs out, making quick work of drying off, too. "It's us, Gia, Celine, Abbey and Harper. It's no different."

My glance flicks down to Luca's left hand. Like a slap, it hurts. *His wedding band is back on.*

"But it *is* different now," I challenge him. I may be wearing his jeweled collar. I may never take it off, but I will speak my mind. "It'll be obvious. Gia will sense it. Abbey and Celine, like all women, can smell a secret a mile away. They're going to know."

Luca lowers his brow. "Let them wonder. I don't answer to them. And we always act innocent around Gia. She can *never* know about us."

226

I catch Zar over Luca's shoulder, raising his eyebrow my way, like an "*I told you so*" while he tugs on a fresh pair of boxers.

And I want this to work. This will take time. Luca won't change in one night.

"Okay," I answer. "For Gia," I tell him before he leans down, tenderly kissing my cheek.

"We'll greet you in the lobby at noon," he insists. "Take your time."

They leave. Zar must get dressed in the bedroom while I remain in the bathroom, and I do take my time. I want this brunch to be perfect.

I want to win.

Yes, I want love, family, and husband, and I want it with Luca. It feels right. It has to be right with the way Luca looks at me. And I want Zar with us, too, if that's what he wants.

But either way, patience is required to win this fight. I can endure for months.

Why?

Because the brunch outfit Luca had Zar deliver to me in a Mercier Hotel white and gold garment bag is breathtaking. Luca even sent fine lingerie, too—white silk lace panties and a matching strapless bra.

Call Julia Roberts. Tell her I'm giving her a run for her money because I feel like a pretty woman with auburn hair, a ruby necklace, and a grumpy, dominating client.

But my dress is sapphire, not red like hers was in the movie. Mine is strapless and made of satin crepe with soft drapes, snug around my waist and hitting below my knee. It's elegant, showing off my tattoos and new jeweled collar, too. The silk tag inside says "Alex Perry," and I don't know who that is, but I know Luca picked this out. This and the new Louboutin nude patent pumps. I know their red sole. I binged *Sex in the City*. I know they're ridiculously expensive.

Giving me these luxurious clothes is Luca's way of making it up to me. Like, I wouldn't notice that his wedding band is back on.

We may love it when he degrades me on Saturday nights. I'm

honored to be his "whore," to be his sub, too. I get off on it. He does, too.

But by day, in front of others, he's dressing me like a lady—*his lady*—who belongs on his arm. And he doesn't want me to hide who I am. Now that he knows the story behind my tattoos, he wants me to wear them with pride.

I pluck out my make-up bag from the suitcase I packed yesterday for our big night and wear a bit more than usual. Carefully, I blow my hair out, too, letting it fall in natural waves. When I'm ready, I study myself in the mirror's reflection, and it's obvious.

I *have* changed.

I may be a proud girl from a trailer park, but I also look like the beautiful rich bitch who owns this hotel too.

God, I wish Maren and her cunty crew could see me now.

It's noon, and the golden elevator takes me down two quick floors to the lobby. When they *ding* open, I'm greeted by a vision that blooms a smile across my face.

"Well, hey, Champ!" Wade, my mentor and the first man I worked with at HGR Security is taking the day shift, covering the elevator.

"Hey!" My hug with him is genuine.

If I had a father figure, Wade would be him. We catch up about his wife and kids, then he asks me about work, "They making you dress this fancy to blend in?"

"Yeah," I answer. "It's a rough gig. I suffer in Gucci every day. Is this your new post? Covering days?"

Paint me double-relieved. Brooke doesn't stand a chance if Jameson covers most nights and Wade covers most days.

"Yeah," he answers. "Until Redix Dean starts shooting his new show in Savannah next year. He and Daniel Pierce." He shakes his head. "Can you imagine their crazed fans? We're already planning their security now."

I can imagine.

And I can't escape how my world connects to my friends and job. Charlie, my boss, is married to Daniel Pierce. Cade, my close friend, is married to Redix Dean. And Luca, my new secret Dom who gave my clit torturous pleasure for hours last night, is close friends with Redix, too.

Oh, and I've watched Redix and Cade get fucked by their lover, Silas Van de May. And we're all friends with Stacey and shop at Delta's, so my world is a steamy, forbidden one.

If Luca insists that our relationship stays secret, it will be a powder keg if our story ever blows up.

"Any developments?" I ask Wade.

"Nah." He tsks. "I bet she lays low for months. Even if she sneaks in using a disguise, she'll see us by the elevator and know what's up. Maybe that'll do the trick."

I shake my head. "Brooke Turner won't ever give up. It may take time and patience, but she's obsessed with having Mr. Mercier."

Irony strikes me how much Brooke and I are alike. We want Luca, but we can't have him, so we tempt him, hoping we can make him change. The only difference is that I'm fighting for Luca's heart, while I fear Brooke may take his soul. She may take Gia somehow.

Speaking of...

I quickly wrap up with Wade and turn to see them waiting in the lobby for me.

Once Gia spots me, she runs to hug my legs, and I can't resist. I lean down and scoop her up. "Hey, kiddo." Even though I'm in a fancy dress, I don't care. I rest Gia on my hip, carrying her back to Luca, Zar, and Celine, waiting for me.

"You look pretty," Gia says. Poking my necklace, she asks, "What's this?"

She may be five, but she's observant. I fear Gia can see so much because *this* feels new. This warmth in my heart. This feeling of her belonging to me, too. This terror I feel that something may happen to her and the fierce fight I feel to protect her.

I squeeze her tighter, answering, "It's a gift."

"From who?" she asks while I approach my new...who?

Family? Isn't that what Luca called us? He called me family, too.

And how he's proudly watching me, dressed for him and holding his daughter? Hot rocks fill my throat. Because Zar's looking at me the same, like he cherishes the sight, too, and there are moments I don't know what to believe.

Who is Gia's real father?

And what happened to her mother?

Darby Mercier died on the Ravenel Bridge in a car accident on July Fourth just before midnight. That I know. It's public record.

But what factors caused the accident? And why does Luca feel so guilty about it?

The police report lists Luca, Gia, and Zar as surviving passengers. It says Luca was in the passenger seat, Gia was safely buckled in her carrier in the center back seat, and Zar was seated beside her. It said Darby was driving, but what's shocking is the section of the report that lists "Contributing Factors" explaining how the accident happened...

It's blank.

It's as if Luca's money erased the whole truth.

He says he's a bad man, that he was a bad husband. He may swear he doesn't deserve love, but Luca would never cause an accident that put his daughter, Zar, or Darby at risk. He's not that kind of man; I know it.

"A special person gave it to me," I answer Gia about my jeweled collar before Luca leans down, politely greeting me with a kiss on both cheeks.

"Ma flamme," he dares to whisper, almost breathlessly, in my ear before pulling away.

His fingertips linger on my bare arm, holding Gia. He lets me carry her to our VIP brunch table, and I set her between us. Zar sits beside me, resting his arm across the back of my chair, while Luca does the same to Gia. We're like the woman and daughter they share, and it doesn't feel odd. It feels fated.

Celine gently smiles, noticing everything but not saying a

word. When Abbey and Harper join us minutes later, Abbey grins, noticing, too.

I told Luca we wouldn't be able to hide it, but we enjoy our brunch as usual, catching up on the week's gossip about the girls' school and karate class drama.

When I excuse myself to go to the Ladies' Room, Abbey rises to join me. "You know," she jokes, "since women can't pee alone."

"It's okay with me," she mutters by my side while we weave through the tables in the lavish restaurant. "You and Luca," she clarifies.

"I..." I don't know how to answer her. "I'm not supposed to..." *What?* I stop my shocked stammer because the list is too damn long.

I'm not supposed to fall in love with my client.

I'm not supposed to want to marry a man who still wears his wedding band from his first marriage.

I'm not supposed to be a second sub to the sexiest pleasure Dom who won't fuck me.

I'm not supposed to let strangers make me come instead, per his command, or share his cock and cum with his best friend.

Holy hell, the list is long if I keep going because I'm sure as hell not supposed to tell Abbey about any of it, either. But she lets me off the hook, pushing the restroom door open for us.

"You're not supposed to say anything," she answers, reading my mind. "And it's okay. That's what I mean." We're the only women in the room as she turns to me. "I know how private Luca is. I know how complicated it must be. But I'm happy for him. I'm happy for you. For Zar, too." My eyes widen, and she flits her hand. "I don't need details. I don't judge. I want this for y'all. All three of you. It's about time."

I had no idea Abbey was this wise. And I had no idea she'd support us. I'm afraid to ask her, to insult her sister's memory, but if anyone knows, it's her.

"Abbey, I..." I search for a respectful way to ask. "It's none of my business, I guess, but were Zar and Darby ever—"

"Together?" Her eyebrow raises. "I don't know. Zar loved my

sister. I know Luca knew about it, too. And Luca loved Darby so much. He was her first love. My sister was very prim and proper, but no one's perfect. There was always something between the three of them. They could hide it like the ocean, but she died before I could ever get to the bottom of it."

"So why doesn't Luca hate Zar?"

Her smile is soft. "Because they love each other, too. I swear those men are icebergs. Ten percent, you can see; the other ninety percent, they hide. But you," she reaches, affectionately rubbing my arm, "are hot enough to melt them both."

It rushes over my lips. I have to know. "How did Darby die?"

Grief creases her pretty face. She looks a lot like her sister. "In a car accident on July Fourth. We threw a party, and they all came over. But Luca and Zar got wasted. They were on the beach, fighting about something with Darby, too, and she got upset. She rushed back inside, grabbed Gia, and said she was going home, but Luca wouldn't let her leave without him. Zar either. So the four of them piled into Luca's car, and she drove. But the bottom fell out that night. It was a horrible summer storm, and I guess she lost control. She hit the center barrier and died at the scene. Zar told me she died in Luca's arms."

Sudden tears spill over my lashes. I imagine the horrific scene —Luca's tears, Gia's cries, and Zar's shock.

"But it's been over four years," Abbey eases, still rubbing my arm. "It's past time we all move on. Darby would want us to. She'd want Luca to love again. She'd want Gia to have a family. She'd want Zar to be happy, too. And that can be you. Just be patient with Luca. He still blames himself."

"Why?"

"Because when fate takes someone from you, you blame yourself."

I nod, finding it hard to talk through the strangle in my throat.

I've gone from a girl who tried to feel nothing to a professional paid to show no emotion to a woman now with tears springing from my eyes at the mention of Luca, Gia, or even Zar.

For the rest of our brunch, I'm feeling everything, and I let myself love it. To love them. I love Gia's giggles at Zar swiping whipped cream across her nose. Mine, too. I love how Gia crawls into Luca's lap, and he holds her because she needs a nap. I love how Zar refills my coffee with the silver carafe on the table. And I love how Luca keeps gazing at me like I'm the most beautiful woman he's ever seen.

By the end of our meal, my heart needs a break. I need to clear my head, see my dog, and talk to my sister.

I wish them all warm goodbyes before I'm finally alone, fishing for the keys to my car at the bottom of my purse before I stop at the sight of the man in the parking deck, leaning on my car.

Waiting for me.

"You broke the Red Rule," Jameson says once I'm feet away. His beefy arms cross his chest. His ankles are crossed, too. He's leaning on my driver's door, confronting me. "He's making it obvious," he warns, "and you're going to get fired or worse."

"The Red Rule" is the nickname the officers at HGR Security have given for the rule that says you don't fuck a client. Why?

I guess it's for the red "inappropriate behavior" slips bad students used to get in school. I earned a lot of them growing up.

"We're not fucking." Still, I try to lessen the lie.

"And I'm not breathing," Jameson huffs. "And since when do you go for a man like him? Richer than god? A possessive alpha asshole who has to prove something? And he's a father? He acts like a family man, but he's got dark kinks, I can fucking tell."

I shrug. "Since when are you the jealous type?"

"Fine," he confesses. I forgot how sexy Jameson's green eyes are. "Yeah, I'm jealous. I wanted us to work, and I fucking tried, but you bailed. You took the HGR job in Atlanta and mailed me a 'let's just be friends' card."

"And you weren't mad about it. So why are you being a dick now?"

"Because you need this fucking job, Scarlett." He leans down, dangerously close to me, and I sense the camera on the concrete beam to my right, aimed right at us. "I know how much we get paid, but it's not enough to afford that necklace, those clothes, and whatever you're hiding. He's not worth losing it all for. You're good at this job. The best fucking at it."

"I need *more* than my job," I sneer.

"Well, you may lose it and him and someone's life if you keep this shit up. You know better. Fucking is a dangerous distraction. That little girl can get hurt."

I step to him. "I'll kill anyone who tries."

"What if it's you?" He's inches from my face, making my heart pound at the truth. "What if you hurt her by fucking her father? You know how shit can go south on this job. What are you thinking?"

"I can control it, Jameson. Don't worry."

I don't fully believe myself, and he reads it in my eyes.

"Listen. I'll protect you," he swears. "I'll protect that girl. Fuck, I'll even protect your Daddy Dom because I'm paid to. But so help me, if your secret gets out of control and lives are at risk, I'm going straight to the boss."

I snarl, "Don't tell Charlie."

"She'll understand," he argues. "Hell, she fell in love on the job, too, but she'll need to know. She'll have to replace you."

"No." I clench my fist. "I won't let her down."

"No." He lurches, making me stagger back before he starts to storm away, warning over his shoulder. "You're letting yourself down."

Luca

CHAPTER SEVENTEEN

"WHAT IN THE HELL IS THIS?"

I've never seen so much brightly colored fur and plastic shit in my life.

"Baba, it's a Furby," Gia huffs, exasperated with my exasperation. "I want the purple one, and Spencer gets the orange one."

"We're here to buy *him* a birthday present," I explain. "It's not your birthday until May."

"But I want one, too." Gia uses that cute I'm-twenty-seconds-from-tears face that I can't resist.

"Yeah, Baba." Scarlett grabs the purple plush toy off the shelf for her. "She wants one, too."

"I had a black and white one when I was five," Zar piles on, and I'm outnumbered. "I really liked it when it said 'Pet me' all day long."

I snort. He's being a smartass, and it's hot. But Scarlett, standing beside him, pushing the red shopping cart, looks even hotter.

Rolling my eyes, I surrender, grabbing the orange one, too. "Fine," I growl. "Do they have gift bags here?"

"It's Target," Scarlett scoffs, "they have everything except your favorite Dolce and Gabanna."

"It's D&G, darlin'," Zar corrects her, and she punches his arm.

Gia grabs my hand, content that I caved on the toy for her while I lead the way, guided by Scarlett and Zar behind us.

"Go up three more aisles, then take a right," Scarlett tells me before she mutters to Zar, "I can't believe he's never been in a Target."

"He's never been in a Walmart, either," Zar adds over my shoulder. "Which is a damn shame because the owner's granddaughter is quite fine."

Scarlett chuckles. "You did *not* date the heiress of Walmart."

"Nah," Zar teases. "I sure didn't *date* her."

"Baba," Gia tugs at my hand, "can we go to McDonald's, too?"

"Gia, we don't eat fast food."

I swear, this is episode two of *What Is Happening To My Life*.

It's been a week since that night with Scarlett...and Zar. And it's taking me days to process. I still don't think I have. The memory of Scarlett and Zar on their knees, sharing my hard cock and cum keeps flashing into my mind at the most inappropriate times.

And I want it again tonight.

And I want this now.

The four of us are toy shopping for Spencer's sixth birthday party in an hour. This part is fun. This feels like family.

But I want to go to this birthday party like I want my balls punched, but I can't be an asshole. Maren, Spencer's mom, invited the entire karate and school class. I won't deny Gia the fun day, though it will be hell for us.

The only thing that makes it worth it is Gia's spending the night with her cousin and aunt. She'll be happy and safe there, and that will free me to do everything I want tonight. I even gave Celine the weekend off.

"But I'm hungry." Gia skips beside me, tugging my hand again so I have to look down and fall victim to her adorable extortion. "And Harper says McDonald's has the best French fries."

"They do." Scarlett makes it worse. "And their chicken nuggets with barbecue sauce are finger-lickin' good."

"Wrong chicken." Zar chuckles.

"Wrong dinner." I turn around, grinning at Scarlett. "I'm feeding you a Greek tonight." Then I glance at Zar. "You too."

Scarlett blows me a covert kiss.

Yes, I want them on their knees again, but that's as far as we ever go. I can live forever with their mouths drooling over my hard cock, though I don't like the idea of their tongues touching. It's too much like kissing, and no one gets to kiss Scarlett.

And fuck, I need to stop imagining it.

I'm in Good Dad mode today. Not Dickish Dom.

"Please, Baba, please," Gia begs. "Can we go to McDonald's on the way to Spencer's?"

I can't win with these three, so yes, we buy the annoying toys and big birthday gift bag, and then I have to bite back my bark at the innocent worker in the drive-thru, taking our order for fried crap to feed my daughter. And, of course, she devours it, and now she's hooked.

Gia sings *The Little Mermaid*, happy in the back seat with Zar, while I endure hell, driving back over the bridge toward Maren's house, also in the French Quarter.

But my life finally feels right again.

I finally have the family I want, one I never imagined was possible, but like before, like this spot coming up on my left on the bridge, I fear I'll lose it all again.

"Hey, Gia," Scarlett calls out from the passenger seat beside me, "let me play a song for you and Baba. I'll teach you the words so you can sing along."

Glancing Scarlett's way, I force a smile while my hands sweat. They shake, too, guiding the steering wheel. Dark memories flash, like the red lights surrounding us that rainy night on this bridge, while Scarlett quickly taps away on her phone.

I know she's doing this for me. I know she's figured out some things about the crash, but I will never tell her the truth.

She can't know how evil I was, or I'll lose her, too.

"Here, y'all." Scarlett presses play, and a country violin kicks in. "This is 'Wagon Wheel' by South Carolina's proud son, Darius Rucker."

"Yee-haw!" Zar calls out before Scarlett starts howling the catchy lyrics, and I glance in the rear-view mirror.

The smile on Gia's face lights up my soul. I forget where I am for seconds because this is all I need. Her. Happy.

We make it over the bridge, singing and playing the song twice while god must like me today. I find a parking spot only a block from Maren's Historic Charleston home.

Proudly, I enter with Gia holding my hand and Scarlett and Zar behind me. The screaming kids contrast with the stately antique furniture. Gia runs to join her friends gathered in the back courtyard while Maren greets us with a smile as genuine as cubic zirconia.

"Welcome," she coos, offering me a glass of punch while I politely kiss her cheeks. "I didn't get your RSVP for *four* today."

"We have a business meeting in an hour," I lie to Maren before I turn and give the punch to Scarlett.

Let that be my covert signal because as much as I want Maren and everyone to know Scarlett is mine, she's my family, too, just like Zar, I can't. No one can know about us. They may call Charleston the "Holy City," but it's full of devilish tongues.

If I didn't have to protect Gia's reputation and my family business, I'd proudly hold Scarlett's hand with Zar brushing my shoulder beside me, wearing his collar, too.

Zar's not a holding-hands or a snuggle-under-the-covers kind of man. At least, I don't think he is. But we have exchanged deeper looks this week. We didn't discuss what happened when we left the suite last Saturday night. Why should we? We know it will happen again, and we know we enjoyed it. *Greatly.*

"Abbey is taking Gia home after the party," I fill Maren in. "They're doing a cousins' sleep-over."

"That's nice." Maren bats her lashes. "Why don't you come back then, after your meeting? I still owe you crab cakes."

"I'd love some crab cakes!" Zar loves pissing off Maren. At one point, it was obvious Maren was attracted to him, too, but never. She's not his type.

Scarlett's our only type, and right on cue, she joins Zar. "Why, yes, Maren. I'd love some crab cakes, too."

I can't fight my grin at these two.

Every preppy, traditional parental duo fills Maren's home today, buttoned-up in Charleston's uptight Southern style.

But not me. Not us.

I crave fine white linen and relaxed denim on my skin for the weekends, Scarlett in that black Prada sweater dress, and Zar in those jeans and black Tom Ford sweater. I gave it to him for Christmas last year. Yes, I also lavish Scarlett in couture fashion because both belong to me now.

"Well," Maren pouts her new lips, "perhaps another time." She touches my sleeve. "When it's just us, Luca. I have some photos of Darby I found. I want to put them in a custom photo-book for Gia."

When it comes to my daughter and her mother, I'll never refuse. "Of course," I tell her. "Some other time, and yes, that would be very kind. I love Gia having pictures of her."

Maren swishes away, joining her seersucker crew, while Zar muses, "I bet if we bought her a giant dildo to fuck, she'd finally get that little stick outta her ass."

Scarlett laughs, tossing her head back.

This entire week, I couldn't rip my eyes away from her. If she's not protecting my daughter and making her giggle, too. If she's not sipping the coffee I make for her, gently thanking me. If she's not ignoring the shit from people like Maren with strength and grace. If Scarlett's not standing by my side, dazzling me with her smile and wearing my jeweled collar, I'm watching her in my cameras.

Don't think I missed her tense exchange with her colleague and former fuck-boy, Jameson, in the parking deck. I've watched it several times, my blood boiling hotter with each play. She did nothing wrong, and I can't wait to punish her tonight.

"It's *Luca,* not a giant dildo she wants." Scarlett lowers her voice, telling me, "Maren's so horny for you, she's ready to kill me to get you."

Even though kids race by with Nerf guns in hand and parents sip mint juleps and sweet tea, I'm not feeling sweet. I feel something else when I lean to whisper in Scarlett's ear, inhaling a whiff of her sandalwood-scented strands.

I need her to know, to be sure. I'm not leaving, and she's never leaving me.

"It's *you* who gets me, my belle." I vow, "You get my heart now. You get my torture later. You get my pleasure in your sweet pussy and tight ass tonight. You get my cock in your dirty mouth, too." She sighs against my cheek. "Is that what my sweet whore wants? Every torture Maren can't have?"

"Yes," she sighs back.

"We're late for our meeting," Zar declares. He doesn't need to hear what I share with Scarlett to know my tone.

An hour later, we find Gia surrounded by kids at the large dining table. The birthday boy is opening his presents with Gia beside him and her cousin beside her.

Abbey gives me the *I-Got-This* wink before I squat down and kiss Gia goodbye.

"Bye, Baba," she chirps. She's excited about tonight, not worried about leaving me, and that's how it should be.

But then she surprises me. She lifts her gaze, searching for Scarlett standing behind me. "Bye, Scarlett." Gia lifts her arms, beckoning a kiss from Scarlett, too. When she leans down to give her one, Gia wraps her little arms around her neck. "Will you be with Baba at brunch tomorrow?"

"Of course," Scarlett assures her. "Have fun tonight with your new Furby."

"Bye, Zar!" Gia waves to him, too.

"Bye, my girl." He says it every time because it's true.

She's mine. She's his. She's our world. We could've lost her, too, so with an open heart, I share Gia with him.

Zar insists he never wants to marry or have kids, and why should he?

He has us.

We belong like this, me on one side of Scarlett, Zar on the other, enjoying an afternoon stroll. I aim our steps down the sidewalk, back toward my car, but then I keep walking.

"Where are we going?" Scarlett's curious, so I rest my hand on the small of her back, allowing my pinky to caress her ass.

"Shopping," I tell her, leading our path under wrought iron balconies above and black shutters on our right, framing window boxes spilling with pansies for the coming mild winter.

Quickly, they figure out our destination. Delta's is only a few blocks away, and our silent anticipation adds to the tension.

I called Stacey Evans yesterday. I've paid a handsome sum to have Delta's open only for us this late afternoon. Though everyone who would judge us is back at Maren's home, I can't afford the risk of running into anyone who truly cares about us.

It's a Saturday. Redix and Cade could be here, shopping with Silas. They enjoy their throuple, and I wish I could be as open as they are. Redix suffers no secrets nowadays. They're toxic. I know.

I die with my secret every day.

But now I have this bringing me back to life.

Zar pushes the iron gate open while I guide Scarlett up the wooden stairs. Instantly, my body remembers the last time we were here, and it simmers in Scarlett's eyes, too, as the same massive bodyguard lets us in.

"Well, hello," Stacey politely greets us in the parlor. It seems she and the bodyguard are the only staff this afternoon.

Though I must keep Scarlett and Zar a secret, I trust Stacey's discretion. She'd go out of business if she didn't protect her clients' privacy. I kiss her cheeks before introducing Stacey to Zar. Of course, she's already met Scarlett, and I catch what Zar instantly admires.

Stacey's long blonde hair is twisted in a French knot. She's wearing black silk pajama pants with matching high heels. But her black silk pajama top drapes open, proudly revealing her see-through black mesh bra, her nipples greeting us, too.

It's the perfect, elegant outfit for a woman who owns the most exclusive sex shop in the South. Stacey is not shy, and neither is Scarlett, her gaze dropping to admire Stacey's ample breasts.

I lick my lips, remembering the show Stacey and her men gave us. I lick them again, remembering last week how Scarlett writhed, blindfolded over my naked hard cock. Scarlett knew by touch that Zar and other men and women served her that night. She's into both, and I'll allow them to pleasure her on my command.

But no one fucks her, especially not me.

"Please," Stacey offers us flutes of Champagne before directing, "the upper floors are all yours. Take your time and ring the gold bell by the doors if you need anything or have any questions."

Delta's is familiar, and I feel like the tour guide leading us up the grand staircase. Scarlett steps beside me, and I can't resist. My palm lands on her ass, guiding her up the stairs, and Zar chuckles behind us. "Darlin', you sure have a sweet set of cakes to admire."

But Scarlett teases him over her shoulder, "Yeah, he sure does have some hot cross buns, doesn't he?"

I grin, leading our steps to turn right at the top of the stairs. "Keep talking about *my* ass," I warn, "and I'll show why they call anal play a Greek art."

"Promises, promises," Zar mocks.

And suddenly, it shoots straight to my cock.

I've been close. With my hard cock wedged against his flexing, pumping ass, I've fucked Zar's crack. I came on his back while he fucked a very-willing Harvard Economics professor. She was hot and couldn't get enough of our college games.

That should've been my warning then that what Zar and I share is powerful. Women want it, and we want it, too.

But that feels like a lifetime ago.

With Scarlett joining us now, I don't think I could survive that temptation again. I'll definitely kill Zar if he fucks her, and I'll definitely break if I get tempted to fuck his ass, too.

So I control us.

"We each pick something for you to wear." I direct Scarlett

toward the ivory lacquered drawers featuring the finest lingerie, ranging from naughty to nice to role-play to raunch.

"Three outfits in one night?" Scarlett asks.

"No." I pull open a drawer. "Tonight, my stud has earned his turn. Next week, it's mine, and if you're good, you get our third Saturday. Then we'll take turns."

I know what Zar craves. One of his many fantasies. Maybe he's fulfilled this outside of our Saturday nights, but my heart doubts it.

No, I'm sure.

Zar's been waiting—waiting for me, waiting for us to find the perfect woman. His first choice was tragically wrong, but Scarlett feels so right.

So now, how far will we go? What does Zar want with me? I'm not sure. But I know what Scarlett wants, though none of it matters. We get the punishment I deserve—no one gets what they really desire.

I select a soft, tight black pleather teddy. It's cupless and crotchless. Looking like the dominatrix Zar craves, too, Scarlett's exposed breasts and pretty pussy in this will taunt him while I strap him to his cross.

Tonight, I'll teach Scarlett how to whip him. How to make Zar come. It's the hottest sight when his hands and ankles are bound, his chest and thighs red with welts from my flogger, while he stares at my hard cock, exposed for him, and he comes without a touch.

Silently, Zar searches through the finest lingerie collection I've ever seen.

On the circular glass table in the middle of the room, Stacey has a half dozen open black gift boxes with ivory ribbons and silky paper inside, waiting to wrap our selections. She anticipates I'll make a generous purchase, and she's right.

Zar makes a smirking show of setting his selection in a box. It's a red bow teddy to wrap Scarlett like a present I can cut open with my favorite scissors.

He knows me too well.

But it's Scarlett's silent selection that drives me mad. It's beyond perfect. It's a long, sapphire silk nightgown with thin straps and a slit up the thigh. I choke down a moan, imagining how she'll look like an elegant lady, bound by her neck, wrists, and ankles against her metal tower, while I rip that gown apart, reminding her that she's my whore too, teasing her pussy all night long.

We select other items, too.

I ask Stacey to send the box with a black leather saddle and its remote-controlled dildo, just like the one she rode for us, straight to my office this afternoon.

Zar selects two open-mouth ring gags for him and Scarlett to wear for my cock fucking their throats, and I fight back my growl.

Scarlett tempts me, too, smiling while she sets nipple and clit suckers into a box. Those and a glass thruster dildo, designed for one to receive and one to hold the long handle, delivering the pounding pleasure.

My mouth is watering. I almost can't speak. When we're done, we stand in the front parlor of Delta's with bags and boxes to be delivered immediately to my hotel, courtesy of one of Stacey's discreet bodyguards, but I'm past caring.

My cock is hard. So is Zar's. And by the hooded look in Scarlett's eyes, our shopping has her soaked with anticipation.

With all that we can play. With all the kinky options we can explore, courtesy of Delta's, I can keep my grave promise while I satisfy my darkest demands forever.

Our heightened arousal doesn't escape Stacey Evans, either. In the hour we spent shopping, she summoned two of her men. I think her blond man, Luke, serves in the Army. He's not here, but it seems we've inspired a night of play for Stacey, Ford, and Mateo, too.

"Enjoy your night." Mateo offers his hulking hand. He's a gentleman wrapped in a thin white T-shirt, revealing the dark warrior tattoos from his collar to his wrists.

"Thank you." I shake his hand, then Ford's. Zar does the same, while Stacey offers a kiss on Scarlett's cheek that lingers longer than polite. It's sexy, and we all enjoy it.

"Dayum," Zar huffs as the door to Delta's closes behind us, and we step into the mild evening dusk. "Kink is in the air tonight." He sounds thrilled while I hold Scarlett's hand, escorting her down the stairs and back through the iron gate.

I can't fight the semi I'm sporting, and Scarlett's glance has her licking her lips at it.

"When we get back, go to our suite," I tell her. "Put on the leather outfit I bought for our stud. Wear my plug, too. Then get the black leather flogger. The one with red suede straps too, then we'll—"

The phone in my jacket pocket rings with a tone that skyrockets my pulse.

It's Abbey.

"Hello?" I answer her call, knowing something's wrong.

"Gia's sick." Abbey sounds calm. "She threw up at the party, and she's crying. She wants to go home. We're on our way there."

"Bring her to me now!" I quicken my steps. I'll get my car later. "I'll meet you at the door."

It might be a five-star hotel, but The Mercier is my home. I rush there with Scarlett and Zar on my heels, all plans for the night shot because Gia's our focus.

We're only a few minutes, a few blocks away, where I meet Abbey's car, pulling under the porte cochere of The Mercier.

"Baba!" I hear Gia crying from the back seat of Abbey's Range Rover before I can even yank the back door open.

"It's okay, my kóri." I reach for her, unsnapping her from her seat beside her cousin's.

Harper, my niece, looks as distressed as I feel because Gia's covered in vomit. And I don't care, wrapping her in my arms.

"She doesn't have a fever." Abbey rushes to our side, handing Gia's overnight bag to Zar. "She just ate a bunch of junk. They all did. At a kid's birthday party, candy buffets may look fancy for Maren, but it's hell on little tummies."

Gia whimpers in my arms, and I can tell by my hand cupping her sweaty curls that she's not warm; she just feels awful.

"I got her," I assure Abbey, quickly wishing her and Harper goodbye before I rush Gia through the glass and gold doors being held open by our bellhops.

"Scarlett." Gia holds her little hand out for her. "Zar," she pleads, too.

And yes, Gia's my blood. She's my daughter because she needs them as much as I do.

Scarlett

GIA'S LITTLE HAND REACHES FOR MINE, AND I GRAB IT. Her distress pulls me to her, into the hotel with Luca and Zar, too, but something slides up my spine, snapping my gaze to the right.

There.

Down the sidewalk.

That woman standing in dusty rose, trendy joggers, and a matching hoodie watching us is *her*. It's Brooke. Even under a white baseball cap, I can spot her anywhere.

But I don't have time. I cover my mark.

Because she's more than my job.

Gia is mine. This feels like my life now while I follow Luca calmly striding through his fancy lobby with his daughter in his arms.

Stares follow us. Whispers, too. They're not disapproving. They're admiring. So am I. The sight of the towering, stern Luca as a tender, protective dad, too, is one to behold.

We halt at the elevator, and he cradles Gia's head against his chest.

Wade and Jameson stand at the new Lobby Lift podium. They're changing shifts while I nod, getting their attention while trying not to raise Gia's.

"Outside," I snarl, and Jameson immediately reads my eyes, dashing as fast as he can without drawing attention to try to catch Brooke. Though I doubt it. She's probably already gone.

"Is Miss Mercier, okay?" But Wade keeps his post, reading the situation in Luca's arms.

"She'll be okay. Thank you." Luca's polite to him.

The elevator doors *ding* open. Several hotel guests dressed to the nines step out before we step in.

Once it's just the four of us, I enter the code for the penthouse, and Luca softens. "My kóri, how's your tummy?"

"Yucky," she replies, mumbling against his chest. "I threw up gummy bears on Ms. Maren's carpet. French fries, too."

"Atta girl." Zar gently pats her back. "That place needed some decorating."

I bite back my laugh. So does Luca.

The doors to the penthouse slide open, and Gia warns. "*Babaaa*...I feel yucky again."

"Okay." Luca quickly enters the code to the front door and rushes her in his arms down the hall to his bathroom.

"I got the crackers and Gatorade," Zar announces, walking toward the kitchen.

"I'll get her some fresh clothes." I know what to do, too. Twice, a stomach bug went through my sisters and me when I was growing up.

In Gia's bedroom, I search her dresser until I find her pajamas. I grab her favorite dinosaur set before I notice the framed photos on her dresser.

There's a picture of Darby, beautiful and pregnant with Luca caressing her belly. A photo of Darby holding Gia. They're in the kitchen here, and Darby's laughing at Gia's smiling face, which is covered in green baby food. Then there's a professional photo. It was taken on the beach with Luca holding an infant, Gia, and Darby kissing her downy curls.

Tears bite at my eyes, but it's not jealousy. I can't imagine the pain. The grief. Everything that Luca had and lost. It swells my heart with patience and compassion.

He needs time.

But when I work my way to his bathroom...

HOLY SHIT...

I need to remember to breathe.

Luca's stripped down to his black boxer briefs. He's drenched and kneeling in his shower with Gia, a pile of her soiled clothes beside them, while he gently washes her hair, getting the gummy bear bits out of it.

His onyx hair drips, hanging in strands over his eyes, but his only focus is his daughter. Her small hand clings to his big bicep while his carved muscles tense with concern, carefully wiping her cheeks clean.

"Baba," she cries, "I don't wanna be sick again."

"It's okay," he soothes, his big body shielding her tiny one from the pelting water. "You have it all out of you. You'll feel better now."

It's the sexiest, hottest, most tender sight I've ever seen, and my ovaries burst.

I'll wait a million years to make that man mine.

When Luca catches me, standing with my jaw on the floor, he grins. Like sheepishly, and *who is this man?* And can I grow old and gray with him, please? Can I have ten of his babies, too? My pussy can take it, I promise, because my heart knows Luca is the father everyone dreams about.

Before he left, my dad was good, but Luca is great. He'd do anything for Gia. Luca keeps his promises, for better or for worse, and for my sake, at least it means he'll never leave.

He turns the shower off, and I hand him Gia's unicorn-hooded bath towel from the towel bar before passing him a plush white one. He secures it around his tan Adonis belt, making my mouth water, before he carefully wraps Gia like the cutest burrito, scooping her up.

And there bursts my backup pair of ovaries.

I didn't know I had them until now.

"Let Scarlett get you dressed," he eases, "while I put on my pajamas, too."

Quickly, Gia reaches for me, and my heart leaps, taking her into my arms. "Will you spend the night?" she immediately asks, and I don't know how to answer.

Gently, Luca gazes down at me through his dripping onyx strands, sharing, "Celine *is* off this weekend. I could use the help."

"Zar, too." Gia looks over my shoulder, and Zar stands in the bathroom doorway with crackers and Gatorade in hand.

"Let's do a sleepover," Zar insists. "Since Gia didn't get hers with her cousin, let's all put on our PJs, watch *Moana*, and snuggle in bed."

What progressive version of Full House *am I living in?*

I thought Zar didn't do families and picket fences. I stare at him wide-eyed, not recognizing him because he's not full of mischief. Nope, he makes it sound perfectly wholesome and normal.

"Please," Gia softly begs, squirming in my arms. "We can all sleep in Baba's bed."

What the...?

"Ahem." Luca clears his throat. "I don't know if that will work."

"We'll make it work." Zar's not a sub tonight. He's taking charge, and I don't fight him because this suddenly feels natural to me, too.

First, I stand Gia on Luca's bed and get her dried off and in her pajamas while Luca gets dressed in his closet. Then, Zar feeds Gia a tablespoon of Gatorade before offering her one Saltine.

"My girl gets a cracker and a tablespoon every fifteen minutes," he soothes, and Gia gently chomps the cracker, trusting his care.

And I marvel, "When did you get so domestic?"

Zar cocks a grin. "My mom was a pediatrician with three sons. I was always her nurse with my little brothers."

Does Zar burst my ovaries like Luca? No. But he warms my heart. He makes this cozy and easy.

Once Luca gets settled in bed, resting with Gia in the crook of his arm, under the covers, he clicks on the flatscreen while he tells me, "In my dresser in the closet, second drawer from the top, are my T-shirts that'll fit you like a nightgown."

Zar disappears to go to his suite for his pajamas, while with his permission, I wander into Luca's custom closet, admiring the neat rows of black, gray, and dark blue suits. Under them hang rows of starched white shirts, swaying over polished fancy men's shoes. It's pristine in here. And it smells like Luca: citrus and cypress.

I don't recognize the bottle of cologne on the gold tray on his dresser. It's written in Greek, but I lift the bottle to my nose and inhale him, noticing the framed photos on his dresser, too.

There's an older picture of his parents' wedding. A picture of Luca as a cute boy, sitting in a blue rowboat, probably in Greece. There's a picture of him, Zar, and Darby. It looks like a selfie he took while they're laughing, lying in a pile of autumn leaves. Then there's the same photo Gia has on her dresser—Luca holding her while Darby kisses her daughter's head.

Still, jealousy doesn't find me.

No, I'm full of hope.

That could be us.

All of us.

I just have to wait.

Grabbing a gray, weathered HARVARD t-shirt from the neat stack I find in his drawer, I grin. It's like the last time Luca bought activewear was in college, and it's pretty adorable.

I take off my dress and bra, draping them neatly over a velvet hanger in his closet. I get a warm fuzzy feeling hanging my dress next to Luca's suit before I take my hair clip out, the one Luca gave me, and set it on his dresser.

When I emerge from his closet in his T-shirt skimming my thighs, Gia's eyes are glued to the screen, while Luca's crystal eyes are glued to me, crawling with a grin across his bed.

"My god, my belle," he murmurs, watching me nestle on the other side of Gia.

Minutes later, Zar returns to the bedroom with a tray loaded with snacks: more crackers, Gatorade, banana slices for Gia, popcorn for us, and whisky, too.

But what amuses me is the Harvard joggers Zar sports like PJs. They match Luca's. Both wear thin, V-neck white T-shirts, too.

"What did y'all do?" I tuck the covers around my legs. "Raid the Harvard gift shop when you went there?"

"Yep." Zar flops down on the foot of the bed. "Euro snob here didn't own sweats until I made him buy some."

Luca grins while I watch in awe at how Zar comfortably props up on his elbow, resting by our feet. Pulling the blanket at the foot of the bed over him, he forms a cozy nest of our bodies, surrounding Gia with the headboard at the top.

Gia alternates between snuggling with me and Luca and crawling down to snack off the tray Zar brought us, letting him feed her tablespoons to stay hydrated. After her full day, she's subdued tonight, seeming as content as I feel.

Though I keep catching Luca watching me with a look so intense, it sets butterflies alight in my chest, fluttering through my body.

HIF #14: I'm almost afraid to believe this bliss. This future. No way can my life be this perfect.

I have fleeting childhood memories of a warm family feeling. I was very young. My mom was happy, my dad was there, and my sisters and I were safe.

But that feeling faded in my heart like an old photo.

Now, this rush of love with the four of us together is technicolor, and I pray it will last.

We sip whisky, watching *Moana* as Gia's eyelids droop until they finally close. She's nestled beside Luca. We're all tired, so Zar sets the tray on the floor before resting his head by Luca's feet and draping his feet over mine. Like he's perfectly happy, Zar closes his eyes while Luca tells Alexa to turn off the lights.

Darkness gently falls over his bedroom, but I can still see Luca with the dim city lights streaming through the white sheers.

Gia's fallen asleep between us, but Luca's awake. Silently, he reaches over, his fingertips gently brushing a lock of my hair off my cheek.

Surrendering on my side, I let him do it. I let Luca make me fall helplessly in love with him. With *us*. There's no turning back. I don't want any other life.

I let him caress my cheek until I have to close my eyes at the tender flutter in my heart, making happy tears well in my eyes.

I love Saturday nights like this, too.

𝓜

SLEEP MUST'VE CLAIMED ME. I awake a couple of hours later, I guess, with my bladder talking to me.

Carefully, I climb out of Luca's bed and quietly pad into his ensuite. I don't turn on the lights. There's a window in here, too; I can see well enough to find the water closet with his porcelain throne. Then I grin because I find it so cute that Luca has kids' flushable wipes in here. After I'm done, I use one, afraid to flush, but I do, hoping I don't wake up...*my family?*

Is that this perfect feeling that has me smiling in the dark?

Yes.

As quietly as possible, I wash my hands in Luca's marble sink and dry them using his white hand towel with a gold *M* monogram.

Oh my god, I even love his bathroom.

If my MMA friends could see me now.

This bitch is getting soft over kids' bath wipes.

But then I turn around, gasping, my fighter's instinct tensing at the towering figure looming in the doorway.

"Shit," I softly gasp. "You scared me."

It's Luca. I'd know his gargantuan silhouette anywhere.

Quietly, he closes the bathroom door behind him. When he locks it, too, I softly gasp again, seeing the shadow of his growing erection hanging heavy in his joggers.

I whisper, "What are you doing?"

Closing the distance between us, he doesn't answer. Reaching over his back, he yanks his T-shirt off, tossing it on the floor before he presses against me, ripping the air from my lungs. I'm trapped between Luca's cool marble vanity and his rock-hard heat.

"I need you." His whisper is gruff. "I need everything about you." Taking my hand, he guides it under the waistband of his joggers. "Do you feel this? How much I fucking need you, Scarlett?"

We're not playing Dom and sub tonight. We're playing desperate, aching need because that's how I feel, too.

Gripping his swollen shaft, I moan at his heft. At how hard and thick Luca gets for me. This is more than sex or kink. It's so powerful between us that it's hard to breathe.

Guiding my hand to stroke him, his other hand wedges his joggers down until they hang from his hips. "Luca," I sigh at his exposure, at his urgent need, at the rush of wet lust I feel for it.

"God, my belle." With his cock, jutting high and demanding between our bodies, together our hands wrap around it, stroking him. He sinks his other hand in my hair, pressing his lips to my forehead. "God, Scarlett, how I fucking need you. All day. All night. I need this life with you. Promise me, my belle."

I need it, too, so I free my hands, quickly yanking my T-shirt off. I stand before him in my black lace panties, and he groans when I lick my palm for him and spit in it, too. Grabbing his thick shaft, I start pumping my slick hand while he guides me again, growling with his swollen cock wedged between our almost naked bodies.

"Scarlett," he grunts, his grip on my hair getting tighter, his breath thinning, rasping against my strands like he's losing his mind. "Fuck, I can't feel this way and be this close to you and not have you," he confesses, gently thrusting his hips in my grasp. "I can't watch you in my life, in my family, in my bed, and not have every inch of you. Always."

It wets my pussy instantly. His passion. His hard cock and body. His ache, so vulnerable. His heart so soft. He desperately needs release, and it's so damn hot to give it to him.

I press my breasts against him, letting him feel my hard nipples urging over his flexing abs. I try to rub every inch of me against him; I can't get enough of him either. His satin skin. His concrete form. His tense need. His wild breath.

"I kept getting hard for you all day." His lips confess, steaming over my scalp. His heat burns through me. "I can't watch you be so goddamn beautiful and perfect for me and not have you. Please." He's dripping for me, so I smear my thumb through his precum, swirling it over his swollen velvet tip, and he shudders. "*Fuckkkk*, Scarlett, I need to be so deep inside you."

"You are, Luca," I sigh back. "You're inside me. Feel this with me."

We can do this. We can imagine everything we can't have together, not yet, but we will one day.

I understand Luca's pain. I'll protect it. I live with that void of losing someone you love, too. You're afraid to open your heart again, so I'll wait for him. I'll make him change. Fate cracks across our flesh whenever we're near; we belong together. He can't keep fighting me.

Pressing his huffing lips to my hair, he gazes down with me at the desperate fervor in our pumping hands, giving him what he's shaking for.

I love it when I make his thighs shake, his lips, too, but I've never seen Luca like this.

He's not a Dom tonight. He's a lonely dad. He's a man who's denied himself for so long, and how it makes me ache because I'm the one he needs.

"I'm yours, Luca." I give him everything. I grab him and our future, and I take it so hard I make him grunt, lurching forward about to release. "You have my body to torture. You have my pussy that's so wet for you." I'm watching. He's watching. He's panting, thrusting for it, and I give it to him. "You have my heart, Luca."

"Scarlett," he grunts before silence falls over him. His body locks while he growls back his roar, barely letting go with a deep, urging groan from his throat before he spurts, drops hitting my chin, my breasts too, but I keep giving. I squeeze, pumping more of his breath away, and he quakes, moaning and spilling over our fists, coating my hand with his cum.

He drags in three deep, ragged breaths before he grabs my drizzled hand and demands, "Take me, Belle." Quickly, he shoves our cum-coated hands over my pussy. "Put my cum inside you," he demands. "Now."

With his sticky hand cupping mine, he guides my fingers to plunge inside my slick heat. Pressing his palm over my hand, his grinding force gives my clit the pleasure it's aching for.

Urging his hard body against mine, splattered in his cum, this is so erotic and beautiful. I gaze up at him, the shadows falling over Luca's exquisite face, his eyes searching mine, and his full lips still shaking with desire. His cock hasn't fallen soft yet, but I'm going fast.

I want Luca too much.

I need Luca too much.

My clit is electric. My pussy starts clenching, but my fingers aren't enough. I'm pumping two inside me and aching for more of him. *So much more.* So I hang on to the promise in his eyes, to the dream I want so badly with him, and that takes me over the edge.

"Luca," I moan, trying to be quiet while I fall into a million pieces, coming over our hands. My thighs shake. They get weak. But I'm pressed between the vanity and him so I don't fall.

Well, my heart does. She falls to the bottom of his ocean.

Because Luca gently lifts my glistening hand in his, pressing it over his pounding heart. Mine is, too, while he whispers in my hair, "You know the word for this, Scarlett. The word I feel for you. The one word I wish I could say."

Then he lets go of my hair with his other hand, wrapping his arm around me and holding me tight, cleaving my body to his, my head on his hard chest while I fight back my soft tears.

I feel every word between us.

Ache. Passion. Pain. Happiness. Hurt. Peace. Fate. Family. Lust.

Love.

Scarlett

CHAPTER NINETEEN

How can someone smirk and eat shrimp 'n grits at the same time? I don't know, but my sister, Ruby, sure has mastered the skill.

She blew up my phone this morning with texts. It's like she could sense my life was in danger of love.

Luca couldn't ignore the buzzing of my phone, charging on his nightstand, so when I assured him it was just my sister, he insisted, "Invite her to brunch with us. I'd love to meet her."

I warned him that's like inviting a lit red flare into a fireworks store, but he didn't listen.

"So tell us some stories." Zar sounds too thrilled, bantering with my sister across from him. Our family brunch is different today. Celine's not here, and Abbey and Harper aren't here either. Harper's tummy is still sour from yesterday's party. "Tell us how many boys in the neighborhood Scarlett beat up."

I shake my head while Ruby laughs. "She's not always like that. Sometimes she'd do the craziest things to make us laugh like—"

"Please don't." I'm afraid of what's about to fly out of Ruby's unfiltered mouth.

"Please do," Luca gently commands, smiling with his arm draped over Gia's chair on my left.

The way he gently caresses his fingertips over my shoulder, too, keeps our connection from last night.

I've never seen Luca this happy for so many hours. He's been smiling all morning, so forget kinky toys and collars. Happy family Luca dominates me the most.

"Well," Ruby looks like a shaken soda bottle about to burst, "she liked to do this thing with tissues and the fan by our bed."

"Oh shit," I quietly groan, then wince, remembering Gia's beside me.

"She'd shred tissues into strips, shove them up her nose, and let them flutter in the breeze." Ruby chuckles. "She called it the 'booger dance' just to make me and my sisters laugh."

Gia giggles, Luca laughs, and Zar drawls, intrigued, "There's *more* of y'all?"

I elbow him. "Don't even. Or you'll find your neck in a ninja choke."

"Yeah," Ruby replies, "there are four of us, and Scarlett was the ring leader. She'd do anything to make us laugh. She can do the best armpit farts in the world."

HIF #15: Kill me now. I'm trying to be all elegant and shit while my little sister slays with stories of my Body Part Art.

"I want to hear *that*." Luca shocks me. He's too relaxed around my sister and amused by what I'll do for him when hell freezes over.

"What's an armpit fart?" Gia's curious, too.

"Scarlett will show us," Luca taunts.

I'm about to flatly refuse at the risk of death by embarrassment, but a new plan forms—one I'd never imagine—one that would be the most hilarious and dangerously tender moment *ever*.

"Alright." I confront Luca with a grin. "I'll show Gia an armpit fart if you do it, too."

Peels of laughter bubble up Gia's throat. "Yeah, Baba!" She's too excited. "Fart with Scarlett!"

I double over, laughing so hard I'm crying. We all are because this is too ridiculous. This is too much fun and like family, and I love it.

Ruby shares more mortifying stories at my expense while Luca caresses the strands falling over my shoulder. He lets anyone witness his quiet affection for me, including Ruby, who turns her focus on Zar. It's like she wants to solve the whole puzzle of our arrangement.

"So, Zar," she probes, "where do *you* live?"

"I have a suite on the fifth floor," he beams. "I have a paltry view of the harbor and a place on the Isle of Palms, too. Just a little fishin' shack."

He teases Ruby because we all know there are no shacks on the Isle of Palms. Every square foot on that coastal island is worth thousands.

"Uh-huh." Ruby smirks. "That's a shack of B.S."

I can tell Zar's admiring Ruby. She sits across from him, wearing a burgundy wrap dress, with her auburn hair piled high on her head with tendrils falling. She licks her glossed lips because Zar has that effect, Luca even more so. And I don't blame my sister. Window shopping is allowed.

"Baba," Gia asks, "what's B.S.?"

"B.S. is..." Luca searches for an appropriate answer.

So Ruby jumps in. "B.S. is beach sand."

Zar snorts, setting his linen napkin on the table. "Yes, my girl." He leans over me, pulling Gia's attention to his smiling face. "I'm full of *beach sand*."

His answer knits Gia's brows. The adult banter confuses her, so I quickly suggest, "How about after brunch I'll take you to meet Crimson, my puppy?"

Then I flinch, realizing I should've asked Luca first. I'm not her parent. I can't take her for the day. I'm her protection officer, and her...*what*?

I don't know because that fell from my lips too easily. I just want to take care of Gia.

"Is that okay?" I ask Luca. "Would you like to come with us?"

I glance around the table. "Everyone? We can go to the aquarium, too."

"Yay!" Gia bounces in her seat. She's feeling much better today.

"I'd love it." The heat in Luca's eyes answering me makes global warming even worse.

"I can't," Ruby sighs. "I promised Rose that me and Cherry would help paint her new condo. The shi—" She catches her curse. "The *stuff* I do for my sisters."

"I can't *wait* to meet them." Zar sounds flirty, playful...and kidding.

Though I'm not. I'll kill Zar if he fucks with my sister's, too. But he'd never cross that line. He wouldn't hurt me that way. My sisters are off-limits, he knows.

But other women? I'm not sure.

I know Luca's committed to me. I know he means it; I'm the only woman he wants. Even if he won't share everything with me, I'll be here when he finally breaks.

But with Zar?

Untethered is the feeling I get with him. Like no matter how Zar submits when he chooses to, you can't tie him down. Not forever. He won't allow it.

Proving my point, Zar leans back in his chair. "I can't go. I have work. We have a private event. A VIP has rented out the King's Club for the game tonight."

"Game?" I scoff. Since when does Zar's job as the CFO have him managing special events? "What *game?*"

"Sunday night football," he huffs like I should know. "Atlanta versus Arizona."

Still, I'm confused, so I glance at Luca, reading his expression. He's searching Zar's eyes for an answer, too, but Luca's not scowling about it. The silent words they exchange are intense but calm like they're confident in what they share.

"Football?" Ruby perks up. "Do you need a *cock*tail waitress to help?"

"Maybe," Zar drawls. "The VIP is a Carolina Panther out on injury. He's home this weekend, watching a game with his boys."

"Since when are you into football?" I pry.

Mischief lights up Zar's deep brown eyes. "I'm *not*," he goads. "I'm just curious about our VIP guest."

What is he up to?

It sounds like Zar's serious. Like he's trying to make Luca... *jealous*? And with another man? An NFL player? And since when are NFL players out as anything but straight? And if one isn't, how would Zar know?

I swear, the mysteries surrounding Zar and Luca keep haunting me. Yes, we're getting close. Yes, we snuggle like a family, watching movies in bed. But yes, when Zar is free, he's up to something. And yes, Luca can share so much with me, but it's not everything.

I want more.

Including answers.

Two hours later, Luca's propped beside me on the grass, his legs stretched before him, while we watch Gia play "dog trainer" to Crimson.

Families spill out of the aquarium. Tourists too. It's a bright, crisp late November afternoon with the sun warming us in the park.

Gia commands, "Sit!" and Crimson patiently plays along. I hold the handle of his long leash securely in my left hand, propped behind me. Then my heart flutters when I feel Luca's fingertips gently caress my right hand beside his in the grass, hidden so Gia can't see our intimate exchange.

"I love this," he mutters. "Thank you for inviting us."

Gia looks happy with Crimson. She's so enthralled she can't hear me ask him, "Will you get her a puppy now? You know she's going to wear you down."

His chuckle is deep. "*We* have years to wait."

We? Years? Wait?

Is he talking about Gia and a puppy? Me and him? Or all three of us? Or four of us?

"So," I ask, "what's going on with Zar?"

"I allow him to explore." He states it so calmly, I'm shocked.

"But," I blurt, "he's with *us*."

"*Yes*," Luca soothes, "he *is*."

"So, why did he make it sound like he's on the hunt? Like he wants to score an NFL player, too?"

"Because he can."

Luca sounds too Dom, too confident about our relationships, but I'm not. I sit up. I want answers but don't take my eyes off Gia, so I ask over my shoulder. "And that doesn't bother you?"

"No," he answers. "I know he's mine, but he needs more." His tone lowers. "Does it bother *you*?"

"Yes," I stammer. "I mean, sorta. I thought we were a family now—the four of us: me, you, Gia, and Zar."

"We *are*," he insists.

"But then, why is Zar allowed to leave us?"

And why is my heart clenching? Why am I grabbing at something right in my hand? We had last night together. We'll have next Saturday, too. Why am I suddenly feeling like I'll lose this?

Luca sits up—the warmth of his big hand presses into the small of my back. Gia can't see it, but I sure feel it.

"He's not leaving us," Luca assures, "and I'm not leaving you. I know you have scars from your father, my belle, but we will never hurt you. We're yours, and you're ours. I'll make sure of it."

"But..." I stutter, my thoughts tripping over past pain. "What if Zar finds someone else?"

Luca doesn't answer at first. Gia's distant giggles fill the air before he replies, "Maybe he should. I want him to be happy. I have you now, so he should have someone, too."

"But you and Zar have each other, too. You've been together for so long. Aren't you worried you'll lose him?"

Silence falls over our dilemma.

"Shake!" Gia kneels before Crimson, gently tugging at his paw, and he lifts it. "Good boy!" She's so cute. I can't bear to lose her, Luca, and what I'm finally loving.

"Listen to me, Belle." Luca's voice nears my ear. "I'm his Dom.

I always will be, and that means I serve him, too. So, when I can't give him *everything* he needs, I want him to find it with someone else. That's what he's searching for, and that's how much I love him. I owe him."

"Why do you owe him?"

"Because," his voice gets gruff, "I wouldn't let him have what he needed before, and it hurt him. He suffered for years, and I did, too. I'm not making the same mistake. He deserves what he needs."

Words can't find me, though I think I understand.

This has something to do with Darby. With whatever Luca and Zar were fighting about that night on the beach. The night Abbey told me about. The night Darby was killed. Or died? Or had an accident?

What exactly happened, I don't know.

But I've had this feeling since this all began that I'm the first for Luca, I'm his primary...*whatever*...and Zar is second. And not once has Zar seemed upset by it.

No, it's like it's what Zar needs. He needs freedom. He needs Luca to be okay. He needs Gia to be happy. But Zar also needs something Luca's not willing to give.

Will I be the same?

The question hangs heavy in the light autumn air.

"Baba, watch!" Gia circles her finger like I taught her. "Roll over!" She commands Crimson, and he does it with a doggy grin.

"Good job!" Luca praises her. "Now give him a treat. Reward him."

Gia walks over and takes the dog treat I pluck from my waist pouch when I walk Crimson. She returns, gingerly offering it, giggling when his muzzle tickles her palm. Then, she goes back to more rounds of "sits" and "shakes" while my silence must trouble Luca.

"Please tell me, Scarlett," he rumbles low, almost tender by my ear. "Tell me I give you what you need. I give you my world. I give you my family and every dollar I have and pleasure I can. I promise. I want you to be happy, too, but you're *not* Zar. You're more than my sub. I will never share your heart with anyone else because...you have mine."

Last night, he didn't say it, but we felt it—love.

So, I let him see me nod. I let him reach for my hand and squeeze it tight. I let him gently peck my cheek and make my heart accept it.

I may not have the love I need, but Luca gives me the love I want. The love I've never had before, though he may never say it. I don't need him to.

I need him to show it.

It feels more than good enough as we stroll with Gia back down the walkway, heading toward my condo building. It's a short walk, a half-block, while I let Gia hold Crimson's leash and I guide her shoulder.

But instinct has me suddenly squeezing her tighter, protecting her, because...I sense it...the tingling up my spine, raising hairs on my neck.

Someone's stalking behind us.

And I know exactly who she is.

"Take Gia into my condo," I whisper to Luca. "You know my code. Take her and Crimson inside and secure the door."

Luca protests, "But—"

"Don't make a scene," I mutter. "Brooke's behind us, and that's exactly what she wants. Just take Gia into my building. You can secure her there and wait for me."

I glance and catch Luca clenching his jaw. He wants to turn around and fight Brooke, but he trusts me. We're a team effort; he trusts me to do as I'm trained.

I walk with him and Gia up to the entrance of my building, my muscles tensing, knowing Brooke's lingering feet behind us on the public walkway along the river's edge.

I wait until Luca's entered my code, the glass door swinging open to my building's lobby. Gia and Crimson bound inside, excited, while Luca ushers her safely in.

Yes, Luca has the size and skills and ferocity to kill for his daughter. There's no doubt. But he can't protect her and chase down a threat at the same time.

That's my job.

Once the lobby door latches closed behind him and I know they're secure, I whip around so fast that Brooke's startled. She's wearing the same dusty rose jogging set from yesterday and the same white hat like she didn't go home. She's been stalking, waiting for us to leave the hotel, and her eyes widen with shock that I'm not running *from* her.

No.

Here I come, bitch.

The squeal she lets out is almost comical, but she's fast. And she has the advantage. She turns and knows where she's going.

Racing through the tourists and locals crowding the popular destination, Brooke weaves through them, but I'm on her heels.

I'm not armed with a gun and don't need one. Because I swear, once I get my hands on her, I have plenty of ammo. All that Luca's PIs and HGR Security have dug up on Brooke, her husband, and their kinky judge friends. I'm locked and loaded once I catch her.

Like any obsessed stalker, she's not thinking. Brooke is ruled by impulse. She races up the block, making a foolish mistake because I know where she's going. I slow down because she's headed back to The Mercier like she can't stop herself. Like she's drawn to Luca, not logic.

We have a protective order against her. Once she's on the hotel's property, she violates it but doesn't seem to care.

Darting down the side street beside Luca's hotel, she aims for the parking garage entrance, running right past the barrier arm and up the first ramp, but she doesn't even make it inside her car.

Scrambling for her keys, she gives me vital seconds to catch up to her. With a fearless leap like I'm back in the fighting cage, I'm on her. Clamping down on the back of her neck, I slam her skull down on the hood of her white Mercedes. We both get bruised by the crash, and I fucking love the pain.

"Bless your heart," I hiss, shaking her neck. "You should've listened, Brooke. Don't fuck with what's mine."

She laughs manically, her face smashed against metal. "He's *not* yours, and you know it."

I could debate her, but I don't...because deep down...she's right.

The fact makes me rage. With my free hand, I torque her arm, pinning her wrist against her back with enough painful pressure while I kick her legs apart. When she jerks, trying to resist, I crack her finger in my grasp, threatening her bones with a break, and she cries out.

"Hush," I tell her. "Fight me, and there's more pain where this comes from."

Torturing her hand, I let go of her neck while I reach in my pack for my phone. The screen scans my face, and with a quick tap across it, I send the distress beacon through my HGR app. Whoever's on duty in the hotel lobby will be here in a minute.

"You can play house with him all you want," Brooke taunts. "His girl may love you and your mutt, but Luca loves *me*. I saw it in his eyes."

"Uh-huh," I huff. "Seems there are lots of men who love you, Brooke. Your husband. Judge Culter. Judge Anson. Judge Williams. You've been very public with your pony play." She stiffens, and I smirk. "Bitch, I ain't judging your kink. But take it inside because we have drone footage that caught your last outdoor breeding in the paddock of your husband's ranch, and I'm impressed. I don't mind a riding crop, either, but I draw the line at wearing a saddle for men to ride. But at least it covered that tacky tattoo above your ass."

"You wouldn't," she fumes.

"Oh, I *am*." I dig my elbow deeper into her spine. "Those judges' wives and their congregations don't know how they like to breed you like a filly twice a month, but I'll be happy to share the gospel truth with everyone unless they lock you away."

"Don't," she snivels. "Please."

"Too late," I growl. "I'm warning you. You need help. You

need to spend a few months behind bars to get it through your obsessed skull—stay away from Luca and his daughter. *Forever.* Or I'll be your death sentence. I'll be the accidental slip and fall in the night that cracks your neck."

The pounding of steps, running across pavement, turns my head.

It's Wade. He's running up the ramp our way while the distant wail of approaching sirens fills the air.

"Neigh," I hiss in Brooke's ear, "if you think I'm fucking bluffing."

CONSIDERING CHARLIE'S QUESTION, Luca taps his gold pen on the boardroom table.

It's Monday morning. Gia's safely at school. Brooke is behind bars, for months at least, and my boss has called this necessary meeting.

"Mr. Mercier?" Charlie asks from the intercom at the center of Luca's table. "Do you need more time, or are you prepared to decide now?" Luca looks at me with an intensity that burns while she asks, "Do you want Ms. Jones to remain on her assignment though the threat to you and your daughter has been temporarily eliminated?"

I purse my lips, anxious for his answer.

Luca was consumed with rage yesterday once he safely returned to his hotel with Gia. Then, he was relieved when he found out I caught Brooke...for now.

Then, once Gia was asleep, he held me so tight in his kitchen, overwhelmed with gratitude. "Forever, my belle," he murmured into my hair. "Forever I am indebted to you."

His embrace, his need, his body against mine—it was overwhelming—and his restraint, too. I couldn't take it. I needed Luca so badly right then that I had to go home.

Yesterday evening, Jameson followed up with several surprise appearances at three judges' homes, showing them drone footage photos, assuring their compliance. Brooke will be sentenced to almost a year in prison, so now what?

Is it over?

I don't want to leave Luca and Gia.

But if Luca is no longer my client, I won't be breaking the Red Rule. But it will break my heart if I can't see him and Gia almost every day.

"In your assessment," Luca asks Charlie. She can't come to an in-person meeting or do a video chat. She's home, feeding her month-old son. "Are all threats eliminated?"

Charlie's sigh is audible.

I sit between Jameson and Wade, as HGR staff on one side of the conference table, while Luca and Zar sit across from us, waiting for Charlie's opinion. She's had so much experience with this, we trust it.

"You're a handsome billionaire who's very lucrative for the paparazzi." Charlie doesn't bullshit. "Too many people target you. You couldn't live a safe and secret life even if you tried."

At the mention of a "secret life," Luca's burning stare flicks back to mine. I know what he fights to keep safe—Gia and his public life as her widower father, and me and Zar in his secret life as our Dom.

Will he ever be free?

I feel bad for Luca. Has he ever known a life where he isn't being someone for everyone else? An heir and loyal son. A young CEO. A faithful husband. A dedicated father. A devoted friend.

That's why his Dom side keeps him sane. It's just for him, and I understand. Only with Zar and me can he be himself. Though a ghost keeps him starved for true freedom.

That's why he answers Charlie, "Ms. Jones stays. We need her."

Jameson doesn't miss the quiet sigh of relief from my lungs. He sits beside me, nudging my foot under the table.

"I'll stay instead," Jameson offers. "Ms. Jones is rare. I'm sure she's needed on another detail, so I can cover the mark. Your daughter is comfortable with me now."

Luca silently seethes, fury dripping from his smirk. I'm glad Charlie's not here to witness it. She'd catch on immediately. Jameson's trying to protect my job. He knows what's going on.

"No," Luca cooly replies. "Gia's most comfortable with Ms. Jones. *She* stays."

Wade clears his throat. He asserts his seniority. "Yes, Ms. Jones is an exemplary Protection Officer, but she can't stay forever." Wade knows, too. He long ago figured us out. He's warning me from his heart, "Something will change one day. Best prepare for it."

I chew my bottom lip, afraid of the questions in my heart.

Who will change? Me? Because my heart can only fight for Luca for so long. Or Luca? Because he'll finally bury his guilt.

"It'll be fine," Zar assures with his warm gaze on me. "We'll make it work, and it will for a long time."

Is he talking about my job or our family with Luca and Gia?

I don't know what Zar did last night, but he found the time to text me dozens of "badass bitch" memes once he found out about Brooke.

"It's settled then," Charlie announces. "Unless you object otherwise, Ms. Jones, are you willing to stay on your detail?"

My eyes anchor to Luca's crystal gaze, and I don't care if my colleagues can tell. He doesn't, either. Deep shadows fall over Luca's face, and they're not sexy Dom ones. They're the shadows of a man who's lost so much and needs me now.

So I answer Charlie and his waiting eyes.

"I'm very willing."

Luca

CHAPTER TWENTY

NEW EMOTIONS STORM THROUGH ME.

Not that I'm a dick, I've just never felt this much esteem for a woman: this much attraction and awe at the same time.

I'd rip someone's throat out if they hurt my daughter, and now I've found a woman who's the same, a woman who's my true match. I felt it the moment we met, and now Scarlett's proven it.

After Gia went to bed last night, I needed to hold Scarlett, unwilling to let her go. She didn't even know she had a small bruise welling on her cheekbone. She got it, tackling Brooke, slamming her against the hood of a car. I watched the video, shocked by how it hit my heart and hardened my cock, too.

My need for Scarlett feels dangerous.

I didn't get my dark Saturday night with her. I didn't get my tender night with her either. After holding her for so long, she left, and I understand why.

We're both fighting what we want so much, but I'm not fighting this...

In front of her colleague, Jameson, the one trying to cockblock Scarlett from staying, I demand, "Ms. Jones, meet Mr. Rollins and me in my office. We need to *come* to a new agreement over terms."

Charlie, her boss, ended our call minutes ago. Wade, Scarlett's mentor, just left, but Jameson loiters, eyeing Zar and me like he doesn't trust us with Scarlett.

And he shouldn't.

Scarlett chews her petal lip. She knows my tone. It's the same one I use when I have her bound by the neck.

"I'll join you." But Jameson's got balls. I size him up. He'd put up a helluva fight. He insists, "I'll always backup Ms. Jones."

But he's no match for my power. For the dark sea raging inside me. My smirk is evil. My directive clear. "You will leave. *I* have Ms. Jones's back. Now and forever. Every part of her works for me. *Not. You.*"

I glance to my left, and Zar smirks at him.

Fuck, how I want Jameson to watch what I'm about to do with Scarlett, how Zar will serve my demands, too.

"I'm not your fucking whipping boy." But Jameson's on to us. "And she's not your bitch. Take your pain out on someone else."

His nostrils flare, but I see right through him. "Oh, but secretly, you'd love my pain. You'd love to submit to me, wouldn't you?" My glare can tell. "You'd come so hard while I break you."

"I sure do." Zar's proud. "No one Doms your ass like Luca Mercier. He sure makes Ms. Jones enjoy it many times, too." And no one shames Zar. No one taunts like him, either, not in that deep drawl. "Care to *come* with us, Mr. Grant? Your hard cock won't stop thanking his whip all night long."

"Gentlemen," Scarlett huffs, annoyed, "drop your damn swords. Yes, they're all big and shiny and sharp, and you want to stab shit all night long. We get it. So quit fighting over it." She turns to Jameson, touching his arm. *She'll pay for that.* "I got this," she tells him. "It's *my* job, remember?"

Jameson leans down, too damn close to her, whispering something in her ear, and my molars threaten to crack, red rage veiling my eyes.

"Now!" I roar, and Jameson leers my way.

"Hurt her," he snarls, "and you'll pay."

"Touch her," I vow, "and you'll die."

He leaves with a shake of his head, and Zar chuckles low.

"Fuck, I get so damn hard when you're jealous, even if it ain't over me."

Oh yeah? I aim my fury at him. "Where were you last night?"

The corners of Zar's lips lift, his eyes taunting with thrill at my possessiveness. "Whip my ass, my Owner, and find out."

Oh, these two. They're past due for their punishment and need a nasty dose.

"In my office," I demand. "Now!"

"We have a meeting with South Beach in fifteen minutes." Zar reminds me of our weekly video check-ins with my properties. It's routine, but today sure as fuck isn't.

"I'm well aware," I seethe, my steps eating the ground between my board room, down the hall, and toward my office with Scarlett and Zar on my heels.

"Yay." I hear Zar over my shoulder, teasing Scarlett, "We're in trouble."

He revels in my fury, and I can't fight the grin he gives me and the semi rousing in my pants.

Once we're in my office, I lock the door.

"Pull up our meeting," I command Zar. He knows how to open the laptop on my desk and start the video call.

"Ms. Jones," I turn to find her eyes coquettish, aiming my way, "you're joining us on the call."

"But I'm not on your executive staff."

"Yesterday, you earned a promotion." I stalk her way, my fingertips grabbing the pearl button on her ivory silk blouse and rip it free. Her gasp is soft while I tear open all the ones not tucked into her black skirt before I sweep the silky fabric aside, loving how this hardens my cock.

Yanking the ivory lace of her bra cup down, I let my fingertip graze her hard nipple before I leave her breast exposed. I tease the other one the same way, making her lungs pant at my touch, so I circle her nipple. "What did your former fuckboy whisper to you?"

Control is all I know with Scarlett, but not at the idea of another dick inside her.

No one lives inside her but me.

She pauses before challenging me, "Why do you care?"

Suddenly, I fist her strands, tugging while I lick my lips at how I make her naked breasts heave against my chest. "I fucking care about what I own. I take care of it. I control it. I won't abandon it, so tell me what he fucking said to MY whore."

I know how to crawl into her soul. She does the same to mine, confessing, "He said I deserved more, someone better."

The sudden crash of guilt through my chest breaks something inside me. It's everything I've known and feared. "Is that what you need, Belle? Someone better?"

"No."

"You want him waiting on you?"

"No."

This pain is all too familiar. I won't survive it again. "Do I give you enough? Are you mine, Scarlett?"

"Yes, Luca. I'm yours." Her sapphire eyes fight back. "I'm *waiting* for you. *Only* you."

I press my forehead to hers. I'll never break my vow, but I need to break something. I need her so much.

"Show me, Master." And she understands me. Scarlett pounds through my veins, demanding, "Give me what I deserve."

I pull back, adoring her. She needs to prove it to me as much as I need to feel it with her. Dragging my thumb over her supple bottom lip, I vow, "You deserve to be on your knees for me. You deserve to be my whore for this meeting and forever."

I tug her hand and lead the way.

Zar has taken his usual seat behind my desk. I don't miss his intense stare witnessing our exchange. He deserves more, too, but I'll give him what I can.

My desk is large enough for three people to sit behind it. The camera on my laptop captures the view from our waists up while we recline in our executive chairs.

It's the usual for our weekly property meetings, but I have a new toy under my desk. I usher Scarlett around and point at it. Her eyes get wide, and Zar's eyes dim with lust because he spots it, too. Then I show her the remote for it, the one on my desk, before I slide it into my pants pocket.

"You'll do your job, Ms. Jones. Clasp your hands behind your back." She obeys as I reach inside my jacket pocket, pulling out one of the black silk monogrammed handkerchiefs I always carry. Her eyes question, not sure, so I ask, "What is your job, my whore?"

She grins. She can't be broken. "To serve you, Master." I cock a brow. "And..." she huffs, her nipples hardening even more, and I get a wicked idea, "to come when you make me come, Master. To be your dirty pleasure slut."

"Oh, Ms. Jones." *I'm so full of love and rage.* I pull open the top left drawer of my desk, plucking out two large, golden paper-clips. "You deserve a *big* promotion today."

Lifting my handkerchief to her panting lips, she submits, letting me gently stuff it into her mouth. "Can you breathe?" I make sure, and she nods. "That's for your screams, Ms. Jones. Don't let my staff hear what a sweet little whore you are for me. Do you understand?"

She nods again.

I lift the thick paperclip to her pearled nipple, and she watches. I glance over, and Zar's watching, too. He hasn't pressed the button to start our video meeting. He knows better.

Carefully, I pry open the paperclip and slowly let it close, pinching tight over Scarlett's excited nipple. It makes me lick my lips, my cock soaring in my pants, while her muffled scream fills my heart with joy.

Her lungs start huffing. So, before I pinch her other nipple in this lewd display, I ask, "Did your little fuckboy ever make you feel this good?"

She shakes her head no.

"Did he wet your pussy like I do? Did he make your cum drip down your thighs like I do?"

Again, she shakes her head no.

I hover the other gold clip over her nipple. "Do you like how I use you, my belle? Do you deserve to be my dirty office slut?"

"Umm," she moans with my silk in her mouth, her eyes and chin demanding yes, so I pinch the other one, and she shudders, her flesh blooming before my eyes.

"Lift your skirt for your Master." Because I can't. After touching her nipples, I'm fighting the urge to fuck her so hard. For hours. Letting everyone hear how I make her scream. The paper clips pinching her nipples are driving me mad.

She obeys, wedging her tight skirt to where it's bunched around her waist. "Good girl," I praise. "Now rub your naughty pussy. I know it's wet for me, so soak your panties with your cum." Her fingers follow my command, grinding over her lace-covered clit before I tell her to stop. "Now, take them off and hand them to me."

Quickly, they fall to the floor, and she bends over, stepping out of them, still wearing her heels, before she places her soaked ivory panties in my outstretched palm.

"Now, kneel over your saddle," I command. "Wedge it into your tight little pussy but not all the way. You can't fuck it until I yank your collar."

The lust in Scarlett's eyes is intoxicating. Lowering to her knees, perching over her new saddle between my chair and Zar's, she doesn't take her eyes off of me. She's been trained.

Before I let Zar begin our meeting with Scarlett covertly kneeling between us, hidden by my desk, I taunt him, "Does the sight of my beautiful whore please my stud?"

"Yes, my Owner." His eyes comb over Scarlett with her breasts exposed and jutting out, paper clips blanching her nipples, while her naked, pink pussy hovers over a beige dildo, soaring from a black saddle with her nude legs spread open. It makes him taunt, "Oh, fuck, yes. I like your gorgeous slut."

"Show me," I demand, so Zar drags his zipper down. "Take it out. Show me how much you want to fuck what's mine."

Zar obeys, wresting his curving length out, freeing it from his black boxers. It soars hard and hungry from his navy suit pants, and I lick my lips while Scarlett moans.

I want to know where he was last night. I want to know who he was with if anyone.

Most of me needs Zar to be happy. My heart wants him to be free. But my cock wants to claim him; I never truly have, and it gets so hard at the sight of his arousal. It warms my heart, too. Deep down, Zar's always been mine.

So I drop my zipper, too. Lifting my heavy shaft, I free it for their gaze. The way they stare with starving hunger at my hard cock makes it drip, so I make it worse. I loop Scarlett's panties over my cock, letting them drape around my swollen base.

"Umm," Scarlett moans at her creamy lace wrapped around what she's desperate for.

So, I stroke it for her, scolding, "Shh, my horny, little slut," before I direct Zar, "Begin our meeting."

He clicks the mouse, and on the screen appears a conference table surrounded by my South Beach staff: the General Manager, the Head of HR, the Director of Operations, of Housekeeping, too, and the Front Desk Chief.

"Good morning, Mr. Mercier. Mr. Rollins," Javier, my G.M., greets us, and the meeting proceeds as usual, with each department checking in.

I wait minutes, tapping my gold pen over my notepad while Zar struggles to take notes on his. His exposed cock, hidden by my desk, is so hard it's distracting him.

We need more punishment.

With my right hand, I reach down and tug my jeweled collar on Scarlett's neck. Slowly sinking down the shaft of the dildo, she starts her ride. I glance at her with a grin, and she knows. She obeys. She keeps her eyes on me while I click the remote hidden in my pocket.

The gentle hum of the saddle may be audible to my staff, and I don't care. I can chalk it up to the A/C kicking on.

But it's Scarlett who kicks in. She loves it—*my sweet, beautiful whore.* She makes it harder for me, bracing her hands on the front of the saddle, she presses her arms together, and it juts her tits up even higher, pinched with paperclips, and I can't fight the urge. I reach down and tug on one.

"Ummm." Her muffled moan gets me off.

For minutes, I make her ride her dildo while I don't let go of her paperclip. It pulls her pinched nipple taut, making sweat start to sheen across her chest.

When the front desk chief reports a glitch with our reservation system, I ask, "Mr. Rollins, would you care to add something?"

Zar knows. He leans forward, suggesting a system update through our IT department in Paris while his left hand reaches down, tugging at Scarlett's other nipple.

Her thighs start shaking. Her chin drops. She's fighting her orgasm until I give my command, and she's earned it. My sweet whore has earned everything I can give.

So I let go of her paperclip and yank her collar, almost choking her as she bucks on her saddle, rewarding her pussy with its first orgasm.

While Zar distracts my staff with a droning conversation about seafood and beverage costs, I glimpse Scarlett gazing at me with desperate lust and deep gratitude.

These meetings take thirty minutes to an hour, and I make sure she keeps coming the entire time. I let go of her collar and click the remote in my pocket again, and her eyes jolt with the hum of the saddle whirling into a higher pitch. I can tell she's fighting another orgasm, so I smirk, shaking my head *no* while I stare at my laptop's screen.

"I'm sorry," Javier interjects. "Mr. Mercier, does something displease you?"

He caught my gesture, so I answer, "Not at all. I'm very pleased with this performance. I'm just reflecting on how valuable clams are, but they're worth it. Please continue."

Zar smirks at my clam reference. He can play all day, too, but Scarlett loses her patience. I'm not letting her come, so her left hand reaches, wrapping around Zar's hard cock.

He coughs down a groan, covering his mouth with his fist, his body lurching at her disobedient tug. I squint down, and she's riding her dildo, her milky cum glazing the shaft while her mouth drools over my handkerchief, her nipples screaming with pleasure, but her sapphire eyes challenge me.

Her fist wrapped around my stud's cock, any man's cock, unleashes my wrath. I rip the kerchief from her mouth. Dropping it on the floor, I snake my right hand into her strands, yanking her head down to my lap.

She better fucking serve me.

And she does.

Like she's been craving my cock all along, she starts sucking it like a hungry whore behind my desk, and I try gagging her on it. Relishing how she's trying to be quiet, I don't care if my staff can hear her choking on my dick.

And fuck...her hot, wet, hungry slutty mouth feels so good.

I fight not to roll my eyes while I fist her strands so hard, feeling her drool douse my dick and pants. Yanking her off, I don't look down. I hold her here, staring up at me while I demand, "Alright, team. Good job. Let's wrap this up."

I've heard enough because I'm just getting started.

Scarlett keeps stroking Zar's cock, and his grin is laced with lechery, loving their disobedience while I start fucking her mouth again, impatient for this fucking meeting to end. Her tongue does that thing, laving up the thick, sensitive vein in my shaft before she flicks her tongue over my swollen tip, and I gnash my teeth to keep my moan from escaping.

As soon as we log off the video call, I yank her head back up, glaring down at her. Spit webs from my fat crown to her swollen lips. Mascara weeps from the corners of her eyes, and she's so damn beautiful when I make her cry, choking on my cock.

"My sweet whore," I growl. "Let go of my stud's fucking cock before I strangle you with mine."

She grins, taunting, "Make me."

She has too much fight in her. She believes in our bond too much, and she better because I'm never letting her go.

Proving it, I palm her skull with both hands, her hair like silk ropes pulled in my grasp. With my hips thrusting brutally, I fuck the back of her throat, her slutty *glucking* sounds filling my office and heart. Her fist won't let go of Zar's cock, like she wants to taste my punishment, so I give it to her.

It doesn't take long. I want her too much. Zar watching us with his hard cock fisted in her hand, does something to me, too. "Look at my sweet whore," I jeer with her teary eyes locked on mine, the swelling of my cock maddening. I'm almost there. "Your slutty nipples are pinched for me. Your naughty pussy soaks a dildo with your cum for me. Now, open your dirty mouth for my cum, too."

Her lips part, her drool webbed from them to my tip, and I don't need to jerk my shaft. I just stare down at what's mine, at what I love, and I let go.

"*Fuucckk*," I groan, watching my cum spurt, pooling over her tongue, splattering her cheek, too. "*Belle.*" More releases. I fill her mouth, my heart holding so much back for her—so much control. But now, "Swallow me," I command, and she does it with pride in her eyes.

It overwhelms me. I know Scarlett can fight me, but she doesn't. She wants me. She accepts me. So, I drag her up by the arm, making her grip release Zar's cock. Her shameless, clipped tits bounce while I whip her around, choking her neck with my chest pressed to her back.

"You let my whore stroke you?" I bark at Zar, and he licks his smirking lips with a nod. "Then clean up her cum."

Dropping to his knees, he doesn't hesitate. He leans over, sinking his mouth over the dildo that's still thrusting into empty air. Zar groans, licking Scarlett's milky cream off the phallus while I make her watch him.

"My stud loves my cock in his mouth, doesn't he? He loves tasting your cum on it."

"Yes, Master," she answers for him. "We love your cock. We love your cum in our throat," she adds, and Zar moans his agreement.

"Get up!" I bark at Zar while I bend Scarlett over, pushing her head down, her sexy mop of auburn curls spilling over my desk.

She wants this. She steps her legs apart for it, standing over the saddle she's creamed on, with her perfect face smashed against my white linen files.

And I hold her here.

I hold my heart in my hand.

When I see Scarlett like this, bent over my desk, her pussy splayed open and glistening for me, I need her so much I'm in pain.

From my cock to my heart, I am. Scarlett doesn't know what she means to me. She doesn't know she's second in my heart. That space used to be occupied by a ghost, but now, I feel Scarlett there. Still, my ghost haunts me. I made a promise to her grave, and I can't break it. I fear if I do, I'll be punished again. I'll lose Scarlett, too.

So, I seek Zar's help. He knows how to make me survive. How to satisfy the dark needs I have while I honor a promise that kills me, too.

He's equally enthralled, gazing down at Scarlett's wanton display, staring, too, at how my cock will barely go down. I need this too much.

"Come on *my* whore," I tell him, and with a gratified grin, he starts jerking off. "Come on her wet pussy, while I fuck her tight ass."

Scarlett's moan is shameless, too. I hold her head down while I reach again into my drawer, pulling out another new toy and lowering it to her trapped gaze.

"Do you remember this, my belle?"

It's the glass thruster dildo she selected, and I bought for her at Delta's.

"Yes, Master," she gasps. "Yes, Master," she begs. "Fuck my ass, Luca."

"Spread your cheeks," I snarl. "Spread that ass for my fuck and that pussy for my stud's cum. We're going to make you the sweet, dirty little whore you are for me."

Scarlett arches her back, her palms stretching her sex open for my thrill. She wants this, too, while I relish, for minutes, just watching her submit like this.

"Look at my dirty whore." I keep sighing, praising her, worshipping the sight she fills me with. "Look at how she needs me in her ass and pussy."

It drives her insane with soft mewls, making Zar grunt softly, jerking off to it.

Scarlett starts getting me hard again when I spit over her tiny, puckered pink hole, watching it drizzle down her cunt. Still, I fist her strands. I'll never let go of her while Zar stares, obsessed with our crude spectacle.

Soon, my cock is jutting, swollen again. It's near his tip, aimed at Scarlett's weeping pussy. She drips with my spit and her cum, and as I gently tease the glass tip of the dildo into her tightest hole, her glazed pussy drips even more.

Slowly, I start fucking her ass with the glass shaft, and quickly, Zar gets off on it. "Say it," I command Scarlett.

She can read my soul. "Yes, Luca." She growls, "Fuck my ass. Make me your whore for him to watch."

The way she pleases me, the way Zar's breath thins, his grunts getting shallow, I know his every sound of pleasure and pain. I love it. I live for it. So, I give it to him as I thrust the dildo in and out of Scarlett's pink hole while I ask him, "You want me fucking your ass, too?"

"Yes, my Owner," he finally confesses to me. "Please, fuck my ass."

"Then ache for it and come on my whore." I torture him. "Come on my hard cock, too."

"Oh fuck," Zar groans, his tip spurting creamy ropes across my shaft, splattering Scarlett's open pussy, too. She flinches, in the best way, as he paints her with his warm, pearly cum.

"Yes, my stud," I praise. "Now, be my bad boy, and let me watch you clean up your mess."

Zar drops to his knees while I bury the dildo in Scarlett's ass as deep as I can without hurting her. It's not. I can tell. She's moaning, writhing for it, spreading her cheeks for more.

Pushing the saddle farther under my desk, Zar clears his spot to kneel beneath Scarlett's dripping pussy. He does it, facing me while I stand over them, so I can gaze down at his dick that's not going soft because he's craved this kink for too long, too. Zar loves my cum, my desire, but he's never cleaned it off a pussy before, and this is going to get me off so damn much.

Yes, we've been waiting for this. We've been waiting so long. We've been waiting for her, ma flamme.

Scarlett

CHAPTER TWENTY-ONE

"CLEAN HER," LUCA COMMANDS ZAR, AND I'M ACHING FOR real touch.

So, when the firm tip of Zar's tongue gently laves over my lonely clit, I groan, "Oh my god."

I try silencing my voice, my lips drooling over Luca's files. Paper clips bite at my nipples, pressed against the cool wood of Luca's desk. My legs are spread open in heels, shaking at Luca's relentless fuck of my ass with a glass dildo that's the perfect width, lusciously gliding in and out.

But something about the warmth of Luca's hand, caressing my hair, gently holding my head pinned down on his desk, makes me need this.

I need him.

Everything wrong we do feels so right. That's when you know you've met your soulmate. Because, be it heaven or hell, you belong together.

Nothing feels as right as Luca inside me, as him kissing me and holding me tight. I still remember my awe at the power of our bodies connected. How it made me cry; it made him cry, too. We were destined to be together.

But I trust Luca's promises, which means I can never truly

have him. The ache is killing me, but at least he gives pleasure beyond my wildest fantasies.

I can't believe I'm here, letting myself be held down and degraded by him, and it's heaven.

Zar's lips start sucking my excited clit, his warm tongue laving through my sticky lips, and Luca starts to growl.

"Fuck yes," he praises us. "Look at my stud," he groans. "That's it," he taunts Zar. "Lick your cum off my whore's pussy; she loves being used." He tugs at my hair. "Don't you?"

"Yes, Master." It's so true.

Luca thrusts the dildo faster into my ass, and stars start shooting across my vision, the brutal pounding shaking my thighs. Zar's tenderly sucking my clit, and my next orgasm is building so high and fast.

"Oh, my whore needs to come." Luca coaxes, "Doesn't she? Say it."

"Yes, Master. Please," I pant. "I want to come with your cock fucking my ass and your mouth licking your cum off my pussy, please."

I understand Luca. I know what he needs to hear. That every pleasure I receive is from him, and it's my truth.

Zar may kneel between my legs, but I'm Luca's. Every inch of my flesh belongs to him. I come for him. I fall apart and wake again, only for him.

The thrusting stops. It leaves my body trembling before Luca guides my hand to grab the base of the glass dildo. "Fuck your ass for me, my belle." His accent changes. He sounds gruff and pained with lust. "Fuck your ass for me to watch while I come on it for my stud to devour." He smacks my buttock hard, making me jump. "And once your pretty pussy is dripping with my cum, I'll let my whore come, too."

I moan. I obey. I shudder. Watching him over my shoulder, I slowly plunge the dildo in and out for Luca to relish, and he's obsessed. He's hot as hell watching me degrade myself for him, fuck myself for him. So, I make it hotter and harder for him.

"Look at my ass gape for you, Master." I pull the dildo out, the exposure to *only* him thrilling me. "Do you see? I'm yours. I'm so open for you, Luca. I'm waiting for your cock to fill me with your cum."

"Fuck, Belle," he groans.

It's the truth, and it torments us. But I see him cracking, his eyes bewitched and unable to resist me. His fist starts jerking his gorgeous swollen cock so fast, and Zar's moan fills the room.

I suspect they've never done this with a woman, and we'll all lose our minds to it. It'll bind us even more, so I start thrusting the dildo faster, making Luca grunt while Zar's tongue flicks across my clit, giving Luca the lewdest, most erotic show.

"Luca," I start begging. "Luca." I keep saying his name because I'm right here. I need him. I need to come. My pussy aches for him. He must be staring right at it. "Luca, please, fuck me," I beg for us all, and he grunts.

Hot splatters coat my sex again while Luca groans, "Scarlett." His palm falls beside me, catching the weight of his body while he heaves, releasing with a grunt that makes Zar groan. I can feel it. I can feel Luca's cum dripping from my lips while Zar laps it up like he's been dying for his taste.

"Luca," I plead again because I can't stand it. The pressure in my ass. The screaming of my clit. The ache in my empty pussy. The heat of Luca leaning over my back. My heart is crying for him.

"Luca, *please.*"

I beg, and he delivers. He takes over. Pushing my hand aside, he starts plunging the dildo into my ass again while he leans over, whispering in my ear, "Come, my belle. Feel me inside you. Come for me. Squirt for me. Want me. Need me like I need you. You're mine, Scarlett, and you love it. *I* love it."

Love.

It bursts.

I clench my teeth to keep my scream from escaping, groaning while the explosion through my sex buckles my knees. The painful pulsing, the sweet spasms in my core ripping my sight and breath away before I feel Zar's hands grab my thighs, holding my body up while I shake with an orgasm so intense, I whimper with need dripping down my thighs.

"Share it with her," Luca commands. But he doesn't sound evil; he sounds eased, adoring, and satisfied. Gently, he lifts me, guiding me down to my shaking knees beside Zar.

While Zar cups my cheek, kneeling and poised over my open mouth, Luca caresses my collar. "You have me, my belle. You have *us*," Luca promises as Zar drizzles the flavor of our bond over my waiting tongue. "Taste my devotion to you," Luca vows. "I'll give you all you deserve. Always."

THE CHOICES on the Greek menu overwhelm me. Usually, Luca orders Moussaka for us, but I'm starving for something more today.

"Is the Stifado good?" I ask.

"Everything we serve is good," Zar boasts. This restaurant is my favorite. My second favorite is our restaurant in Seoul. It's the Best Bulgogi in the world. And if that ain't a fact, God's a possum."

Luca chuckles. "You're getting more Texas by the day. What's happened to you?"

"I'm happy," Zar croons. "Ain't you?"

It's Friday. It's been the usual week for us. I take Gia to school. Luca trusts me to do it daily while he and Zar are busy with the end-of-year reports. It feels like business and family, routine and perfect.

"Yes." Luca even sounds it. "I'm happy."

"What about you, Clipper?"

Zar tosses that nickname out for me, and I stomp his foot under the table. Not hard, just enough. "Call me that," I answer, "and I'll call you 'Chipmunk' for all the cum you can store in your cheeks."

Luca snorts his water, but Zar strums his fingers, highly amused. "Sounds like a deal to me."

"Sounds like your *death* to me."

"You two, keep it down," Luca warns with a grin. "You're making it obvious."

"No," Zar leans back in his chair, "she's making it fun."

"Speaking of fun..." Luca signals for the waiter. "Let's do a movie night with Gia. Let's make it a Friday tradition on Celine's night off."

I reach for his thigh beside me. No one can see while I gently caress it, feeling Luca's hand fall over mine. "I love that idea," I share, so punch drunk on love that I'd suffer *The Little Mermaid* a thousand times.

But Zar's tone drops. "I gotta pass."

The waiter arrives to take our orders while it stirs in the air. *Something.* Zar's hiding something.

"Why?" I ask once we're alone again. "Do you have a hot date?"

"No," Zar answers.

"A random hookup?"

"Nah."

"Then what is it?"

"He always goes out on Friday nights." Luca makes it sound okay.

"Where do you go?" But I probe, dying to know. "Can we go with you?"

"I always go alone," is all Zar offers as the light in his eyes dims.

He's hurting. It makes me reach for his hand with my empty one. "What's wrong?"

Gently, Zar holds my hand on the table while Luca squeezes my hidden hand on his thigh.

"Scarlett." Rarely, Zar calls me by my name. Rarely, he commands me, "Don't ask."

"Why? I don't understand. What's wrong?" I turn to Luca. "Do you know where he goes?"

Luca shakes his head, genuinely innocent, but not really. He guesses something. I can see it twisting his brows.

"If you two don't tell me what's going on..." I start pulling my hands away, but Zar grabs, not letting me go. Luca, too.

"I go to the movies," Zar confesses.

"So..." I stammer. "Why is that a secret?"

Again, he doesn't answer. Neither does Luca. And you can cut the sudden tension with a chainsaw.

"I'm not doing this." I shake my head, literally feeling pulled between them. "Tell me what's going on, or I swear I'll—"

"Because he used to go to the movies with Darby on Fridays." Luca's voice drops to an octave rife with pain. "Because I was always too busy, so Zar would take her. He'd give her a little break and the attention she deserved while Abbey watched Gia."

I turn my gaze back to Zar. Grief twists his face, so I squeeze his hand. "Why is that such a secret?"

For the first time, shame strikes Zar down. He drops his chin. Forever, he doesn't answer, and Luca doesn't help him, which is rare.

"Because," Zar finally lifts his beaten stare, "I go to Darby's grave every Friday night, too."

The breath I need to draw hurts. It burns through me. For Zar's sake. For Luca's. My stare searches between them as they lock eyes but don't say a word.

"Why?" I softly ask.

"Because I loved her." Pain shakes Zar's voice; all his swagger, gone. "Because I love him, and I loved her, and I go to pay my respects. I tell her about our week, about Gia and—"

"Stop."

There's not an ounce of anger in Luca's tone. Only compassion. Only pain. He doesn't want Zar to say what hurts him. Who? Both men. I can feel it, but I still don't understand.

"Do you go to her grave?" Gently, I ask Luca, squeezing his hand, too. It's starting to sweat in my grasp.

"No." Grief sounds like glass in Luca's throat. "It hurts too much. And Gia's too young to go. It confuses her. When she's old enough, I'll go then."

"So I go for us," Zar helps him. "I bring her fresh flowers every week. Irises were her favorite and…"

Luca leaves me fresh flowers on my desk every day.

A tear suddenly escapes over my lashes, surprising me. Zar sees it, gently wiping it away with his thumb. "Don't cry, gorgeous." His grin is instant; it's tender. "You'll fuck up your mascara."

"That's my new nickname." It falls over my lips, wanting to light up his eyes. It works.

"Yes, Gorgeous," he cocks a full smile, "it sure is."

"I'm not mad at him." Tenderly, Luca tugs my hand, turning my watery stare to his.

I don't know this emotion crushing my heart for them; I just know it's bittersweet.

"I loved her," Luca explains, "and I love him, too. I knew he loved Darby, and I'm thankful he did because I became a very angry young man and a bad husband. I was an asshole. I didn't know how to handle the grief of my dad dying, the stress of taking over the family business, of being a new father and a good husband, too. I didn't know how to handle it until I had no choice. But I was never angry with them. I was angry with myself. I left Darby feeling lonely and abandoned, and she deserved better. She deserved to feel loved."

Luca's thumb caresses my hand, the grief in his eyes trapping me forever.

He's trying to confess to me, but he's not. He's trying to tell me, but he won't. He says, "Like you deserve love, too, my belle."

Like he's trying to warn me…

Because I agree.

Luca's giant hand grabs a fistful of popcorn. Amused, I watch him shovel the snack into his waiting mouth, pieces falling into his lap, but he looks like Gia's twin. Both have their eyes glued to the flatscreen.

I convinced them to watch *Brave* as our Friday night Disney movie, so they're enthralled. They've never seen it.

It takes Luca minutes to realize I'm watching him, not the animated movie. When he finally busts me, he winks, "It's the best."

"What? The movie about a fiery redheaded girl with good aim?" I smile back. Leaning against his upholstered headboard, I love our new tradition.

"That and..." He's so sexy when he smiles at me. "This." He drops his greasy, buttery fingers over my hand.

I roll my eyes, grinning, while he turns his attention toward me, letting Gia dance excitedly in front of the foot of his bed. She has this cute habit of moving her body the entire movie while her eyes won't move from the screen.

Zar left a couple of hours ago.

To Gia, it was normal, but to me, I felt something shift. Something was different in the way Luca offered to walk Zar to the door, so I peeked around the corner from the living room and watched.

I couldn't hear what they whispered, but Luca grabbed the back of Zar's neck, and tentatively, Zar reached for Luca, holding his waist while Luca's kiss ghosted Zar's forehead.

Then, they fell into a tight embrace, and the lump in my throat was instant. Love, forgiveness, and passion seized their muscles, their bodies cleaving together until Luca kissed Zar's cheek.

Like it was a blessing.

Then Zar left for Darby's grave, and I trust he'll return.

Sometimes, though, I fear Luca's heart will be forever trapped at Darby's grave.

The movie blares in the background while Luca studies me, too damn intensely and hot. "Do you have a passport?" he asks.

"No." I take another sip of Ouzo and water. I'm getting addicted to many Greek flavors, especially him.

"Let's get you one." He squeezes my hand. "I'll have it expedited in time for some trips."

"Trips?"

"Yes." His thumb rubs over mine. "Come with us to Paris for Christmas. Meet my mother, and then we'll go to Mykonos for the New Year."

I'm afraid to agree to this paradise. I've never left the country, and now Luca wants me to embark on a new global life with him, Gia, and maybe Zar.

Funny, I've stared down worthy opponents who wanted to beat the shit out of me, but the idea of a family vacation scares me. It's all my heart desires.

And fuck, I need to pick an emotion to wear on my face because I confuse Luca, whose voice drops. "You don't want to go with us?"

"Oh, I want to go. I'm just afraid I won't want to come back."

He smirks. "You're afraid I'll romance you in Paris?"

I smirk back. "You're afraid to see me naked in Mykonos?"

With a cute scowl, he teases, "*Not* in front of the children."

"But you said nudity is natural and normal in Greece."

He lowers his gaze, all sexy as-fuck. "I'm half French, too, so I'll get a full boner watching you naked on the beach, and my hard cock's so big, it's *not* family-friendly."

I snort because he's right. Then I blush because I really want a very adult vacation with him, too—just me and him. But that may never happen, and...

"Bali," he commands, tugging my hand. "I'm taking you there in April for your birthday—just me and you."

How the hell did he know my birthday? And how the fuck did he read my mind?

HIF #16: More accurately how-I'm-NOT-fucked.

I shake my head, imagining a tropical paradise and celibate hell all in one magical location. Like a convent in the middle of a swingers resort with me and Luca, naked and aroused, and him not fucking me.

I'd feel rejected if he didn't make me feel so adored.

"Scarlett." He reaches for my cheek, reading my mind again and freaking me out because he turns my heart into defenseless mush. "I don't want to go anywhere without you. I want to *be* with you. I—"

"But you won't *be* with me, Luca," I whisper. "Not totally. I'm waiting on you, but for how long and—"

"I can't." His dark brows knit with regret. "You know why and—"

"Baba." Gia whips around, her brows knitted, too. "Why did my mommy go to heaven?"

I swear, the temperature drops. The room is suddenly cold. A shiver blooms down my flesh like Darby's beautiful ghost that haunts Luca's soul is suddenly standing in the room with us, the timing not lost on me.

"Because," Luca sits up, clearing his throat, "the angels needed her."

I glance over Gia's shoulder and, inwardly, kick myself. I forgot this movie is about a daughter and mother. And I should never be allowed to be a mom because I should've known better. Gia's not ready for this.

She only grows more confused. "But *why* did the angels need my mommy?"

"She died, my kóri." Luca's tone drops deeper than I've ever heard. "So the angels needed her up in heaven to watch over you."

Gia looks at the ceiling. She's not sad, but I see grief twisting Luca's handsome face.

Has he talked with Gia about this yet?

"How did she get up there?" Gia asks the ceiling. "I don't see her."

"We don't see angels," he answers. "But they're always up there, loving you."

But I glance down.

Luca still wears his wedding band every day, and every day, I notice. Sometimes, when he's intimate with me or being so Dom, I see it, but it doesn't feel wrong. It's *not* wrong. It's powerful. It bonds me to his pain. I'm trying to honor his promise and trying to be honest that I don't know how long I can. But I love him, so I keep fighting.

"Baba?" Gia still stares at the ceiling. "How did my mommy die?"

Though his tan is permanent and deep, the life drains from Luca's face.

"She died in an accident, my kóri."

"Why?"

"The car was going very fast."

"Why?"

"She didn't mean to drive that fast."

Gia cants her head, aiming her stare on him, her smart little mind working to make sense of it. "Was she grumpy? *You* drive fast when you're grumpy, too."

It hitches Luca's breath, his daughter's questions dredging up the pain he tries to bury.

"No," he mutters. "She wasn't grumpy." He pauses, his lips tensing. "She was happy. She was laughing with me and didn't mean to go that fast."

He's lying.

I can see it.

I can hear it.

I pray Gia can't because Luca's doing it to protect Gia's imagination about her mother.

But since he's lying, the opposite must be true.

Darby was driving fast, but she wasn't laughing. She was... crying? Yelling? Those are the only emotions I can imagine making a driver lose control of a car, particularly in a torrential downpour.

"Will she come back like Merida's mom?"

See, I'm a horrible person.

I should've protected Gia from this movie. The fantasy about a mother who suffers a spell made by a witch, turning her into a bear, taking her from her daughter until the daughter breaks the spell and brings her mother back, is only making reality hard for Gia to understand and for Luca to explain.

The lump in Luca's swallow is visible. "No, my kóri. She's not coming back. She watches over everything you do from heaven. She'll always be your angel for the rest of your life."

With a tiny eyebrow raised, Gia studies the ceiling again. Half of me wants to cry at Luca's grief, but that's not what Gia's feeling. She's too young. She's skeptical. She's concerned.

And...*Gia looks too cute.*

If her mother's angel *can* see her, she'd agree.

"Does my mommy watch me poop?" Gia wonders aloud, and I snort, choking down fits of laughter.

I can't help it.

I worried the same about Santa Claus and the whole "he sees when you're sleeping; he knows when you're awake." I went to the bathroom in the dark for months until my mom got so frustrated that she burst that fairytale bubble.

A sudden smile takes Luca's face, too. "No, my kóri. Angels give you privacy in the bathroom. Anytime you want something, tell your angel."

Gia smiles. Mischief, like Zar's, dances in her eyes. Power, like Luca's, booms from her little voice as she commands the ceiling, "Angel! Give me a puppy named 'Baklava!'"

My laughter escapes. "I told you." I elbow Luca. "She's going to wear you down. She'll make you change your mind."

Relief and joy relax his face. He reaches for my hand. Leaning over, he gently kisses my cheek, promising, "My daughter is the only one who can."

And for months, it's true and happy and perfect between us.

Until...it's not.

Scarlett

CHAPTER TWENTY-TWO

"Even your feet look fancy now." Ruby kicks a bit of sand over them. "Six months of subbing for Luca Mercier has your toenails looking like five-star luxury."

"What are you talking about?"

I study my recent pedicure. It's French. What's the big deal? Yeah, my feet are tanner, too. All of me is. That's what a week in Bali will do to you.

"I'm talking about you. Girl, you've *changed*." Ruby cracks open a can of beer. "Should I have brought Dom Perignon instead of PBR for your belated birthday?"

I take a swig of my beer before fussing back, "Quit giving me shit. I'm the same." I grin, showing her wrists, making her look closely. "Except for these."

Why am I proud to show Ruby the newest abrasions on my flesh? Because they were damn fun to earn.

"Okay." She flops back into her folding chair in the sand. "Dish your Dirty Dom weekly update. I fucking live for your naughty news."

It's late April on the beach. The sun is shining. The temperature is perfect. And I'm a year older, glowing after my vacation with Luca, though it was heaven and hell.

The heaven part?

"Zar surprised me and showed up for the last two days of our vacation," I confide in Ruby. She's the only one I can. "He and Luca had it all planned. The villa we stayed in was over the water with an open ceiling and wooden rafters—"

"Oh my god!" Ruby kicks her feet. "And perfect for ropes, you slutty bitch. I'm so jealous."

"Why are you jealous? You're the one hooking up with half of the Carolina Panthers."

"Two!" She points at me. "Only two. You know I'm a double-dip diva; now finish your story."

I swig my beer again. Sitting on the lounger, I wedge my feet in the sand of Folly Beach, relieved to be sharing. The secret life I have to lead has me bursting at the seams, and not always in a good way.

"Well, they used the rope to bind my wrists overhead, like I was almost hanging, while Luca spanked my ass with a leather paddle for every year I've been alive. He didn't do it too rough, just enough to sting so good while Zar ate my pussy, and they made me come twice and so hard, I thought I'd pull my arms out of their sockets."

Ruby leans forward. "*Then* what?"

I almost don't want to tell her. I mean, is there anything I won't tell my sister? But I need to tell someone. I've been holding so much in.

"Don't ask me how they got it to Bali because I don't wanna know, but do you know what a fucking machine is?"

Ruby's eyes get wide. She nods, eyes glued to mine while she slurps her beer, waiting for more. Like I'm sharing XXX-rated campfire stories, but there's no campfire because it's warm today, and this story is hot.

"Well, that's what I got for my birthday. A fucking machine and a padded stool for me to bend over with my hands tied to it, while the dildo on that thing was a jackhammer from cunt heaven. Oh my god, it felt so good. Then Luca made Zar lick my ass while I stared at Luca and sucked him off, like we were having a kinky foursome with a machine, and..."

I start giggling, covering my face like an abstinent schoolgirl, though I sure as hell am not. That's a teetotal lie.

"And *what?*" Ruby squeals.

"And they did it to me for two days straight. The four of us—Luca's dick, Zar's tongue, that fucking machine, and me—coming in every position and place in that villa. Thank god for coconut oil, ice, and aspirin."

Ruby stares at me like a meteor shower—in awe. "I bet they bought it at Delta's," she marvels, and she's probably right.

"Well, Luca gave me *that* and these for my birthday." I glance around, making sure no one is watching, but it's a Thursday. The beach is quiet this afternoon, so I drop the spaghetti strap of my dress discreetly since I'm not wearing a bra to show Ruby.

"Oh my god!" Ruby gawks. "Your nipples are pierced with diamonds! They're real, aren't they? Luca gave you ten thousand dollar titties!"

"Yeah." I lift my strap. "I suggested the piercings a month ago, and Luca made it amazing, of course. He made it so kinky and sweet the first night we were there. He found this woman, like she was trained and medical, and he had her come to our villa. He already gave me the most erotic massage of my life—"

"Wait? What?" Ruby gulps her beer.

I take a gulp, too, because, yeah, whoops, I forgot this other hot story.

"Yeah, Luca carried me to a massage table outside on the deck of our villa over the ocean. It was heaven. Then he blindfolded me, and all I knew was that multiple pairs of hands were rubbing oil on me. It was like a legit massage at first until it got hot. Oil rubbed on my clit, on my nipples, my inner thighs, and feet. Hands were getting me off and groping me while Luca held my arms overhead, teasing my ear with his dirty ass amazing accent.

"He always worships me and tells me I'm his beautiful whore. He made me come so hard, letting strangers touch me everywhere but where I really needed him. Then, a few minutes later, he took off my blindfold, and it was just us and this woman. She looked like a nurse almost. Then Luca made me cry, telling me how much I meant to him, cracking open a black velvet box with these thin platinum bars and diamonds on each end.

"While the woman pierced my nipples, Luca fucked me with a fancy rabbit vibrator so it wouldn't hurt, and it didn't. It only turned me on so much. He made me come on the massage table, both times as she pierced me, and then she left. And I was naked on the table, pierced for Luca and staring up at him and needing him so much. It was my birthday, and I begged him to please finally fuck me again, but then..."

Here's the hell part.

The storm again. The flood of lust in my body thinking about Luca. The raging love I feel, but it's an ache, too. A heavy, crushing one that's never satisfied. It hurts. I'm drowning. I can't breathe, and I can't deny it anymore.

"Then *what*?" Ruby snaps me out of it.

"Then I couldn't stop crying."

"What?" Ruby's voice gets soft. "Why?"

"Because I don't know how much more I can take. I love Luca, and I know he loves me, but he never says it, and he never fucks me. And I thought I could wait for him to change, but you're right; *I'm* changing. I've gone from having the Fuck Flu to Death by Dick Denial."

"Yeah, but you've died and gone to Kinky Heaven." I love my sister. She's trying to make me laugh. "What if he gave you one night? Or one time? Like for the next holiday or something?"

I stare at the horizon, toeing the sand, mulling it over. My mind is as churned up as those waves. Like a coming storm, my emotions keep rolling in, and they grow stronger and more destructive every day.

Ruby whips out her phone, taps away, and suggests, "May first. It says it's Global Love Day. Tell Luca he has to fuck you for the world's sake or else."

She makes me chuckle, but when I'm honest with myself, "No," I tell her. "That would only be worse. One time with him again, and then nothing? I deserve more than that. I want more than real sex with him. I want us to be together. I want to be a real couple, a family. I want him to be proud we're together, not ashamed and hiding me like I'm trash."

I look at Ruby. I let her see the tears welling in my eyes. Lately, I can't fight them. "Don't laugh when I tell you this."

"I won't."

"I want..." I can't believe I'm going to say it. I can't believe this is my deepest wish. "I want to be *Mrs. Mercier*. I want to be Luca's wife. I want to be Gia's sorta mom. I want us to be a real family, and I want Luca to want it, too."

She rubs my leg. "Talk to him about it."

"I have."

"What does he say?"

I roll my eyes, feeling like an asshole doing it, but that's how frustrated I am. "He says he'll give me everything I want but *that*. He won't break his vow to his first wife. So I cried the night I got pierced, on my birthday, because he made me feel so special, then so rejected. Like I'm not good enough for him to change. Luca's like my cancer and cure. Because, most of the time, I'm happy. Then he tortures me with pleasure, and I love it, then I hate it. It's painful. I want him, and I can't have him. I swear I can't take it anymore, and then he holds me so tight, and I'm okay again."

"All because of his dead wife?"

"Yeah," I mutter, looking back at the horizon. "I can't compete with her ghost. And the sad thing is, I think I would've liked her."

My toe digs a hole deeper in the sand, searching for the courage to say it aloud to myself and my sister.

"What really hurts me, Rubes?" I finally share, turning to tell her. "We got back from Bali yesterday morning, and I went home to see Crimson, get some sleep, and do laundry. But when I went to pick up Gia this morning to take her to school, she was so happy to see me, and I had missed her so much, too..."

This is the part that hurts so much.

The final thing that broke my heart today.

Like Luca dealt the final punch and knocked me down. I can't get up.

I lose.

"Luca was wearing his wedding band again this morning," I tell her, my lips trembling. "He took it off for our vacation; I thought that was his sign that he was changing for me." I fought like hell not to cry when I saw it, but now I do. "But he put it back on when we got home like he doesn't even care if I see it. If it hurts me."

Ruby falls uncharacteristically quiet. We both stare at the horizon where the sparkling ocean kisses the sky.

It's peaceful, but I'm not.

I don't know what to think or what to do anymore.

Yes, it's insane. It's infuriating. Luca's vow to his dead wife makes no sense, and even if it did for a time...

Now it feels like he *is* cheating.

But I don't know on who anymore.

"Well," Ruby finally sighs. "I can share an NFL player or two with you."

I shove her. Forgetting my strength, I almost knock her out of the chair, finally making me chuckle. "I'm not fucking your seconds."

"Seconds?" She scoffs. "Girl, if I told you about the parties I've been going to, you lose track of numbers."

"Parties? What parties?" She does that dumbass thing of zipping her lips and throwing away the key. "You know," I warn, "there's a nerve in your hand I can pinch and make you instantly pee. Like the next time we're in Target, it'll be clean up Ruby's run-off on aisle ten."

She howls back, laughing. "I ain't afraid of you! Miss Phobia of Little Mice."

"Those things are disgusting."

"You only hate them because a mama mouse had her babies in your tennis shoe one night, and then you put your foot—"

"Shut up." My body shudders. "Answer my question: what parties?"

With a guilty grin and eyebrows dancing, she says, "Ask Zar."

"*What!?*"

She shakes her head. "He doesn't fuck. I swear. Don't worry. He's faithful to Luca and you. That's obvious because that man has cock and cunt opportunities galore. But he doesn't take them at his parties at his beach shack, ahem, *mansion*...so the rest of us get to enjoy them. We've kinda become good friends."

"What are you talking about?"

This is kinky news to me.

I know Zar isn't around much. Especially the past few months, since February, and that's another heaven and hell story.

How Luca didn't bring Zar to the Bachelor & Bachelorette party Luca and I were invited to.

It seems Silas, Redix and Cade's lover, found his soulmate, too. So, Redix and Cade threw Silas and his bride, Eily, a joint Bachelor and Bachelorette party at the sex club where I met Luca.

It was like pornified deja vu for us. But, like Zar, I was mad at Luca for excluding him. So I just teased Luca all night at the club, making him watch while I exposed my pussy to him while Redix, Silas, Cade, and Eily gave the hottest sex show I've ever seen...no, wait...there was Stacey and her three men and their show, too.

See! Everyone's proudly fucking in shows and orgies and clubs except us.

So, on the limo ride home that night, Luca and I had our first fight.

"Why can't we be like our friends?" I challenged him. "They're public with their love. They're proud of it. So why do you hide me and Zar? Our friends care about us. They'll be happy for us."

"Because," Luca growled beside me in the limo's backseat, "rumors start. And Redix is a celebrity. In his world, many people accept his lifestyle. And Silas never cares what people think, and his beautiful new wife is an artist. They can get away with the avant-garde. It only adds to their mystique, their cachet."

"Quit using French to explain your bullshit." I was mad. I was hurt for me and Zar. "You're ashamed of us."

"I'm not ashamed of you," he fumed. "I'm *protecting* you. I'm realistic. People will judge."

"Cade's a cop, and people judge her, but she doesn't care," I argued. "She and your best friend, Redix, have a daughter now. They're with Silas and Eily, too. They're all a happy poly family like we should be."

Luca shook his head. I swear he can be so damn stubborn.

"Cade doesn't have to court investors. *I* do," he lectured me. "I have contractors and partners and properties worldwide where conservative traditions reign. If they find out about what we do, that I'm in a throuple with you and Zar, it's over. The Mercier Hotels will be boycotted. Properties will shut down, and people will lose their jobs. My family's legacy will be forever tarnished, not just for me, but for Gia."

He had to go and throw that logic down, using Gia to make his point, and I got it, though I hated it.

"My belle." He reached for my hand, and I let him take it. "I'm not ashamed of you." But I wouldn't look at him. I glared out of the window. "You don't know how proud I am of you always. Gia wants to be just like you, and I can only dream for that to be so."

And *that* melted me.

I turned to look at him, and like a sexy devil, he smiled. "Stop being mad because it gets me hard when you're feisty."

"Not hard enough to *fuck* me." Still, I was sassy.

He laughed and said, "Oh, I'll make it up to you."

And that's the night Luca and I made the biggest mess in his restaurant kitchen of Margot's after everyone left. Together, we made Baklava and got powdered sugar everywhere. Then, he laid me nude across the marble baker's table, and that's the first time, the only time, since our first night at the club, that Luca really touched me again.

He swirled the honey for the Baklava around my nipples and coated his fingers with it, too. I knew a small amount is good for your pussy. I read it somewhere. But apparently, Luca was well aware of its power. Because he sucked my sweet nipples and fingered me so hard, I came, I cried, I gushed all over his honeyed hand. And then I begged to devour his cream with honey, too, and he let me. He kept his fingers pumping inside me while he came in my mouth. He roared so loud that anyone in the lobby could hear him.

We were a sticky mess, laughing like teenagers, sneaking onto the elevator to his penthouse. Then we snuck into his bathroom and silently showered together.

Luca washed my body and hair, so I insisted and washed him, too. His lips kept gliding wet over mine, but he never kissed me. It would've been so perfect and romantic if he had made love to me then because that's how we felt, holding each other under the dark rain shower. He was hard, and I was soft, and it felt like love.

But he wouldn't.

He won't.

"Uh! Earth to Scarlett!" Ruby shakes me out of it again. "Where the fuck did you just go?"

I blink at the horizon, not believing the past six months and not knowing if my heart will survive the next. "Rubes," I sigh. "What am I gonna do?"

She lifts her beer can and makes me raise mine for a toast. "You're gonna have a Happy Birthday, bitch. Because I love you and your bougie pedicure and your diamond nips, and you're my badass big sister who'll figure it out. Talk to that hot-ass daddy Dom of yours and lay it on the line. Make him choose. His past or his future? What do you have to lose?"

Everything.

Luca

CHAPTER TWENTY-THREE

I HATE BOW TIES. EVEN WHEN I WEAR A CUSTOM TUXEDO, they still strangle, making me tug at my starched collar.

But this black-tie event was my idea, well, sort of, and it's for a good cause, so I put my full power behind it.

"May I have this dance, Mr. Chairmen of the Board?"

The voice over my shoulder is not one I can easily refuse. Maren is quite persuasive. Thankfully, she's been putting it to good use lately.

"Sure." I turn and offer her my hand.

Years of ballroom dancing classes come back in an instant. Resting my hand on Maren's back, I take her other and lead us in a casual foxtrot.

"This was a great idea, Luca." She keeps her voice low. "We've raised seven hundred thousand so far. Just three hundred more to meet our goal."

It was Maren who nominated me to join her on the Board of Directors for our kids' school. It was my idea to accept only if the board agreed to create a full scholarship fund for at least fifty percent of future students. So they appointed me as the Chair. Then, it was Maren's idea to have a black-tie dinner and dance to raise the money.

So here I am.

I'm raising thousands for a worthy cause while my fucking feet are killing me. But Maren's a good dancer, so it's not that bad. We twirl across the dance floor, other couples stepping out of the way.

Of course, I offered to host the event in The Mercier ballroom, and of course, Maren and her friends took over the details. I didn't care. I give two shits about chair covers and centerpieces. I just know good taste, and Maren knows Charleston's style, so it worked.

The event is a huge success.

"I should be offended." Maren jokes. "You're the belle of the ball, but *I'm* the one who organized it."

"You did a great job." I smile at her, and I mean it.

Maybe divorce made Maren bitter for a time, and I understand. I have no room to judge. But these past few months, she's mellowed. It's actually been easy working with her. We've had dozens of meetings and playdates. I swear something comes up every day, and Maren needs my opinion.

"And to think?" She rolls her eyes, laughing. "The Brenners wanted this to be a dry event. I mean, really? Josh Brenner has deep pockets but short arms. He just didn't wanna chip in for the open bar."

I laugh, too, because she's not wrong. The drama on our Board makes a soap opera seem sedate.

"Do you have plans for Gia's birthday this month?" Maren grips my bicep tighter. It's part of the dance, but it makes me lower my hand on her back.

"Yes." I lead us to an open space. "We're taking her to Disney World. It's a surprise."

"We?"

"Yes. Me, Abbey, Harper, Celine, Zar, and—"

"And *Scarlett*," Maren mutters. "Luca, I'm sorry, but she's not right for you."

"Ms. Jones and I are professionals."

"No, you're not. And you have a right to move on. I want you to be happy. *Darby* would want you to be happy. But Scarlett doesn't fit in, and the poor thing knows it. She's proud, and I don't blame her, so don't make her suffer when you know how others treat her."

"How *you* treated her."

But I don't disagree with Maren. When I took Scarlett to Paris, then Mykonos, we got stares. Maybe they were for me. Maybe they were for her beauty. But they made Scarlett uncomfortable, almost insecure, which isn't like her.

"You're right," Maren answers. "I got caught up in the petty gossip of some of the moms, and I should know better. I haven't been my best self this past year, and I apologize."

"Thank you." I aim for another spot where we can move. I can't believe this crowd. I can't see the edge of the dance floor.

"But Luca, you should hear how they talk about her. All her tattoos and just the way she stares—it's rather creepy. If she ever hears it, it's going to break her poor heart. Women around here can be so cruel. Don't put her through it."

"Maren." I'm annoyed. And fucked. I never should've said anything. "Scarlett and I are not together. I'm not with anyone. Not since Darby died, and it'll stay that way. I still wear my wedding band for her."

More like...I was so lonely until I finally found the happiness with Scarlett that I don't deserve. I get so lost in her. I take my ring off for her, for our time together, but then I have to put it back on. It keeps me tethered to my family, to my grave vow.

I don't know how to move forward, so I dance with Scarlett in circles of pleasure and pain. I used to love my punishment, but now I'm punishing Scarlett, too. It killed me when I made her cry on her birthday.

No matter what I do, I seem destined to hurt the women I love.

"If you and Scarlett aren't together," Maren mutters, "then why is she looking at us like that?"

Like what?

I scan the room. Of course, Scarlett is here somewhere. I invited her. She's here with Gia and everyone except Zar.

Zar's been gone a lot lately, and I know why.

Months ago, I hurt him, excluding him from Silas and Eily's party at the club. Zar said he understood why, and I sure got an earful from Scarlett about it. But I thought I made it up to her. I thought I made it up to him.

Every Saturday night since, I've been pushing my limits. I've changed our rituals for them. Zar gets to pick the toy I fuck him with; Scarlett does, too. Our aftercare is more intimate. I stay longer. We hold each other. We take baths together, too. I don't sneak away until dawn, and that's only for Gia's sake.

But I'm not a dumbass.

I can only give Zar so much, so I suppose he goes elsewhere for the rest, and I can live with it.

But not Scarlett.

I can't lose her. She knows I love her. To say it would be breaking my vow. My words could curse us, too, so I try to show her every day. I try to keep my past promise and have a future with her, too.

I saw Scarlett an hour ago but got yanked to the dance floor. I've been here ever since, and it's packed. I'm not dumb enough to ask Maren where she spotted her. That would be a dead giveaway, so I dance around searching for her.

I need to find her as the song changes. It's a slow song, a love song. The piano softly plays, and the lyrics hauntingly sing from the grave...

"Hello. It's me."

My feet stop.

My heart, too.

The strangle on my throat is instant. The room falls away, and suddenly, I can't see. Memories drop like velvet curtains over my vision.

"Hello" by Adele plays, and Maren mourns. I can barely hear her ask, "Remember? This was Darby's favorite song. I asked them to play it for us."

"I remember." It's all I can say, all I can see, because air can't fill my lungs, and movement can't find my feet.

Music does that to you. It drags your beaten soul right back to your past and buries you there.

So Maren urges, her feet making mine slowly move. Her hands land on my pounding chest, her body and the music taking me. The lyrics, too.

They don't mean the same anymore.

Not when Darby used to belt "Hello" in our kitchen, looking so cute, using a wooden spoon for a microphone and making me laugh. Not when she'd sing it in the car going over her favorite bridge, rolling down the window for the world to hear, making me proud as I drove. Not when she used to play it on our piano, and I'd sit on the bench beside her, holding Gia in my arms. No one sings like Adele, but Darby sounded like the angel she is now.

Her voice always stopped Gia from crying.

And now?

I am.

I'm hearing Darby's voice singing again from her grave. Lamenting. Praying. Haunting. *Can you hear me? About who we used to be? When we were young? And free?*

Her wails from the other side. My wails of I'm sorry. Over and over.

For everything that I've done.

For breaking your heart.

The guilt suffocates. The burning flood behind my eyes is sudden and it kills me, too. It embarrasses me. Like Gia, like our beautiful daughter, I stare at the ceiling, searching for her mother there, begging my tears not to fall. Begging my lips to stop trembling. My hands, too.

I'm a grown man. I can't fall apart in the middle of this ballroom where I met Darby. *"You're beautiful when you're miserable."* It's the first thing I said to her. *"You're cute when you lie."* She took my heart with those words; it was love, perfect and flawed until she was gone.

And I can't stop hearing my shouts that night. They're like

this song haunting my soul. It plays, and I hear Darby wailing in the rain. Then it was instant—the collision. Darby was on the other side; she was gone. I reached over to brush the long brown curls off her face, and I can't stop seeing her blood on my hands. I can't stop hearing our daughter's cries from the backseat. I can't stop worrying about Zar's groans of pain.

It was all my fault.

And I'm so fucking sorry. A thousand times and from the other side. I'm so sorry I broke your heart.

"Luca?" Lights blur. I can't hear anyone but Darby. The room spins, and I sway. Dizzy. "Luca?" Maren holds me tighter, so I hold her back so I won't collapse. "Luca, are you okay?"

"Give me a minute."

It's all my pride can growl to save me. To keep my feet moving. To maintain my dignity. I will not fall apart in front of everyone. *Not* in front of our daughter.

She's here somewhere.

Maren didn't know. I didn't either.

I didn't know my beautiful ghost was waiting to sing to me again.

"Luca? Talk to me." For all of Maren's flaws, she's not horrible. She cared about Darby.

"Just give me a minute." I need for this song to end. I need for this all to end. The pain. The guilt. The memories. But they won't. They never will. That's not how life works for the living. Only the dead are free.

Until finally...the song fades.

A joyful Stevie Wonder song plays next, lifting the mood, and I swallow the razors in my throat. My focus slowly returns. My voice, too. But not my composure. I keep dancing with Maren until I can catch my breath.

"Luca, I didn't mean to upset you." Maren sounds sincere. "I'm sorry."

"It's okay." It's not, but it's not her fault. "Just..."

I finally see her.

Scarlett.

She's all alone. No one's standing with her in the shadows against the dark wall. She looks breathtaking in her strapless white dress, our clip in her auburn hair in an elegant twist, and our necklace sparkling around her throat.

Gia and Harper dance feet in front of her, but they laugh, ignoring her, while Scarlett's stare is frozen and focused on me.

On my hands clinging to Maren.

I haven't danced with Scarlett tonight. I won't. I can't. No one can know about us. But I know the crushing anguish breaking across her beautiful face. I know the tears welling in her lonely eyes.

Because I love her, and I can't.

Because I'm promised to another woman, not her.

Because I can never give her all she needs.

"Maren." Politely, I kiss her cheek. "Excuse me, please."

My steps leave Maren on the dance floor, trying to close the distance between me and Scarlett, but guests stop me, blocking my way. Well-wishers and congratulations. Admiration and praise. I don't want it. I don't deserve it. But I get stuck. I get grabbed, palms shoved into my hand, shaking it. Pats on my shoulder. Kisses to my cheeks. It takes me too long, and by the time I turn to find her again, Scarlett's gone.

"Baba!" Gia comes running. "Dance with me!"

I scoop her up and spin her around. She giggles while I ask, "Where's Scarlett?"

"Her tummy hurts."

"What?" I'm grilling an almost six year-old for intel.

"She said her tummy hurt, and she went home."

Oh fuck. I hold my daughter while my heart drops, but for her sake, I hide it. I swing Gia around the dance floor. She makes me dance with her for two songs, and I make her laugh until I find Abbey. She's standing with Celine and other parents.

When she sees us approach, Celine's face lights up. She loves dancing, so she whisks Gia from my arms while Abbey angrily scowls at me. I lean down and let her whisper, "Scarlett just left."

"I know. Gia told me."

"Luca..." Abbey scolds. "She was crying."

ONE. Three. Five.

That's Scarlett's code to get into her building. She told me it was her featherweight when she won her last title, so I punch it in, praying she's here.

It took me two hours to leave the party.

Yes, I wanted to run after Scarlett immediately. But no, that's not my life.

There were hands to shake—thousands of dollars in donations for kids to secure. And there was my daughter, who wanted two more dances until she finally fell asleep in my arms, so I took her upstairs and tucked her into her bed, and then I raced here in my Lotus.

The elevator to the tenth floor of Scarlett's building takes forever.

Do I knock on her door? Or just use the same code to open it?

I'm not sure. I'm not good at begging.

I'm used to demands. To power. To control.

But when I stand on the other side of the door to 10D, I hear voices. Her muffled voice and another. It's not her sister. No, I know that deep baritone, and *he better fucking not*.

"Scarlett!" I pound her door. Fuck, her neighbors. She has five seconds to open it, or I'm kicking this fucking thing down.

Shadows fall under the threshold. "Open it!" I demand. "Now! I know he's in there!"

The door flings open...

And it's him.

"Keep making an ass of yourself, and the cops are coming," Zar snarls.

But I brush past him, my glare aimed at Scarlett. She's sitting on her sofa, in the same dress, with her eyes puffy from crying, but now she looks pissed.

"So you go to him and not me?" I demand to know, but that stoic stare drops over her eyes. The one when she can't show emotions, but I sure reveal my rage. "Answer me!" I shout.

"Don't yell at her!" Zar shouts back.

So I whip around. "I can't fucking believe it," I seethe. "You're doing it again, and you fucking know it."

Zar glares back. "Fuck you," he growls. "That's *not* what this is."

"Sure looks familiar," I yell. "The one night when I got caught in a shitshow and hurt her feelings, and I didn't mean to, yet again, here you are. The knight in shining armor to save her from me, right?"

"But you won't stop hurting her, will you?" Zar sounds too calm, too right. "Because *YOU* won't stop hurting. That's what you do, Luca, right? *You* hurt, so *we* hurt? You make damn sure of it. Hell, you get *off* on it."

Fuck, that punched my soul. "Go to hell."

"We're going together," Zar snarls. "Remember?"

"Stop it." Scarlett barely speaks. "Both of you. Just. Fucking. Stop."

I turn back to her. "Belle, I'm sorry. It's not what it looked like. I had to dance with Maren, and then that song played, and it's my wife's favorite song and—"

I catch myself.

I did it again.

I make tears suddenly spill over Scarlett's lashes. She stares at me with disbelief, with pain. "Luca, she's dead."

I swallow hard. "I know."

"No, you don't. Because you still wear your ring. You're married to a ghost. You're faithful to a lie."

"It's not a lie. It *was* my fault."

"How?" Scarlett pries, "How was an *accident* your fault?"

I clench the truth between my teeth, keeping it in because Scarlett lifts her chin and won't back down. "Tell me," she demands. "Because I know you lied to Gia. You said Darby was

315

laughing and driving too fast. But she wasn't, was she? She was what? Yelling like you? Crying like me?"

"Stop." I seethe; my past and present are about to crash again.

"Tell her," Zar urges. "Just tell her."

"No! She'll hate me, too."

"I won't hate you," Scarlett pleads.

"Yes, you will."

"It was just words," Zar implores.

Blood pounds through my veins. Love chokes my heart. Anger clenches my fists. Guilt crushes my skull and my chest, too, holding it back because I can't admit it.

Words matter. Words scream. Words bleed.

"What did you say to her, Luca?" Scarlett stands. She reaches for my hand, but I pull it away. "Luca, tell me." She's so beautiful, and I'm about to lose her. Scarlett begs, tears streaming down her cheeks, "Please, I deserve to know why I'm not good enough for you. Why you'll never love me, too."

That's not true.

"Tell her!" Zar shouts, impatient with Scarlett's pain.

I am, too.

I can't take it anymore.

I hate myself. I hate that it wasn't me. I deserved to die for what I said to my wife. To the mother of our beautiful child who *will* find out one day what I called her mother, and she'll hate me, too.

They're the last words Darby heard...

"Whore!" I shout in Scarlett's face. "She told me what she did, that Gia may not be mine, and I called my wife a fucking whore. I told her I never wanted to touch her again, to kiss her again, or fuck her again. That I didn't love her anymore, and I made her cry so hard she wailed. She sobbed and closed her eyes and lost control of the car, and I killed her."

"But..." Scarlett stammers. I watch the collision I feared crash across her face. The damage, instant. "But that's what you call *me*. You call me a *whore*."

I'm not worth defending.

If I explain it to her. How when I say it to Scarlett, it's not an insult; it's an exalation. How it's praise, not pejorative. How I love it about her; I need it from her. How she was made for me. How I'm free with Scarlett; she's my true match. It only damns me more.

But Zar tries. "It was my fault. I slept with Darby. One time. One night, she was lonely, and I was weak, and the guilt ate us alive. Until that night, July Fourth, Darby told me she wanted to tell him, but I told her, 'No.' I got mad at her that day about it. I warned her that he was under a lot of stress and—"

"Don't defend me," I growl. "I was wrong and drunk and angry. You were drunk and being a dick to her, too. And I didn't understand why, and we fought about it on the beach until Darby got upset and started to leave, so we went after her. We climbed in my fucking car and..."

It breaks my voice.

It breaks my heart.

"With our *daughter, too*..." It chokes my throat. "And she sobbed, going over the bridge, confessing to me, saying she was so sorry, but I shouted at her. I broke her heart. I killed her with my words, and we all could've died because of me."

"But we didn't." Zar reaches for me, too, but I pull away. "It was an accident."

God, how I've made him suffer ever since, just like I suffer. I hurt him for it, and we both love it. We need it.

And every time I look at Gia, I see her mother. I see what I took from her, forever, and I deserve a fate worse than death.

I deserve to live with this agony.

"That's why," I answer, turning to confront Scarlett. She looks so hurt, so I finish the fatal damage I started. "That's why I promised to Darby's grave that I would never kiss, or touch, or be with another woman. That I would never love again. Because I can't take back what I said. I can't bring Gia's mother back, but at least I can suffer with her. I can suffer the last words I swore to her that night for the rest of my life."

Scarlett

THERE'S A RINGING THAT FILLS YOUR EARS; IT SCREAMS through your brain when you're knocked down. When your face is on the mat, and you're bleeding and can't focus. For a moment, you have two senses: what you hear and pain.

I hear every word from Luca. From Zar, too. And the ringing is here, too. It's damage from my previous fights, but this pain is new.

It's excruciating.

Every word they say to me makes sense, and they land like punches, so I cross my arms over my body to protect myself, but my heart is beaten.

I'm still stuck on that same word—*whore*—the word Luca has condemned his soul for saying. And it's odd.

It doesn't hurt me.

No matter what he says, I know how Luca makes me feel when he says it. Revered, not reviled. Worshiped, not condemned. I feel like I'm finally found in Luca's loving arms, and he moans with me like he's holding his truth, his soulmate.

But what finally defeats me?

Still.

Luca leaves.

He puts on his ring and goes back to Darby's ghost every time.

And I'm left staring at the window, *at a widower*, hoping he comes back to me.

"Scarlett?" I hear Luca's voice through the high pitch in my ears. My name suddenly sounds foreign in his accent, like I don't belong in his world—I never did.

I'm going to miss him.

I'm going to miss so much.

"Can I see her?" I ask Luca, not caring about the tears I can't stop. "Can I please see her sometimes?"

"What?" Luca softly shakes his head. "She's dead."

It's his truth. I'm not even here because, in his mind, Luca's still married to Darby. He won't let her go, and the pain makes my lips tremble.

"Gia," I beg. "I don't want her to think I abandoned her. I'll always be here for her, so can I still see her sometimes? Please? I love her, too."

"What?" Luca stammers. "What are you talking about?" Finally, he sees *me*. He hears *me*. He confronts the truth he can't hide, and his face falls. "Belle...don't."

"You leave me no choice."

"Why?"

"Will I ever be good enough, Luca? Good enough for you to love?"

"You are." He chokes. "I'm not."

I nod, hearing what he'll never say to me.

Salty tears pool over the seam of my lips, but I don't care. I'm still that broken-hearted girl with her chin up and fighting back.

"You know," I confess, "I used to wonder what I did to make my dad leave. I felt guilty about all the times I misbehaved with my sisters. Or that we cost him money he didn't have. So, I'd barely eat for days so that my sisters could, so he wouldn't leave to go to the store. Then, I tried to be so perfect, so strong after he left, hoping that would bring him back to me..."

"Scarlett..." Luca steps toward me, but now I pull away.

This fight is over.

"But there's a moment you realize it wasn't your actions," I explain, "it was *you*. *You* weren't good enough for him to love. And—"

Luca rushes, "That's not—"

But I put my hand up. "And that's what you believe as a child. That's your pain until you grow up and learn you can't *make* someone stay. You can't *make* them love you. That it's not your fault. You know it. You just don't *feel* it. Because you're still that little girl he left waiting by a window."

"Scarlett, please. Don't do this. Don't leave." Pain brims in Luca's eyes. I glance over, and it's filling Zar's, too. "Don't do this to us." I look back at him. "To me. To Gia. We need you. Don't make us go through this again."

"Then answer me...Luca." That name. *His name.* I already feel his fresh scar on my heart. "Decide: will you live with me, or will you die with her?"

That pushes him over. His tear falls, but the darkness that falls down his face frightens me more.

"Never," he strains. "I can't, and I won't. I lost her. I lost me. In a way, I lost my daughter, too. I never want to know the truth if Gia's not mine, because in my soul, she is. I'm committed to my wife, to her mother, to the family we had together. And if I break my promise to her, I'll lose all I have left."

"You already have," Zar answers.

FUCHSIA PETALS from the crape myrtle trees form a bright carpet over the grass. Crimson rolls around in them, making Gia laugh.

If I focus on her, I can almost fight my tears. I can almost ignore Luca, sitting alone like a dark shadow on the bench across the park.

"So, kiddo." I've practiced this. I ran it by Abbey, who approved. She's pissed at Luca, worried about him, too, but she understands. I'll reach out to her from here on when I want to see Gia. "I have a new job."

"But you work for Baba." Gia sits in the grass with me.

"Well, actually, I work for Ms. Charlie. Remember her?"

"The fat one?" Gia scrunches her nose. "The one with a baby in her belly?"

"Yeah, but her baby is here. He's a baby boy, and she needs my help. I'm going to work for her, but I'm gonna visit you all the time, okay?"

It's not entirely true. Charlie and Daniel are fine. They have their detail. But I called Charlie and said since the threat to Luca and Gia has been contained for at least months, I was ready for a new assignment. And Charlie does need me. There's a new series being filmed nearby with three famous brothers, a former pop trio. Their security will be a nightmare. I'm already dreading screaming teenagers.

No, I'd rather be singing *The Little Mermaid* with a six year-old.

"But what about Baba?" Gia pets Crimson. Dutifully, he lies down for her. "If you leave, he'll be sad."

I'm sad, too.

It's been two weeks, and I'm broken beyond what I knew was possible. Telling Luca and Zar to leave that night took everything I had.

At first, Luca refused. "I won't leave you," he growled. "You're mine, and you know it."

"No," but I stood up to him, "you were never really *with* me. You never gave me everything like I gave to you. I only belong to someone who'll love me back, who'll say it, and be proud about it, so leave." He wouldn't move, so I put all my pain in my words, not my fists. I screamed in his face, "Leave, Luca! I'm a whore, right? I'm not worth your love, your kiss, your touch, or your fuck, so leave! I fucking hate you for hurting me, too!"

It was the right and worst thing to say, but it worked. It punched his jaw to the side, the death blow real. Anguish and shame took his face, so he silently turned and left, slamming my door behind him.

Zar gave me a hug and a peck on the cheek. He promised, "I'll watch after him. I won't kneel for him. I deserve more, too, but I'll make sure he's okay."

"Please." I meant it, hugging him back. And he kept hugging me until my sobs finally stopped.

I'll always be bonded with Zar, and I didn't want to hurt Luca. I'll always love him, but I love myself, too, and I don't want to hurt anymore.

Or, at least, maybe one day I won't.

"Your Baba will be okay," I assure Gia. "He loves you so much, and he may be grumpy for a while, but he'll get better. I promise."

I tug at the hem of her navy uniform dress. Gia only has a week of kindergarten left, and I've hated not driving her there.

Zar told Gia I went on a vacation with my sister when, really, I've been lost. I took time off. Every day, I run back and forth over that bridge. It's five miles and designed for pedestrians to enjoy, but I don't. I'm just trying to find peace.

"Will you be okay?" I ask Gia. I need for her to be. "I'm right here, okay?" I point to the building she can see from the front door of The Mercier. "You can ask your Aunt Abbey to call me anytime, and we can do a playdate."

"What about Zar?"

"Zar can play with us."

"But Baba can't play with us?" She looks back at him, glaring our way behind sunglasses. "Is he still your friend?"

Oh fuck. Please don't do it. Don't cry.

I kept my piercings. They sometimes hurt as I do, but I left my collar and hair clip with the concierge last week. I made sure Luca got my message with no note—he didn't choose me, so I'm choosing myself.

I don't belong to him anymore.

"When your Baba ever feels like playing again,"—*loving again* —"he can be my friend."

But I don't trust it. I won't break Gia's heart, but I don't trust Luca won't always break mine.

Broken people break people.

That's what my mom used to say.

"Will you still come to my karate classes?" she asks, and I stare, treasuring every freckle dusting Gia's nose. She deserves someone to love her like a mom, and I feel like I am because this hurts so much.

"Of course," I croak, fighting to keep it together. "I'm so proud of you. You just earned your yellow belt. Next is orange. You may earn it by Christmas."

Gia nods. "I'm good!"

"You sure are!"

"Gia!" That voice booms, shaking my soul. On instinct, I turn my head and follow it.

Luca's standing on the edge of the park, far enough away to make this worse. His hands are shoved in his faded jeans. His thin, V-neck T-shirt hangs soft on his bronze body, but his voice is harsh.

"Gia!" He shouts again. "Let's leave."

Leave.

He said that on purpose.

Luca could've used other words, but he swears by how much they hurt, and now, he's using them to hurt me, too.

"Bye, Scarlett." Gia jumps up, wrapping her little arms around my neck, but I don't get up. I let the pain pin me down.

"Bye, kiddo." That's what my dad called me; I hear it now, so I squeeze her tight. "I'll see you again soon. I promise. I'm not leaving you."

She pecks my cheeks, as her dad does to all but rarely did to me, before she runs away, and I watch.

I watch a little girl grab her father's outstretched hand before she turns back, waving goodbye to me.

But Luca?

He doesn't look back.

Luca

CHAPTER TWENTY-FIVE

SEVEN MONTHS LATER

"BUT SPENCER WAS MEAN, SO I PUNCHED HIM."

Gia scowls, folding her arms, sitting in time out on the bench where her Sensei told her to go for ten minutes.

"You are *not* in karate to punch people." I squat to her level, scolding with the voice she *used* to listen to. "You're here to learn to defend yourself. Do it again, and no more karate."

She narrows her eyes. "You're mean all the time."

"Gia Anaïs, speak to me respectfully and behave, or you will lose screen time for a month, too."

What the fuck has gotten into my daughter? She's gone from a cute little ninja to an angry punching nightmare.

"But Spencer started it!" she protests. "He said you and Ms. Maren are getting married. But I said you're married to my mommy in heaven, and he said that's dumb! Dead people aren't married."

That logic hits hard. I love my daughter but hate my life. All I do lately is go through the motions and put out little Gia fires all day.

A tap on my shoulder turns my chin.

"Got a minute?"

It's Abbey, fighting her grin.

"Gia," I turn back to her, "you have eight more minutes. And you *will* behave and you *will* apologize to Spencer, Ms. Maren, and your Sensei for your behavior. Understood?"

She glares at me, so I raise my eyebrow.

"Yes, *Baba*." She sounds so thrilled.

"What the fuck has gotten into her?" I side-whisper to Abbey once we have some distance.

As usual, the dojo is packed—more than ever, it seems. I don't recognize some faces and some I can't see because it's so crowded.

"You're kidding me, right?" Abbey laughs. "Luca, it's Parenting 101."

"What?"

"Gia's pissed about you being up Maren's ass all the time. And quite frankly, I feel like punching dicks about it, too."

I glance across the dojo, wincing at the red face of Spencer, still huffing tears with an ice pack over his little pecker. I'd be proud of Gia for standing up for herself, but... *Maren's* son? Really? Of all pricks to punch?

Everyone, please, line up to fuck my life, but be warned. The wait is long.

"I'm not up Maren's ass," I growl, and Abbey snorts, swiping my nose before I bat her hand away. "What are you doing?"

"She left a little shit on your tip."

"I'm not ass-diving anyone, thank you very much."

"Speaking of," Abbey keeps rolling, "have you heard from Zar? From Scarlett?"

Even though Abbey always pisses me off so much that I laugh, this subject's not funny.

"Sorry," Abbey mutters. "Too soon?"

"Never will be the right time."

I let that hang in the air while I fight the sudden clench of my heart.

I see Zar every weekday for work. That's it. He's relaxed and aloof, and it hurts because he's made it clear. If Scarlett's not with me, *he's* not with me.

But I know he doesn't hate me. He gave me the biggest gift I never asked for this July Fourth, on the fifth anniversary. It was like Zar gave me a silent ultimatum to change for Gia's sake.

So I'm trying.

And Scarlett?

I think of her all the time, then force myself not to. Her collar and hair clip lie beside the cologne on my dresser. I make myself see them every day, then look away.

It's different when you lose someone who's still alive. When you love them, and they hate you. It's almost as bad as them dying because that's how I feel without Scarlett. Dead inside.

I know it's been hard on Gia, too, so I'm trying to live a normal life, hoping it will feel right one day.

I glance again at Maren. She's shaking her head my way, so I mouth "sorry," and she gives me a soft shrug like she understands.

"And *that's* why Gia's a holy terror lately." But Abbey catches me. "You're playing house with Maren, and you're a hemorrhoid about it. Scarlett and Zar kept you from being a real pain in the ass, but, *hmmm*, for some *strange* reason, they're not around, and your assholery has swollen to epic proportions."

"God," I huff. "Your husband needs to sail home and give you some back-door boogie because ass is all you think about."

"Back-door boogie?" She chuckles. "What is this? The 70s?" She elbows me. "Yes, I need John to come home and bury his bone in my backyard, but we're talking about your bitchy dog right now and it ain't Gia."

Maren may behave like a saint with me, but Abbey still swears she's the devil.

The Sensei claps once. "Gia," he calls, and she stands, bowing to him. But then I catch her fighting not to roll her eyes while she makes a dramatic show of going over, stoically shaking Spencer's hand, then Maren's.

Gia's so genuine, it's fake and Abbey snorts. "She's just like her."

"Who?"

"You know who."

Scarlett sees Gia every Sunday. Abbey takes her, and I stay home. But every Saturday night, I walk alone through the French Quarter.

I walk by Delta's and remember. I walk to the park beside Scarlett's building, and it's empty. I walk around to the side of her building where her balcony is. I stand out of the lamplight, letting shadows cloak me while I watch. Because every Saturday night, she's there on her balcony. She's too far away for me to see much, but it's enough.

I still spend my Saturday nights with Scarlett.

"She's lost a lot of weight," Abbey laments.

"I know."

"You've seen her?"

I don't confess about my weekly watching. No, I debrief her on official business. "We had a security meeting last week, and Scarlett was there. Her boss and colleagues, too."

"Why?" Abbey sounds worried.

"Because Brooke Turner was released on parole this week."

"Your stalker?" Abbey asks, "Does that mean Scarlett's coming back?"

Long ago, Abbey figured out Scarlett was not my assistant. Of course, my protective sister-in-law looked her up and found Scarlett's title fights on YouTube.

"No," I answer. "They don't think Brooke's as much of a threat as before. Her husband's ranch is in foreclosure. Their life is in a scandal, so hopefully, she's learned. But, just in case, we have security on the elevator again. And Charlie, Scarlett's boss, is searching for another woman Gia will trust."

"Luca," Abbey groans, "just get *Scarlett* back. You know you want to. You know you miss her."

"She told me to leave, so I moved on," I tell her. "It's what you told me to do, for Gia's sake, right?"

Abbey can hear my tone. I'm not fucking around. I'm not in the mood. I'm not a Dom or a man trying to control. I'm just trying to be the father Gia needs, even if doing the right thing feels so wrong.

"Well," Maren appears beside us, "*that* was more drama for the day."

Abbey steps away on my left while Maren closes in on my right.

"Sorry," I tell her. "I've spoken with Gia. She's just going through a phase."

"It's been a very *long* phase." Maren's voice strains with judgment. "I've tried so hard with her. Spencer, too. But Gia tries my patience. She's acting like a—"

"And that's what parents do," Abbey jumps in. "You use your patience, and you deal with it. You don't get a goddamn trophy for being the mature adult you're supposed to be."

Oh fuck, Abbey's defending her niece, and *oh fuck*, Maren's going to be pissed.

I'm caught in estrogen crossfire.

"Yes, of course," Maren answers tersely. "I'm a good mother, a good woman. I know all about patience." Resting her hand on my arm, she eases. "Luca, let's bake cookies with the kids tonight. Let's go to the market after class and get a bunch of icing. They can decorate together and get along just fine. It'll be perfect."

Abbey nudges my arm, and I flick my eyes at her.

When Abbey shakes her head no like that, she looks exactly like Darby. Like in one silent gesture, she's seething, "Oh, hell-to-the-no. I do NOT approve."

But this is me. This is the life I'm trying to have. I'm not happy, and Gia certainly hates it, but at least I'm trying to have a future.

I've learned some painful, lonely lessons lately. I'm using my power to fix the past, at least what I can. I'm secretly trying to make some wrongs right.

The proof?

I'm not wearing my wedding band anymore.

Scarlett

CHAPTER TWENTY-SIX

"WHAT DO YOU MEAN A 'NAUGHTY NEW YEAR'S PARTY?'"

"I mean," Zar drawls, his voice filling my car and heart. "You're coming to one of my parties."

"My sister sure loves them." I'm not joking. Ruby raves about Zar's parties.

It seems months ago when Luca excluded Zar from Silas and Eily's party at the club, Zar was inspired to start hosting private events at his beach house.

Was it to get back at Luca? It sounds like his parties are so hot; who cares?

"She sure does," Zar admires. "There's no slack in your sister's rope. She's one of the few women I'll allow."

"Are you in love?"

"Do I have a death wish?" He laughs. "Hell no. I'm never fucking your sister. I'm not fucking anyone. I'm..." He pauses, and I feel the same. "I'm trying to be happy. At least this dog is on the hunt while I bet there're cobwebs on your pretty kitty."

I don't fuck Zar. I don't fuck anyone. I finally feel numb, and I'd like to keep it that way. Fuck you very much, Love.

It's simple math. No fucks equals no Fuck Flu.

Zar knows this. We talk all the time.

"Just what am *I* supposed to do at one of your private orgies?"

"Check IDs at the door. Be my hot bouncer with bouncing titties."

I laugh. "Fuck you!"

"Fuck someone, please." He taunts. "And by the way, it's not an orgy; it's an *opportunity*."

"An opportunity for what?" I turn left. I'm past due for stocking up my fridge, and I'm bingeing a new show this weekend. Beer and chips are required, though I lost my appetite months ago. "Are you inviting me to a kinky fuckathon with the NFL's finest?"

"They are *fine*." Zar drawls again, "*Dayum* fine. One in particular is..."

His voice drops as I pull into the parking lot of my local market. I park, feeling the ache in his silence.

"It's okay," I tell him. "You're allowed to move on. You can love someone else."

"You gonna swallow that pill, too?" he asks while I stare out my front windshield. I can't see anything but all the love I never had.

"I'm not ready," I answer. "Though some of y'all won't listen."

"Oh," Zar croons. "Who? Who's ringing your chimes for a different answer?"

I grin because I'm saying it to piss him off. "Your favorite: Jameson Grant. He calls me all the time."

Zar falls silent. My engine idles. I don't turn the car off or Bluetooth either until our phone chat is done.

"He'll kill him if he finds out." All mischief drops from Zar's tone. "You know that, right? Luca wasn't kidding. *You* may have left, but he never leaves. He's still watching you. He always will."

I don't know it, but I sense it.

Every Saturday night, I stand on my balcony and get lost in the view and memories. I get so lost, I feel like Luca's there with me, but I'm alone.

And I'm lonely.

I don't want to know if or how Luca's moved on because I

know he can't hide who he is forever. No one can. Eventually, he'll need someone to torture again.

Just please, God, don't let me know about it.

That's the worst part. When they move on, leaving you behind. Like your love was a lie.

"It's not what you think," I answer Zar. "Jameson's a friend. We just talk. He's going through some shit right now." And it's not for me to share, so I leave it there.

"Well, then," Zar soothes. "Come just be my friend, too. Come sit on my back porch in a rocking chair beside me. Come watch the ocean and ring in the New Year with me while we hear others fucking and being happy about it, even if we aren't."

"You got a ring with that proposal because I just might accept it?" I talk to Zar and the bustling parking lot. "Me and you? Like a celibate nun and monk, growing old together, while we host secret society parties for closeted NFL players. Hell, yes, I'm game."

"You want diamonds or pearls?"

"Darlin'," I'll always tease him, "you know I deserve both."

"Only if you show up. New Year's Eve. Nine o'clock. If you're not here, I'm kidnapping you. And please, beat my ass when I do because my Mister Happy sure needs a hard pounding."

"Good night," is my answer with a grin.

"Night, gorgeous."

He ends our call and I turn off my ignition.

It's a Friday night on a December weekend. The grocery store is packed with people buying wine and party foods. Good for them.

I want a party like I want a kidney stone.

After scoring on the beer and the snack aisle, I wind my way to the frozen section. Walking past the cliché ice cream for a solo date, I crave waffles for company. They'll taste like shit with beer, and that matches my mood.

Scanning the freezer case, I spot different kinds of waffles, but the ones from Disney's *Frozen* make me smile. *I know someone who'd love these. Me, too, now.* I grab a box, letting the freezer door slam shut while I drop the waffles in my cart, needing real maple syrup and...

"Scarlett!"

I look up. Gia's running down the frozen aisle, aiming for my legs to hug.

"Well, hey, kiddo." I bend down to hug her because she wraps around me so fast. I'm so surprised that I lose my logic for too long to protect myself.

She can't be here alone.

"Gia!" That voice booms through the market, and my soul quakes.

Please, no.

One work meeting with him was enough. I couldn't even look at Luca. Not once. I focused on Zar. I focused on the security report about Brooke Turner's release. I focused on finding another protection officer for Gia while I pretended I could breathe for an hour, but I couldn't.

I wore my clothes. I wore my stoic face. I died inside, tender pieces of me starved for oxygen while Luca's fire burned right through me; with what emotion, I don't know.

I left the meeting so fast, with Wade and Charlie by my side, and I didn't look back, though Luca's glare scalded my back.

But now?

"Gia?" His voice softens at the sight of us hugging. "Hey," he says tenderly, but who is it for?

Luca stands at the top of the aisle, his face relieved like he'd been chasing Gia through the market. And he's breathtaking. He's massive and magnetic with crystal eyes grabbing me through his onyx strands. He's wearing those same faded jeans, but it's winter. Luca traded his white linen shirt for a sweater. The vintage, cream, Greek fisherman's sweater I bought him last New Year's in Mykonos.

He still wears my sweater? It softens something inside. Hope flutters my heart. He looks happy to see me. *Does that mean he still—*

"There you are!" Maren appears, and I hide my gasp, the agony instant.

No...please, no.

Maren's pushing a brimming grocery cart with Spencer on her heels.

Please don't do this to me.

She's wearing a white preppy sweater, jeans, and high heels, too, like she matches Luca.

Not her.

She looks perfect, like she belongs with him, and that's when I remember my hair's in a messy top knot, and I'm still in my sweats. An old faded baggy set that's red and green with Crimson's muddy paw stains and the Grinch's smiling face on them, too, for the merry fucking season.

I look as pathetic as I suddenly feel.

Hell stands on higher ground than me.

"Scarlett!" Gia squeezes my legs again. "We're decorating cookies tonight. Wanna come?"

We?

I look down at her, sudden pain choking my voice. I don't know how to answer, how not to hurt her or me. And when I glance back up, I see Maren strolling my way with her smirk so big, her makeup so flawless, her long, straight brown hair so elegant. Her hazel eyes dance on the grave of my dreams with Luca, mocking everything I ever wished for. It all dies instantly as I rip my shocked glance from her.

To *HIM.*

Because Luca stops, he stands beside Maren, his arm barely brushing hers. They look like the couple, the family they are now, while my teeth grab my trembling lip, feeling disgraced, while Luca stares at me like he doesn't even recognize me.

But I know who I am.

I'm that girl, alone and left at the window, and I can't see anything but this blinding pain. It's all I can see because Luca's trained me too well. For him, I'm too observant. My shattered heart noticed before my teary eyes did...

He's not wearing his wedding band.

It's degrading. It's insulting. It's every scar I have ripped open. Every insecurity shoved in my face, trying not to cry.

For Maren, he took it off. For her, he moved on. For her, he's willing to try. For Luca, Maren is good enough.

I lost.

Maren won his love.

Humiliation buckles my knees, but I recover, squatting beside Gia, fighting it, clinging to my last shred of dignity, the last ounce of fight I have left. For her, I will...

"Some other time, kiddo," I answer her invitation.

But it happens because deep inside, I feel that girl crying at the window while I'm staring at this little girl I love so much, *and her father left me, too.*

My tear falls.

I can't fight it.

"Why are you crying?" Gia's worried, her little hand landing on my cheek.

I swallow, forcing my smile. "I'm just so happy to see you."

I can't look at him. I won't. No man gets my last piece of pride. I'll die with it.

Gia wraps her arms around my neck, and I bury my face in her curls. She squeezes me back before pulling away. "I get my orange belt tomorrow."

"You do?" I make pride, at least for her, fill my voice. I keep my eyes on her. She's all I have left of that dream, even in pieces that are too small. Even though I can smell Luca's cologne. Citrus and cypress mock the nights I slept in his arms. Even though I can see his shoes, the ones I used to kneel before.

"Will you come?" Gia asks.

"Of course." It will kill me to have to watch Luca loving Maren, but for Gia, I'll give my life. "What time?"

She's six. I don't expect her to know or answer. He does. "One."

His body looms, his voice falling over me, too, like I'm on my knees for him again, but no, never again. I keep my eyes on Gia, not him. I fake a smile for her.

"I'll be there. I promise." I kiss her cheek. "Night, kiddo."

I let my body lead. I trust it, not my heart. Turning as I stand, I walk away, leaving my full grocery cart alone in the aisle while I take my beaten pride with me.

Ignoring why I was here and everything I used to fight for, I remember the only one who'll be there when I get home. I disappear down the dog food aisle and grab a bag for Crimson. The only kind moment I'm granted tonight. The one thing that's not *HIF #17* being shoved down my burning throat is the empty self-checkout I find and quickly, I pay.

I make it to the parking lot. I make it to my car. I make it to my hatch, popping it open. Tossing the bag on the mat, I throw my purse beside it. My phone falls out as my hands fall, and my tears fall, too. I brace my palms on the car mat while I let one sob escape.

So I can breathe. So I can gulp for the air, love, and happiness I can't find. So I can still feel alive, though my soul just died.

"Scarlett."

Please, stop.

Luca's standing behind me, making this worse, making another sob rack up my spine, but this one, I fight. I bite my bottom lip so hard I make it bleed, iron and salt filling my mouth.

If I'm not good enough for his love, he's not good enough for my tears—no more.

"Scarlett."

Not even my eyes. My stare that he used to demand, his crystal eyes locked to mine, he doesn't get that either. I keep my back to him.

"Leave," I demand.

"Just—"

"Leave," I insist because all I can see is how, in the store, Luca's wedding finger didn't have a pale ring around it—the one I used to see. No, it's gone. His finger is tan. He gave Maren his love all summer. "Leave. Be happy. Gia deserves it."

"Look at me."

"Never again."

I won't say his name, either. He'll never hear it from my trembling lips. I reach for my keys that sprawled across the mat. I look for my phone that fell out of my purse next, and it rings. The screen lights up the night and I glance down at it by my bumper.

JAMESON

I see who's calling me. Luca must see it, too. Good. Let him hurt as I do. I'll drag him to his knees with me, both of us beaten and bloody.

Zar said Luca would be furious if I'm with Jameson. Well, let him feel defeat. Let him suffer like me.

Jameson's ringtone blares, demanding an answer, but I let Luca hear it. Adele sings "Someone Like You" on my phone. It's an inside joke Jameson made about me and the girlfriend he loves, but Luca doesn't know that.

Luca's moved on with his life, with his heart, with his daughter, too, so let him believe the worst about my life, too.

I let the song play, taunting the air until Jameson's call rolls to voicemail. Then I shove the phone in my purse and grab it before I slam the hatch closed, and still, I won't look at him.

"Belle," he growls.

"Leave," I command. "I'm the Master of my heart now."

Luca doesn't answer.

I aim for my driver's door while his footfalls fill the air. He walks away; he leaves while I drive away, too.

I make it home. I make it through a night walk with Crimson. I make it through five old episodes of *Schitt's Creek* trying to cheer up, but it doesn't work.

It's almost midnight when my phone buzzes with a text on my nightstand. I flip it over.

SEMEN DEMON

No one is like you, my belle

Luca's torture never ends, and I don't know what that's supposed to mean.

I don't answer him.

I go out on my balcony and let the night hear the cries I've been fighting. I let the river take my sobs. I let the stars glisten like my eyes spilling with tears until it's all out of me. The wails. The pain. I don't care who hears me. Who sees me.

There's nothing left but me, the darkness above, the street lamps glowing below, and tomorrow, when like hell will Luca Mercier ever make me cry again.

Luca

CHAPTER TWENTY-SEVEN

I'M STARING AT A SEA OF KIDS AND FAMILIES IN THE DOJO. Excitement fills the air, but I'm exhausted. I didn't sleep last night.

But it was worth it.

Fate had lost her patience with me. She wasn't subtle. She took a baseball bat to my life, hitting me with sign after sign.

Maren spit nails because I ran after Scarlett. We didn't make a scene in front of our respective kids, but Maren gave me the evil silent treatment while we left the market, and I dropped her and Spencer off.

Why? Because I didn't apologize for running after Scarlett.

Seeing her was my first sign. She looked so real and tender in her cozy Grinch sweats, with her hair in that cute knot. My gaze landed on her, and I didn't see my past. Scarlett suddenly looked like my future. I saw her hugging Gia, and I saw the one thing I could change.

My one chance to make it right.

But Maren made it worse.

She was smug while Scarlett suffered. Watching her abandon her cart, Gia tugged my hand. I lifted her, and she whispered in my car. "Baba, I want Scarlett."

It was another sign, so I whispered back, "Me, too, my kóri," before I pecked her cheek, set her down, and ran after her.

Did I know there'd be hell to pay?

Sure. Thank god I'm a billionaire who doesn't give a damn.

Though no money will fix how I've hurt Scarlett, how she won't even look at me.

Cookie night was canceled, and Gia seemed thrilled to have me to herself. While I cuddled with her and watched *Frozen*, Maren tried to start a text fight with me like we're thirteen.

> **MAREN BANKS**
>
> Don't ever embarrass me like that again

> > Speak to your son like your boy. Not me

> **MAREN BANKS**
>
> I thought you threw that white trash away months ago. Seems I was wrong

> > Yes, you're very wrong

> > Goodbye

So I ended the fight like I'm thirty and no one's bitch, because it didn't take but a second of jealousy for Maren to reveal her true toxic self again.

Then I waited for Gia to fall asleep. Since it was Friday and Celine's night off, I had only one other person I trusted with her.

> > Will you watch our girl?

> **STUD**
>
> Not for you

> > For Gorgeous

> **STUD**
>
> There in 60

Zar lives at his Isle of Palms home now, not his suite on the fifth floor. He sees Gia every day, but I'm like a ghost to him.

And I deserve it.

When he finally arrived, his customary chill was gone. He seethed, "Are you finally making this right?"

"She's with that fuckboy, Jameson, now."

Suddenly, Zar's eyes sparkled with mischief like he knew something I didn't. "Well then," he smirked, "be the raging bull with the biggest balls and go fight for her."

But before I made an ass of myself twice and barged into Scarlett's building and killed Jameson Grant, I checked her balcony first. Her lights were on, so I texted her about that song.

Another song from Adele.

It was another sign: the slap my face deserved.

A moment later, Scarlett was on her balcony. From a hundred feet above, I could barely hear her sobs, but they crushed me.

Scarlett was alone, but I swear someone stood beside me.

Hello? Can you hear me?

It was my beautiful ghost.

That bridge spanned the horizon from where I stood by the river, calling to me, hearing another woman crying because of me, and I started to walk.

It was the final sign, and I listened.

I walked the path I've hated for so long, curving and climbing for miles until I stood at the center of the Ravenel Bridge, as close to *that spot* as I could.

The memory will never leave me, and it shouldn't. Because you can love someone and let them go. It was time. It was okay. Darby was singing to me. She was telling me to. From the wallet in my back pocket, I took out my first wedding band. I'm saving Darby's wedding ring, her diamond, for Gia one day.

But the gold wedding band?

It belongs with the angels, too. I gave it the river, with a prayer and some tears, and finally said goodbye.

When I got home, I found Zar in my bed, and Gia curled up

with him. So I laid beside her, too, and slept an hour before Gia woke us up.

Once she hopped off the bed to go to the bathroom, I reached for Zar. I held his cheek. "I'm sorry," I told him.

He trailed his fingertip over my lips. "Did she hear that, too?"

"Not yet. It was too late last night. But she will. I promise. I love her. I love you."

He cocked a smile. "I love you, too, you fucking asshole." Then he paused. He had to tell me, "I found someone."

"Good." I meant it.

"I still want you. I still want her. But I belong with him like you belong with her." Then he always has to be a sexy smartass. "And I swear if you don't get her back for us, I'll be showing *your* ass the business end of a whip."

I laughed. He laughed. Gia raced back to my bed, jumping on it, jumping on us until it all felt right, except for the one person we miss the most.

"Someone put Meow Mix in the Chex Mix today."

As usual, Abbey stands beside me in the dojo, her snark making me laugh.

The belt ceremony is a celebration, so snacks and punch are being served. Zar was supposed to come too, but we woke up to Gia, our truce, and an earthquake in Naples, so he took a flight to assess our property there so I wouldn't miss this for Gia.

Celine's here, too. She's been flirting with some kid's single granddad, and good for her.

I look across the dojo mat and see what Abbey's joking about. There, Maren stands, right back to her old ways of gossiping with the moms. This time, their clawing eyes swipe my way.

While kids scurry around, I mutter to Abbey, "I think I started a pussy fight."

"Started?" She scoffs, "This is the championship round because look who just walked in the door."

Immediately, I see her, too, the breath ripped from my lungs.

Holy Shit, it's the real Scarlett Jones.

Not the one pretending to be my demure assistant, or a proper lady fitting in, or a woman dripping in French couture. No, this is Scarlett in full effect, making all eyes turn her way while she smirks back at Maren.

Long auburn hair in a fiery mane. Black leather pants and boots. A sleeveless ivory mock turtleneck. Scarlett's showing off her tattoos, her lithe muscles, her amazing breasts with proud nipple piercings, the diamonds I gave her. You can see their outline through her tight shirt with no bra, and my cock roars to life after being silent for months.

The hisses from Maren's clowder are instant, but this time, Scarlett stalks their way, blowing a kiss to the other moms before she yanks Maren's hand into a covert hold.

I'd give half my fortune to know what she's whispering in Maren's ear, but it looks like Maren is about to piss in her paisley pants.

"Fuck yes," Abbey mutters, watching as Scarlett leaves Maren visibly shaken. "The kitty just met the lioness."

I can't take my eyes off her. Scarlett finds a spot to stand by herself, and there's so much I need to say to her. I know she'll make me pay first, and hell, yes, I'll probably enjoy it.

Gia runs across the mat. It melts me how she asks Scarlett to fix her ponytail. It's fine. I fixed Gia's hair this morning, but she misses Scarlett. I do, too.

The Sensei claps, and three dozen kids in gees form three lines. The dojo is stuffed with proud families, too, so one of the staff thankfully props open the double glass doors at the front to let in some mild winter air.

Still, I sweat at the sight of Scarlett. I don't hide that when I'm not watching Gia, I'm watching her.

But she won't look at me.

Like I've hurt Scarlett beyond repair.

"Gia Mercier."

Sensei calls her forward, swelling my chest with pride, watching Gia demonstrate her kicks, punches, and blocks. She gets a big smile when it's her turn to chop a board as thin as paper, but it's the gesture that counts. She does it with a fearless

"Keeyah!" and it's too cute. We clap when Sensei takes her yellow belt, replacing it with an orange one, and I glance over.

Scarlett's watching her, too, blooming heat through my chest because it's not with her stoic bodyguard face. She's smiling, proud, and teary-eyed for Gia.

Like a mom.

It takes an hour for the ceremony to end, and then mayhem ensues. Kids run everywhere. Families crowd the floor for pictures. Punch gets spilled on the mat, and Gia's running between Abbey and me, to Celine, then Scarlett, then to giggle with her friends.

Finally, I work my way to Scarlett in the crowd. She sees me coming and looks away like she's searching for Gia.

I'm not known for patience or for being a kind man when I want something.

Something that's mine...

But I try.

I close the distance between us. The crowd presses against us, and she won't look at me, but she lets me lean in to whisper.

"Would you like to demonstrate your black belt by kicking my blue balls?" I swear a smile ghosts her lips, but she fights it. "Or you can break boards over my dick, though I'm warning, it stays hard for you."

Her face is stone, her eyes scanning the room, her chin starting to pivot. "Your girlfriend sure would hack up a furball over that."

"I'm a grown man; I don't have *girlfriends*. I claim the *woman* who's mine, and it's you."

I watch it dawn over Scarlett's eyes how I'm not standing with Maren, how Maren's glaring our way because I'm seeking her again.

I want her back.

I'm about to demand Scarlett look at me, but she demands, "Where's Gia?"

Panic laces her voice, and I whip around, searching the crowd, too.

Kids are screaming. Parents are laughing. The dojo has speakers set up with music playing. It's wall-to-wall people.

I don't see her either.

"Gia!" I shout into the crowd while Scarlett turns toward the open glass doors.

"Shit!" She starts rushing that way, and I see it, too—my world being taken from me in slow motion.

I watch the nightmare in the parking lot through the glass wall of windows. Brooke Turner is trying to drag Gia by the arm across the pavement, but Gia's kicking her shins.

Scarlett pushes through the crowd to get her. I do, too.

"Baba!" Gia screams for me as we rush outside, leaving the din of the dojo behind.

"Gia!" I start running for her, but Scarlett grabs my shirt, yanking me back, and I halt, suddenly seeing it, too.

The driver's door of Brooke's white Mercedes is open, and her husband rises from his seat, raising his right hand with a black gun aimed our way.

"Twenty million!" He shouts while all I can hear is Gia screaming, "Baba!" and "No!" and "Keeyah!" She's kicking Brooke, who's dragging my soul toward the car.

"Get her. I'll get the gun."

Scarlett says it so fast. She acts so fast because she is faster, but I act, too.

Together, we run, rushing them. It makes Brooke and Gia scream at my approach. I can only focus on my daughter and the blur on my left that's Scarlet, racing faster than me right toward a gun. And I don't have to stop what's about to happen. *Give me my daughter.* I reach, grabbing Gia's hand, while my fist lands across Brooke's face.

Then, a blast, a gunshot pierces the air.

It's instinct. Gia screams, and I take her down with me. I shield her body with mine, covering her, holding her tight, my reality a blur with her safely in my arms.

Brooke screams. She's on the ground beside us, her nose

347

pouring blood from my punch, but she's not looking at me. She's watching, and I look over my shoulder at the spectacle, too.

Scarlett has Brooke's husband on the ground. He's a big man, but she's wrapped around his back while he tries to fight her. He's reaching overhead, punching at her skull, dragging their bodies across the pavement, but Scarlett's arms trap his neck in a choke-hold, her legs coiled around his waist. She's not letting him go.

Or breathe.

"Bitch." He's spitting. His face is red, eyes bulging with no air because Scarlett fights. She squeezes her arms tighter, choking off more oxygen to his brain with her right bicep over his neck...and that's when I see it: blood weeping from the gunshot wound through her arm.

"Scarlett!" I call out, but I hold Gia. She's crying, whimpering under me.

I search the pavement for the gun. Scarlett's kicked it away from the man's grasp, but she's not taking chances.

"Go night, night, motherfucker," she growls, and with one final squeeze of her bicep, making it gush blood, he collapses.

Sirens near. The screams from the dojo hit my logic. The Sensei blocked the doors. He kept everyone safely inside, and it's wise until Scarlett does how she's trained.

She kicks the man's body off hers and drags to her feet, plucking his gun from the ground before aiming it at him and Brooke.

"Luca," she huffs for breath, "clear the scene. Secure Gia inside."

She's right, so I pick Gia up with me. "Scarlett!" But she starts crying, reaching for her.

"She's okay, my kóri. She won the fight." I hold Gia tight, racing back toward the building and Abbey, who pushes past the Sensei, reaching her arms out for her.

It happens fast. Police cars swarm the parking lot with two ambulances behind them.

Scarlett sets the weapon down and puts her hands in the air. At first, officers aim their guns at her, but I run back toward the scene. "Not her!" I shout with my hands up, too. "She's my body-guard! It's them." I nod to Brooke, crying on the ground, and her husband starting to wake.

The police take no chances. Some keep their weapons drawn while others put cuffs on all three. It's protocol, but I don't care.

Calmly, I approach the officer, cuffing Scarlett while my blood boils. "She's Protection Officer Scarlett Jones with HGR Security. I'm Luca Mercier. She was protecting my daughter and neutral-ized this kidnapping attempt. Uncuff her now!" Scarlett winks at me but staggers, the color draining from her face. "She needs medical care!" She's trying to calm me down, but it's not okay; she's about to pass out.

The officer realizes it, too. "Medic!" She shouts, and EMTs appear, then it's a blur.

Scarlett's on a gurney. Officers secure the scene. A medic asks to check on Gia, too, so we climb into the back of the other ambu-lance. Gia wants me to hold her the whole time, and I do. She's physically fine but shaken, asking me several times, "Is Scarlett okay?"

"Yes, my kóri," I keep telling her while I watch them whisk Scarlett away in another ambulance while we stay parked in the lot. I know she'll be okay, but someone tell that to my heart.

Once Gia is settled down, admiring the stickers an EMT gave her, an officer approaches.

He takes my statement. I give him the basic information before I insist, "Please contact Charlie Ravenel of HGR. She can fill you in on the details."

I don't want my daughter to hear them, to be scared. I'm not. We're safe. Brooke and her husband will be locked up for good.

The officer is gentle with Gia. "So," he eases, "Gia, have you seen those people before?"

"No," she answers, sitting on my lap. "But they were mean, and Scarlett beat them up for me."

The officer hides his chuckle. "She's your bodyguard?"

Gia shakes her head. She's never heard that word used for Scarlett.

"No," she answers proudly. "Scarlett is my mama bear."

Hot rocks choke my throat.

Gia got that from the Disney movie we watched with Scarlett, the one about the brave, fiery-haired girl and her mom, but this isn't a fantasy.

It's my final sign.

"Yes, she is, my kóri."

Because I'll make sure it's real.

Scarlett

CHAPTER TWENTY-EIGHT

"Want me to wash your pussy, first?"

I roll my eyes, lifting my right arm wrapped in plastic. "No, just wash my pits. I stink."

Gently, Ruby wipes with a washcloth, careful not to get my bandaged arm wet. It doesn't really hurt. The bullet missed my bone, and I've suffered worse in fights. But I wanted a shower so bad. If the hospital is making me stay another night, I can't stand feeling this gross.

Carefully, Ruby washes my breasts, fighting her grin. "Where did your ten thousand dollar titties go?"

"They took out my jewelry for surgery."

"You better get 'em back."

"I did. They gave me my clothes and jewelry in a bag."

"No," she says, squatting to wipe my legs next. I could do this myself, but my morning nurse is a five-star general. She ordered Ruby to help me shower. "I mean, you better get HIM back."

I don't answer. She finishes washing my body, handing me the cloth to, yes, wash my pussy, too, while Ruby starts on my hair.

"He's waiting outside, you know. He was here last night and back this morning."

I know. I could hear Luca barking at the nurses and doctors,

351

demanding scans that aren't necessary. They got the bullet out. I just have to stay pumped full of antibiotics and stay another day for observation before they send me home tomorrow.

"I don't want him back," I answer her.

HIF #18: Yeah, I can't convince myself, either.

"Uh-huh." She smoothes in conditioner. "He's got red roses," she taunts. "He's dressed in a suit and tie for you, too."

Images of the final scene of *Pretty Woman* fill my head. The one where the grumpy hero goes after his escort-turned-love to win her back. But I refuse to believe Luca watched it for me.

"And if you don't take him back," Ruby teases, "there's a mess of horny nurses and doctors out there, creaming their canyons for him."

"Eww!" But I laugh and lie. "Let them have him. I'm not accepting Maren's seconds."

That hurts worse than the wound in my arm.

Luca fucked Maren.

Luca kissed her.

Many times, probably.

I can imagine all the passion he shared with her since he's been waiting so long, and it hurts like hell. I can't breathe every time I think about it.

Ruby pinches my uninjured arm. "Ouch!" I flinch.

"Listen here." She points a finger at me. "We're the Jones sisters. It don't matter what number we are; no one fucks better than us."

"How do *you* know?"

"I've been told my male-catcher is championship level."

"We don't fuck the same males." I can't believe I'm having this spat.

She turns off the shower, grabbing a towel before patting me down. "Zar sings your praises. He's had pussy galore and won't fuck other women now. He says yours is the best."

"I never fucked him."

"Point proven because he's still whipped for you." She snorts. "Literally."

"Shut up and help me put on a sexy hospital gown."

Once I'm settled back on the bed, Ruby towel-dries my hair. "You need to see him," she mutters. "You've been miserable for months, and there's only one hot-as-fuck reason why."

With my left hand, I tug the blankets around me. "I got nothing to say to him."

"Well, Luca's got something to say to you. You know, for saving his daughter's life and all. And he may be an asshole Dom and a widower with a celibate vow that makes no damn sense, but that man will *not* stop until he speaks to you. You know it, so yank the Band-Aid off and get it over with."

But I don't see him.

Ruby leaves, and I eat the nastiest hospital lunch. The afternoon nurse comes in and checks on me, too. I talk on my phone. I debrief with Charlie and HGR. I waste as much time as I want watching Animal Planet on the hospital's TV until an evening nurse comes in.

While she checks my pulse, she laughs. "Mine would be up, too."

"I'm sorry?"

She eyes me over her glasses. "Honey, if that fine ass man was out there, waiting to see me—*all day* apparently—my pulse would be racing almost as fast as my little legs to catch him."

"Fine," I huff. "Send him in."

When the door closes behind her, all my emotions enter, flooding my pounding heart. I hold my breath as the door pushes open, then closes behind him.

Energy crackles, the heat rising in the room, in my cheeks, too, because Luca swallows the space, wearing a crisp black suit, a white starched shirt, and a tight scarlet tie. The red roses he holds have bloomed open. His onyx hair is the same, his crystal eyes, too. They search mine like he's been waiting forever on me, but I don't speak first.

"Thank you," he insists.

"How's Gia?" I rush, temporarily forgetting that I hate him.

"She's fine. She's home. Abbey and Harper are there. Celine, too." Carefully, he sets the roses on the table at the foot of my bed. "She drew this for you. She wants me to FaceTime with you, too, but I told her you were sleeping."

He reaches into his jacket pocket, pulling out its contents: a folded sheet of white paper and his black kerchief.

Tingles prickle my flesh. My body remembers. Liquid heat floods my core with the memory of what Luca did to me, how he made me come with paperclips on my nipples and his kerchief in my mouth, but he puts it back in his pocket while I raise my left hand for the drawing.

Fine. My body may forever lust for him, and it may want him back so badly, but not my heart.

I don't trust him.

"She uh..." Luca stammers, and it's not like him. "Gia drew you as a bear."

A smile fills my heart, studying her drawing. It's a stick-figure girl with long brown curls, standing between a tall stick-figure man with black hair and a brown squiggly blob with red hair and furry arms and legs.

I understand immediately. "Like from *Brave*," I mutter. "I'm the bear."

"Her *mama* bear," Luca adds. "That's what Gia calls you now."

I can't.

I squeeze my eyes and let tears spill for her, and I love it. I love how this little girl lives in my heart. She's made it so tender.

"Scarlett," Luca eases. "She's right. You *are* her mama bear. And I'll never be able to thank you enough for protecting her. I can't fix everything I've done, either, but I..."

He stammers again, so I look up from the drawing. He's reaching into his other pocket.

Luca looms feet from my bed, his beauty and cologne filling my senses. His trepidation, too.

Why is he afraid?

He pulls out another piece of paper. It shakes in his hand. "I don't know if I did the right thing," he says. "But I tried. All summer, I did. I couldn't live with myself, feeling like I left you. I know you told me to, and I understand why. So, I hope this doesn't upset you, because I had to do something. I had to make something right for you."

I look down at the paper in his hands. It looks like a letter. "What did you do?"

He swallows, locking his gaze on mine. "Scarlett, I found your father."

The ringing stabs my ears. I didn't hear him right. "What?"

This can't be true.

"Your father," he soothes. "I found him. He's alive. It took my PIs months, and it wasn't easy. He's been living off the grid in Alaska for years."

I can't see through my sudden tears. I can't breathe. "But...I don't understand. We thought he might be—"

"He spent twelve years in prison in Louisiana for armed robbery. It seems he tried to rob a bank."

How can this be?

"Does my mom know about this?"

Thoughtfully, Luca shrugs. "I don't know. I didn't want to overstep my bounds too much. Once I found him, I wrote him a letter. I told him I was a..." He pauses, choking on the word. "A *friend* of yours, trying to help you find him, and he wrote back. This is his letter to you."

My throat burns. "What does it say?"

"Don't *you* want to read it first?"

"I can't." I can't focus through my tears. I've never felt this vulnerable, this shaken before in my life. Not since my dad left me, and now he's back.

And Luca found him for me.

"Read it to me."

Carefully, Luca reads my dad's letter aloud.

Something about hearing my dad's apology in Luca's accent shatters me in the best way. The pain disappears. The little girl is okay. My dad is sorry. He's ashamed. He confesses that he made a stupid mistake, robbing a bank to get us money. He says he failed us. He couldn't face us, so he told my mom to tell us he was dead. Then he served his time and disappeared so we wouldn't be disgraced by having a felon for a father.

"But if you want to talk to me," Luca reads my father's words, his voice shaking, too, "I would be honored. Your nice friend said he'd fly me to you or whatever you need. I want to see you, kiddo, and tell you I'm sorry. That I love you."

Luca lowers the letter. "I'll do whatever you need, Scarlett. I'll bring him here or send you there, or I'll just leave this letter with you to decide one day."

He sets it beside the roses on the table.

"Why?" I wipe my tears. "Why did you do this for me?"

He pauses, his eyes caressing over me. Not in a sexy way. It's warm. It's adoring.

"Because I've watched you, Belle," he answers. "From the first night I met you, my eyes opened, my heart, too, and I witnessed the strong, beautiful woman you are on the outside and the tender, loving girl in your heart. I know it sounds odd, but it's true. And if I wouldn't let me take care of the woman you are, then I'd take care of the girl. The one waiting at the window. Because I'm never leaving her or you, Scarlett. You may never be with me. You may tell me to go, and I respect you; I will. But I will always be watching you, taking care of you, and—"

"But you're with Maren."

He shakes his head, swearing, "I'm NOT with Maren. I've never *been* with Maren. I was trying to give Gia a normal life, playdates and dinners and all. But I never broke my vow with her. I never even kissed her or—"

Half of my heart heals, but still, I argue, "But you took your wedding band off for her."

He glances down, studying his hand, how the tan line is gone, how I made the assumption.

"I took it off for Gia." He looks up at me. "All these years, I wore it to make it true. That *I* was married to her mother. That *I* was Gia's father. Though Darby slept with Zar, I needed to believe we were a real family once. That I was a good husband and a good father. I couldn't let that dream die, too."

A soft grin lifts his lips. "But of course, Zar defied me," he explains. He took a sample of my hair and Gia's, too, from our hairbrushes and had a DNA test done. On the fifth anniversary of Darby's death, Zar wanted me to know, with no doubt, that I *am* Gia's father. I didn't need to wear a ring to make it true."

He steps closer to my bed. The nurse left the side guards down, and my guard is down, too.

I'm overwhelmed.

I can't fight him, and I don't want to. All I hear is everything I need, everything I should trust.

I let Luca take my left hand. Gently, he holds it.

"I'm so sorry, my belle." It sighs over his lips. "I'm sorry I hurt you. That I denied you for so long. I asked you to fight for me, to make me break for you, and I only broke you instead. I can't make you forgive me. But you won. You make me love you, and I'll never stop."

A grin brushes my lips. "I *make* you?"

"Yes," he grins, lowering to one knee, holding my hand, and I can't believe my eyes. "I love you, Scarlett Jones. You are the master of *my* heart, and I'm begging for another chance to make you fall in love with me again."

My lips tremble. So does my hand in his. But my pride replies, "You asshole." I smile. "You think you can *make* me fall in love with you again?"

"Yes." He's too confident, too sexy, too powerful, and too humble right now. "Scarlett, I want to make everything right with you instead of being trapped in all I did wrong. Darby used to say, 'Choose hope.' I hear her now, and I choose you. I'm going to spoil you. I'll court you for everyone to watch, to see me proudly on my knees for Scarlett Jones. All the paparazzi. Charleston. Paris. Mykonos, and Maren, and her catty friends. They'll all see. I will prove to you and the world how much I love you. How much my daughter loves you, too. Then I'm going to ask you to marry me..."

My heart stops.

I can't stop staring at his eyes while he says, "I'm going to ask you to honor me. To please be the mama bear to my daughter. To be my family forever. To be Mrs. Scarlett Mercier, my beautiful wife, the only woman in my heart, and—"

"Ask me now."

He pauses, and my heart pounds. My world is spinning. My dream is coming true, and I know what I need.

What I deserve.

And when that sexy darkness falls over Luca's face. The one that makes him rise from his knee. The one that makes him smirk like an evil Sex God. The one that makes him let go of my hand so he can lean over and sink his hand into my hair, his lips lowering to mine...

I'm about to get it.

"I won't ask you, my belle." He nears. "I'll fucking prove it to you."

Suddenly, Luca's mouth is on mine, his warm kiss tearing my breath away while he gives me his. His lips seize. They take, they play, they part and pierce me open, his tongue finding mine, claiming it, too. His hands in my hair lift, making my body rise to take him.

After so long, our deep kiss is a flame and a flood. I moan into it, and he moans back, pressing deeper into me. It's hot. It's wet. It's us finally together again, but he halts, panting over our lips, "I don't want to hurt you."

"You're not." I grab his tie.

"Your arm," he worries.

"Fuck my arm." I mean it. "And fuck me right now, Luca."

It's all he needs to hear. To unleash. To let go. Like a feral animal unchained, he's on me. He's hunched over me, devouring our kiss. He's been starving, and I'm famished, too. I can't get enough of him consuming me.

I sink my left hand in his hair and demand. I push his mouth to my neck. It's my permission and plea, and he grabs it, tugging at my gown, groaning when he finds it untied. It's nothing but a thin sheet over me while he kisses my neck, biting it, too, ripping my gown down.

But he pauses, afraid to take it off my bandaged arm, so I do it. I tug the gown off, dropping it by the side of the bed before I lie back, naked for him, and Luca stops.

He hovers over me, his chest heaving, his pupils dilated. His stare ravages the sight of me. How my nipples harden for him. How my thighs fall open for him. With the remote dangling from the side of the bed, I press the button and lower it.

My body lies prone for him to take. I spread my knees wider, tilting my hips so he can see. I make him lick his lips at how my pussy gets so wet for him, too.

Tugging at his tie, Luca rips it off, then his jacket, too. Tossing them on the recliner in the room, he turns back to me, his stare pinning me down with his fists clenched.

He growls, "You make me so fucking hard for you, Scarlett, it hurts. I've been waiting so long for you. I..." His erection threatens to rip his pants, to rip me open, too, and I'll relish it.

But I know what he's thinking. Why he won't touch me yet. I know the final thread holding him back.

"I am, Luca." He won't say it first because I do. My wound doesn't hurt. Only this does; I ache for him. With both hands, I pinch my nipples for him. "I *am* your whore. I'm your proud whore who loves it when you say it to me. When you make me do dirty and degrading things for you. When you fuck me like one for anyone to watch. It's not an insult. You make me feel beautiful. You make us feel right, like we belong together. You make me want you more. You *make* me love you."

I sink my right hand between my legs, proving my arm doesn't hurt. I finger my wet pussy for him while I demand, "You're going to say it while you fuck me. You're going to make me come when you call me your whore. And you're going to come, too, because you need me. You love me, and you need me to be your beautiful whore, too. Say it, Luca. Say who you really are."

He yanks my slick hand away, replacing it with his, ramming two thick fingers inside me, making me cry out, making my back bow. His sudden, curling touch, pressing into my walls, makes me forget. It makes me moan. He feels so damn good; I slam my eyes closed, but he growls, "Look at me!"

I do. I open my eyes to find him over me, his fingers buried, jerking brutally, lusciously inside my slick cunt, his palm grinding over my swelling clit.

"I'm your Master, Scarlett," he swears. "It's who I am; I'm your *only* man. I'm going to fuck you now and forever and make you come like my whore, like my wife, like whatever I want you to be because it pleases me. I'll give you so much goddamn pleasure, too; you'll always beg for me." Ruthlessly, he pounds his hand, claiming my sex. "Now put my name in your mouth, Scarlett, in your breath, on your soul, where it belongs forever."

"Luca!"

He leans over, claiming my nipple, too. He sucks and licks it, biting my breast, while the pressure in my pussy is maddening, his power pulling me to places only he can. I can't stop. He does it to me so fast. He bites my other nipple, the pain thrilling my flesh before he glares at me, demanding, "Whose pussy is this?"

"Luca!" I crack. I come. I stare into his eyes while I shatter, gushing over his hand. He breaks my dam, and he's just getting started.

"Taste," he demands. "Taste how you're my only whore." Pressing his dripping fingers into my mouth, he makes me moan; he makes me thirst for my watery cum. I suck it off his fingers while his other hand unfastens his belt. With a furious tug, he snaps it free, tossing it on the chair before he drags his zipper down.

But no, I've waited too long. He's teased me too much. I pull back from his tangy fingers in my mouth. "Take it all off," I insist. "Fuck me as bare as I am for you."

My commands make him smirk, and I trust that on many nights to come, I'll love it when he punishes me for it. But now?

He strips naked while he glowers, almost scolding me, "Are you really bare? Or are you still on birth control? Have you been bad? Did you give my pussy to some little fuckboy who doesn't deserve it?"

"Yes and no." I make his eyes narrow, his nostrils flare. I love taunting him, too. "Yes, I'm still on the pill. And no, I don't fuck *boys*. I've been waiting to please my man, my Master."

The pure dark lechery and bright light in his eyes—it's all Luca. All Dom and Dad and the man I love, how he loves those words from my mouth.

He towers nude by my hospital bed. Smooth bronze skin. Heaving pecs. Hard nipples. Carved flexing abs. Trimmed black pubic hair framing his thick, veined cock, jutting out, demanding and hard.

We don't care who enters the room because they're not here. Only we are.

I'm soaked for him.

Caressing his hand up my thigh, he vows, "I'm going to fuck you, my belle. I'm going to fuck your mouth, your pussy, your ass, *your mind*. I'm going to fuck every inch of you in front of our friends, too, just as you desire. They'll watch how I own you. How much I love you. Zar, too. I won't hide it anymore. I'm proud that you're mine. That this pussy is mine."

Savagely, he spreads my lips wide open, relishing how my clit thrills at his raw exposure, savoring how my vulnerable cunt drips for him.

"And then," he swears, "after months of using you, after I play with my whore however I want, making this pussy come so many times, I'll make you my wife, and you'll stop taking the pill. I'm going to breed you and mount this sweet pussy so many times a day until you have our baby." He smiles. "Or four."

Softly, I giggle.

He makes it sound so crude and cute. "Promise?" I ask him.

His smile slides into a smirk, leaning over to bite the inside of my thighs. I gasp while he vows, "It's already done," before his warm tongue finally, slowly, lusciously laves over my tender clit again.

I moan, "Oh my god, Luca, yes."

"Watch me," he demands, hunched over me. "Watch me eat your pussy. Watch me make you come on my tongue. Squirt your cum in my mouth, my whore, then I'll fuck you. I'm too hungry for you. I need to make your cunt dripping wet for me so my cock can rip you open to satisfy it."

With a vengeance, his mouth plunges, feeding on me, dragging groans up my throat. His tongue licks. His lips suck. Luca spreads my thighs, holding them open, pushing them back to my chest. I'm shamelessly splayed open for him to devour, from my ass to my cunt to my clit; he doesn't stop growling into the meal of my arousal, greedily lapping up sweet slurps of my desire.

But he tortures me, too.

He doesn't put his fingers inside me. He fucks me with his mouth, and it's not enough, and he knows it. It's excruciating ecstasy while he stares at me with lewd love in his eyes, furiously flicking my clit with his tongue for me to lift my head and watch, to relish the pleasure he gives. He tightens my core. He clenches my walls. He bites my delicate clit, and I buck. I come. I cry out for him, "Luca, please!" I'm pulsing. I'm shaking. I'm aching for him in starved voids only he can fill.

And finally...

Luca returns to me.

He climbs on top, like he did our first time, pushing my thighs open with his knees. His cock is so swollen. It's hard and angry. I bite my lip, knowing how he destroys you with pain and pleasure, his wide crown pressing, stretching, urging into my entrance. Desire and greed fill his eyes, peering down at me, but still, he cares. "Watch your arm, my belle. Tell me if it hurts."

Luca doesn't get it.

How he's tyrannical and tender. How he's everything I want to suffer and savor. I know love brings pain, too, and I'll take it all with him. So I lift my arms, proving my strength. I'm tough.

"Make it hurt, Luca," I insist, grabbing his back with both hands, my fingernails sinking into his tight, satin flesh. "Fuck me, and never stop. Make us hurt until we're healed."

Drawing in a savage breath, he locks his glare to mine, and I'll never look away. He's too beautiful, too brutal as he thrusts, not yielding to my resistance because I have none.

"*Fuuckkk*," he grunts, driving all the way inside me, exploding my breath away, my ache gone.

"Yes, Luca," I cry out.

"*Fuuckkk*, Belle," he grunts again, thrusting in and out, staring into my eyes, driving into my center like he can't believe it. I can't either. Luca burns. He stretches. He fills. He hurts so damn good, I groan, fighting back the tears.

"Fuck, Belle," he groans, too. "Fuck, you're so swollen for me. So wet and mine and so fucking tight. Clench for me," he growls. "Yes. That's it. Clamp this hungry pussy around my cock."

I wrap my legs around his flexing ass. I use my strength and hold him so tight against me, letting him deep inside, my fingernails marking his back, too.

"Fuck, yes, you feel good." His lips praise. They kiss and brush and huff over mine. He won't stop. "Fuck, I missed you. I missed your kiss. Your taste. Your pussy. Damn, Scarlett, how you take me. *All* of me."

It's more than his cock I have. It's his heart. His love. His life. I see it in his eyes. They shine, facets of light and dark claiming me.

Yes, he's mine, and I'm his.

Our bodies match. We writhe. We rise. We move together. He braces himself above me just enough so we can feel it. So we can watch it, too.

For minutes and forever, Luca moves inside me. "Scarlett," he keeps sighing. He keeps kissing my lips. "My belle." He's not fucking me like he did our first night. Our only night, he swore it then.

No, he's claiming me now for all time because that's what we have. Forever, I'll be with him.

Our grunts and groans fill the room. The bed squeaks and strains with our shameless search because we don't care. We need to find this together. We've waited too long. We need this too much.

Rising on his knees, he pulls out, gazing down at where our

bodies join. "Oh, my sweet whore," he praises. "I'm making you cream on my hard cock." He boasts, rubbing his thumb over my clit, "Look at you. Look at your pretty pink pussy gaping open from my thick cock inside you. You're a hungry little whore for me, aren't you? You want all the dirty fucking things I'm going to do to you, all the ways I'll play with you." He spanks my clit. "Beg for my cum and punishment."

"Luca." I will. I am. I lift my hips. I'm going to come again. He knows my body. He knows my breath. He knows how to control my orgasm. He's about to thrust inside me and make me do it, but the door swings open.

We whip our stare to the nurse, who is clearly not as pleased as me.

"Y'all, stop this mess right now," she snaps. "The whole floor can hear you two. Don't make me call security!"

I try to snap my legs closed, but Luca suddenly smirks, looking so erotic and evil that God would sin for him, too. Hooking his arms under my thighs, he yanks me lower, holding me open while he starts hammering his cock inside me, taunting the nurse.

"Call security right now," he commands, slapping his hips against my thighs. "I want all of them to watch me fuck the hell out of my future wife because she's mine and they'll never stop me. Hear how wet I make her sweet pussy? Look at her taking my big cock. See her cream on it? She's too damn tight, too damn perfect for my cock not to fuck forever." Viciously, he goes faster, harder, making my tits bounce. I can't believe it. It feels so good. We're so wrong and right. "She's such a beautiful whore for me. Isn't she? Such a dirty slut for my cock. Letting you watch me fuck her. Look at her," he growls. "Watch. Don't you agree?"

I moan.

I love this.

I love him.

"Ma'am?" The nurse is flustered. Angry and worried. A little amused and aroused, too. I glance at her and can tell. No one can watch a bronze, hard, naked Luca fuck like a demonic God and not want to sell their soul for his ruthless cock. "Are you okay?" she asks. She's doing her job.

"Fuck, yes, I am," I pant, grabbing Luca's flexing pecs. "I'll even marry him if he makes me come right now."

Luca turns his smirk from her to me, his hips not stopping, his cut ass flexing for her to admire, I'm sure.

"Well, I never," the nurse huffs.

"Well, you should." Luca smiles down at me. "Fucking this pussy cures everything."

She storms out of the room, and I almost want to laugh, but Luca falls over me, burying his cock so deep inside that I gasp before I groan. He finds that sensitive spot high in my core, rubbing my tender cervix like only he can.

Only Luca reaches me.

Only Luca does this to me.

Only he's allowed this deep inside my body, in my heart, too. I lose my mind. I lose everything to Luca when he's here with me.

"Say it, Scarlett." I want to thrash, but his pleasure pins me down, the stimulation in my core maddening. I can't escape it, and I don't want to. His hips relentlessly grind harder, his mass pressing in. He fists my hair, so I scratch his back. He's going to take my whole body. My whole life. "Say you'll marry me so you can come."

He tilts his hips, and his swollen tip rubs my cervix even more, erasing my mind. I scratch deeper, hanging on. "Say it, my sweet whore." His breath rasps, his back muscles clenched in my grasp, tensing for release, too. Luca blazes like white heat deep inside me, coiling our bodies so tight, my pussy burning to release. "Say it," he groans. "Say you'll be my wife so I can come inside you."

He grinds on my clit, hitting that spot inside me, too, and I ignite. "Yes, Luca, yes." I combust. I brighten. I let the pleasure flames roar, scorching through my body. Luca makes me come so hard the spasms scald, and I cry out. I love it. I love him. My muscles, my bones, everything turns to ash. My eyes, too. He watches me burn for him, and he does, too.

"Ma flamme," he groans, stilling his cock deep inside me. His body locks, his spine braced. He can't stop it either. He stares at me, love consuming his eyes, the release straining the sinews in his neck.

"Luca, do it. Let go. Fill me with your cum," I beg him. I make him. For so long, he's held back, and now he explodes.

He roars, throwing his chin up and coming so hard his cock jumps inside me. It shakes his thighs, his lips, too. "Scarlett! Fuck!" He starts thrusting again, chasing it, reveling in it, loving it, loving me. "God, Belle," he marvels, not stopping, still fucking me. "Fuck, yes, Belle. Make me. Keep making me come inside you." He lets it all go, pumping his hips until his warm cum spills from me, until he barely softens and finally collapses into our kiss.

We find our breath here for moments before he presses his forehead to mine. Tears well in my eyes, and they gloss his, too, but he smiles. "I heard a 'yes.'"

"No." I smile. "You heard wrong. You heard a '*yes, Luca, yes.*'"

"So you'll marry me twice?" He kisses me. "Once in Charleston." And kisses me again. "Once in Paris." And again. "Then we'll honeymoon in Mykonos, then Bali." And again. "I promise to fuck you all over the world."

I linger my fingers down his back, loving the welts I've left behind that he'll love, too. The pain in my right arm returns, but I don't care. "Is that your big plan for us?"

"It's my big dream for us," he answers. "I never had a wedding, and now I'm going to give my beautiful bride the biggest one. Twice. Gia will love it, too."

"They're in there, Officer!"

Our eyes get wide. The angry nurse is outside my door. Apparently, she did call security, but sorry, folks, the hot show is over.

"They're carrying on like shameless heathens." The nurse doesn't sound too mad about it. "We can all hear them!"

I laugh, still feeling Luca inside me. "We are SO in trouble."

"No, my belle." Tenderly, he kisses me. "We are SO in love."

Luca

CHAPTER TWENTY-NINE

"Hmmm," I study Scarlett's face, "your nose needs to be browner."

She laughs. "Said no one about me, ever."

"Baba." Gia brushes my hand, holding a makeup sponge, away from Scarlett's face. "Bears have black noses, not brown. Look." She points to my phone beside her on the kitchen island.

"She's right." Scarlett glances at the YouTube makeup tutorial paused on the screen. "We all need black bear noses."

"Can you make my hair like that?" Gia asks Scarlett.

The model has it pulled into cute hair puffs, mimicking ears. "Sure!" Scarlett declares. "We'll *all* do our hair like that."

I nudge her foot. "My hair's not long enough."

She winks back. "Think again, Papa Bear."

Scarlett sits on the barstool beside me, knee brushing knee, while Gia sits on the counter before us, leading the transformations. But we have to help her. If not, we really will look like we've been brown-nosing.

The front door beeps, and I grin, rolling my eyes. "Here comes trouble," I warn Scarlett. "Watch, we'll never live this down. You'll find honey jars on your desk from here until eternity."

"Zar!" Gia jumps down and runs for him.

Stepping into the kitchen seconds later with Gia on his arm, the look on his face defines a "shit-eating grin."

"Well, my, my, my," Zar drawls. "What do we have here?"

He's too damn happy at the sight of me and Scarlett, looking like Goldilocks's adult playthings.

"We're taking a picture," Gia plays with Zar's whiskers, "to tell everyone that Baba and Scarlett are getting married. That Scarlett's gonna be my mama bear forever."

She's been so excited since Christmas Eve when we took her to Build-A-Bear and gave her the exciting news—we're getting married this summer. Twice.

Zar plops down on the other stool beside me with Gia on his lap. "Looks to be some kind of picture." He teases, "Like Smokey The Bear's in for some fiery role play."

I kick his foot, and he laughs because Gia's too young to catch the dirty reference.

Of course, Zar knows about the wedding. He was the first person we told. We called him from the hospital.

So, after Gia was fast asleep on Christmas night and Celine was home to watch her, the three of us snuck down to the suite to celebrate.

It was more like a reboot because Scarlett and I have no boundaries now, but Zar has new ones.

He still wants me as his Dom. He still comes for my whip. Zar still craves the taste of me on Scarlett, but I'll never let him fuck her, and that feels right to us. Scarlett understands. Sharing her with him in that way drags us into our painful past.

And we're moving forward.

I feel free.

I *am* free.

I've hit the jackpot of love and lust with Scarlett. She's everything I need, and I want to give Zar what he needs, too—sex with him. Lately, I get aroused by the idea of finally fucking him. Zar does, too. Scarlett said she'd love it. The three of us talked about it, but Zar wants to wait.

He's met another man. He doesn't know how they'll work yet, and we understand. He'll always be welcome with us.

We'll always love him.

And Gia certainly will.

No, Zar isn't her father, but he's her family. Our family. He loved her mother, too, and she's the daughter he may never have. She sure has him wrapped around her little finger.

"But Gia, remember." I use the voice she's back to obeying. "We're not sharing our picture or our family secret yet. Scarlett needs to tell her boss, Ms Charlie, that she's not working anymore."

"I remember," Gia chirps, hopping down from Zar's lap. "Can I have some Kourambiethes?"

She's seeking the cookies by the stove. They're vanilla and covered in powdered sugar; she can't resist.

I nod yes, as Scarlett corrects, "Oh, I'll be working, just not for HGR anymore."

"Yeah," Zar taunts, "we'll keep the new Chief of Security for The Mercier Hotels *very* busy. She'll need fancy gold handcuffs."

But she elbows *me*?

Fine. I'm guilty. I thought it, too. We're three peas in a kinky pod.

"Just know, I'm not dressing like a French secretary anymore," Scarlett warns. "For my new job, think French *assassin*."

Scarlett points at herself, and once again, I admire the bandage on her right arm and the ring I put on her left hand. It's a rare pale blue diamond. Finding one that size is not easy, but when you know the CEO of Harry Winston Jewelry, you get it sent by a special secured courier the next day.

I wanted to propose to her formally, but I had no patience.

We've waited long enough.

So I had Celine keep Gia busy Christmas morning, making chocolate madeleines while I proposed to Scarlett in the shower.

Don't judge.

It was the only privacy I could trust for an hour, and she looked too beautiful. The water hid our tears while I swore to love her, to live on bended knee for her. I slid the two-carat diamond on her ring finger and stayed there, on my knees, proving how much I'm devoted to her, to her pleasure, too.

"So, when are you two shackin' up?" Zar asks.

"Not until we're married." I reach for Scarlett's hand. "I'm old-fashioned that way."

That gets Gia's attention. She's back on task. "Baba," she puts her hand up, "stay there. I'll get the stuff for our bear hair."

She marches off to her room, on a mission to destroy any ego I have left, right in front of Zar, who waits until Gia's out of earshot.

"Old-fashioned?" Zar scoffs. "Please. You're so damn kinky you have to unscrew your britches to take them off at night."

Scarlett laughs, and I chuckle, too, muttering, "Fuck you."

Zar winks. "Not yet."

I stare him down even though I probably look like Winnie the fucking Pooh. "Just let me know when you're ready to find out why they call it 'Greek Style.'"

"Shh!" Scarlett nudges my foot because Gia returns to torture us with hairspray and hair ties. And I allow it, even my mortifying hair puffs as ears, too, with Zar here to witness.

Yes. This must be love.

I let him take the picture of me, Scarlett, and Gia on the terrace. The late December afternoon is mild. It's perfect. I hold Gia in one arm, my other wrapped around Scarlett while I kiss her lips.

Zar quips, "Say 'honey,'" to snap our pic, and I mutter to Scarlett, "Told you." But he captures our smiles.

Fuck, we're not even married yet, and I've never been this happy.

Later, we clean up after Zar leaves for his beach house. I hold Gia's hand. Scarlett does, too, walking down the sidewalk through the French Quarter, warmed by the afternoon sun, dappling through the bare, twisty oaks.

"Baba," Gia skips between us, "when Scarlett becomes my mama, will Crimson be my puppy, too?"

Scarlett laughs. "Told ya she'd wear you down."

"Shit," I grumble. "Am I in control of anything anymore?"

"Nope!" Scarlett laughs even harder.

We're on our way to walk her dog, and yes, that cute mutt will be living with us, too.

While we play in the park and Scarlett and Gia teach Crimson how to jump through a hoop, my phone buzzes with notifications.

I check it, excusing myself, worried about what's blowing up social media. I have a fake account to monitor posts about my properties, but I follow a few hashtags because I care.

I care about the celebrity going viral again.

I call him. Twice. Each time, it rolls to voicemail, and he doesn't call me back until Gia's asleep and Scarlett and I are enjoying cigars on the terrace.

"Hey dude," Redix greets me. "What's going on?"

"I'm checking on you dickhead," I answer. "It seems someone's having a *very* Happy New Year's trip."

Scarlett grins, puffing away because she saw what went viral, too.

Fans busted Redix on a private holiday he's trying to have with his wife, Cade, and their partners, Silas and Eily. It seems Daniel Pierce, his wife, and our friend, Charlie Ravenel, are with them, too.

Fans posted pictures of Redix and Daniel at some pirate museum in the Bahamas. But in the posts, Daniel didn't look thrilled about it, and I know Redix too well. He looked worried. They're co-stars. Their show is number one, and they can't escape the press or the rumors.

I understand. I feel bad for them.

"Fuck, man," Redix groans. "I can't go anywhere without it going viral."

"You sure as hell can't go anywhere with Daniel Pierce and expect it *not* to."

I never blow sunshine up Redix's ass, and he doesn't mine either. We've shared too much.

I talk to him while I admire Scarlett sitting across from me, curled in a chair, wearing my Greek fisherman's sweater over her black leggings. And I feel my joy, my freedom. I feel it's finally time to share it all with Redix.

I joke a bit with him, giving him hell about the orgy the six of them are obviously having on Silas's superyacht. Though I know it's much more. They share a deep love. They follow their hearts, not the rules.

I do, too.

Yes, I believe in vows and traditions, but I've learned the hard way some rules can kill love.

Love can't be contained in words, covered by graves, or confined by rings. Love is bigger than any person. It was here before us. It lives on after us. We change for love; love doesn't change for us.

My gaze worships Scarlett while I tell Redix, "I want to finally show you and everyone I care about...*who* I love." Then I think of Zar with us, making my cock stir. "And I want you all to watch... *how* I love them."

Redix replies with shock, with a volley of questions. I've been keeping him guessing about my love life and sex life for quite some time. "You want Silas to send the chopper for you?" Redix also sounds impatient. "You can show us tomorrow."

"No," I chuckle. "I've waited this long. Let's find a weekend this month when you can join me as my guests."

"At your golf resort?" he asks because we usually meet to play a round there.

But now...

My mind is crafting the most elaborate, erotic, dark, and sensual group play. It's making me hard and Scarlett chew her lip, her sapphire eyes sparkling in the night.

"No," I answer Redix. "At my Charleston hotel." My dick swells more, imagining it already. "There's something I want to show you."

"Show who?" But Redix is cautious. I've been so private for so long. "All six of us? You want Daniel and Charlie there, too?'

This is perfect. Scarlett needs to tell her boss anyway...

"Yes, Charlie Ravenel definitely needs to be there." She's a stunning woman, too. "If her husband wishes to join her, that's even better. It will only add to the scene."

I tease Redix, but I make sure he's okay, too. I'd kill for him. I'd kill for anyone I love. I make him laugh, promising me it's a date, then I end the call.

"Just what are you planning?" Scarlett rises from her chair. She keeps her cigar in hand while she straddles me, grinding on my erection. "A night where all our friends are in the suite, and I walk in with your collar on and tell my boss I'm quitting to be your sub for life?"

I brush an auburn tendril from her face, tucking it behind her ear before lingering my fingertips down her bare neck. We haven't put her collar back on.

She needs to earn it again.

I sink my hand in her silky strands, pulling just enough to make her mewl, to make her open her neck for my bite.

"I'm giving my treasured fiancée the engagement party she desires." Gently, I bite, I kiss, I lick her neck before I steam over her ear. "They're going to meet my beautiful future wife and admire her ring." Carefully, I bite her ear, too, just enough to make her shudder. "Then they'll meet my sweet whore, and admire how we'll fuck her all night long."

Scarlett
CHAPTER THIRTY

"Nope, you're not allowed."

Damn, my sister is persistent, but so am I.

And damn, I was a dumbass to tell her about my XXX-rated engagement party tonight.

It's been two weeks since Luca invited our six friends. He's invited other guests, too, so he said he needed time to prepare the suite. By now, I'm expecting it to be a Taj Mahal dedicated to tits, tail-fucking, and torture, but I'm not allowed to see it...yet.

Neither is Ruby.

Ever.

"You're such a cunt blocker," she huffs. "You get to have a hot guy-n-girly show with some of the sexiest men alive—like *People* magazine said so—and I can't go!"

"My sister is not watching me fuck. Period."

"Yeah, well, I hope you start your *period* in two minutes."

I stare out of the window of my room on the third floor of The Mercier and laugh. *I love this bitch.*

"Why are you jealous? You have your weekly watch-n-jack NFL parties, and my cunt ain't crying about it."

"But come on," she whines, "It's *Daniel Pierce*. It's *Redix*

Dean. I'm staring at them, and—holy fuck my tail-gate—*Silas Van de May* is across the lobby, too. Girl, yes, you're marrying the Dom-est one of them all, but those three men and their hot wives are porn personified. I won't watch you, I promise. I'll cover my eyes and peek through my fingers and only watch them."

"No. You're not watching my future husband fuck, either. I gotta draw the line somewhere, and in-laws are definitely it."

"Oh, come on! Zar gets to go upstairs. And Nick's joining him."

I haven't met Zar's new man, but I'm excited to. Ruby watched their love story bloom, but it's still early. Zar's sweet about how slow he's going with him. So this is a big step: Zar inviting Nick to join us. At our debut S&M show, nonetheless, but hey...

Tell me when Zar's ever been ashamed about sex.

"Quit asking me, Rubes. I'm not changing my mind." I walk naked, in white Louboutin heels, toward the bed where my dress awaits. I need to be ready. Luca will be here in five minutes to escort me downstairs to the lobby bar, where Ruby is waiting, too.

"If you don't let me come to the *real* party on the third floor," Ruby pauses, and I can't wait to hear this, "I'll put a pregnant mouse in your sneaker again."

Fuck, I shudder every time. "God! You're the only hell our mama ever raised."

"Sure am."

"No."

"Pretty peep-show, please."

"No."

"Me love you long time."

I laugh. "No!"

"I hope you queef and die."

"What a way to go."

"I hope you get a yeast infection so bad your puss has to open a bakery."

"All can enter but you."

"I hope a dildo gets stuck inside, and you have to walk bow-legged for the rest of your life."

"Don't need a dildo for that; I'm marrying Luca Mercier."

She sighs. "I hate you."

"I love you, too, skank. See you in a minute."

I drop my phone on the bed and gather the long ivory satin slip with spaghetti straps. It could be worn as an elegant wedding dress, which makes this night perfect. The soft dress settles down my body. Its neckline gracefully drapes low. The back is open, too, with a slight train sweeping the floor. My arm has healed, though I have a fresh scar through it.

But I already feel like Luca's wife.

And I'm definitely his sub.

He sent a glam team to get me ready, his spa staff, too. He bought all he wants me to wear tonight, and it's not much. I'm not even wearing lingerie, and it thrills me.

But what thrills me more?

Maren will be downstairs. Luca invited her and her friends, and Maren would be too disgraced to miss this exclusive event. He even invited Jameson to rub it in, but he doesn't know Jameson's bringing his girlfriend. I do, and it'll be a way to curb Luca's jealousy.

Wait. Who am I marrying?

Luca drinks Jealousy for breakfast with two sugars and cream. Daily.

Other adults will be there, but no kids. Gia's staying at Abbey's tonight. Celine is off for the weekend.

Luca has promised to make the announcement and the toast quickly. Then, we'll have one round of drinks with everyone before we leave, and discreetly, our select friends will join us in the suite, too.

A gentle tap sounds at the door.

He's early. He's excited.

I don't have a clutch to carry or jewelry to wear but my new ring. Whenever I gaze at the rare sparkling diamond, I see Luca's eyes. I see the rest of my life.

Using his keycard, he doesn't wait for me to let him in. The suite belongs to him. I do, too. I stand in the middle of the room and let his gaze feed on me while he stalks my way.

Luca dons his usual attire—a severe black suit, a crisp white shirt, unbuttoned, and no tie—but he doesn't look the same. Happiness adorns him now, and it makes him inches taller, wider. He steals more breath from any room.

"Ma flamme," he sighs, kissing my lips. "Let's do this fast because the rest of the night needs to last long."

I let his heat wrap around me, his warm hand caressing my bare back, leading the way. We make it to the elevator, and the request, the fantasy burning inside me, can't wait anymore. Now's my chance to ask. We're alone, so I tug his hand, and he grins at me. "Yes?"

"I have one wish tonight." He arches a brow, making me stammer, "Just tonight. I know you have strong feelings about it, but I do, too. And you know I love you. Only you. I mean, I love Zar, but not like our love and—"

"I know what your wish is." He squeezes my hand, lowering his lips to my ear. "So, be my lady at the party now, and I promise I'll share my whore for the night."

Is this a good time to be commando?

Hell no.

I fear I have a damp patch on my dress. My nipples are hard, my cunt is starting to slick, and Luca knows it. I swear, he can smell it while he kisses me. The elevator doors *ding* open, and I lift my chin, letting him proudly guide us to the crowd awaiting in the lobby bar.

Honestly, the hour is a blur, punctuated by moments of clarity.

Like our six special hot guests, a couple of them famous, kissing my cheeks with congratulations.

Like Charlie, my boss, confessing she's not surprised I'm leaving HGR to take over security for a global hotel brand. But she laughs, whispering that she's more surprised I let Luca put me on my knees. "No judgment." She pecks my cheek. "I let Daniel do it, too."

Stacey and two of her three sexy men are here. I'm thrilled they'll be joining us upstairs. We owe them the return favor of a show. And when she glides her hand over my exposed back, Stacey sends goosebumps up my spine, introducing me to Vivian.

It seems Vivian works at Delta's now, taking the most elegant boudoir photos. Of course, Luca's hired her before, and I chew my lip, knowing Vivian's taking our taboo pictures tonight.

Luca doesn't abandon me in the crowd. He keeps me on his arm, so I delight when I find Jameson towering over the others. I gently nudge Luca. "I want to introduce you to someone."

Our well-wishers are in the dozens. It takes minutes to work our way through the crowd. When Luca finally sees Jameson's secret I've been keeping, "Oh," he murmurs at the sight, genuinely surprised.

Jameson's date is young, and she's famous for it. With the hottest make-up line in the world, she's the country's youngest, newest billionaire CEO.

Yes, she's barely twenty-one. Yes, Jameson's almost forty. Yes, he was her bodyguard and also broke the Red Rule for her. And no, Charlie didn't fire Jameson either because, one, she made the same mistake with Daniel, and two, it's not a mistake if it's love.

I make the introductions, though Soriya Hahn doesn't require one. She's been on the cover of *Forbes*, and so has Luca.

I've already met Soriya. We had too much wine and a long girls' night, discussing Jameson and how they could make this work. She'll always be a target, and he's sweetly obsessed with protecting her.

"You're welcome to join us upstairs." But Luca surprises me, inviting them. He lowers his voice, politely pecking Soriya's hand. "I have a private celebration planned to *share* my fiancée tonight." Jameson's eyes narrow with desire. He doesn't miss Luca's choice of words. It's Jameson's secret fantasy, and Luca clocked it, clarifying for Soriya, "We're a very intimate and consensual group. You are welcome to simply watch and enjoy."

Oh my god, HIF #19: My slut butter is now melting under my dress.

I glance down and thank the horny gods there's no stain. Because Soriya is stunning. Long brown waves. Exquisite brown skin. A fuchsia dress caressing her curves. But her sexiest asset is her business acumen. Yes, she's only twenty-one. So yes, she's an adult woman perfectly capable of making every decision about her sex and body; thank you very much.

But what is Luca doing to me? He's serving a buffet of temptations I can't possibly devour in just one night.

Jameson leans down, whispering in Soriya's ear, and she nods yes.

"Thank you." Jameson's voice gravels with lust. "We'll be happy to join you."

Like a Dom with diplomatic ease, Luca leads us away.

"What are you doing?" I ask, thrilled.

Gently, he squeezes my waist. "I'll teach them who they are tonight while I show them how I pleasure what's mine."

Yes, please, my daddy Dom. I'm so in love.

We have one final guest to greet tonight. For the past hour, she's been spitting venom through her smiling fangs at us. But once she sees us aim her way, her eyes dart nervously as if she wants to slither away but knows better.

See?

I've trained Maren.

I schooled her in the dojo that fateful day. I took her hand, pinching a special nerve that, depending on my pressure, makes you want to pee or die.

"Now, now, Maren," I whispered in her ear. "You and your cunty crew will behave like adults and quit talking shit, or I'll make you piss your pants like you're two." I tightened my pinch, and her eyes got wide. "Feel that?" She whimpered, nodding. "Good girl. Now play nice, and I will, too."

Then I kissed her cheek, giving it a little tongue. It freaked her out, and I laughed, making a mental note to send my new friend a huge vibrating dildo from Delta's.

It arrived three days ago. I just got the confirmation from Stacey.

"Luca. Scarlett," Maren coos at our approach. "Bless your hearts. I hope you two will be so happy."

Southern translation: Eat shit and die.

"Thank you, Maren." Luca kisses her cheek. "How's Spencer?"

"He's fine." Maren smiles, her tail rattling. "What a beautiful dress, Scarlett."

Southern translation: You look like a whore.

Global newsflash: I can't wait to be one in about thirty minutes.

"Why, thank you." I mirror her, canting my head so much that IQ points threaten to fall out of my ear. *Why do some women do this?* "We hope you'll be at our wedding this June."

I'm hiring a plane to write her invitation in the sky over Charleston.

Maren bats her lashes. "It's at our Baptist church, right?"

Leaning forward, I gossip with my new fuck-you-friend. "Honey, with the filthy things Luca likes to do with me? I may burst into flames in a church." Maren gasps. "But he does make me come so hard I scream 'Hallelujah,' so at least he's saving my pussy, if not my soul."

Luca chuckles, shaking his head. He's so past giving a shit, too. Maren may spread rumors. Or she may jump off the hypocrite train and live a little and come a lot. It's her choice, and we don't care.

Yes, there are things we will always keep private. But me, fucking my future husband, is not one of them.

Me, fucking a dozen of our friends?

Well, that's our little secret.

"Good night, Maren." Luca slightly nods. "I'll see you at the board meeting Monday."

Finally, Luca's holding my hand, leading us out of the crowd. I can see our friends have already snuck away. Zar's waiting for them in the suite, but down here, there's a band, a DJ, free drinks, and sumptuous Greek treats served to our guests on silver trays all night.

They don't need us to enjoy themselves.

We make it to the elevator, and relief fills me. The podium is gone. We don't need covert security anymore. Brooke and her husband will spend the next twenty years in jail.

"Hey!" But a shout across the white marble lobby makes us whip around. "Think you can leave without saying goodbye?" Ruby looks stunning, walking our way in her velvet emerald dress.

Luca leans down, his smile genuine, kissing both her cheeks. "We'll see you tomorrow at brunch, right?"

"Yeah," she answers, her voice lowered. "But you and your hot studs are about to fuck my sister so senseless, I won't recognize her tomorrow."

"No one fucks my future wife but me," he growls, and I'm confused. Luca said he knew my wish, if only for one night. But I'm swept into Ruby's arms before I can ask.

"Have fun, Ho," she huffs into our hug. "I hope you get so much bukkake in your eyes that you go blind."

I laugh, squeezing her back. "I love you, too."

THE NIGHT I first discovered Luca's kinks at this white door to his secret suite seems so long ago. Now, we share them. Now, we stand together, and I hear voices, relaxed but laced with excitement on the other side.

"Scarlett," he caresses my cheek, "remember your words tonight."

"Luca," I answer.

Hooking his finger under my chin, he meets my stare. "I meant it downstairs, and I vow to you always; I am the only man inside you, as you are the only woman for me. Forever. I will allow others to please you tonight. Whatever pleases me, too, but your pussy is mine. No one fucks it but me. Ever. Do you consent?"

"Luca." Desire pounds in my pulse for what that means.

"Do you want to earn your piercings back tonight? Your collar, too?"

My nipples ache for his diamonds. He asked me to take them out this morning and give them to him; now I know why. My neck has felt naked, untethered, and lost without his collar, too.

We ache for this ritual tonight, so I answer, "Luca."

He leans down, his lips brushing mine. "If I give you your fantasy tonight, will you give me my dream and awake in my arms tomorrow and always?"

His kiss is loving, sensual, and slow. The rest of the night, he'll be brutal. He will dominate and degrade and display me, and I reach for him, cupping his cheek, too. He moans at my possession, at the power I give him, too.

"Luca." I give him my answer...forever.

Pulling away, he takes the black kerchief from his pocket. Tonight, he blindfolds me with it. "This is just until I have you in position," he says.

Though I can't see, I trust. With Luca's hand wrapped around mine, there's no place I fear.

Voices drop to a murmur when we enter the suite. The temperature, familiar and warm. The smell, sandalwood and ginger. The music, the same erotic songs. Blindly, I tread over plush rugs. Other aromas and colognes, leather and lavenders fill my senses.

On my right, "She's so beautiful," I hear a woman softly admire, and I can't tell if it's Eily, Silas's wife, or Soriya, Jameson's girlfriend. They're both younger.

I already sense that the large room is different. I already know Luca spared no expense redesigning it, and it feels right. Like our new life, we have a new suite. This will be one of many nights shared here, I'm sure.

"Step up." Luca gently guides my elbow, and I step onto a solid platform. It's deep enough for Luca to turn us to where he's standing behind me, his warm, hard chest pressed against my bare back.

Even though I can't see, I know I'm facing our audience.

"Thank you all for joining us." Luca caresses his hands over mine, lingering his touch over my wrists. "We want you here tonight...*I* want you here tonight to show you how much I love this beautiful woman." Like a feather, his fingertips brush slowly up my arms. "As you can see, I am a very lucky man." His palms warm my arms, his touch pausing over my bullet scar. "Tonight, we celebrate that Scarlett Jones will marry me. She will be my wife. She said, 'Yes.'" Tenderly, he jokes with me. "*Right?*"

"Yes." The blindfold can't hide my smile. "I will marry you, Luca Mercier."

Our guests chuckle, and I feel safe, happy, and loved. When Luca caresses the top of my shoulders, playing with the thin straps of my dress, lust floods me, too.

"Scarlett will be my wife forever." His lips press to my ear. "And she will be my *whore* tonight."

He slips one strap down, exposing my breast, air thrilling my nipple. My flesh tightens at the taboo; at the eyes, I can sense watching us.

Palming my breast, he cups its weight. I gasp when he nips my ear. "Tell them what you beg when you consent. When you love being my whore. Who is your Master?"

He pinches my nipple, and I gasp, "Luca. I'm your whore, Master."

My other strap falls, my dress skimming my waist while he cups my breasts, lusciously pinching my nipples. I moan while he commands the room, "Please enjoy her, too. Please relax and watch how she serves me, how she pleases me. I may ask some of you to help, but you can refuse. And when I'm done, you are welcome to join us, with one rule..."

He releases my screaming nipples. Yanking my dress down, he leaves it pooled around my ankles. Wrapping a hand around my neck, my naked flesh excited to be seen, Luca plunges his other hand between my legs, spreading my lips, exposing my clit for them to witness his claim, "This is *MY* beautiful pussy," he growls. "Fuck her, and you die."

I bite my lip because I trust every person in this room, and I trust Luca means it.

Gently, he unties my blindfold.

Soft, golden light makes me blink while I find my focus. When I do, I gasp, not believing the sight.

Luca's completely redesigned the suite. We're standing at the top of the room on a large one-step riser, like a stage, but it's covered in black suede. I glance over my shoulder, and the familiar black leather platform bed behind us is large enough to welcome most of our guests.

But Luca's thought of that.

That's what the new riser is for.

He tosses his black jacket on the bed while I scan the room.

First, I see a panorama of people reclining on wide, tufted, blue velvet barrel chairs. Six of them are arranged in a curving row, and knowing Luca, they swivel, too. He designed it so the audience could enjoy every angle in the room and themselves.

Our glass curio cabinets are still in the corners. The brass tables and the drawn blue velvet drapes are the same, but there are more mirrors. Almost every wall has floor-to-ceiling mirrors; you can't escape a spectacle.

Zar's padded whipping cross is still on the wall to my right. My torture tower still stands beside it. All the nights we've shared, bound and beside each other, make me search the room for Zar first, just as Luca summons him.

"My stud," Luca calls. "Please let me introduce you, too."

Zar rises from the far right chair while the man whose arms he was in remains.

That must be Nick.

I smile because Nick's a mass of pure power and muscle, like the hero of an NFL team's defensive lineup. He's sexy, but what makes him cute is the smile he gives Zar and how he slowly lets go of his hand for him to join us.

Joy blooms in my chest at the comfort of Zar's approach. On our Saturday nights, he wears the same black pleather pants and no shirt. He always looks fierce. But tonight? Luca's thick black collar is back around Zar's neck. Zar took it off for the months I was gone, but like me, it's back. And I know, on a cellular level, that no matter our future or who's there, Zar will never leave us.

It's beautiful how, once he's by our side, Luca reaches, cupping Zar's neck, gently kissing his cheek. But they don't kiss on the lips. *Not yet.* Zar said he saves his kisses for Nick. *For now.*

But Zar will always crave Luca's touch. Luca's power. Luca's domination. He told us last night how he needs Nick to understand this, to hopefully accept it and enjoy it, too.

Tonight is the test.

Luca stalks behind Zar, his arm brushing mine. He grabs Zar's neck, his other hand slowly groping Zar's abs, teasing down his dark trail. Luca makes him pant while he announces to our guests, "This is *my* proud stud. The man who found me. The man who saved me. He serves me, too, and I love him for it. I always will."

Dragging Zar's zipper down, Luca bites his neck above his collar while he frees Zar's hard cock. Stroking it, he makes Zar moan, letting us watch for minutes before he commands, "Who do you serve?"

Zar rasps in Luca's choking grasp, "You, my Owner, always."

"Get our whore ready for us," Luca commands Zar, who gathers his breath before he steps down.

Proudly, Zar walks with his cock exposed and hard across the room toward one of the cabinets while Luca's shadow falls over me. Caressing my naked buttocks, he spreads them open, to my delight. He makes me pant while I confront our guests. I admit shyness finds me, but my desire is stronger.

Next to Nick on my right, who sits alone on his chair and looking content to watch, are Jameson and Soriya.

They watch from their chair with Jameson cradling Soriya across his lap, her cheek resting on his bare chest, her hand caressing it, too. She's still in her silky dress, but Jameson's stripped his shirt off. No doubt to show his brute power to Luca and secretly?

I love the competition between the men.

Jameson loves Soriya. She was forbidden to him for years, and he waited to have her finally.

But some of us always want the one who got away, too. That's what Jameson jokes that I am, but Soriya's won his heart. It's obvious with how he kisses her hair and rubs her arm.

I've witnessed much of the story of the three couples next to them, too.

Daniel and Charlie are in their chair, Silas and Eily are sitting on their right, with Redix and Cade on the other side.

I watched Redix win Cade, his soulmate, back. I saw how Silas selflessly helped it happen, and they became a beautiful throuple. Then I watched how Silas finally found Eily, his innocent princess, and she joined them, too.

But now, the six are together.

Daniel and Charlie are with them, too. How and in what ways? I'm unsure, but I know each couple is married and committed. Together, the six share a tragic history, making their bond powerful.

It's love, and my nakedness heightens.

Licking my lips, I realize Daniel is nude. Though I know him well, I've only seen a naked Daniel on the screen, acting like he's fucking Redix, but I've never seen him buff like this in real life. And I've worked for Charlie for years, but I've never seen her so hot like that, either.

She's reclining between Daniel's massive legs, his hulking chest her pillow. She's wearing a sexy black bondage bra with a matching strappy black panty.

And that's when I realize, scanning the couples, that Eily, sitting beside Charlie, and Cade beside Eily, and Stacey, on the other side of Cade, are all wearing the same black luxe BDSM lingerie.

Luca planned this.

Stacey helped, I'm sure.

Desire wets my cunt because I stand naked with Luca biting and kissing my neck, his hands clutching my hips, while I realize that Silas, with Eily on his lap, and Redix, with Cade on his, are naked, too. They're concealed, but soon, we'll witness their proud arousal.

I've seen it before.

The same is true for Stacey's men, Ford and Mateo. They sit on my left. Their chair is wide enough for Stacey to nestle between them. I've always admired Mateo's stunning black ink. I've always admired Ford's sculpted, hard form, too. Luke, Stacey's third man, is stationed abroad, but if he were here, I'm sure he'd find a way to fit between Ford and Mateo with Stacey draped over their laps. The men love each other, and they love sharing her.

I scan our audience, left to right, and that's five hot, nude men with women on their laps. That's Jameson and Soriya, looking half-concealed and completely thrilled. That's Nick, looking relaxed in faded jeans and a grey t-shirt.

And there's Vivian, our photographer. She's still wearing her camel-colored, cashmere wrap dress. With a camera strapped around her neck and her tawny hair in a messy ponytail, she's here to work, but I don't know how she does her job, snapping pictures of Luca groping me for all to watch. Because when Luca Mercier's in charge, nothing is safe for work.

Proving my point, Zar returns carrying white leather straps with gold hardware dangling from his grasp.

Usually, Luca restrains me in black leather.

But those are white and gold.

Because now...

I'm Luca's bride.

"Hand me her bust harness first." Luca takes it from Zar's hand. Wrapping the white binding leather strap under my breasts, Luca buckles it in the back before reaching around, lifting the center strap between my cleavage. It has a collar, and he secures it around my neck, kissing it while he vows, "Be my proud whore tonight, and my bride will wear her jeweled collar in the morning."

Luca loves fucking me in the morning.

Actually, at that magical hour, it feels like he's making love to me. I wake in his arms, and he holds me tight, my back to his chest, while he goes so slow, so deep, sighing in my ear. He caresses my breasts and rubs my clit; he's so gentle with me.

The first time he was inside me like that, we watched the sunrise through his bedroom window, and he sighed, "For so long, Scarlett, I lived in a lonely, darkness that wouldn't end. But you are my light. My belle. My dawn. Every day, I awake to love you."

But now?

He's not gentle. He fastens the collar tight around my neck. It doesn't choke, it excites me.

"Spread your legs," Luca demands, and I watch Zar kneel before me. He helps me step out of my dress. "Keep her heels on," Luca commands. "My whore loves wearing them for me."

I grin, remembering my first fight with Luca about heels and my attire. And now?

I lust for Louboutins while he's railing me.

With his fingertips admiring my thighs, Zar wraps a white leather cuff around one, then the other, securing each with their gold buckles. The leather is soft but thick. Luca spares no expense on our gear.

Stepping beside me, he's trained me, too. I raise my wrist so that Luca can bind it with a wide padded leather cuff that Zar hands to him. While Luca kisses me, blindly, he secures it to my thigh cuff, then he walks around and kisses me, cuffing my left side, too.

When he steps back, the shutter of Vivian's camera explodes, capturing me nude, with my hair free but my body bound. My wrists are cuffed to the outside of my thighs, my naked breasts are hoisted high in a white leather harness with a collar, and my engagement diamond sparkles on my finger.

I've never felt so proud and beautiful.

And loved.

Luca towers behind me, turning my chin to claim my kiss, too.

He'll never leave me, as Zar kneels before us. And for a moment, we silently pose, kissing and revealing our secret, our love.

Then...

Luca hooks his finger in the gold ring on my collar, and our engagement party *really* begins.

Scarlett
CHAPTER THIRTY-ONE

LUCA ADMIRES MY BODY AND RESTRAINTS, HIS GAZE HEATED while he hooks a finger through my collar. His other hand carefully helps me step down from the platform while Zar rises from his knees and joins us. With his left index finger tugging the gold ring of my collar, Luca hooks his right finger through Zar's ring and teases us with a playful jerk, "Mine."

Leading us, we begin our exhibition around the room. And I love Luca's pull, his control. I love how he's proud to do this with us now.

So are we.

All Zar ever wanted was for Luca to claim him proudly. All I ever wanted was for Luca to love me freely.

First, he presents us to Stacey, Ford, and Mateo.

Releasing our collars, Luca shocks me, slapping my bare breast twice, and I moan, the sting shooting straight to my excited clit while he taunts, "My whore owes you a show."

Yes, I do.

Stacey winks back. Mateo and Ford nod.

Caressing his hand over my bottom, Luca pinches it before he reaches behind me, under me. "Show them how you serve me," he commands, so I step my thighs wide apart. Arching my back as much as I can, I open my sex for him to play with, right before their eyes, while he commands Zar, "Prepare me."

Luca's middle finger lightly tickles my clit. Stacey watches him tease me, my nipples responding, too, while Zar unbuttons Luca's starched shirt. Pulling it open, he licks and sucks Luca's nipples, his tongue circling while Luca circles my slick entrance before Zar lowers to his knees.

Ford and Mateo lower their gaze, too. Like hungry wolves, they watch Zar unzip Luca's pants. The moment Zar's fist wraps around Luca's hard cock, lifting its weight, freeing it from its confinement before he allows it to surge before us, Luca thrusts his fingers in my slick pussy, making me gasp.

"Yes, look at how well they serve me," Luca praises, pumping his thick digits into my cunt while I writhe over his left hand, and Zar kneels on his right, admiring his soaring cock. It mirrors Zar's.

"Yes, they do," Ford agrees. "I bet it makes her wet when he strokes your cock, too."

It's a request, not a statement, and Luca smirks, nodding at Zar to begin. It *does* make me wet. How I can't move my hands while Luca fucks me with his fingers, matching the tempo of Zar's pumping fist. How Zar licks his lips at his shameless effort, showing other men how he loves Luca's cock, while Luca finds my clit. Spanking it hard for Stacey's gaze, he jeers, "Does my whore crave my cock, too?"

"Yes, Master," I sigh.

Quickly, Luca unsnaps my right wrist cuff, freeing my hand to serve him, too. Stacey licks her lips, admiring his ferocious width, his terrifying length, how my hand and Zar's stack, choking Luca's cock with room left to stroke him.

I thrill his swollen tip while Zar lavishes Luca's thick base. We make him muffle his lustful grunt, enjoying our service.

"Gives me big inspiration," Mateo admires Luca's command, sipping his whisky. He's hard for this. So is Ford. But they refrain, for now, enjoying our show.

Luca does, too.

For minutes, he makes us stroke him with his hooded stare on our guests. It's like we're unraveling Luca, exposing him, revealing his full power. His cock is so hard, displaying his pleasure, but his restraint is epic. It's seductive. It drives Stacey to finger herself, her men helping her, sucking her nipples, too. We perform for her until we make her come, her moans wetting my sex.

Then, Luca growls, "Get up," and Zar stands.

"Thank you," Stacey coos while Luca snaps my wrist to my thigh cuff. Then, he leads us by the collar rings again. He takes us next to Redix and Cade, Silas, and Eily, too. He centers us, standing between their chairs.

Luca orders, "Kneel."

Since my wrists are bound again, my balance is precarious, so Zar helps me. He holds my uninjured arm while I kneel on Luca's left, and then Zar lowers, submitting on his right.

"Look at them," Luca commands everyone, so I lift my eyes; Zar does, too. It's not degrading to see. It's loving, proud, and arousing how Redix, Cade, Silas, and Eily regard us, and we stare back at them.

There's no judgment in their eyes, only admiration, watching Luca gently caress my hair and Zar's waves, too.

"Now you see what I've been hiding," Luca confesses. "But I won't anymore. This is who I am. This is *who* I love. This is *how* I love."

He affirms us, displayed before them. He declares himself, exposed to them. He reveals the secrets he's hidden, his guilt, and his love for me, for Zar, too.

Last week, Luca told me how he shared everything with Redix: the past, the crash, the guilt, the vow. They had a long talk, and now, Luca's showing him, too.

"It's beautiful, man," Redix replies. "She is. He is." His gaze combs down Luca's hard body. "*You* are. We're happy for y'all. You don't need to hide your love from us anymore."

Luca brushes the back of his fingers across my cheek. "I won't. *We* won't. I'm proud to have her. To have him."

"You can have us tonight, too," Cade adds. Pointing to their sixsome, she says, "We've talked about it. We have some boundaries, but we're honored to celebrate with you. To share some things with you."

Oh, my god. Finally!

HIF #20: I've died and gone to orgy heaven. Oh, how I'm about to get SO fucked by SO many.

There's so much I desire, so much I've fantasized about. My pussy wets even more as Luca starts stroking his length at their tempting offer, explaining, "My man is promised to someone else."

I steal a glance at Zar. He grins, loving Luca's acceptance. Luca's support. Yes, Zar will always want us, but he also wants to save himself for Nick.

But me?

I want to share every pleasure with Luca. More than the sex, it's the trust required to do this. The love, too. Luca is very private. He has to be. He's very possessive, too, and I understand why.

But in this room, in our future together, Luca gives me love and trust like he's never shared. He gives us freedom, too. To be who we are. To explore what we desire with no shame. He's willing to change for me, and I'm willing to be all he'll ever need.

He slowly squats behind me, tugging my pearled nipples while he offers, "Would you like to join me and share her tonight?"

"Yes!" Eily blurts. "I've never been with a redhead before," she admires my bound body, "and you're *so* beautiful." She makes me smile.

Silas does, too. He chuckles at his wife's enthusiasm, caressing Eily's long brown hair. "Whatever my wife wants." He adores her. "Within reason," he warns her, too. Silas looks relaxed with his long, sun-streaked hair in a knot, but he has limits.

We all do.

Redix echoes him. "You've watched *us* before, so take your time." His gaze relishes my kneeling body. Luca's rising body, too. They desire us, it's obvious, and I chew my lip, anticipation becoming a delicious ache in my core. "So enjoy yourselves," Redix eases, "and let us finally watch you, too."

But that was also a dare, a taunt between men. *Horny men.* It makes Luca chuckle deep. Fisting my hair, he gazes down at me, demanding, "Show them, my belle. Take your time and show them what I love to watch."

"Yes, Master," I answer, shifting my body.

"You, too," Luca commands Zar. "Show them how proud we are."

Zar smirks, confident, as we face each other with Luca's cock towering between our mouths. I dart my tongue out, licking his sensitive seam, while Zar drags his tongue down Luca's shaft.

We make him hiss. We drive Luca crazy, teasing his cock for minutes, loving how his hands palm our skulls. So, he teases us back.

"Stroke that dick. Show them how you get so hard licking my cock," he orders Zar. "Spread your thighs wider, my whore," he controls me. "Let them see how hard your little pink clit gets, tasting drops of my cum on your tongue."

We obey. We moan. My tongue dances with Zar's, our mouths meeting, slobbering up and down Luca's shaft.

Out of the corner of my eye, I see Cade's head in Redix's lap. She's sucking him off, too, and I glance, seeing Eily's doing the same to Silas.

But it's the look in Redix and Silas's eyes; their lips parted like this is an erotic performance amongst men. Aroused men. Hungry men. Hard men. They lust for Luca.

We all do.

I gaze up at him, ravenous like they are. I take him first, letting him fuck my throat while he praises, "My sweet slut, so thirsty for my cock fucking your mouth, aren't you? Show them how you drool for me."

Lust drips over my lips. It drips from my pussy. The men are moaning, watching Luca fuck my face with my wrists bound, and I love it. I moan, too, with him deep in my mouth before he yanks me off and attacks Zar's waiting lips.

"My sweet skull pussy," Luca growls. "Show them how you take it. How you're my throat goat." He's brutal with Zar. He's brutal with me, and we relish it.

"Fuck yes." I hear Silas groan like he's about to come, telling Eily, "Baby girl, don't stop."

Luca raids my mouth again. "Show them, Belle," he demands. "Show them how you choke on me. How you give your beautiful face for me to fuck. How my cock in your mouth makes you my wet little whore forever."

"*Fuucckk*, man," Redix grunts, and Cade moans. He must be coming in her mouth. "Fuck yes, woman, swallow it."

Grabbing my hair, Luca holds me still, barely gagging on his mass while he taunts our audience, "She fucking loves this. Every inch of my cock and pain she craves in her tight little holes."

Yes, I do.

"Such a dirty girl," Silas groans at his wife, at me. His next rough grunts thrill me, hearing how we make him come, too.

I love this.

I love that every night, Luca will please me; every morning, he'll love me; and every day, he'll care for me. I surrender my throat and let him ruthlessly fuck it, my shameless *glucking* filling the air.

"Dayum," Redix admires Luca's fervor, "I want some of that."

Who does Redix desire? I'm not sure.

"I want her, too," Cade confesses, and yes, it turns me on. I'm attracted to her—to all six of them.

"I'll share her." Luca tugs at my hair. "But not yet." He plops my swollen lips off his cock. "Crawl," he demands, guiding us toward Charlie and Daniel, Jameson and Soriya, too.

Zar can obey. He crawls, but with my wrists bound, I can't. I have to walk on my knees and gaze up at Luca, admiring me, while Daniel's blue eyes savor my submission. Charlie's impressed, too.

She's letting Daniel plunge his hand in her panties to our show. But there's something in Charlie's eyes, watching me. We can speak with no words. She's stunning, and Daniel is jaw-dropping. But they're a boundary I don't want to cross. Charlie feels the same.

We all have them. We all honor them. We don't have to share everything except trust.

Luca summons us to kneel before Jameson and Soriya.

It's half sweet and half sadistic.

It's sweet because Luca's including Nick. He wants what Zar wants: for Nick to watch and hopefully support this.

It's sadistic because we're centered, inches from Jameson, who'll have to witness this, too.

And the sight will certainly impress because Luca strips before him, tossing his clothes away. He towers, bronze and shredded and naked in front of everyone, his cock still glistening with our spit as we kneel, once again, before him.

Caressing Zar's dark waves, he gently orders, "Tell your man what you need from me."

Luca wants Zar to have a love like Luca and I share. Will Zar ever change and want to marry? Maybe. But it begins with respect, and Zar gives that to Nick.

"I need to serve my Owner," Zar explains. "I always will. But I asked my Owner to let *you* have me first, so I'll always be yours, too."

It tightens my raw throat. Zar rarely gets this vulnerable. He's usually so full of swagger, but this is his tender heart, hoping he can have the love he's been searching for.

Zar made a tragic mistake with Darby, but Luca understood. He forgave him and loved him. Like Luca has moved on with me, he's let the pain and past go; Zar wants to move on with Nick, too.

We truly are starting new lives together.

"Please, babe." Nick sounds sincere, secure, aroused, and assuring Zar, "I like it. I want it. Go ahead. Show me the real you. It's okay."

"Show him." Lovingly, Luca urges Zar, "We have no shame. Show him how you like to serve me. How you'd like to serve him one day, too."

It's immediate. It's intoxicating. Sharing this intimate act always connects us. We come so hard every time.

Luca turns, his cock hovering over my parted lips while he

gives his backside to Zar. I can't see from where I'm kneeling tonight, but I've watched them do this before. How Zar loves to get on his knees and spread Luca's cheeks, serving him, rimming him until it makes Zar come. Sometimes, Luca comes, too.

But tonight, Luca throws his chin up, groaning as I gaze up. He's so beautiful like this, overcome with lust. Then, it makes him glower down at me; his eyes darkened more than ever because he's finally letting all know, all watch his desire. "Put my cock in your mouth, my belle. Suck me," Luca growls. "Serve me, too."

Proudly, I do. I stretch my lips and plunge down his length until I gently gag on it, loving that Jameson's watching, that everyone is.

"Yes." Luca grabs my hair. He reaches around and grabs Zar's, too. "Lick my ass. Suck my cock. You fucking love it."

"On my god," Soriya mutters. "God, y'all are so fucking hot."

"Do you want to touch her?" Luca rumbles, asking Soriya while I moan. "Hear her? She wants you to." He coaxes Soriya, "Scarlett wants you to play with her while she gags on my cock."

Fuck, this turns me on because, *holy shit,* she does it.

Soriya doesn't ask Jameson for permission. She crawls down from their chair, but I don't abandon my efforts. I keep licking and sucking and loving Luca's cock. Zar's behind him, devoted to him, too. I can feel Zar's kneecaps brushing mine under Luca's spread legs. I can hear Luca's breath changing, loving it, too.

Then I feel Soriya kneel behind me. I feel her heat on my back. Her warm hands start to caress my breasts, hoisted high in their leather harness, and Luca praises her, "Good girl. That's it. You like her, too, don't you? You like playing with my whore's hard nipples."

"Yes, Mr. Mercier," she sighs, pinching my nipples with no shame.

Oh my god. Oh my god. She's into this. This is her kink, too. I have to look. I have to glance left.

And I do. And I moan with Luca's cock in my mouth.

Jameson's watching his girlfriend fondle me, and it's making him fondle his hard cock. He's taken it out, proudly stroking his length.

"Play with her sweet pussy, too," Luca commands Soriya, and he's so damn Dom, all obey.

"Yes, Mr. Mercier." Soriya sounds like she *wants* to obey him, but she hesitates.

And this is what Luca meant. Of course, he recognized Soriya and Jameson's desire to submit, maybe before they knew it themselves.

It's how Luca found me, too.

And Zar.

"Don't be shy," Luca coaxes her while I suck his fat tip, my eyes rolling at his filthy taunts. "You're a little slut just like mine is. You love being dirty, so show your *boyfriend* how much."

Soriya's voice stammers with desire. "Yes, Mr. Mercier." Her breath steams over my shoulder, pressing her breasts, covered by her silky dress, into my back. Her eager hand lowers, her fingertip circling my clit while her other hand pinches, tugging at my nipple.

My groan is deep, muffled by Luca's mass, while he gazes down at us with his evil, erotic smirk. "Good *fucking* girls," he jeers. "Now, tell me how wet my whore is, on her knees with my cock fucking her throat."

"She wants you. She's soaking my fingers for you." Soriya's digits slide slick through my folds, woman to woman; she knows how to do it, and I shudder. I groan. I'm getting so close.

"Make her come on them," Luca orders. "Just like that. Yes, pinch her pretty pink nipple, too." And Luca's so dominating, fisting my hair while he makes another man's woman kneel and be nasty for him, too. "Show your boyfriend," he commands Soriya, "how this gets you off. How this gets you wet. Finger your pussy for us. Show him how you like obeying me, how you like playing with my whore's sweet cunt while you play with yours, too."

Holy fuck, Luca's so dominating, he's dazzling.

Tears leak from my eyes because I adore him.

The way his sexy glare makes Soriya let go of my nipple. The way his power makes her rustle under her dress. The way, even without his touch, he makes her want to touch herself while she moans, playing with my clit, too.

Yes, Luca loves me; he's devoted to me, but he can control anyone.

We both gaze up and obey him, and it makes Jameson groan at our submission, at how Luca's dominating me and his woman right in front of his face. He's getting off on it. I can hear his panting breath, his jerking fist.

"Show your *boyfriend*." Luca cuckolds Jameson more, urging Soriya, "Show him how you're a good little girl who likes to play with pussies for me, for a *man*. That's it. Show him how I let you touch my whore's wet pussy, but he can't. Go faster with your fingers. We can hear how wet you are. Let him watch his slut come for me. Good girl. That's it. Come for us."

Oh my god. I'm on my edge, feeling Soriya shudder against my back. Luca's taunts make her come so fast and hard that her lips moan into my shoulder.

"Take it." Burying his length in my mouth, Luca holds me here. "Yes, use those fucking tongues," he commands me and Zar, holding his head, too, while he gazes down, adoring me. He can see I'm desperate to come. "Now show Mr. Grant," he commands Soriya, "how you can make my whore's pussy come for me, too."

"Mmm." I hear Zar moan, loving this. He must see Jameson jerking off to Luca's power, to his bullish demands. How he dominates three of us at once.

It makes Luca fist my hair tighter, locking my gaze to his while he entices Soriya to strum my clit. I'm about to come, and he is, too. His shaft swells against my lips, burning at his relentless fuck.

"Come with my cock in your mouth, my belle," he growls. "Come with my stud licking my ass. Come with a good girl playing with your sweet wet pussy, too. Show him," he snarls. "Show Mr. Grant how you're *MY* whore while I come on your tongue."

"Goddamn." In awe of Luca, I hear Daniel groan in his deep British accent. *Is he coming, too?*

"Yes," Charlie moans. *They must be.*

"Fuck." Nick's enraptured, too.

Click, click, click. I hear Vivian's shutter capturing my submission.

They're all watching me, watching us, and it's too much. It's too taboo. I love it. I can't fight it. I gaze at Luca with his cock in my mouth, and I come. I let him use me. I let him cuckold a man, making his woman finger clit, making my body buck, then shatter, gushing over Soriya's flicking hand.

"Fuck, Belle. Yes, my whore," he praises me. "Fuck yes, lick it." He praises Zar. "Fuck, you two." Then he stills, coming and grunting and grunting again, flooding my mouth while his thighs shaking. Then he finds his breath, growling his command. "Show him. He wants to see it. He gets off on it."

Yes, Jameson does. Luca knew it all along. He's that bad, he's good.

Because when I turn my head, showing Jameson Luca's cum on my tongue, it makes Jameson come, too. "Damn, girl," he groans.

"Yes, Daddy," Soriya coos.

Is that also their kink? It must be because I swallow, making Jameson's eyes roll back, coming more to Soriya taunting, "Yes Daddy, I'll be so bad for you," while she crawls back onto their chair, kissing him while Luca caresses my cheek.

I can't help but look up and smile. Luca does, too. He smiles down at me with that secret *told-you-so* grin only couples share.

Carefully, he helps me stand. He helps Zar rise, too, kissing him on the cheek. "Get ready for me," he calmly commands Zar, who turns toward his cross.

Then Luca turns back to me. Cradling my face, he takes my mouth in a deep kiss, moaning at his taste on my tongue.

I assume he'll lead me to my torture tower beside Zar, but he surprises me. Scooping me up, Luca carries me to the platform.

Scarlett

CHAPTER THIRTY-TWO

CAREFULLY, LUCA SETS ME DOWN ON THE EDGE OF THE plush platform. Smoothing my hair, he insists, "Let me get you some water, my belle."

A round brass table by the platform contains full pitchers, crystal glasses, lube, condoms, vibrators, and wipes. It's what we usually have here, but Luca has quadrupled the supplies for our guests.

While he fetches my drink, I get my bearings, still dizzy, still buzzing, my skin alight with the last scene with Soriya.

I search for her and find her naked in Jameson's lap. They're lounging, kissing, and recovering.

Nick looks intrigued. He's focused on Zar, who's dutifully standing by his cross on the wall, waiting for Luca. But what traps Nick's stare is Zar's hard nudity with his hands clasped behind his back. He strips for this next part, and the sight is mouth-watering.

I scan left, and Daniel's still playing with Charlie, his hand disappearing under her black panties. It's sweet how he takes care of her. Titillating her. Worshipping her. Whispering in her ear and making her laugh, then moan while he nuzzles her neck.

Beside them, though?

Silas is serving Eily. More like she's serving him her pussy in his face. Standing on the chair, she straddles his mouth, grabbing his long hair. "Please, Silas, yes. I need to come. Yes, make me come. Oh god, yes. Like that. Don't stop! Don't stop!"

It sounds like Silas is moaning *and* chuckling into his wife's hungry sex, able to quickly satisfy her with his tongue because she shakes, crying out, "Silas!" So, he grabs her buttocks, holding her over his mouth until she's thoroughly relieved.

"Thank you." She collapses on top of him. "*God*, I needed that." She kisses him, and she's so cute.

I understand. We've created so much pent-up desire in the room.

It has Redix fingering Cade, their mouths moaning into their kiss.

It has Mateo and Stacey stroking Ford. He's in the center, praising them while they watch us.

Vivian seems heated, too.

She's stripped off her dress. Poor woman must've been sweating like a whore in church. *No, wait, that's me.* It is getting warm in here, though, in the best way because Vivian's nipples are hard under her coral lace bra. Her matching panties capture my glance, too.

Damn, she's hot, and I'm clearly in heat. I must be ovulating like those mating lions Zar always teases us about.

Luca returns, squatting before me, offering a full glass with a straw, and I obey. I drink the whole thing for him.

"My belle." He rubs my thigh. "Do you want more?"

Is he kidding?

HIF #21: I don't want more. I want it ALL.

I reach for his fingers on my leg. Though mine are bound, I grab his and gently squeeze, answering, "Til death do us part, Luca."

Like a flashbulb, a smile brightens his face. It hits his eyes, too. They sparkle.

Guess that was the right answer.

He gently takes my lips in a long kiss before he stands, taking the glass of water while his steps aim for the cabinet in the opposite corner.

I take the moment to check on Zar again. While Luca's not looking, I blow him a kiss. He pecks the air back. We do this all the time. When we take breaks, we can be so disobedient, and it's fun.

Now that our friends know, I can imagine all the fun we can share with them. Not just nights like this. I want days shared on the beach. I want barbecues and babies. I want birthday parties and beer around a fire pit. I want to bitch about the families we love and the jobs we enjoy. Hell, I want to pick paint colors for a house.

Who the fuck am I?

Ruby's right. I am getting fucked senseless...

And I haven't even been fucked yet.

I make myself chuckle, but when I see Luca returning, I'm stunned by arousal. His cock is rousing again. He's got that dark look in his eyes. A long gold bar with gold leather cuffs hangs in his grasp, and I know what it is, though we haven't used one before.

Without a word, Luca kneels on the platform before me. Uncuffing my wrists from my thighs, he takes a moment to rub them, making sure my restraints aren't too tight.

"Luca," I answer the flash of concern in his eyes, so he continues with my consent.

Leaning down, he buckles a cuff around my right ankle. Adjusting the metal bar to my width, it spreads my thighs almost as wide as they'll go before he secures the end of the bar with its cuff to my other ankle.

Of course, he leaves my heels on while softly commanding, "Lie down, Belle." With my wrists free, I lower to my elbows before I rest on my back.

The black leather platform is warm, supple, full of salacious memories, and about to make more.

Lifting the spreader bar from its center, Luca slowly pushes my knees toward my chest, and the thrill, my shameless display, makes me eager, my body singing for this degradation.

I submit my wrist cuffs for him to bind to the center of the bar. The *clicks* of the gold snap hooks send goosebumps down my arms.

Then, Luca rises from the platform, and I breathe in his heated gaze. I feel what his eyes covet. I'm bound, my sex splayed open, my heeled feet in the air, my thighs braced far apart with my hands able to grasp the golden bar between them.

"Scarlett," he sighs, lingering his fingertips down the back of my thigh. "You're so beautiful for me." Slowly drawing his touch through my slick, spread lips, his reverence for my vulnerability opens me more. There's nothing I won't do with him. I can feel Luca's love, his stare burning my entrance, warm air licking at the void he hasn't filled yet tonight.

Luca makes me live, dying for him.

"Stay," he commands. "Let them stare at what's mine and wet and waiting for me to fuck."

He pulls me by my thighs to the edge of the platform. I'm spread-eagled, my arousal dripping down my cheeks. I can't see my audience, but I can feel them. Their stares are flicking my raw, exposed clit.

I've made Luca raging hard again. Leisurely, he strokes himself at the platform's edge, insisting, "Tell everyone who you are, Scarlett."

"I'm your whore, Master," I answer. My nipples scream it, too. "I'm your whore who's wet and waiting for you to use me, to fuck me, please." I pause, caught in the devil and delight in his eyes. "And I'll be your wife, too, wanting you like this forever."

His nostrils flare, but his eyes soften. "I love you," he rumbles, wanting to take me now. He's hard for everyone to watch, but like he's proven for years, he can wait. He can take care of the ones he cares for first.

Kissing the inside of my ankles in the air, he leaves me exposed to everyone, for the clicking camera, too.

But in this luscious, degrading position, I can turn my head and watch him like everyone else does, I assume. Or they're staring at my shameless glistening pussy and vulnerable ass. Probably both while I admire Luca's cut, naked ass flexing for my delight.

He aims for Zar, making Nick turn in his chair because it's a powerful sight. Luca's hard and naked. Zar's hard and naked. Their skin tones are similar, their appearance, too, but their roles are opposite.

Shoving Zar to his knees, Luca demands, "Make this cock so fucking hard for you. For the punishment you want."

Zar eagerly obeys, grabbing Luca's thighs. He chokes on his length like he's been starving, but really, it's his pain he seeks because Luca lets him do it until Zar gags. He drools and moans. Then Luca drags him up and slams him back against his cross, the padded X on the wall. Binding Zar's wrists, Luca straps his ankles to the cross next. It spreads Zar open, similar to me, with his sex, his eyes, hungry and desperate for Luca, too.

I glance at Nick. *Is he okay with this?* I don't know him yet, but I worry.

Luca does, too. After he retrieves his red and black leather flogger from the cabinet, he approaches Nick.

"This is what he wants," Luca tells him. "It's what I need, too." He pauses, something tender filling Luca's eyes. "But I need your permission. If you want to join us, I need your consent, too."

Nick nods, his stare finding Zar's.

But Zar doesn't speak. He's a good sub. He looks willing and wanting, so Nick answers, "Yes, he wants this, and I want it, too. You have my permission to please him. Show me how he likes it."

Luca nods before he turns to drag his flogger down Zar's bound body, making Nick's eyes fill with wonder. I'm sure others do, too, but I can only turn my head to see Nick, Jameson, and Soriya on my right.

Soriya admires Luca. Jameson does, as well, but he keeps glancing at my exposed pussy. Jameson's seen it before. He's fucked me before. But Luca's right.

No one but Luca owns me now.

And with the first whizzing *thwack* of his flogger, Luca proves it. All eyes are on him and Zar. Because their dance is practiced, it's perfect. It's tough and tender. How Luca whips Zar's naked thighs. How Zar groans for it. How sweat starts to sheen across Luca's muscles, and Zar's muscular body shines the same.

They can do this for so long. I've watched, marveled, and come watching them. Because Zar's cock curves up, hard and begging for it. Because Luca gives Zar the sight he craves, too. This makes Luca's cock so hard he drips when he whips him.

But it's more intense and intimate because they no longer do this out of guilt. Or grief. They're free now. They do this all out of love.

"Do you love this?" Luca requires.

"Yes, my Owner." Zar writhes, holding back his release.

"Do you love *me*?"

"Yes, my Owner."

Precum drips from Zar's tip, and it makes me wet. Their pleasure would arouse anyone. I hear the heavy breath, the stirring bodies in the room. I search the mirrors and see many roused stares in the reflection between Zar's cross and my tower.

Is it Zar's desire? Is it Luca's torture? Is it Zar's greedy cock? Is it Luca's broad muscles ripping across his naked back? I study our guests. I read people well, and the revering look in their eyes makes my core ache, too.

It's hard to define.

It's Luca.

He's a molten explosion. A volcanic wonder. His heat. His power. His force. He's destruction and creation. He's everything you fear and need.

God, I love him.

We *love him.*

"Show him!" Luca commands Zar. "Show your man how much you love my whip. Show him how you come for my pain. For my pleasure."

Zar groans with his nose down, his eyes glaring, but his lips shake.

"Now!" Luca roars.

His last lash is brutal. It's what Zar often begs for. It strikes Zar's raw cock, and he cries out, fountains of his cum, spurting, splattering the bare wood floors beneath our torture chambers. "Yes!" Zar roars and Luca gives him one more with a backhand of his flogger. One more stinging whip. One more ferocious swipe of pleasure. One more creamy release.

"That is hot as fuck." I hear Silas's praise.

"Bloody right," Daniel growls.

"*Mmmm*." Ford sounds impressed, aroused, too.

"Yes, it is," Nick agrees. He accepts, and it's what Zar needs to hear. He's panting. He's sweating, but he smiles at him. Then, he smiles at Luca, who tenderly kisses his cheek before he unbinds him, guiding him to rest and recover with Nick.

Tossing his flogger on the floor, Luca looks possessed, his pecs heaving, and I chew my lip.

Everyone's quiet.

Everyone's anticipating.

He stalks toward the cabinet. Off the glass shelf, he grabs a large gold bowl. I've never seen it; wanton worry crawling between my thighs, wondering what it is.

Luca aims my way. He sets the large bowl on the platform beside me before he situates our bodies such that I'm in his lap, between his thighs, my head resting against his erection.

Memories of our first Saturday night flood my body. It feels so long ago, but my heart trusts him the same.

He pinches my nipples, making me groan while he demands, "Who will give my future wife pleasure while I give her a little pain?"

"Oh fuck," I mutter, loving this, realizing what he's about to do.

A sultry voice answers, "I've always wanted to."

Oh my god, it's Stacey.

I hear her heels click my way, then I see her in the mirrors on the ceiling above us, then on the horizon between my legs spread open by a golden bar. Ford and Mateo approach, too, standing much taller behind her.

Stacey caresses my open thighs. "I think we have a show to finish, don't we?" She smiles, and I nod.

Looking like a sex kitten, her blonde hair is piled in a messy French twist. Her large breasts spill from her black bra before Ford pulls the cups down, giving us a lip-licking look at them. Mateo drags her panties down, too, but leaves them around her ankles.

It happens so fast. Mateo bends her over. "Our woman needs to taste what she's been fantasizing about." Grabbing her hip, he makes her hands brace on either side of me, his other hand shoving her gorgeous face into my open pussy, while he shares, "She tells us about it while we fuck her ass like this."

"Oh my god!" I cry out to the carnal compliment. To the pleasure of her tongue meeting my clit. To her moans while Mateo claims her. To Luca, spraying my nipples with cold saline water to clean them and his fingers holding a platinum bar.

They must've prepped Stacey already. She's not in pain. She's loving it. She's moaning, licking my excited clit while her men kiss, and Mateo fucks her.

And I gaze up at Luca, trapped in this pleasure and trust. I trust Luca's care. I trust this will bind us even more. I trust that he'll wait to re-pierce me until Stacey makes me come.

I do not doubt this man's love for me.

I'm certain of our lust, too.

Luca's erection presses against my neck, and Ford's soars hard, watching Mateo take Stacey's ass. Then Ford taunts her; he taunts me, "Our woman's never eaten a pussy before, but she sure wants yours. Since our show for you, she's wanted to taste you. We make her come confessing it."

Stacey moans, and my thighs start shaking. My eyes anchor to Luca's staring down at me with such love, such desire, while Stacey's plump lips eagerly suck my clit with Mateo thrusting, nudging her face deeper into my pleasure. "Lick it," Mateo taunts her. "Let me see your tongue flick her clit for me."

"Luca." I need him. The pleasure. The pain. I need it all. I'm almost there. My core is binding tight.

And when Ford nudges Mateo aside, taking his turn with Stacey, sharing her ass, my edge is razor thin. I'm going to fall into Luca's eyes and Stacey's ravenous mouth.

"Luca," I beg him, and he adores me, pressing the cold bar poised against my tender nipple. He's found the original mark we created and is ready to retake it.

Smack. Ford spanks Stacey's ass. "Eat that pussy," Ford orders her. "Come on, our little slut. Make her come while I make you come fucking your tight ass." He spanks her again, and she moans, and I let go.

"I'm coming," I cry out. I can't stay quiet. Lightning sparks in my sex like the light in Luca's eyes. I stare up at him, and he does it.

"Forever, my belle." He pierces me, and I scream. I come to a soft, fluttering tongue on my clit and a sharp, fiery pain in my nipple. The ecstasy. The agony. White light takes my vision. Quickly, Luca re-pierces my other nipple, too, making my orgasm scream longer through my body, making the bar rattle between my shaking thighs, making Stacey groan like she's coming, too, staggering back into Ford.

I can barely focus, my vision blurred but I catch how Mateo sweeps Stacey into his arms. They disappear from my view because I can only gaze up at Luca, who gently caresses my flushed cheek.

My nipples are hot and tender, like the look in Luca's eyes. "Do you want more, my belle?" He soothes me, but I'm on fire.

"Don't stop," I demand. He cocks a dark eyebrow. "Please, Master, give me more."

Luca knows what I ultimately want and will happily endure every pleasure to get it.

He frees my wrists from the bar before shifting our bodies around again. I'm like a chained rag-doll in his grasp. He puts me on all fours, on my hands and knees in a whirl, with the row of chairs on my left, my stare facing my tower.

The bar still spreads my thighs. Arousal dribbles down my legs. My sex is exposed and pulsing for more. My breasts sting. My neck, my wrists, my thighs, they're still bound in cuffs.

I love this.

Tugging my hair, Luca kneels behind me, making me turn my head toward our guests. His taunt is vulgar and devoted. "Who wants her next?"

"We do."

The voice is deep, masculine, and lulling with a sexy Southern drawl. I find my focus and see Silas carrying Eily my way.

"Put her under her," Luca respectfully commands Silas. "Let your wife taste her, too. I need her pussy soaking wet for this."

"My pleasure," Eily offers with a sexy grin. Silas sets her down on the platform, and she crawls under me, turning sideways on the platform, too. Silas kneels between Eily's legs. He's hard and looks eager to watch us.

I'm in that trance state again, euphoric, but I have enough logic to guess correctly, to love what Luca's about to do to me.

He rustles behind me. I can hear him and see in the reflection how he's rolling a condom on before he snaps open a bottle of lube. He coats his hungry cock and fingers with it.

"Help me get my whore ready," he kindly orders Eily. "She needs to want this so bad because this hurts so good."

"I can't reach her." Eily sort of giggles, and Luca softly chuckles. Silas grins, too, patiently stroking his impressive cock while he watches us arrange our bodies to fit.

I glance around the room, and all eyes are on us. They can watch the profile of our bodies lining up to do this.

Unlatching my ankles from the spreader bar, Luca tosses it aside. With a *clank*, it lands on the rug. Gently pressing down on the small of my back, he offers my pussy to Eily's mouth. "Let her pleasure you, my belle, while I get your tight ass ready to be fucked by me and our friends."

Yes, I heard that right.

Yes, it's what I want. It's so obscene; I love it.

And yes, it takes every ounce of trust, love, and pride to do this, and that's all I ever feel with Luca now. I want to thank him, to kiss him, but his fingers are too fast, and Eily's tongue is too good.

Luca penetrates my tightest hole while Eily laves over my clit, and I moan, lust blooming goosebumps down my flesh. I want to taste Eily, too, to pleasure her, but she's too petite. We're in the hottest sixty-nine, but our bodies don't align. I just have to submit and squat over her face and let her do what she enjoys, too. Because she spreads her thighs for Silas to admire her slick cunt, and he does.

"Such a cute little slut for me," he praises, and his voice makes Eily moan into my folds, her tongue expertly working my clit. Where Stacey felt new, like she was exploring me, Eily's mouth is deft and delicious.

Yes, in her sixsome, she has acquired some skills.

Confirming my guess, Silas taunts her, "You can't get enough of this, can you, my naughty wife? You like to give as much as you get."

Yes, she does. I moan, staring at Silas's seductive body while I feel his wife's tongue lavish figure eights over my clit. It's heaven as Luca coaxes, "Yes, my belle loves this, too. She loves being used." Pumping his fingers in my ass, he admires Eily's efforts and her moans. Mine, too. "Yes, that's it. Good girls. Get her ready for my cock."

I am. I really am.

Straddling my legs with his, Luca hovers, barely urging inside my ass while he demands, "Look at our guests, my belle. Let them see how much you love this. How my whore craves my cock fucking her ass."

Oh my god. My eyes find Jameson's, and I moan my submission. I moan, letting the man I'm destined to be with, the man I love, claim me before his eyes.

Luca always burns. He always stretches. He always pleasures. He always hurts before he heals, but Eily's gentle suck of my clit makes the pain pleasing.

"Luca, yes." I start begging him. "Master, yes." I can take it. I want it.

With Eily's help, he opens me. He breeches me, going past that stinging ring while Eily sucks my clit harder, and I scream, my thighs shaking, my sudden, shattering orgasm surprising me.

"Fuck yes, take her ass like an animal," Silas admires Luca crouched over me, grabbing my hips, humping and thrusting while I'm panting, staring at Daniel. He looks voracious, like a hungry wolf watching us, too.

They're all watching Luca fuck my ass like a wild initiation, and it feels like one. "Yes, Scarlett," Luca growls. "Take it. Take all of me. Moan for my cock in your ass, my belle. Tell them how you love it."

And I do. "Yes, Luca, I love it. I love you." My submission complete. My pledge sealed.

I belong to Luca Mercier.

Eily kisses my clit like she's leaving as Luca seats deep inside me, making breath hard for me to find. My thighs shake. I can't escape his blinding pressure, his maddening pleasure. All I can feel is him and the ache in my pussy for him to fill, too.

Luca gently lifts my shoulders, hugging my back to his chest and grabbing my neck. Thrusting into my ass, he sounds cruel and caring, his lips pressed to my ear, "Ma flamme, do I burn inside you as you do inside me?"

"Yes, Luca." From the tips of my ears to my toes.

"Do I satisfy? Am I all you deserve? All you can take and love?"

"Yes, Luca." I'm dripping. "Forever."

"Thank you." Luca controls his tone, addressing Silas, "Please thank your lovely wife for me while I fuck my bride."

It's so crude and cute. How Silas yanks Eily to the edge of the platform. She squeals with delight before he mounts her, taunting, "So hungry for cunts and my cock, aren't you, baby girl?" Then he starts fucking her, making her cry out, wrapping around him while Luca turns our bodies.

He turns my chin, too, flooding me with a kiss that takes my senses while his hips don't stop, his hand moving from my neck to caress my jeweled breast.

Is he fucking me in the ass for all to watch? Yes.

Am I in orgasmic heaven? Hell yes.

"Stud," he summons Zar, who appears moments later. Without his command, Zar knows. He lowers, his mouth finding my clit to lavish while Luca ravishes my ass, and I groan from depths few achieve. It doesn't take long. This orgasm will destroy me. My shaking eyes search our admiring audience. I'm getting my ass fucked for them, and the man who owns me, who loves me, knows my next cry. His name shreds my voice while he holds me tight, letting me gush in his grasp and over Zar's awaiting mouth.

"Give me her cum," Luca demands, and Zar rises. In an almost kiss, he shares my watery reward with Luca, dripping it over his lips. I watch in the mirror and can't stop moaning.

They're so beautiful together; we're so beautiful together.

I expect Luca to keep going, to make me come again like this, and I will, but he pulls out, leaving me gaping from his claim.

I'm kneeling, panting, open, and not sure what's next. Then, Luca lies down beside me, on his back, before he snaps off the condom, tossing it on the floor.

"Crawl on top, my belle," he summons me, gripping his surging shaft. "Give me that beautiful pussy. It's mine."

Yes, finally. I swing my trembling leg over and straddle Luca. Then, suddenly, wildly, he pulls me into him. Into his kiss. Down on his body. Taking his cock, his heart, his life, his future, his everything. Luca wraps his arms around me, driving inside me, filling me, overwhelming me, making happy tears leak from my eyes.

"Do you want more?" His lips brush mine. "Can I give my sexy bride, my future wife, my beautiful whore, my best friend, *ma flamme*, my Scarlett, everything she desires?"

I lift, bracing my hands beside him, his diamond sparkling on my finger, his crystal eyes shining beneath me, too, and I answer the heaven and hell in his eyes.

"Luca."

Luca

CHAPTER THIRTY-THREE

LOVE.

That's all I feel with this woman, in every expression of the word.

My heart reaches for Scarlett, and I find her; I finally find myself inside her. She takes my body, my heart, my life, and my soul forever.

When we lose someone we love, we fear we can't live without them. It's a thousand lonely nights we fear we won't survive.

But love never dies. Wait, trust, and when it returns to you, it's a dawn, a brilliant fire, more beautiful than ever because you've been humbled.

Now you know. Now you believe.

Love: it's what I'll give Scarlett forever. Deep. Devoted. In beautiful ways that will make her smile, laugh, or cry those tender tears I cherish. And yes, I want others to watch me do it. To watch us share this. To witness how she makes me a whole man; every piece of me is hers.

Gazing down at me, I let her see it in my eyes.

Love: that's what I give her now because I'll give her this. I'll give us permission for one night to lose control, to fuck our tempting, true friends. I'll grant her wish because it's my desire, too.

I let myself change for her.

I let her love consume me.

Grabbing her hips, I stare into her eyes and insist, "Take me, Belle. Show them how you love me, how I love you."

But fuck, she's so beautiful above me. So damn wet and swollen around my cock. So tight and hot. Our games with our friends have her ravenous for me, so I hold on. For her, I can. I've honed my control to a painful degree, and she's always worth the wait. I'll give her everything she wants before I finally have what I need, too.

The platform shifts beside us, and it thrills me.

On my right, Silas is fucking his cute wife, and the way his power takes her petite body is almost taboo; it's intoxicating. I love hearing her pleasure, his pleasure.

Though I'm on my back, guiding Scarlett's hips, watching her fuck me in the mirrors above, I can't see him. He just stepped away, but I know he's always there. "Stud!" I call. "Come share the first turn with her."

Scarlett moans. It thrills her, too. Her eyes roll back before she knows to obey, watching me while Zar appears in my line of sight by the platform's edge.

This isn't just Scarlett's fantasy—it's Zar's dream, too. We've never done this, and she's the only woman we will ever share like this. He's been waiting so long. Deep down, so have I.

I went through hell to find her, and I'm never letting her go.

And Zar doesn't need my command. Grabbing a condom from a side table, he rolls it on before he climbs behind Scarlett. Kneeling between my thighs while Scarlett's legs straddle over mine, Zar pauses, his gaze almost not believing we're about to do this finally.

And I need to be sure, too—one last time. I will share her. I'll give her pleasure. I will fulfill her fantasies, but parts of Scarlett are too sacred to me, to us. Her heart. Her pussy. They're mine.

But this? I wrap my hand around her collared throat and hold her gorgeous stare. "Is this what you want, Belle? My cock fucking your pussy, only my cock, while I share your ass with my stud?"

"Yes, Master." Her answer is quick and begging with lust. "Please, Luca."

"Go slow," I order Zar, hoping I've opened Scarlett enough so the pain is gone and only the pleasure remains.

He obeys. Carefully, Zar presses in, and...

Goddamn, I can feel him. Holy fuck, she feels so fucking good and tight.

"Fuck," he grunts, feeling it too. "I can feel your cock inside her, too."

"Yes," Scarlett urges us. "Do it. Don't stop. It doesn't hurt. It feels so good. Please, Luca, don't stop."

It's incredible. It curls my toes and thins my breath. I have to fight not to come while Zar matches his thrusts with mine. We don't do it hard at first. He knows better. We go slow. This is for her pleasure.

Scarlett falls over me, taking us, moaning against my pecs, her teeth gently biting me, too. She starts moving her hips in my grasp, seeking more, wanting more. I know my woman's desire; I've mapped its every contour.

"Harder," I order Zar. "Fuck her harder. She wants it. Right?" I squeeze Scarlett's throat, lifting her so I can watch this. "You want our fuck, my sweet whore?" With my other hand, I circle my thumb over her clit, and she doesn't stop arching for us, grinding her hips, moaning, taking our cocks, and seeking her end.

"Yes. Fuck me harder," she begs with my diamonds sparkling from her peeked nipples. "Fucking give it to me. Give me those cocks."

Fuck yes, this is MY *woman.*

"Damn, gorgeous," Zar growls, holding her elbows, bowing her back while he thrusts lewdly into her. "You take our cocks so good. You're so fucking good for your Master, letting me fuck your ass, too, while he owns your sweet pussy."

"Yes." Scarlett rides us faster, her hips greedy, her arousal dripping down to my shaft. Staring at me, she begs, "Fuck me, Luca. Fuck me like your whore. Harder. Harder motherfucker."

I groan, my eyes rolling, my soul singing, my heart kneeling, thanking every god for this woman. She's more than my fantasy. She's my vow, my forever.

"Damn, I wanna come in her," Zar growls. He begs, "Damn, my Owner, please, I wanna come inside your whore. She's so fucking dirty and wet for us."

He'll always have to wear a condom, but I'll give him this. It's my fantasy, too.

"Do it," I order. "Share my whore with me."

Zar's groan is deep; it's carved into my soul, too. His satisfaction, his happiness, and his heart mean everything to me. And so does my woman. She's right there with him but holding back, waiting for my command.

God, I made her wait too long, and now...how I'll give her everything until my dying day.

"Do you love it?" I squeeze her neck harder. "Do you love it, my belle?" She's shaking. I'm thrusting my hips and she's soaking my balls. Her gorgeous eyes are cracking before me. "Do you love being our whore to fuck? All night, they're going to take your ass while your sweet pussy is mine. Do you love *ME* for it?"

She bucks. "Yes, Luca."

"Show me you love me, my whore. Come while we fuck you."

She does. With a deep moan, her neck strains in my grasp. Lurching, she shakes, contracting around my cock, her arousal streaming down my shaft. Her fingernails dig into my pecs. "Yes, Luca." She gasps for breath. "Yes, I love you. I love you."

Zar collapses, kissing her shoulder. He stills behind her while I grab a breath, too. Carefully, he withdraws. I can feel him leave her body, and it keeps me so hard. It makes me want more from her, but I make sure. "My belle?"

"Luca," she answers my unspoken question.

"I want her next." A deep woman's voice almost purrs it. I'd recognize it anywhere. I've admired her for so long.

Cade steps up to the platform wearing a black strap-on, and I focus, looking around me to see that we're surrounded. They were all watching us.

The clicking shutter of Vivian's camera hasn't stopped. Silas is spooning his wife at the top of the platform. They're satisfied and finished, watching us continue. Nick has joined Zar by the platform's edge. He's wrapped his beefy arms around him. Jameson has Soriya kneeling on the platform to my right. He stands behind her, kissing her neck and caressing her breasts.

But when I look to my left, what blood I have left surges to my cock.

It's Redix, standing behind Daniel. He's stroking Daniel's hard cock. *Oh fuck, he's fucking Daniel's ass, too.*

Goddamn, that turns me on.

They're watching us. They're getting off on us. It looks like Daniel's about to come on his wife, Charlie, lying on the platform before him. She's fingering her pussy. It sounds like she's going to come, too, watching Redix fuck her husband.

Damn, this is what those six have been up to.

"Keep going," Redix coaxes me. "My wife wants to fuck your woman, and I want to watch her do it. And then, it'll be my turn."

Moans fill the air at his taunt. I can't see them, but I hear Stacey and her men. It sounds like Mateo or Ford; I'm not sure who, but someone, more than one, is getting fucked on their chair, watching us.

Scarlett looks around, her eyes finding focus and the truth, too. "Oh my god," she sighs, and I agree.

I never knew it could feel like this. For so many years, I hid, buried in guilt and grief. And the years before that, I was buried in shame and secrecy. I knew who I was, and it was a man I feared others would hate. They'd revile—all but Zar.

But I was wrong. I was lucky. Fate took everything from me, and then she gave it back. And more.

Now, I have this. I brush my thumb over the lips that make me trust in love again, that make me proud to desire this.

"Scarlett, look," I share. She does before she gazes down at me. "Do you feel it, my belle? Do you feel how much they love us, how much I love *you*?"

"Yes." Tears almost take her eyes, but Cade kisses her shoulder, caressing her waist.

"Do you want this?" Cade asks. "Because we sure do. We've been waiting for you to get together for a long time. You're really fucking beautiful together."

"Please," Scarlett grinds on my cock, sighing for Cade. "Yes, we've been waiting, so please fuck me, too. Show my Master what a dirty little girl I am for him."

That stirs me. That ignites us again. Scarlett knew it would.

"Oh, my dirty girl." I thrust my hips, sticking my thumb in her mouth, too. She starts sucking it while Cade starts pressing in. "You want a woman to fuck you, too?" Scarlett nods, moaning while I feel Cade's dildo, not as thick as Zar's cock, urging inside her, too.

Damn, Cade is stunning. No one is as beautiful to me as Scarlett, but Cade was a model. She still wears her iconic short hair, her long bangs cloaking her purple eyes, and those breasts bound in that BDSM bra; she looks born to be Scarlett's dominatrix. If only for the night, or maybe more.

While sharing Scarlett with Zar felt natural, erotic, and destined, like we will surely share it again, this feels dirty, naughty, and new. And I crave both.

Cade reaches around, cupping Scarlett's breasts. "Does my cock feel good?" She steams over Scarlett's ear. "Do you like me fucking your ass?"

"Yes," Scarlett sighs.

Cade circles Scarlett's nipples. "Can I play with your pretty diamonds, too?"

'Yes," Scarlett begs, grinding again, seeking my cock and Cade's dildo.

Fuck, these women are hot.

Fuck, I can't believe my future wife.

"Yes, my belle," I praise her. "You're such a sweet slut for us, letting Cade take a turn in your ass."

"Luca," Scarlett groans. She's loving this, and I'm loving her.

Cade carefully plays with Scarlett's nipples, kissing her collared neck while she starts pounding faster, slapping her hips into Scarlett's cheeks. I can feel the maddening rhythm, the dildo thrusting against my cock squeezed tight in Scarlett's wet heat.

"Fuck," I growl.

"Yes, Master." Scarlett sees my pleasure, too. What man wouldn't fucking love this? "Thank you," she taunts me. "Thank you for sharing me. Thank you for letting her fuck my ass."

"Damn, y'all feel good." Cade sighs over Scarlett's ear, praising her, "That's a big, hot fucking Dom you're going to marry. You get his thick cock, fucking your pretty pussy every day? And you're his sweet, little whore, too? Letting him spread your pussy open to tease us all night? You make our mouths water."

"Fuck, yes, you do," Daniel thunders. I glance over. He's taking a pounding from Redix, who's grabbing his shoulder while Daniel stands and takes him in the ass. He loves it. He clearly loves watching us, too. "Yes," Daniel growls. "Fuck our asses. Fuck yes. Fuck us."

Charlie moans. It sounds like she's coming, and Daniel will, too. Once Redix lets go of Daniel's hard, bobbing cock, without a touch, Daniel roars, coming on his stunning wife.

"Oh my god," Scarlett cries out. She's watching them, too, and I'm gnashing my teeth, holding it back. I stop thrusting my swollen cock, so I won't come inside her yet.

But Scarlett's coming. Her thighs shake, and that makes Cade come, too. It sounds like it; both women are moaning and huffing for air, and I'm grabbing for breath, too. I want this next part too much.

No, I don't want to fuck Redix, and he doesn't want to fuck me. But just once, there's something about this that feels right. That feels like we were always going to find ourselves here.

Redix and I have shared too much pain, but we survived it and want to share this pleasure, too—this love.

Cade kisses Scarlett's cheek. "Congratulations," she teases, and Scarlett smiles.

"Thank you," she rasps.

"My husband wants to congratulate you, too," Cade says.

"And I gave him my permission. Just this once. This is our engagement gift from the six of us."

I feel her leave Scarlett's body. Redix has left Daniel's, too. Daniel has pulled Charlie into his embrace. They nestle at the top of the platform. I crane my neck to see them beside Silas and Eily while Redix snaps off the condom he used and grabs another before he stalks our way with a bottle of lube in hand, too.

Pulling Cade into a deep kiss by the platform's edge—*those two define soulmates*—Redix loves no one more than Cade, but he's a generous man. Everything he sacrificed for her. Everything he gives to the ones he loves.

All six of them. Their love overwhelms us, but ours does, too. We've captivated them.

We've captivated Stacey and her men, too. They gather on the riser, a tangle of limbs hugging while they watch us. This is the final round, and we need it.

Redix takes his position behind my woman. He brushes her arm. He'd never take this from anyone. He's survived too much. "Do you want this?" he asks Scarlett. "Because I'd be damn honored to give it."

"Yes," Scarlett gazes down at me, answering him, "I want it. Fuck me but save yourself for your wife. There's only two men who totally share me."

I cup her cheek. We both turn, and of course, he's there. Zar nestles in beside us. Nick takes his place behind him. They hold each other while they watch us, too.

The heat of the bodies surrounding us makes me sweat; it makes me need this. It feels like the ultimate domination and surrender.

The cool lube Redix pours over Scarlett's ass drizzles down to coat my shaft, too. She's going to need it. He's that hung, too. But I trust him.

I hold Scarlett's neck, not choking, just admiring, worshipping the look in her sapphire eyes, the feeling of Redix pushing into her ass, his mass gliding against my cock clenched in her swollen pussy, too.

"Damn, Luca," Redix growls, resting his hands over mine, holding Scarlett's hips, too. It's intimate. It's hot. "She's so fucking tight with your big cock in her, too. Fuck," he huffs. "Fuck, y'all feel good."

"Oh my god," Scarlett gasps at his size meeting mine. Filling her. Stretching her. "Oh my god, yes." Her lips shake. Her gaze locks on mine. "Luca."

"Yes, Belle." I squeeze her neck. "Let my friend fuck you too. I'll let him have your ass while I take your pussy."

Her nipples are screaming hard. Her diamonds sparkle, they beckon. Vivian's shutter clicks, capturing this as Soriya nears. Bodies press around us as Stacey joins her, too. Teasingly, they lick Scarlett's jeweled nipples. I think their men are fucking them, too. I can't see because all I want to watch is Scarlett and how her arousal floods her gaze. It's drenching my thighs, too.

My woman has taken so much, and we've given her so much. This is what she wants. Her fingernails dig into my abs like I'm her anchor.

I match my tempo to Redix's. We start going faster, harder, and it feels like I'm fucking Redix too, and we won't ever do it, and that's what makes this so damn hot. That and two women licking those tits that belong to me, too.

"Yes," I groan. "Treat her like my whore. Fuck her like my whore." Scarlett moans. "She loves it. She's soaking my cock for it."

"Oh fuck, yes," Redix groans. "Oh, she can fucking take us. Damn, she's hot. She's wet. She's grinding back on our hard cocks."

"Yes," Scarlett strains. We're making her come fast; I can see it. I'd give my life for it. Her pleasure is my mission, my purpose. "Yes," she cries out. "Fuck me. Fuck me." She stares at me. "Thank you, Master. Thank you for fucking me, for sharing me with your friends. Thank you for making me your whore, for making me come for you, Luca."

Oh, ma flamme.

I thrust so hard she bucks, shattering in my grasp, her eyes rolling back. She can't take much more. Her satisfaction. Her arousal. Her submission splashes over my thighs.

"Fuck," Redix huffs. He feels her spasms, her squirting pussy and bucking body, too. "Fuck, I gotta stop."

Carefully, he withdraws, respecting Scarlett's request, but I'm not done. Not yet. Not ever.

"Give her to me," I growl. "She's fucking mine." And the women recede. Bodies pull away.

Once I have her to myself again, I wrap Scarlett in my embrace and flip her over. Everyone moves, making room for us. Digging my knees into the platform, I spread her thighs and sink my fist into her fiery strands, and she lifts her hips for me. This is our ritual, first and last. I hold her tight and she opens for me. She takes me, pounding hard, and I'm gone.

The room falls away when I'm inside her, staring into her eyes. It's only me, allowed so deep inside her like this. I reach that place inside her; I find her heart. She's everything I seek, all I'll ever need, and together, we burn. Our friends, total strangers, the whole world can watch us couple, or breed, or fuck, and it doesn't matter.

I have one truth. It's Scarlett and me, now and forever.

Scarlett

A YEAR AFTER OUR WEDDINGS

"WHAT DID YOU CALL THIS DESIGN?" Luca scoops up Gia. She's excited, too. We've waited a long time for this.

"I call it 'Beach Chic meets Fancy Greek,'" I tease him because he's been patient.

Luca bought me our beachfront "shack," *ahem*, mansion, for our first wedding gift in Charleston. Then, for our second wedding gift in Paris, he declared that I had to remodel and redecorate it.

"Make it ours," he said, and boy, did I ever.

It took a year.

HIF #It's Been A Minute, I've Lost Count: This bitch likes to decorate. Thank god, I married a billionaire who put me on all of his accounts.

But Luca trusts me, and he should. You can take the girl out of the trailer park, but I can still pinch a penny so tight, I give ol' Abe Lincoln a migraine.

What challenged his patience? I forbade Luca to see it. I know

427

the sneaky, sexy fucker drove by all the time. Zar's home is three houses down. But Luca was forbidden to enter.

Only me, Gia, and our friends-turned-decorating assistants, have been allowed inside, working with crews and teams to get this right.

It's our forever home.

Well, one of them.

For our honeymoon, Luca gave me a little "villa," *ahem*, ocean view mansion in Mykonos, too.

I swear, my husband went on a spending spree when we married. For years, he spent little. He changed nothing.

But now?

He's changed. I've changed. His wallet's changed...

"Baba," Gia insists, "let me show you my bedroom first."

Luca sets her down in our new front yard, a carpet of Bermuda grass lined with sago and windmill palms, azaleas, and boxwoods.

"We have a whole house to show him, kiddo." I take Gia's hand. Luca takes her other as we climb the steps to the front porch.

"I like the Grecian blue front doors," he admires. "The gold hardware, too."

"Hmm," I wonder aloud, tapping in the security code to enter. "Wonder where I got that inspiration? Now close your eyes."

"Let me! Let me!" Gia bounces at his feet. So, Luca scoops her up again and puts her on his shoulders.

Her little hands cover his eyes before he grumbles, "Don't poke them out, my kóri. I need them to see what you've done with the place."

"It's pretty," Gia assures. "Scarlett spent millions!"

"Shhh!" I cut her a look with a smile. "That was our little secret."

"It's not a secret." Luca laughs. "My CFO kept me appraised of the damage."

"Shut up," I mutter, laughing, too. Guiding him by the elbow, he stoops through the front doors with Gia on his shoulders as I lead him inside.

The front doors automatically close and lock behind us. It's part of the sophisticated security system I installed, along with the guard stationed outside by the beach, twenty-four-seven.

What'd you expect from the Chief of Security for The Mercier Hotels?

Luca still has his obsessed fans.

But now, he has his badass wife, too.

"Okay." I take a breath, excited for him to see this. It's an open-concept design with floor-to-ceiling windows to the dunes and ocean. It's all warm white walls, plush Grecian blue furniture, gold hardware, glass fixtures, and reclaimed wood floors. *God, I hope he loves it. I can't return this shit.* "Open his eyes!"

Gia lifts her hands. "Opa!" She shouts.

He blinks and looks around.

"This is the foyer." I'm nervous.

"Oh," he's not smiling, "is that what they call entryways?"

His accent sounds strained. His handsome face scowls. His dark brows pinch.

Shit, that's the look he and Gia get when they're mad.

I huff, "You hate it, don't you?"

This was my fear. I went more casual than Luca's five-star luxury style. But it's the beach. It's South Carolina. It's our family home. And I guess all my taste is in my country mouth because he hates my interior design.

"I don't *hate* it," he grumbles.

But tears threaten. I've worked so hard on this. And I'm so emotional lately. Hell, I cried when I got a damn papercut the other day when I used to take bullets with no tears.

"My belle," he sees me getting upset and cracks his stunning smile. "I don't hate it. I *LOVE* it. It's perfect."

I swipe away my little tear. "You..." I want to curse, but I'm a mama bear now. I have to watch my salty tongue. "You poopy head! Don't mess with me."

He leans, chuckling before he plants a big kiss on my lips. "I'm a Harvard-educated man. I know better than to piss off Mrs. Scarlett Mercier. I value my balls too much."

"Baba," Gia chirps from his shoulders, "what balls?"

"Testicles," he answers.

"Remember?" I wink at her. "I showed you how to punch them to defend yourself."

Gia nods. "Yeah. But Zar didn't like it too much."

"Yeah, well," I shrug, grinning from ear to ear at that memory, "that's what he gets for being my sparring partner."

"Show me around." Luca pats Gia's leg. "Where's your room?"

"Hang on." I tug his arm. "Before we go and tour six bedrooms, seven baths, a home office, a home gym, a roof-top gazebo and spa pool, a—"

"Cha-ching! Cha-ching!" Luca teases, following me through our new living room with sofas and seating galore—perfect for Friday night movies and more Disney hell.

"Quit pitching a fit," I warn. "You told me to fix this place up. No more beige walls and carpet."

"Speaking of walls." He pauses while I slide open one of the glass doors to the deck, pool, patio, fire pit, and ocean outside. "Where did they go?"

"You told me to make it ours." I point to the open chef's kitchen on the far side of the first floor. It sprawls into a window-wrapped breakfast nook and sunroom.

"Cha-ching!" He admires the new wing of our home.

"Luca!" I stomp my foot.

He starts laughing even harder, and that makes Gia giggle, too. "I'm teasing you, my belle." He beams. "Spend all our money. That's what it's for. I can make more."

Securing Gia's legs under his arm, he reaches down to slap my ass. Of course, I let him. Lucky for him, our girl is around, or he'd be in for a real fight-turned-hot-fuck-fest.

"I want to show y'all something." I soften my tone, and he takes the hint.

Winking, he carries Gia outside.

I lead us across the new elevated sun deck and down the stairs to the ground level. The pool has been replastered. The patio has been re-tiled. The entire yard is discreetly fenced and lined with a screen of beach grass and low palms for privacy and security. Still, there's the long boardwalk to the public beach, so HGR will keep a guard outside at all hours.

We no longer have active threats, but protecting my family's more than my job.

At the yard's edge, I lead us to the special garden I had designed. Luca pauses, setting Gia down. He recognizes the gesture immediately. It makes him speechless, gazing at me.

"Gia," I take her hand, "these are irises." I point to the enormous bed of rare, heirloom colors I planted. Purples, periwinkles, reds, pinks, oranges, yellows and whites. It's every breath-taking variety I could find.

I squat beside her and share, "These were your mommy's favorite flowers. Your Baba gave her some on their first date. Like these pretty pink ones. He said he gave her white ones like this to hold for their wedding. And when you were born..."

I trail off, watching Luca swipe away a quick tear.

"And when you were born," I choke up, too, but I keep going because this is love and family and life, "he brought her a huge bouquet of these rare lavender and pink ones. They're called 'Mother Earth Irises.'"

"They're pretty," Gia says. "Like my mommy."

"Yes, they are." I peck her cheek. "And they'll come back every summer, and we can plant more if you like."

"Can I put one on in my new bedroom? In a cup with some water?"

"Sure." I rise, taking her hand. "I bought us a bunch of vases for them."

Gia picks a pink one, and I snap its thick stem. Proudly, she carries it up the deck stairs while Luca pulls me into a hug.

"Thank you." His voice is gruff, but his words are tender. "It's beautiful like she was. Like you always are, ma flamme. I don't know how I got so lucky. Twice."

"Maybe because under all this sexy, bossy Dom exterior," I mutter into his linen-covered chest, "is a heart of Grecian gold."

"Maybe it's because I met this beautiful, fiery woman who fought for me."

"Did I win?"

"You have my ring and my heart," he says, keeping his arm over my shoulder. "And my billions. Come on. Show me how else you bankrupt me."

"*Luca Andreas...*" I warn.

"Oh no," he mocks as we trod up the deck stairs, "she's getting feisty again. She's using my middle name and accent, too."

But I know he loves it.

He loves the new kitchen's white marble countertops. He eyes them, teasing, "Perfect place to make Baklava and babies."

I don't comment.

He loves our new dining room and the custom table for fourteen I had made. But he jokes, "Are we going to be one of the uptight families who always leaves it set like that?"

He mocks the centerpiece and table laden with plates, glasses, and flatware.

"No, Mr. Harvard. We're having a housewarming party tomorrow. Remember? Everyone's coming, and I'll be too busy to fuss with this."

When I say everyone, I mean only the friends we like and the family we love. I refuse to suffer the "polite" company of Charleston's elite any more than I have to.

We wander upstairs, where Gia disappeared a while ago. She's obsessed with her new bedroom. I let her decorate it, and it looks like a Disney Princess Theme Park...with a bunk bed.

When we find her in there, she's playing with her mermaid dolls, splashing them in the full sink of her ensuite bathroom.

"My, my." But Luca spots them first on her bathroom vanity, choking down his laughter. "What do we have *here*?"

Then I spot them, too.

"These are their beach towels," Gia answers. "They're playing on the beach today."

"Gia," I speak, then snort, then speak again. "Those are my *maxi* pads."

But tell that to her. She's got four mermaid dolls cocooned in my Always with Wings.

Luca falls back against the wall, crying because he's laughing so hard, and I don't want to embarrass her, but I laugh, too.

"But I found them in you and Baba's new bathroom." Gia's confused. "They're little sticky towels."

"Kiddo," I smooth her ponytail, "you can play pretend with them, but they're not for dolls. They're for big girls and women."

"But I'm a big girl."

"Oh god, no," Luca mutters. "I'm not ready."

"Yes," I answer her. "You're getting older, and you'll need them one day, too."

"When?" she asks.

I cut a glance at Luca, and he shrugs, grinning with a this-is-your-fish-to-fry look.

"I'll tell you tonight," I promise.

We leave her content to play with dolls and maxi pads in her bathroom while I show him the rest of the guest rooms.

"This one's ready for my dad." I show it to Luca next. It has its own deck and a great ocean view.

"What time is his flight?" Luca asks because he can't remember anything if I don't put it in his busy calendar.

"We're picking him up at nine."

I've seen my dad several times this year. The first visit was tough, I can't lie. I had a lot of anger and tears and questions. Me *and* my sisters did. But he stuck with us. Dad understood, and now he's loving having his family back.

He sends dolls to Gia and chew toys to Crimson every month.

I take Luca's hand and show him our owner's suite. It's serene with its own deck, too. The ensuite we have has all the luxuries Luca requires. Of course, he also checks the bed, pressing on the mattress, taunting me. "You sure this can handle us?"

"That's what this room is for."

I enter the code and unlock the white door off the side of our bedroom. Vivian and Eily helped me decorate most of the house. Eily's indigo art is everywhere, featured in our home and Luca's hotels. Vivian's touch is on the furniture and lighting. She can find great deals. But Stacey helped me with our private sex room.

It's not like the suite we still use at the hotel. Our friends coming to tomorrow's party often come there, too. *Yes, I meant that pun.*

But this is a smaller room with a sex bench and chaise and a few toys, too. The walls and ceiling are papered in dark blue damask. It's cozy and all we need since we have the hotel suite, Delta's, and we've also enjoyed Silas's superyacht.

Luca admires the room, gazing around. I glance down, and his faded jeans reveal his rising approval.

"Pace yourself, Mr. Mercier," I warn. "I have one more room to show you."

I take his hand and lead us back into the wide hallway.

Sunlight spills in from the skylights above, and Gia's chatter with her dolls can be heard from her room on the other end of the long corridor.

Resting my hand on the brass door handle, I say, "Close your eyes."

"Why?" Luca obeys. "Is this Crimson's doggy palace? Barks-and-Bling themed that cost us a billion, too?"

"God made you sexy because you ain't funny," I lie. "No, Crimson will be happy in his doggy bed in Gia's room. We'll bring him here tomorrow, but I wanted you to see this first."

I open the door and gently nudge him to step inside.

My waterworks start before Luca even opens his eyes to see the white crib. He blinks at it before a sexy smile blooms across his face. "Belle?" He turns and clasps my face. "Are we...?"

"Yes," I answer. "Twelve weeks."

"Why...?" he stammers. "Why didn't you tell me sooner?"

"Because," my lips tremble, "I wanted to surprise you. And honestly, I'm worried I might lose it."

His kiss is tender. He understands me. "You won't lose. You have me. You have Gia. You have your family and dog, Zar and

Nick, and all our friends. No matter what happens, you're not losing us. We won't leave you."

"I know." I nuzzle my nose against his. "It's just that we're so happy, I worry something will happen."

"Things will always happen." His thumb brushes my cheek. "But that's what our love is for. Okay?"

"Okay."

"So," he won't let go of my cheeks, "when you said you were bloated from too much Moussaka and that your breasts hurt from my bites, you were lying." He won't stop smiling.

"Yes, Master," I confess, "I was lying."

"And we've been to the suite several times these past few months and Zar's private parties, too, but you were pregnant the whole time?"

Zar's parties are epic, not for what happens, but for who's there. It seems a tight group of NFL players have to be closeted as gay or bi, but they're not at Zar's place. He and Nick make sure of it.

And there was that hot night, long before I was pregnant when Zar finally gave himself to Luca fully. God, I'll never forget it. Nick and I were there. We joined them. It was one of the most erotic nights we've shared, and it bonded the four of us even more.

"Yes," I answer him, "I didn't want to say anything. I wanted to surprise you like this, in our new home. And besides, our sex life doesn't end because I'm pregnant or whatever."

"But it *will* change." His tone drops. "I'll always want you, my belle. We'll always be who we are together, with no shame or secrets. But I also vowed to care for you, to protect you, too. You and..."

He pauses, glancing down at my little bloated belly. You can't tell. It's June, and I'm wearing a flowy sundress.

"I know what we're having," I tell him. "The technician was pretty sure. Do you want to know?"

"No." He caresses my belly. "I just want you to be okay. You and our little gift."

"Oh, come on." I laugh. "Don't make me keep this secret for six months."

He kisses me. And maybe it's because he made us wait for so long, but Luca's kiss still takes my breath away. I smile across our lips, "Come on, Daddy Dom. I know you wanna know."

"Fine." He pulls back, his fingertip grazing the gold jeweled collar around my neck. "Tell me another way you'll make me love you."

"*Make* you?"

He just cocks his dark eyebrow...and smiles.

"Okay, fine. You can pick the first name, and of course, we'll share your last name, but *his* middle name is 'Pyrrhus.'"

He pauses. Tears suddenly well in his crystal eyes. "We're having a boy?" He kisses me. "And you want his middle name to be Greek, to mean red like a flame, like your name?"

He makes me cry, too. "It's perfect, right?"

"No," Luca kisses me again, "Scarlett Mercier, you are."

And again. And again. And...

Sometimes a fuck is worth it.

The joy you feel is incredible—how it heals your heart so much.

Because you can fall in love with someone after just one night and love them for the rest of your life.

NOT THE END

Do you that night when Luca is finally with Zar, too?
And sneak peeks of more to come?
Get your free bonus chapter - ZAR'S NIGHT -
at KellyFinley.com.

Dear reader,

Thank you for giving this story your time & heart. Please, if you could leave your honest review, it means so much to me.
For more of Luca's forbidden world and friends, browse my other spicy books. They are free to enjoy in Kindle Unlimited.

"The Queen ♥ of Spice"
KELLY FINLEY BOOKS

-All Interconnected Books Available in Kindle Unlimited-

Charlie & Daniel

THE COME FOR ME TRILOGY

(SPICY, ROMANTIC SUSPENSE, ALPHA HERO & BADASS HEROINE)

Pierce Her

Hunt Her

Chase Her

Redix & Cade

ALL FOR YOU DUET

(ANGSTY SECOND CHANCE TO A SPICY MMF WHY CHOOSE DUET)

After Him

With Him

Silas & Eily

A FORBIDDEN, V-CARD TO POLY LOVE STORY

(STANDALONE ROMANCE)

All For Him

Stacey & Her Trio of Men

A MMMF ALPHA HEROES & SASSY HEROINE REVENGE

(STANDALONE ROMANCE)

Tempt Her

Silas & Eily; Redix & Cade; Charlie & Daniel

A Spicy, Lots of Friends To Lovers RomCom

(Standalone Romance)

Holiday For Six

Luca & Scarlett

A Single Dad / Alpha Dom Why Choose Romance

(Standalone Book)

Make Him

Beau & Blair

A Frenemies To Lovers, Why Choose Sports Romance

Shameless Play

Shameless Game

There is more to come in my spicy book world.

It will feature The Six, Delta's, The Mercier Hotel, secret sports romances, billionaire board rooms, proud poly love, and more!

KELLY FINLEY BOOKS

Join my newsletter at KellyFinley.com
to get the latest sneak peeks, giveaways, and more.

ACKNOWLEDGMENTS

My husband and best friend: I wake up to coffee and your sweet notes. Your love and support keep me writing. I'm lucky I found you, Silver Fox.

My Book Team: Deborah, you are a Proofreading Goddess and always so encouraging. Thank you, Lori, for another gorgeous cover. Hugs to my BTS team, Bree and Brit.

My Beta Team: Dani, Deborah, Heather, Jay, Jessica, Katelyn, and Marsha. I love y'all! Thanks for your comments, edits, and texts. They either crack me up or crack the whip.

My ARC, Spicy Gals & Hype Teams: I love the family we're building. I cherish your posts, reviews, and support. I love our DMs and chats, too. I truly can't do it without you all.

#Bookstagram & #BookTok Followers: It's true. There *is* a community and a world of friends online. I'm overwhelmed by the amazing people I've met. Every day you make me smile. You keep me writing. Thanks for your comments and love.

Author Friends & Mentors: You inspire me. You school me. You help me. Thanks for the Zooms, emails, and chats. You keep me strong.

Best for last - You, my reader: Thank you for giving your time to share this story with me. When welcome your messages, posts, and emails. They are the greatest gifts. And I promise to keep giving you more spice. Big hugs.

Xoxo,

Kelly

ABOUT KELLY
"THE QUEEN OF SPICE"

 Kelly Finley hates writing bios but appreciates that you made it this far. So here you go...

She lives in the Carolinas with her sexy husband and cherished family. A rebel with many causes, she fancies black leather, dirty jokes, big hearts, and smart mouths.

Her books are so spicy that her readers started calling her **"The Queen of Spice,"**...and she wears her crown with pride. Dedicated to writing books with proud love and shameless heat, she's most likely at her keyboard putting the next spicy story on the page for you.

Want to connect with Kelly and her readers? Get her newsletter at KellyFinley.com. Follow her on socials, feel free to message her, or connect using the Discord App.

Use this invite link for Discord = https://discord.gg/H47nZKhWQN

- tiktok.com/@kellyfinleybooks
- instagram.com/kellyfinleybooks
- facebook.com/KellyFinleyBooks
- bookbub.com/authors/kelly-finley
- goodreads.com/goodreads_kelly_finley
- amazon.com/author/kellyfinley

Make Him

Kelly Finley

© 2024 Kelly Finley Publishing, LLC

Visit the author's website at www.kellyfinley.com

ISBN: 979-8-9866222-6-2 (eBook)

ISBN: 979-8-9866222-7-9 (paperback)

All rights reserved.

Proofread by Deborah Richmond

Cover design by Lori Jackson

Cover model: Alfredo Hernandez de la Cruz

Printed in Great Britain
by Amazon

46842066R00260